AF490126

WBT
PUBLISHING

# Welcome to Willouby

# Welcome to Willouby

∞∞∞∞∞

# An American Fairy Tale

By

## Paul Alan Richardson

WB Tree Publishing
USA



ISBN:  979-8-89217-252-3 (ebook)
ISBN:  979-8-89217-253-0 (print paperback)

Book Cover and Design: Kyle Hopkins

Published by Willouby Publishing
USA
www.wbtreepublishing.com

Second edition paperback - June 2025

**For**

mothers,
mischief makers, and
merry men

## Note

All quirks, oddities, fuzzy references, misspellings, Questionable Capitalizations, tense confrontations, letter obsession, use of numbers, swirly punctuation, and kaleido-scope phrases are very much intentional. Everything else is absolutely on purpose. The blame is all mine. But first you must decide who I am.

Forgive me. I couldn't make it too easy, My Wild and Wonderful One.

## A Clue

As your first friend in Willouby, here's a clue for you to get started on this Who Is It of a Who Did It and How and Why Was it Done?

## I am M.

Perhaps M for Mister or Madam or Monster or Magician or another M altogether. That's for you to discover on your adventure.

But careful with M. It's a tricksy. Flip it around in the upside down and it becomes something else Entirely.

Good Luck!

# Monday

# —— Chapter 1 ——

**I saw Jacob** Maymerry on the day he moved to Willouby. He rolled a white sofa up the gravel driveway, balanced precariously on three flat yellow scooters—the kind from PE class. In a charcoal cardigan over a powder blue polo, he looked like a substitute teacher trying his very best after being assigned kindergarten by surprise.

He pushed the sofa cautiously but began a borderline jog once he realized it wasn't too heavy. I saw him pick up speed. His face relaxed, and his eyes brightened into a shine while daring a drift up to admire the sycamore tree canopy. He noticed a large nest in the leaves and relaxed for the first time since opening the moving van.

His confidence was misplaced.

A yellow scooter wheel dipped into a potato-sized pothole. The couch stopped abruptly, and Jacob's momentum propelled him over the end of the low white armrest. He twisted in confusion, rolled atop the back of the couch, landed on the gravel as his body flipped everything sideways, and he finished with three full rotations down a small grass embankment along the driveway.

I was too far away to hear Jacob's *oof* as he hit the gravel rocks or his *squeak* of confusion as he rolled onto the grass. It all played out like a silent Charlie Chaplin episode, and I almost believed he did it on purpose. For my amusement.

Jacob rested on his back, eyes on the clouds, for three seconds—four seconds—five seconds—processing what had become of his life. With a jolt, realizing this was his first day and he needed to make a good impression with the locals, Jacob gained composure, and dusted his pants over his thighs in an attempt to remove now permanent grass stains. After adjusting his mindset to ensure this is exactly what he wanted to happen, he went up the embankment to find the errant yellow scooter which had shot into the neighbor's bush.

It was only then I saw another man moving boxes into the front door. From his angle, this man couldn't see Jacob's furniture debacle. I felt relief on Jacob's behalf—*Don't worry, he didn't see anything. You're cool.*

I thought it was the two of them, and I almost continued on before seeing the third creature moving in—a calico cat perched on one of the mammoth limestone boulders that protruded across the yard like shapeless gargoyle protectors.

A mysterious *aurora borealis* of whites, blacks, and browns, the cat seemed indifferent to Jacob's couch moving plight. She gave only a half-hearted glance in his direction as he rolled down the embankment. Her cat face showed not surprise but boredom. She had seen Jacob flailing before, and considered it his default condition.

The feline look was unmistakable—*What did you expect? Who thought it was a good idea to let him move furniture alone?*

Instead, her eyes followed a wisp of thin white fabric blowing across the yard—a long dormant snake-skin that Jacob swished up in his chaos.

It wasn't until he walked back in the house after failing to find the yellow scooter that Jacob realized his cardigan was covered in leaf crumbs. He was about to grab a back-up but remembered all his clothes were still packed in boxes. It was another two hours before he glanced sideways in the bathroom mirror and noticed a bramble of objects entwined in his hair—a partial bird's nest that a spring robin abandoned along the embankment weeks earlier.

∞

**The old wood** sagged two inches under Jacob's tan slippers when he stepped down on the basement stair. The pine made a *mew mew* sound and Jacob wondered if it could hold a human man.

*Is this how I die?* A death by fall into the basement of a house on Closing Day would be a cruel twist. But at least he'd avoid paying a dime on the loan. Since becoming a homeowner—that very morning—Jacob Maymerry's mind saw death in funny places. Morbid thinking comes with a mortgage, he assured himself. Adulthood has its trenches.

Staring down the basement stairs funnel, Jacob knew he would not die via termite-infested wood, because the home was given a clean bill of health by the bank that required the inspection before giving them the money to buy it. And who was Jacob Maymerry to question Wells Fargo?

The stairs opened onto flat dirt, just as expected when descending underneath a 125 year old, 4 bedroom, 3 bathroom, one-of-a-kind jewel in a charming old town district with lots of potential! Must see!

The 'ol gal sat on the market for three years. Leaves blew in piles through the bare rooms on the day they first viewed her. Jacob was no prude, and he knew she had as much ancient grace and faded beauty in their price range west of the Blue Ridge Mountains.

But there was a reason no one had popped the cork since the bank took ownership—she had let herself go a bit. A cheap kitchen makeover fooled no one, nicks in all the trim and walls, a deteriorating nervous system, and a reputation for looking scary. But Liam fell in love upon opening the car door at the curb and decided they must have it. Thus the die was cast that set Jacob on a path into the basement.

∞

**Alive at the** bottom of the stairs, Jacob realized it was a lair more than a basement. A chalky, partially exposed limestone boulder sat like a king in the center of the boxy room. More than a century prior, jacklegs charged with digging the massive rock out for the house foundation had a moment of extreme clarity, set down their shovels, and simply gave up.

Jacob was drawn to that boulder—it deserved respect. The ultimate owner of this acre of Willouby, Jacob felt that it *was* this acre. Maybe it went the core of the earth itself. His name might be on the deed, but he'd never have rights over that stone. Willouby locals sometimes called the place the Rock House, because the front yard was pocked with limestone peaks of unknown bulk hidden beneath a veneer of grass. The rocks bubbled all over and might have been random hints of the real power that lie underneath the 'ol gal. But mostly it made mowing and trimming an utter nightmare.

But at that moment Jacob stood in the basement. And he had forgotten.

*Oh boy*. Jacob blanked on why he even walked down into the lair. It would soon be filled with things—all the things of their life that belonged down deep. The things for much later, maybe, once a year, or the things they were obligated to keep. Basement things are outcasts. If it wasn't so dirty, and if he put up Christmas lights, this would make a nifty island of misfit toys.

*Focus*. Why did Jacob come down here? He looked at his hands, hoping he was holding something that would reveal what his younger self was thinking a few seconds ago. *Is my brain twisting in two?*

Seconds from walking back up the stairs, defeated, he saw the flashing light on the washing machine. *Change the laundry!*

*How could I have forgotten about the laundry?* The washer and dryer were the only objects in the basement besides the overhead pipes, hot water heater, ancient rake, balled up sheet, metal coal furnace monster, boulder to the center of the earth, and a scrap of dirty newspaper along the stone foundation corner.

Jacob knelt in front of the washing machine and cursed Liam for claiming to be "too tall" to go down into the basement.

*How convenient*, thought Jacob. Though he was content playing the guy under the cap, occasionally emerging, quite reluctantly, to do the astonishing. He still searched for the exact right astonishing thing.

Crouched in the basement dust, tossing whites into the machine, he glanced around and a question struck him—*How on earth did this washer and dryer even get down here? They certainly didn't fit through the pine stairway funnel—too narrow.*

*What black magic?* No no, Jacob saw the answer. There was a cellar door tucked darkly along one slanted ceiling, with two rickety wood steps in the downslope to the dirt basement floor.

The longer he stayed down, the more his eyes adjusted to the dimness, the more he noticed in the deep. Like crisp spider webs, draped delicately across the pipes—the spider architects themselves hidden. A pristine web without a spider is far scarier than one sitting exposed. *Was he being watched?*

Jacob inhaled for five seconds and then exhaled for eight. He recently learned that breathing techniques were nature's best cure for anxiety. To his dismay, he still felt spider stress even after he exhaled. But he pretended it worked, and considered going over to the scrap of dirty newspaper in the corner to see if there was a date on it.

It was then that he felt a flick at his neck, then a longer strand wrapping around his Adam's Apple. Thick, hairy.

Jacob grunted and fell forward from his crouch. His head clunked against the hard plastic washer door, and he slid sideways to the floor, his face half covered in chalky brown dirt. Jacob's first thought was that now he'd have to shower again. He'd already wasted twenty minutes trying to get all of the bird's nest out of his hair from earlier in the day.

*Meow!*

"Eleanor, Dammit!" He mouthed words through dirt lips.

The indifferent cat paused and stared at him for a moment. She resumed after two blinks and pawed herself over his chest as he lay with cheek still in the dust, leaving brown cat prints on his blue polo.

Jacob flipped onto his back, took a four second breath, felt dirt puff into the air, and exhaled for another four seconds. He twisted and watched Eleanor strut along what he now saw was an already-trodden cat path. She had a purpose and was going for the old newspaper scrap. Jacob propped himself up on an elbow, spat on the ground to rinse his mouth, and watched the curious kitty.

Like her namesake, Eleanor Roosevelt the Calico Cat kept abreast of the news of the day. She came with the name, or so Liam claimed when he brought her home from the pound or shelter or wherever she last stalked. That's why he was startled when, instead of checking for top stories, she sat down on all fours, like the Sphinx, and started licking the paper.

Something was off. The hair on Jacob's dust covered forearms electrified. Not only was Eleanor not reading this blank sheet of newspaper, she walked straight toward it and licked it as if it may contain a dash of meat.

*What was it about this scrap of paper?*

Growing intrigued, Jacob popped up but stayed in a slight crouch to avoid the pipes dipped haphazardly from section to section above. They crossed the underside of the beast, the back of the embroidery. Earlier in the day Jacob smacked the dead center of his forehead on one thick pipe, and he wondered if he'd go to his grave with the resulting indention above his eyes. To avoid a repeat concussion, he descended into a duck walk down at Eleanor's side.

*That isn't a scrap of newspaper at all.*
*It's an unglazed ceramic bowl!*

It was not a ceramic bowl. But it would take thirty three minutes of careful digging to uncover. With all tools still packed in boxes, Jacob poked and flicked with the fork he'd used the night before to eat pasta. It was a satisfying meal, but not quite as satisfying as feeling like an amateur archaeologist at the start of what he hoped, *who knows, a boy can dream,* might become his life's quest—*an astonishing adventure.*

Jacob's mind whirred and fogged up, opening itself to the mysterious

doorway into dreamworld, where the voice in his head said inane things like—
*Don't worry, Detective Maymerry is on the case!*

Could the holy grail be buried under a Queen Anne Victorian in a colonial American town at the tip of Virginia? Was it any stranger than Moses finding the tablets on the top of some random rocks in a nowhere desert?

As sweat beads darkened the dirt around him and the single bulb light swayed behind him, Jacob Maymerry and his fork delicately mimicked the work of the dinosaur digs he'd learned about in school and felt through movie screens. His forearms ached by the time he realized his startling discovery.

A skull was buried underneath the house.

# —— Chapter 2 ——

**"Dinner's ready!"**

A voice echoed down the basement funnel, breezed over the disturbed swirl of Jacob's dirt face imprint in front of the washer, and floated into the amateur archaeologist's ear as he kneeled above a mostly uncovered human skull.

"Dinner's ready," Jacob repeated aloud to ensure that Eleanor and the skull both heard.


*Uh Oh. Dinner's ready.* His situation hit him.


He had about 30 seconds. Maybe 45 seconds, little time to ponder what to do next as he knelt under the house staring into empty eye sockets.

Jacob looked at Eleanor who had watched the entire affair with sporadic interest from her throne atop the boulder to the center of the earth. The cat blinked and looked at the fool. Jacob could feel her amusement—she was a deity watching an inferior species waste thousands of calories badger clawing a milky bone that she had already checked for protein. As Jacob's face shifted into panic at the realization that dinner was ready, her cat eyes rolled with the usual tough love—*What did you expect? You got yourself into this mess.*

Jacob stared down at the product of his labors, whatever remained of a human head. He did not see signs of any other bones. He had uncovered a skull. Nothing more. *What on earth?*

Dirt caked in his nails. Mud covered his knees, forearms, and a black watery mush smear dashed across his forehead like a Monday morning ash mark.

He exhaled. Took a 3 second breath in, then a 2 second breath out. As if knowingly walking into a big mistake, he whispered aloud to the bored calico, "Please forgive me. I don't have time to make a more thoughtful decision."

As an attorney, and corporate counsel for the AAMCLDS, he knew that "I didn't have time to make a more thoughtful decision" would not hold up in court. But going against all his jurisprudential instincts, he nodded at Eleanor like a bumbling general who made a decision that would likely cost them the war. Deftly using his left hand, he put a finger to his lips in a *Shhh Quiet,* followed by a zipped lips slide. *This is between us.* Eleanor blinked in understanding, and Jacob began his walk up the stairs, to the kitchen, his dinner, and to keeping a big secret.

∞

**The "Dinner's Ready"** call meant Jacob's basement time was drawing short. Liam came by his kitchen voice honestly as a former sous chef of a Michelin Star Establishment, and the brand new proprietor of the trendy under-the-radar, next-hot-thing in the Shenandoah Valley that he opened one month prior.

The chef did not know that Jacob was under his feet, badger clawing away as dinner brewed. Like all the oldest homes dotted across historic Willouby, kitchens were in the back of the house and they often had two stairwells—one up, one down. A funnel into the cellar below and back stairs traveling up like a hidden spine, providing sneaky access to second floor bedrooms and the expansive, unfinished attic that they were making a suite.

Jacob considered the separate staircase a most delightful feature. He had a penchant for cozy British mysteries, and this Victorian was primed for a dinner party murder. The second stair created opportunities for a scarlet deed to go unnoticed. He imagined soft-footed detectives tapping down the back spine explaining how it allowed the murderer to slink away while the rest of the party huddled confused in the front parlor.

"Let's eat outside," Liam yelled a second command. That meant that Liam already made his own plate, was walking to the porch, and Jacob could join him whenever.

Jacob was a whir of cascading thoughts as he slow walked from the skull—covered by a sheet—up the sagging basement steps, into the kitchen with the spoiled spinach green cabinets that Liam hated, stared at the vegetable heavy soup with some spicy pepper sparking the air above the pot, ladled a handful into an extremely wide but shallow bowl, and tried not to spill it as he walked to the outdoor dining table.

The broth was hot, scalding even. He pursed his lips to let the soup fall back into the bowl as the first bit swished on skin. "Great flavor," he said.

"MmmHmm. It turned out alright, I think." Liam barely heard, staring at the yard with a pre-renovation blush that made Jacob nervous. *What mountain of chaos is that mind bringing down upon us now?*

A man of letters, logical positions, and sensible judgment, chaos was Jacob Maymerry's enemy. Which is why it was surprising that throughout the entire pleasant porch dinner, while watching red and blue birds dart from the apple tree to the maple to the sycamore, through dozens of soup sips, Jacob made not a single peep about the human skull currently sitting in their basement.

Why did he keep mum?

Later he told himself that he carefully considered it all and then made a reasonable choice. But the deep down truth he'd tell no one was that it was a gut decision. Totally out of his control. All the post-hoc justification was a lawyer's trick to make it seem like a good choice.

Jacob Maymerry felt pulled toward his tiny destiny like a thirsty dog drawn to a water bowl.

*If I say a word, then the police might be involved. There's a human skull here, protocol, paperwork. What a mess. I don't have time for that. Who has time for anything these days?*

*An even bigger mess is the fact that a larger dig might be required, which would excavate under the foundation of the house. We can't risk the structural integrity of this historic home over mere bone!*

Jacob emphasized this emphatically with a finger raised in the air during the argument in his mind.

*It's a sense of duty, really. If you see a piece of trash on a walk, do you call the city garbage authorities, make them gas up their trucks, pay overtime, and drive to the sidewalk to pick up the trash to deposit it in a proper public receptacle? No, a good citizen does it himself. I, Jacob Maymerry, have a civic duty to take care of this skull business without draining more hard earned Willouby tax dollars.*

*No need to derail Liam. He's completely overwhelmed at the moment with the final restaurant milestone and plans to re-do this entire house. It would be extremely selfish of me to foist this on him. Far better to think through fully on my own and spare the man another dollop of anxiety atop the already backbreaking load of modern adult existence.*

*We can't let this skull business derail us right now.* Jacob won the argument with himself in a unanimous verdict.

That pesky head was Jacob's cross to wear, ring to bear, pill to swallow, and mystery to unveil for the world. *At least for now,* he thought. He might change his mind after dinner.

∞

**"Night Night."** Jacob heard in the dark from the other side of the bed.

Considering the overflowing pile of nonsense and tomfoolery in his life at the moment, Jacob began his first sleep in the 'ol gal with unusual contentment. He decided to calm himself into sleep by settling on the justification for his actions that day—Dignity. Keeping the skull to himself provided the proper dignity to honor the memory of the sad soul whose journey on this planet must have been a rocky one. He could decide what to do tomorrow, but for now, he convinced himself he'd made the right choice.

∞

**But peace was** not to come that night for Jacob Maymerry. His typical routine was bed at 11pm, wake up at 12:15am for the bathroom, 4am wake up thinking he missed a phone call from Colorado, and then an alarm clock at 6:15am.

Between seconds of occasional peaceful sleep, Jacob dreamed. On the first night of the skull he had an *Alice in Wonderland* fantasy of going down down down. He followed Eleanor to an archaeological site along a river. The cat wore ancient Egyptian garb of white fabrics with blue and gold around her head. Jacob knelt down to admire the regal little creature. But when he did, she made an about face, revealed her backside directly to his nose, and bunny-kicked Jacob into a now raging river behind him.

An idea came not in words but a feeling that Jacob would later call the Flow. He could no more make a different decision than could he paddle against the raging rivers flowing from the Mississippi into the Gulf of Mexico.

*The Divine Miss M! Is that what they call that American River? Or Muddy Missus M?* Jacob would look it up later. The point was that he was on a path that the universe insist be taken. The stars demanded it.

The heavens shone down on Jacob. He closed his eyes and let himself be carried away by the river. He opened them to see a popcorn ceiling with a paper mache protrusion—the remnants of an old roof leak that the home inspector said "is probably fine for awhile," though his work came with no guarantees.

Jacob woke at 4:05am. Usually, he only had a few seconds of sleepy bliss before waking to *The Lion Sleeps Tonight* from Liam's phone alarm. But this curious home was already shifting his subconscious routines. Jacob could not shut off his mind.

*I left a skull in the basement. What have I done?*

Jacob stared at his bedroom ceiling leak divot for two full two hours before the *Weem a Way, Weem a Way*. He waited for a drop of water to fall out and land right in the middle of his face.

He knew he had the dig site to himself the next day. Liam wouldn't go to the basement, because the chef said explicitly that he never wanted to go to the basement. He claimed the ceilings were too low, but Jacob knew an even stronger reason was that Liam possessed an embarrassing terror of snakes. For his part, Jacob found beauty in the slinking and slacking oddities on the planet—including snakes, possums, and hippies.

Deep deep down, *even he, Jaocb Maymerry*, did not know the real reason why he kept the skull a secret. His life felt like snap judgments with mountains of fancy justifications piled on afterward. It wasn't civic duty that kept him silent. It wasn't the mortgage or the ol' gal's foundation or dignity.

Maybe it was laziness. Telling people and dealing with it all seemed like so much work. Life was exhausting already, the last thing he needed was something else. *God almighty, can't I catch a break?*

Or maybe, Jacob suspected, the core motivation for his actions was an unknown shadowy emotion that brewed like a thick fog inside him as he uncovered all that remained of what used to be a real human mind. He had no name for the emotion, a muddy mix of sadness, curiosity, confusion, excitement, and fear.

While forking the skull up, he paused and lightly knocked his own with his knuckles, just underneath the hair. Eventually only a thin layer of skin between the world. One day someone might dig him up. Today it's me, tomorrow it's mud.

If by some hurricane turn of fate his head ended up buried underneath this house—or, even worse, a stranger's house—what would Jacob want to happen?

Privacy. *Leave me be. If my skull ends up down here, it's probably because these ancient stairs gave way. How embarrassing. I wouldn't want some grotesque black and white image of my hollowed out noggin on the front page of a prying local paper like a silly Boy Scout story. Leave me to the snakes, opossums and occasional adventurous cat.*

# Tuesday

# — Chapter 3 —

**Weem a Way,** *Weem a Way* echoed off the attic rafters. Jacob popped up with forced vigor, ignoring the fact that he dripped in sweat.

Ten minutes later, after three sips of coffee, he began that first sunrise in the house on his knees, elbow high in purple kitchen dish gloves, scrubbing an unknown mess that Eleanor either created or dragged in from outside.

Scrubbing Jacob wondered what else had been spilled on this hardwood over the last 125 years.

*Blood? Was this a murder house?*

It was only then that a thought occurred to him that should have much earlier—What if there are many skulls hidden underneath? He avoided thinking about ancient burial grounds, because he was a rational man. *Sure, the house is built on a slight hill. But that doesn't mean it's crumbling on a pile of bones. Or does it?*

Crouched on the old hardwood, purple gloves making his hands sweat, blue cleaning fumes spiraling up his nose, Jacob Maymerry ran headlong to the edge of a mental cliff. If he allowed his mind to wander, he would create a slippery scenario ending with the house deteriorating into worthless pieces down into a sinkhole of historic bodies. Wells Fargo would insist that the mortgage payments were still due, and Jacob's credit score would free fall. Debtor's prison until the end of days.

*Snap!*

A radiator interrupted his digression. In that brief moment of clarity Jacob remembered a lesson from the same video he'd watched about the importance of proper breathing—Face your Fear.

*Are you worried that your new house was built on a burial ground and is structurally unstable? Prove that fear right or wrong and then move on with your life! Now inhale for eight full seconds. Hold for four seconds. Exhale for three. Feel better?*

∞

**Budding Detective Maymerry** sat at a makeshift table on the first floor in the space with most light. A likely dining room, it currently possessed a board propped across containers of Halloween decorations. During the boot up, he stared at the empty walls painted a wet mushroom brown. Boxes piled around him. A weight set in one corner, a bike against another. He noticed a claw-like gash under the picture rail, powdery drywall residue littered on the floor. *Was that there when we bought this? Did someone come in here with a crowbar and cause even more damage? What have we done?*

The Windows log-in prompt buzzed, but before he could type in his password the face recognition got him and opened up his home screen anyway. Jacob knew it made his computer far less safe. But did it really matter? He doubted any international enemies would break into his laptop to steal secret AAM-CLDS information. *Or would they?*

Brushing away the paranoia, he searched—*What to do if you find a human skull in your basement?*

*How is this my life?*

Straight away he noticed that Section 18.2-126 of the Virginia Code considered it a Class 4 felony to disinter or displace all or part of human remains (of which a skull would qualify). But, Jacob's legal eye immediately noticed there was a caveat. This applied only to remains that had been "deposited in any vault, grave, or other burial place."

"A lot of wiggle room there," Jacob said aloud to Eleanor Roosevelt who jumped atop a stack of heavy crates filled with unknown belongings.

"Yes, a lot of wiggle room indeed."

He then clicked from the official state website to an article from a publication entitled, *High Flyin'* that was either a monthly magazine for behind airplane seats or cannabis connoisseurs. The article, "What to Do If You Find Bones In Your Backyard," had the author's smiling picture posted next to her byline. Jacob found her compassionate face reassuring, and for that reason he considered her article to be the highest authority, trumping anything from the Virginia Code.

The author interviewed an unnamed local museum expert who claimed that with bones, "when it comes to private property, the United States is in a group of countries like North Korea in that if it's in our backyard, it's up to us. If you find the Greatest Pyramid of Egypt umder the garage, you can blow them up or do whatever."

Jacob spent the next ninety seconds considering how someone might accidentally find the Egyptian Pyramids in their backyard, let alone get enough explosives to blow them up. They'd be fully liable for all the blasting damage to nearby houses, and they could make a fortune selling tickets inside the pyramids, so it'd be a rash decision.

That was enough information. Jacob was grateful to the unnamed local museum expert, but he found the comparison to scary countries a little hyperbolic. He almost got into a long argument in his head with this expert about the virtue of the US position. But he caught himself and said to the air, "It's not worth it."

It didn't matter, because this wasn't a legal decision for Jacob. He knew full well that the exact letter of the law matters in a courtroom, sometimes, but the wild west of adulthood was far more complicated. Who drove under 65 miles per hour on the highway? He would never tell this to the Virginia State Bar, but sometimes laws were reasonable guidelines with many exceptions.

∞

**Detective Maymerry** drove on.

He began, as he often did, at the very beginning. Even when there was no need. Jacob maintained unrealistic optimism about the speed and skill of his research abilities. A part of him believed he could type on this machine and walk away perhaps an hour later knowing exactly whose skull Eleanor unearthed. He would then know what to do and move on with his life.

After five minutes on one website, a mere 300 seconds, Jacob was relatively confident in his historical knowledge of the region. Willouby sits atop the Shenandoah Valley, which traces a north-south diagonal line across Virginia. Bordered on the west by the Appalachians and the east by the Blue Ridge Mountains. The valley name comes from the river which runs the length of it—the very same Shenandoah River longed for by John Denver in the early 1970s. The Blue Ridge are prized by locals for the natural barrier they provide against invaders from the Atlantic—Europeans in the 17th century and DC suburbanites today.

Humans walked the Shenandoah Valley for perhaps 17,000 years. Jacob considered how many people lived over 17 millennia, 670 cycles of grandmothers and mothers and daughters. An army of feet walking atop this little hill where the 'ol gal sits. How many people through those generations of men, women, and children had stood on the boulder in the basement? *Could Jacob really figure out which one's head was left for him to find?*

A storybook image popped into Jacob's mind of a tired woman sitting on the rock to rest. Tan, shoeless, covered in beads and feathers, she wiped her brow after carrying water from a creek. She slipped, then slept, and nature buried her. Is it her skull down there?

*Focus, Jacob.*

The Algonquian, Siouan, and Iroquoian lived the ups and downs of these lands for centuries. Europeans arrived around 1600 but it was decades before hearty souls mustered the courage to trek over Blue Ridge mountains and into the fertile valley below. *Maybe one of those original explorers finally met their end under this house?*

"This isn't helpful," Jacob said to Eleanor, who was staring at him from unopened boxes of Southern glassware like a fading Broadway star watching an imploding performance from the Presidential box suite.

*No No. You're doing great. Keep going,* she seemed to say sarcastically with her mere presence. *Eventually you'll go back to Adam and Eve and really get to the bottom of this.*

∞

**The problem with** the Internet was that it linked to too much information. The monumental task laying before Jacob was made bare. He took deep breaths, forgetting to count the inhales and exhales, and tried to use what little reasoning skills he possessed to narrow down his list of options.

Willouby was founded in 1744, so it's highly unlikely that the skull was from before. Possible, sure, but if he was playing the odds, then he had to assume this patch of dirt on the hill with the boulders sticking out on top, was mostly empty until folks settled in this area to give it a real name. But that still left 280 ish years of skulls trodding all over the property.

"Jacob, you fool. Speed it up." He whispered these full sentences out loud in front of this laptop. Only a whisper, because he wasn't crazy.

In a final search, he scrolled upon a free digital copy of a text from 1926 entitled "Willouby Virginia and Its Beginnings 1743-1814." It was there he learned the city's first famous resident was none other than George Washington himself. Mister President owned various bits and fields of the place in his younger days—when the hamlet was an English colony and not the little American city described by Southern Existence as "utterly charming, must try the local honey!

"This is progress," he whispered to the screen for no reason. He knew it wasn't George Washington's skull in his basement. Nor was it likely the Brigadier-General who founded the city and who's name now adorned a school, park, and a large stone monument. In the 1860s, Willouby was a cascade of calvary, flags, marching, shooting, running, bleeding, anguish, despair, hope, and victory. Sitting atop the Shenandoah Valley entrance into Virginia proper, the little town transferred hands over 70 times in the Civil War.

*Now we're really getting somewhere.*

The realtor who sold them the 'ol gal mentioned that other neighbors had found various fragments, cartridges, and Minie balls in Jacob's yard. "If you dig anything up, you can sell it on the line. Yes sir, and a Civil War bullet alone can get you eight dollars." He'd said it like a man who made a mini-fortune on memorabilia sales.

Remembering the realtor's comment, Jacob immediately assumed until proven wrong that the skull must be one of the 600,000 Americans who died in those bloody years. Or maybe it was the wife of one of the soldiers, stricken with grief, who sat on the boulder and perished out of despair. Maybe. But it had to be a Civil War skull. *Had to be. When else were so many skulls strewn all across these fields?*

His confidence was misplaced. The Civil War ended 160 years earlier. The house was finished 40 years after the surrender at Appomattox. That left 120 years of history, heads tramping up and over and through the doors. So many possibilities.

"A needle in a haystack," Jacob whispered to the corner spider plant and then popped out of the chair for a trail mix snack.

# —— Chapter 4 ——

**At some unknown** time, Jacob thought about going down to check—just to see—but changed his mind when the phone rang for the third time in as many hours. Another call from Colorado, AAMCLDS Headquarters, Board Chair Gladys Gershwin came in hot, "You won't believe this. Just. Will. Not. But those gentlefellas now want to start a competing line of dance boots," Gladys assumed all Europeans were male. "The nerve. The gall. I mean, no ideas of their own. None. Just ridiculous. Can we stop this?"

The rest of Jacob's afternoon was spent fighting for the rights of American line dancers. "I looked into it," Jacob said on a conference call with the entire AAMCLDS Board that afternoon, "and it turns out we can't stop other companies from making boots. But, we can explore branding issues to ensure consumers aren't tricked into buying inferior products."

Jacob let himself forget the letters AAMCLDS the second he hung up the conference call and his mind went back to the mystery of the skull once more. A mystery which now seemed more important than most other things in his life, even though he knew that was a ridiculous thing to think.

Yet he was most sure that Detective Maymerry would continue the investigation for at least one more day. Another gut decision because Jacob was carried along by Flow. Going with the River. Not fighting the current is sometimes the easiest way to live. That's what he tried to tell himself while drowning the other voice echoing inside his head: *Are you making a mistake?*

**Liam came home** on edge after a grueling kitchen day with two burners on the fritz. He kept it simple with a grilled cheese dinner, which the tired chef considered a cop-out, but a favorite for Jacob.

The budding detective's mood ballooned with the first sharp cheddar bite. They ate from the couch watching an old show about stranded island plane crash survivors. Jacob forgot the skull for two full episodes before they cleaned up and collapsed in the attic.

Jacob had not set foot in the basement the entire day. After his morning research, he knew it best to put the hunk of bone out of his mind. This was for two reasons. First, he really did have a mountain of bill paying work to get through. Second, and more importantly, he wanted to give himself time for plausible deniability. If Jacob carefully dug for two straight days in the basement, then he was fully committed. But by avoiding it entirely he felt he had an escape door in case questions were asked.

*Skull? Skull in the basement? Weird, didn't see that. How odd.*

*Oh that skull? Yes, found it while doing laundry and then totally got swept up in chores and forgot.*

In bed that night, bolstered by the grilled cheese, Jacob shored up his confidence. *One more day to research and think.* Then he'd tell. No harm in that. He drifted away with visions of skeleton smiles dancing in his head.

∞

**The second night** in the attic bedroom brought no peace for Jacob Maymerry. He dreamed of his employer—the AAMCLDS.

A highly regarded institution, the American Association of Modern and Classic Line Dance Society, had served the nation for more than 85 years, though very few people knew. Pride ran deep with The Board which maintained an iron grip on the industry since its founding, or naming, or some such detail which Jacob long forgot.

True professionals knew that the American version of various things were unquestionably supreme: hot dogs, confidence, and baseball. No one needed to vote on this. It was known. It's called the World Series, and words matter. In just the same way, Americans obviously own the premier version of line dancing. It is known. Or was. Until what Jacob dubbed the Kick-Ball-Change Wars began five years earlier. This is not to be confused with the ABC Wars, an ongoing internal AAMCLDS feud.

The KBC War erupted when, after decades of infighting, the Europeans re-grouped, found a previously hidden sense of unity, and joined forces to steal the AAMCLDS's rightfully large majority of worldwide line dance consumer revenue. Out of nowhere, the organization that Jacob served faithfully and nearly silently for years was under attack.

The EAMCLDS—European Association of Modern and Classic Line Dance Society—began holding copycat conferences, competitions, and DVD subscription drives. In two years, a third of market share was gone, and Jacob's employer went from a squirm to a wiggle into a mad panic. Then they began to fight back.

As the only lawyer on staff—and zero dollars for outside help—Jacob Maymerry soon became the most experienced line dance jurist in the nation. His old legal tasks like reviewing wood dance floor rental contracts suddenly morphed into much more contentious and confrontational paperwork flutterings.

Jacob once unsuccessfully sought to copyright the phrase 'line dancing.' The Board was disappointed, and failed to appreciate that their expectations were unrealistic. One Member suggested at the end of a long conference call, "Maybe try to get the word 'dance' overall. I say go for the gold. That's the American way."

"Ok, I'll see what I can do," Jacob said. As he always said. Attorney Maymerry's employers were of a naivete that an opposing counsel once called "breathtaking, almost charming."

**Jacob woke sweating** at 3:15am, having seconds before been arguing in front of the United States Supreme Court about how to perform a proper grapevine. Justice had said "you're on a very shaky dance floor, young man," but Jacob couldn't remember why.

He tiptoed out of bed. One part of himself said it was for a bathroom break, but a deeper part knew more.

Perhaps the river current carried him as he went directly down the spine steps from their 3rd floor bedroom to the 1st floor kitchen. Jacob opened the tiny latch with a finger, propped the basement door with a little help from his shoulder, flipped on the bulb light, and felt the familiar sag of the first step.

"Just wanted to see that you were doing alright," he said aloud, knowing full well that it was a joke. Jacob found himself growing fond of the hunk of bone. He told himself it was because he was new to town and had yet to make a single friend. But he knew that was simply a funny thought, that would appear to others as if he were going crazy. But he knew he wasn't crazy, so he couldn't be. That must be how this all works.

A moment passed before Jacob's senses returned and it struck him how this would look if anyone saw—man in blue pajamas, tan slippers, staring at an exposed skull in a dirt floor basement. He looked over and saw the boulder to the center of the earth. *Is this rock bottom?*

"Meooow"

Eleanor Roosevelt jumped onto the boulder—he didn't realize she had followed him down. He went over to give a pet, grateful that she cared enough to see what he was up to. As he got closer, however, he noticed that her front paws were dark and dripping with black soil. Jacob realized then that Eleanor had not appeared from the stairs but the dark shadows of the basement corner. She was already here before he came down.

And the kitty had been working. Jacob followed the cat prints in the basement dust and saw a scratched hole near the dig site. A small object glistened as the light beam dashed across the cellar.

Jacob looked directly at the object that Eleanor exposed—two feet away from the skull itself. Jacob's archaeological abilities were clearly lacking if he had missed this. Continuing the thread of incompetence, he immediately picked up the exposed object with no care to preserve anything.

"Oops," he said aloud as the thought struck him too late that he should have left it on the ground. He spun the object over in his hand. A flat metal circle, an inch or two wide. The front was textured into some images and wording, but Jacob's mind was in a deep night haze—the dark and dust of the basement made it difficult to figure out what it was. *A button? Part of a badge?*

Jacob Maymerry stood in the basement, the blue of his pajama pants now covered in dirt to the calf, holding an unknown metal object in his hand, staring at an exposed skull, and wondering what gods he offended to have stumbled into this ridiculous situation. Eleanor the calico cat sat on the boulder stuck in the earth with a smirk of pure joy.

He inhaled for 4 seconds and exhaled for 8 seconds.

"Are you kidding me?" he asked whatever listened in the dark.

∞

**Back in bed,** Jacob tried to aimlessly think of anything but the skull. Exhaustion set in like a mist, and he mercifully dozed without knowing.

In the mystery twilight just before sun up, he slept and his mind swirled down to the skull. Jacob walked the pine steps to see George Washington on the dirt, in full Revolutionary War uniform, his head placed exactly where the skull lay in the dirt.

"Hi Jacob! It's Me!" Dream George Washington gave a wooden tooth smile that made Jacob scream himself awake.

But he wasn't screaming—it was an alarm going off somewhere in the pitch black house.

Jacob's exhausted brain fired back up. *Oh my god, the house is on fire.*

# Wednesday

# — Chapter 5 —

*The house is on fire?*

Jacob woke to blackness—and the high pointy beep of an alarm warning of danger. But in the weird mist between dream and awake, he didn't trust his senses. Jacob's eyes felt open but he saw nothing. He heard the alarm, but did he really? For a moment he wondered if he was still asleep before a rustle and garble next to him that Jacob wrongly interpreted as, "What's going on?"

"Do you hear that?" Jacob spoke in a very loud whisper, so as not to be rude. But this had the effect of making his question about fire seem silly. *Who whispers such flammable words?*

"What?"

"The beeping? Is it the fire alarm?"

"What?"

"The beeping. Is the house on fire?"

"What?"

Getting nowhere, and now fully awake, Jacob ignored the final What. He twisted his legs over the side of the bed and used toes to grope for slippers. He searched in the dark for his hanging robe, prioritizing quiet over hurrying to see if the house was really roasting to the ground. Perhaps a part of his inner self cackled, *Let it burn.*

As he made it down the spinal staircase to the kitchen, he grew confident the house was not on fire. But something was definitely wrong. The exact opposite of fire, in fact. Jacob entered Alaska, and his breath puffed out in the nighttime dusk now filtered with milky window moonlight. Jacob hugged his robe tight and went for the thermostat.

"Thirty three degrees!" his whisper roused a startled Eleanor who had been sleeping inside the nook of a dining room chair.

"Meow"

"What's going on here?"

"Meow"

"It's freezing!"

"Meow"

Ignoring Eleanor, Jacob tried turning the thermostat up but realized it was already set at 67 degrees.

An awful silence hit him. The house was cold and it wasn't saying a word. Homes built generations past always made sounds—their vital signs. But this place was quiet—the radiators didn't rattle or jostle or tittle or rumble. The 'ol gal wasn't breathing.

For a moment, he froze. Not from the thirty three degrees, but the new problem that he simply did not have the mental capacity to face at 4:32am on a Wednesday morning in a robe and unhelpful cat weaving figure 8s between his legs.

*Keep your hand on the wheel 'ol boy.* One part of Jacob voiced encouragement to the other. Then an angelic voice sang a few bars of an unknown song that Jacob felt as some siren's call from the back of a church pew. Maybe this was a problem for the universe to solve. Maybe he should cinch tight his robe, walk back up the steps, get under the covers, and see what the sunrise brought. Maybe everything would be warm and back to normal by then.

But his mind strayed underneath his feet, to the bone head still sitting in the dirt like a benign tumor causing no trouble now but poised to savage some day soon. Jacob inhaled for four seconds, exhaled for eight, and sat in silence for ten full seconds. To his amazement, it helped. He knew he was in control

Before he could decide what that meant, Liam emerged frozen at the foot of the stairs. He stood atop the calico prone to sarcasm.

∞

**"Damn, it's freezing,"** Liam discovered.

Jacob nodded. "Uh, yea."

"Boiler must not be keeping up." Liam guessed. "Yea, emergency heat is supposed to be kicking on, but it isn't doing much. I don't really know anything about this stuff."

In an act of *noblesse oblige*, the exhausted chef mumbled, "Let me take a look, I guess," while making his way toward the basement stairs.

A cold sizzle bubbled atop Jacob's skin. *How had he forgotten?* There were problems bigger than a cold house. Bigger even than frozen pipes. Problems like explaining why there is an unearthed skull in the basement.

"Right, right." Jacob was on unfamiliar terrain. He couldn't improvise his way out of an HVAC discussion—he may as well try to speak in Eleanor *Mew Mews*.

With a swiftness that sent Jacob's stomach to his throat, Liam took a few strides, dipped his head under the door frame, and stepped down on the sagging basement pine.

Like a man being walked down the green mile to his electric chair, an immediate resignation fell over Jacob as he followed two paces behind. *There is simply no way out now. I have no plan. I have no story. And he is walking to the boiler, mere feet away from the skull I haven't told him about.*

Air deflated from his capillaries, his neck muscles rubberized, his head flopped forward, chin on chest. *This is it. I didn't even last a week.* Near the bottom of the steps he made up his mind—Confession. No weird story or excuses—he'd tell the truth. He found the skull a few days ago, didn't want to bother him with it, and that was that. *Oops.*

Perhaps the River was trying to tell the skull to disappear from his life. He'd go back to the real world of compromises—calls from Colorado—dealing with the Board so he could shovel money into a bank account that was then shoveled back out to pay for food and fixing up the 'ol gal. He'd repeat that for decades, eventually live in a fixed up house, and die peacefully after feeding ducks for a few years. It was not a bad draw in life, all things considered. So it goes.

Jacob stopped at the last stair and waited to hear the sound of the skull's discovery.

It never came.

*Was it too dark for Liam to see? Was he not looking at the ground? Was he too tired and not thinking straight?*

Mustering courage enough, Jacob walked in behind Liam, who looked stupefied tapping an old dial of some kind on the ancient heating system. Jacob dared a sideways glance in the direction of the skull and only then remembered that he'd covered it with a sheet, rumpling it up casually so as not to draw attention. In the dark of an early morning home emergency, the pile attracted none of Liam's mind.

"Damn. Seems like it's trying to crank stuff out but struggling. Need to call someone, I guess."

"Yes, that makes sense. Pretty much the only thing we can do," Jacob added nothing of value.

And as quick as he came, like Santa back through the chimney, Liam was upstairs with the speed of a man who remembered that snakes may be slithering all around him.

∞

**One crisis averted** only to spawn another. A colony of HVAC folks would be marching down into the basement that very afternoon. It was a minor miracle that Rooster & Sons & Heating & Cooling were available so quickly. Jacob ignored concern about the unnecessary ampersand in their name.

The Rooster folks said they would get there as soon as possible, "after we finish our lunch at the latest." Jacob almost asked them what they were eating—assuming that McDonalds would be quicker than if they sat down at a diner. He needed to know how much time he had. But instead Jacob said, "Sounds great. I'll be here whenever."

Detective Maymerry hoped he had a few hours to think, think, think. What he most thought was: *Should I throw in the towel?*

It had only been two days since finding the skull—he'd decided what to do by not deciding—but now the same options presented themselves. The thought occurred to him that maybe he'd have to make this decision every day, over and over, until his last day. Life was just one damn decision after another.

Jacob inhaled for four breaths, exhaled for four, and then waited for the relief to flow. It didn't so he walked to his second floor office to think somewhere new. He stared at the ceiling in the room of packed boxes, his neck crimped against the top of his chair, and slowly twirled in a circle. If anyone saw him in this private moment they'd wonder how this was the sole legal professional at the head of the AAMCLDS and not a toddler daydreaming about what he's going to do once released from time-out.

His chair spinning stopped when Jacob heard a loud Meow! followed one second later by the Ring a Ding Ding of his cell on the desk. The timing was suspicious, as if Eleanor felt the cell phone vibrations in the air a few seconds early. Cats are spooky.

A text from Liam: **"Delivery didn't arrive—driving to Baltimore to pick it up—we're gonna order in tonight."**

In a flash Jacob struck off one of the options before him. He was not going to tell anyone about the skull. *Why burden another stressed, overworked, project-riddled soul.*

For an indulgent moment, Jacob considered himself a real hero. It faded the next instant when he realized he still had a decision to make—the head's fate rested in him. *With great power comes great responsibility*, Jacob knew from many movies.

Not telling Liam eliminated one of three possibilities. Better but not good enough. The two remaining options remained to Pitch or Investigate.

How to decide? He swore he heard the tick of a clock that didn't exist in his office. *Was that another beep from the basement?* He waited for the sound of gravel indicating the Rooster professionals with the unnecessary & in their name were pulling up the driveway. Was this skull worth any of this silly chaos? Was he taking years off his life by not chucking the thing and moving on?

From nowhere Jacob remembered some ancient bit of wisdom from a forgotten high school class—*No one can make you live in fear without your consent!* He smiled to no one and the most idiotic version of himself whispered in his ear, *Jacob's still on the case. The adventure continues!*

∞

**Detective Maymerry** acted with the speed of a cat mid free-fall. The skull was in danger. Roosters would soon descend the basement stairs, start pecking away at the boiler, and ruin the whole damn thing.

A white sheet over the skull would not be enough—not on an opponent like Rooster & Sons & Heating & Cooling. Male siblings can never be fully professional. Jacob envisioned the youngest Rooster son with the cleanest boots lifting the sheet just to see, or maybe  accidentally kicking it, innocently shattering a fragile piece of history.

No, a sheet would not do.

Moving it from its resting spot seemed out of the question. Lifting the skull and hiding it in some empty closet felt blasphemous, though Jacob couldn't explain why. It was the river. Or perhaps the budding archaeologist finally remembered that the exact location of the fossil was as critical as the bone itself. *Touch nothing more. You are a steward charged with this most difficult of missions. No cheating.*

While waiting for sounds of the gravel driveway, Jacob went to the basement and stared at the skull, hoping a solution would pop into his head. The only thing that did pop in was the notion that he could bury it in the corner of the yard and go on with his life without any of this nonsense.

But he didn't do that. Instead, he inhaled for three seconds, exhaled for four, and walked to the garage to find inspiration there. Jacob's eye drifted to a trash pile—discarded papers, leaves, and other nonsense. Turned over on its side was an extremely old plastic storage bin with matching lid, a large hole in the bottom.

And a hole is just what Jacob needed—about the size of a human head. He grabbed the bin along with the still intact lid, and hauled it down to his basement lair. Jacob said aloud, "If it fits, it sits."

Eleanor was not there, and so the words bounced off the stone walls, heard only by the boulder to the center of the earth. It agreed with Jacob's assessment.

With eyes closed for luck, he lifted the plastic tub, flipped it right side up, and lowered it delicately with the hole directly over the skull.

Jacob felt time slow as the plastic came down.

It fit. Almost too perfectly, with such precision that Jacob, a usually very grounded man, wondered if this was a sign. *But from whom?*

The philosophical matter must wait, because his job wasn't nearly done. He heard it. Gravel. Trucks. Two of them. At least that's what he thought based on the sounds echoing somewhere above him. He imagined an army of young sons emerging from the &&& white trucks, marching down to catch him red-handed.

All of that flashed into his mind in a whiz burr. He recovered as the first driver's door popped open.

No time to linger. The river had taken hold of Jacob. He set the lid on the broken tub which didn't actually look broken now that the hole was hidden flat against the dirt.

Not good enough. It might be moved while the sons worked, and if they tried to move the bin—*Game Over.*

Bricks. He saw them thrown in a corner with old paint cans that he swore he'd never seen down there until that very moment. Jacob haphazardly re-opened the bin, set the old cans and two handfuls of bricks inside, and shut it again. He tossed the dirty white sheet over top of it.

It was only then that he realized he'd spun himself into a web—he'd never be able to explain being caught by the heating and cooling family trying to hide a human head in the basement. Jacob was a blank canvas here, no reputation, and locals might skip, hop, and jump to the serial killer card if one of the Rooster boys started spreading rumors about the new guy storing skulls in the old Victorian rock house on the hill.

"This is tricky," he said aloud to the boulder.

"Meow." Eleanor appeared from nowhere to sit atop the rock with a joker smile up to her eyes.

Moving with as much speed as his cardigan allowed, Jacob bound back up the basement stairs. He glanced out the kitchen window and confirmed the approaching disaster—two white vans. Both decked out in three ampersands—&&&—on each side and the back of the vans. Eighteen ampersands had descended and matching pairs of Rooster Boys would soon be released, down into his basement, to destroy evidence, and start rumors that would ruin their lives. They might even have to move. All because of Jacob's disastrous decisions.

A prematurely wrinkled man in flannel emerged with several grunts, wisps of black hair, a medium pot belly, and decades deep exhaustion.

Jacob ran down for a final check, looking at Eleanor with pleading eyes, hoping for guidance. She remained on the boulder and didn't even do him the dignity of looking, instead pretending to be interested in something inside the washing machine.

*Knocking at the door.*
*More knocking.*

Moving without thinking, he ran to the dryer, pulled out a pile of recently cleaned clothes, tossed them atop the broken bin, and then tipped the empty laundry basket over to create a mess big enough to be ignored by HVAC workers.

A long exhale without any inhale, Jacob Maymerry went back up the stairs to face the Rooster boys and his coming doom.

# — Chapter 6 —

**"So ya gotta** boiler problem," the eldest Rooster crowed as Jacob opened the door.

"Looks like it," Jacob said with a fake smile. "Here, I'll show you down. We woke up to no heat. It's not really my area, but hoping you can at least tell us what needs to be done."

Jacob secretly wanted the Roosters to look, diagnose a problem, then head out. He could deal with a bad boiler for a few days if it bought him time to figure out how to better solve the skull in the basement problem without getting caught.

"Mmm Hmmm. Happy to help. Rog is coming in a second."

Rog, it turned out, was the only son. At least the only son on this job. Two vans. Two men. Jacob allowed himself a pang of hope. The faint traces of wrinkle lines on the young Rooster suggested the family came from a long line of hard workers. He was probably thirty but looked forty five.

Jacob flipped on the light, and walked the two men to the large, clunky, copper machine in the center of the room. The metal monster radiated pipes of all kinds up through the veins of the 'ol gal. Jacob felt lightheaded as he stared at it—a boiler octopus gripping the insides of the house, holding it in place. The pipes almost moved as Jacob stared, the stress of the morning gave way to a woozy exhaustion.

He heard another beep from the deep, but the Rooster men didn't say anything, and Jacob was not about to ask about imaginary sounds. He was already on the precipice of social disaster. No point creating more rumor fodder if they ended up finding a skull that was now clearly trying to be hidden.

*You fool, Jacob.*

∞

**Introductory chat revealed** that the Roosters came from a long line of Rogers. The current patriarch was Roger III and the son was Roger IV. A straightforward family tree of RRs.

Papa Rooster diagnosed the issue instantly, "Lemme guess. It runs, right? It seems to be giving it a good go? But it won't heat? That's it, right?"

"Yep, exactly." Jacob hoped nothing more would be asked of him. His least favorite position was the home idiot, being questioned by professionals exposing his ignorance of even basic topics.

"It happened overnight, when the temperatures dipped, right?"

"You got it." Jacob was getting slightly annoyed at the way this was dragging out.

"You don't know when this boiler was last cleaned do you?" Roger Rooster III flashed a smile of worn teeth.

"Hmmm, unfortunately, nope. Don't think so." Jacob was reminded of law school, when professors kept asking questions to unprepared students who they knew had no answers.

"Well, see, that's your problem," Papa Rooster said and Jacob couldn't help but feel personally attacked.

"Oh yea?" *Man, just tell me.* Jacob's chest thumped and he glanced over at Son Rooster who was looking like a curious toddler at the pile of clothes atop the sheet-covered plastic bin.

"It's a cleaning issue. Build up. Who knows how long it's been there, but boy is that a job. Look at that Roger." He motioned to his son who leaned in and looked at something inside the metal machine.

It took another 10 minutes before they agreed to lightly clean the unit. That was opposed to deep cleaning of the unit, which would take a week or more. But that would prove too costly, because every one of the ten thousand nobs, nozzles, and chunks on the beast would need to be removed, wiped of all filth, and then reassembled. Jacob decided on the band-aid option of a light clean—far cheaper, immediate, and time to plan next steps for the basement skull.

Jacob's stomach dropped under his gut as Papa Rooster said, "We have everything we need down here. It'll be a few hours, but I'll yell for ya when we're done."

"Oh. How wonderful. We really appreciate it." Jacob said somehow.

As he walked up the basement stairs, his head fogged, and he had to press a palm against the narrow wall to stay upright. He almost felt like a poison gas was seeping into him, and he realized he hadn't eaten or drank a single thing since the night before. His body was a ball of twisty adventure thoughts. Life was suddenly more complex than ever before. And now he would be waiting for hours. Waiting to hear a scream from the basement announcing that a curious Rooster had gone and done it. Revealing Jacob's secret and causing an untold number of life twirls.

He reached the top of the stairs, wondering how he would accomplish any work, then felt a flick of hair on an exposed ankle. "Meow."

"This is all your fault," he said to Eleanor's backside as she drifted down to gossip with the guests.

∞

**Thirty minutes into** the Rooster cleaning job, the very basement confrontation that Jacob feared rose as sounds up the spinal stairs to worrying ears from his listening spot in the kitchen.

"Me OW!" An extra sharp Meow.

Psssss. "Meow!" A Meow with an exclamation point.

Hisssssss. An Eleanor hissy fit. Did one of the Rogers step on her tail?

"Meeooooow…" An unmistakable, drawn out Meow of Warning.

"You can get it over here," he heard Roger III say, though he wasn't sure if he was talking to Eleanor or his son. The disturbance quieted and the sounds returned to scraping and metal dinging and Roger grunts.

∞

**"All set!" Jacob** heard a manly yell from the deep.

*Hallelujah.* The Roosters finished 90 minutes later without making any sounds indicating they'd found a human skull.

"Wanna come down and take a look?" The father said in a way that assumed an answer.

*Not really, but thanks!* "Sure thing. One second."

Jacob popped up from the makeshift dining room table where he'd accomplished nothing and bound down the pine basement steps.

Papa Rooster was on his knees, belly touching dirt, shining a flashlight under the boiler beast. "As you can see here…"

By the time Jacob was done, his white T-shirt was filthy, forced to shuffle around the sasquatch metal box, look underneath from various angles, all while mummering "Oh, Yep, I see that, Right, Excellent," over and over without a clue what the Rooster was describing.

Roger IV said, "We almost tried to get it from this side, but your laundry was in the way. And the cat was napping so cozy on that tupperware, we didn't have the heart to move her."

Jacob looked for Eleanor, but she already bored of the situation and dissolved somewhere in the dark.

∞

**Well, thanks for** all your help," Jacob said a little too quickly as the son made another boiler comment.

It was only when they were squeezing their large frames out of the back door that Jacob let himself fully believe that the skull was safe for another day. In his relief, Jacob's muscles relaxed, and he got a little careless. His hand had been twisting the metal circle in his pocket. The piece that he'd found near the skull—the only other artifact that might, possibly, who knows, be some sort of clue to the skull's identity. He twisted it in his pocket, and he pulled it out in front of the Roosters.

"Whatcha got there?" Roger IV said.

*Dammit.* Jacob's mind was still filled with that poison gas, and so he told the truth, "Oh, I don't really know. Something old I found in the basement here. Trying to figure it out actually."

"Lemme see." Son Rooster was sparse with words. But he had a curious mind, like a squirrel with a deep nut interest. Being a polite man, Jacob handed it over.

"Well I'll be. Dad, look at that." He passed it to his father who looked at it with half curiosity. "Yep."

Jacob watched, confused. "You know what that thing is?"

Roger IV smiled. He had dirt on his lip. "Of course. You found it down there right? It's a button or badge, delivery. Coal delivery. Must have been one of the Boyles or Weavers. Those are the only two that did it here."

"Oh?" How quickly the Rooster became interesting and Jacob wanted the man to keep talking.

"Yea, these were on their uniform." He pointed to his chest. "Or here." He moved the point to a spot above his forehead. "Back in those days they wore coveralls and hats. All formal, like a mailman or milkman. They were kinda special, ya know. Like pilot wings. It was a brother-hood."

"You ready?" Papa Rooster wanted to leave and ushered his son out. Jacob followed as they loaded tools into trucks. Jacob peppered the son with questions, trying to decipher what he was saying about the metal object.

By the time they drove away, Jacob's mood thawed—the house was no longer cold, and his skull investigation was getting interesting. Roger Rooster IV explained that the object he'd found very likely belonged to one of four men. That's because heating and cooling work had been practiced by fathers and sons since fire itself was harnessed. And in all the time that coal delivery would have happened in this 'ol gal in Willou-by, only two families did the service—each a father and son. The Boyles and Weavers.

Was he getting close to the end of this adventure? Is the skull a Weaver or a Boyle?

He felt like the river was carrying him wherever he needed to be. *Silly little Jacob, rivers are for trix, or did you already forget?* Jacob thought this from nowhere but shook it away with a shudder.

∞

**Jacob tried to** explain the Roosters on a call to Liam.

"So just two were here. Three and four," Jacob said.

Liam was immediately lost. "What?"

"Just three and four were here."

"Four people were here? That's a lot for one job"

"No, just the two Rogers. Roger three and Roger four. That's their names. It's confusing."

"To be honest, I have no idea what you are talking about."

"I know, it's hard to get straight. There are only two Roger Roost-ers, at least I think. The father is technically the third, and his son is the fourth."

"Look, I really don't care. But they got it fixed, so I'm happy." His voice cracked and didn't sound happy so much as exhausted as he hung up. Jacob wondered if an obnoxious patron had given him trouble today or he had opened the salt shaker and it all spilled into a pot. It was surprising how little Jacob truly knew about the ins and outs of the restaurant business.

A call from CO led Jacob into an hour of AAMCLDS work, both the KBC and ABC Wars had ignited Board President Gladys. But around 3pm, Jacob put his phone on silent and made a gut decision.

Perhaps the river forced him into the decision, but he knew it was the correct one. Because for the first time in too long, he was excited about the future. He knew exactly what to do next and where to go. Jacob Maymerry was headed to the library.

# —— Chapter 7 ——

**Huxley Library sat** as the architectural lion marking the northwest corner of Old Town Willouby. Its copper dome crown rose like a beacon on the city skyline—long ago patinated to a blue-green. Like the Statue of Liberty, it beckoned weary travelers of all stripes—from the tourist to the downtrodden.

A sweeping main lion paw staircase provided a berth wide enough for a kindergarten class to enter hand-in-hand. Jacob carved a narrow path as he cut up the steps, next to two chatting women. Jacob assumed they were deep in debate about the books they had returned. But he instead caught snippets of a bizarre grammar disagreement about the size and frequency of contractions.

Jacob almost needed two hands to yank open the ten foot wooden doors. He imagined entering a busy castle as his eyes adjusted to a small flurry of quiet but diligent activity swirling inside. This was his first time in the Willouby institution, but he hadn't come unprepared. A quick browse of the Huxley website revealed that he needed to head deep down, to the bowels of the feline, to find a woman named Barbara. As the head archivist, she might be the critical figure in this little mystery that his cat dug up. Barbara was the woman who knew things, especially about old things.

At the start of his walk he'd found a single, crisp, tri-folded $1 bill in his jeans pocket, which he took as an omen from the river of good news ahead. He circled his way down the stairs to the deadly quiet Archives, the home of all of Willouby's oldest secrets. Or so Jacob hoped.

The room looked like a museum of information-gathering. Shelves of books dominated the main floor, and a cursory glance revealed these to be tomes of a magical variety. No glossy covers or smiling images. Instead the texts looked homemade, pieced together, self-published, reference books, yellow pages from the last 100 years, reams, rolls, and reels of various sorts. Microfiche in one corner, old card catalogs in another, and stacks of interconnected storage containers that Jacob could only imagine held an ancient tapestry of a famous war won by Willouby locals against invading Englishmen.

A simple desk sat in the last corner, sparse and clean, with a green shaded lamp that made Jacob's heart skip a beat. Sitting behind it was the woman Jacob had come on this adventure to find. He assumed it was her because a simple brown name plate made it clear: Miss Barbara.

∞

**Barbara Johnson was** an institution at the institution. Jacob was not sure of her proper title but *Master of the Archives* or *Keeper of the Keys* rang a bell. Dressed as Jacob hoped in ankle length sweeping fabric of dark red sunset, brown sandals with a dozen criss crossed straps, and twirling an actual ring of keys. *What a delight.* Jacob bubbled inside. *Her hair's even in a bun!*

The 'Miss' title was misleading, as Barbara Johnson appeared in her mid-70s. She carried the iron-weight of expertise that comes with anyone who takes their job seriously and has the same role for 50 years.

Miss Barbara gave a gentle librarian smile as he entered. "Welcome to the Archives. If you could sign in on that form up front, I'd then be happy to help you find whatever you're looking for."

"Wonderful. Thanks so much." Jacob signed, noticing he was the morning's first visit.

"Appreciate you doing that. So what brings you down this way? Hunting for something specific or following a muse?"

Jacob already decided on his approach—honesty with a touch of omission. It was a simple story, he explained to Barbara Johnson, who listened with such rapt interest that Jacob went on longer than he intended. He revealed that he'd found this old button or badge. He mentioned how a local HVAC professional provided the 1st clue.

"Was it a Rooster?" Barbara asked.

Jacob nodded with a smile, explaining that the young Rooster said it looked like a coal company uniform piece. Being new to town and fascinated with local history, Jacob used this little discovery as a reason to make his first visit to Huxley Library, a place he'd seen in a hundred photos before they arrived.

"How wonderful. Well, I'm very glad you made your way here. Let's see if we can help." Barbara responded with just the right warmth, and Jacob shrunk into a child. What a relief. Instead of having to figure out all these boxes and Dewey Decimal configurations, why not let Miss Barbara lead the way.

"Hmmmm. Fascinating. There are a few places we can look," Barbara started walking and talking. *Was she pretending to be less confident than she actually was?* Perhaps showing off her knowledge was beneath her. Miss Barbara Johnson no longer had any ladders to climb, status to maintain, or good old boys to impress.

"Do you mind if I take a peek?" She held out her hand and Jacob dropped the metal artifact. "Splendid. I bet figuring out the origin of this has been nagging at you. These little mysteries always get under my skin." Jacob was already growing fond of the interest that Barbara showed in his mission. It was almost as if she actually felt his internal tug of war.

"For starters, we might want to take a closer look." She motioned toward the microfiche corner, and Jacob noticed that one of the stations included some optical glass-microscope hybrid. Barbara set the button down, and zoomed the magnifier in front of it. She adjusted a knob for focus, took one glance herself, then smiled at Jacob, "Why don't you see."

Jacob was struck by how much his eyes missed. His feeble senses showed this to be a jammed piece of metal with an indistinguishable raised imprint covered in a layer of filth from decades in the dirt. But with the magic microscope eyes, he saw much more.

There was life in this little piece of metal. The light grey stain left color disorientation—an image, numbers, and shapes popped out enough to grasp at their meaning. 1, 9, 0. *And are those letters?* Jacob stared in silence then heard Barbara's voice in his ear from above, like a whispering angel, "Do you see the year, 1903?"

"Yes, I do." Jacob almost giggled it out. "And there are words here too, or a few letters."

"That's right." Barbara Johnson already knew the answer but savored helping Jacob find his own wings.

The more he looked through the lenses, the more he gained confidence in his ability to translate the shapes and bumps he saw into something more. A small picture that might have been a coat of arms or seal—and dashed across that logo were the letters AFOFL. One more message might have been added across the top of the button, but it was too far gone for Jacob to get anything else. He pulled back from the microscope, blinked to adjust his eyes, and smiled at the Keeper of the Keys.

"Pretty neat," she beamed back.

"Absolutely. I made out some letters." Jacob struggled to share what he saw. "Not falafel but a-lafel. Do you know what that word means? Is it even

English?"

With more grace than he deserved, Barbara offered an alternative idea. "It may not be a word but an acronym. AFOFL. One idea is that it's the AF of L?

*Of Course. That's definitely it.* "Hmmm. Perhaps." Jacob needed a little more help.

"The American Federation of Labor." She started walking toward her desk, and Jacob followed. "If you'll give me a minute I believe I have a file in the back that may be useful."

She disappeared through the Archives Staff Only door. Jacob was reminded of a vacation at an all-inclusive resort in the Caribbean. His skin still tingled with the embarrassment of being asked to leave a delicious buffet he found at the resort because it was for Premier Guests Only. He was allowed to carry one chicken strip out on a folded napkin. Jacob learned then that life was different back rooms, all the way down until the end.

∞

**"Got it," Barbara** emerged from the Staff Only section holding a thick manilla folder in one hand.

Jacob watched in growing awe as this master of old-school information revealed a color photo of the very metal object he'd found next to the skull. Or something damn near just like it.

*Bless you Barbara Johnson.*

"So you can see, this version is probably the one. The missing text along the top is visible here—Ice & Coal Drivers Union. I think what you have is the pin worn on the cap of delivery drivers, back when they made weekly stops, before refrigerators and furnaces. Did you happen to find this on or near an old hat?"

Jacob felt such gratitude and comfort in Barbara's presence that he almost blurted like a too-truthful elementary student. *Not a cap, but I did find the man's skull nearby.*

He held that in, and the search continued. "That's fantastic. So neat. I didn't expect to get this much information." Barbara bowed her head like a master musician after a flawless performance.

"Now if you have time, or could point me in the right direction, I'm also hoping to figure out who specifically might have delivered the coal and worn this. The Rooster, Roger Rooster—the son," Jacob struggled out the phrasing, but took faith in a small smile that Barbara Johnson failed to hide. "The Rooster folks mentioned two other families who worked the city, or our neighborhood. I'm hoping to uncover a bit more about that."

Barbara Johnson's eyes twinkled as her fingers tinkled the skeleton keys on her waist. Key chimes echoed across the otherwise silent Archives. Feeling a friendship blossoming as their adventure continued, she playful turned her back to Jacob and said, "You need only ask. Follow me."

∞

**They walked to** a section of bookshelf with homemade binding of yellow pages laid out in order. The earlier the year the thinner the volume, all the way to immediately after the Civil War. Back then the guidebooks appeared more like a children's scrapbook, with random bits of information written, pasted, and stuck inside. The yellowbooks were slightly more organized by the turn of the century, when Jacob's 'ol Victorian was built around the boulder to the center of the earth—four blocks from the basement archives where he now sat.

"Do you mind telling me the address where you found it?" Barbara asked this with the utmost discretion, like the custodian of a Swiss safety deposit box.

Jacob had thought this through. He wouldn't mention the skull, obviously. Instead he shared that he was the new owner of that old Victorian house that was surrounded by rocks. Though Barbara Johnson, institutional knowledge holder of all Willouby, might already know.

"We just bought the 'ol place on Nottingham and Fenway."

"The rock house. I know it well. Congratulations!" Did she just wink?

"Thanks. So far so good." Very original, Jacob.

Barbara asked a few more questions and Jacob gave sparse details. When was the house built? Finished in 1901, maybe. When was the boiler added? Roger Rooster IV said something about the 40s?

She nodded with each answer and pulled assorted peeling faded honey books from the long stretch of shelf. Laying them out on one banquet length table, Barbara opened each to a specific page. She tilted her head in satisfaction, "Yes, that makes sense. Why don't you take a look."

Hoping he wasn't about to fail a test, Jacob walked along the table and noticed they all looked like pages of advertisements. It was alphabetized, and each was related to the letter D. A muppet voice in his head said 'D is for Death.' Followed shortly by 'D is for Danger.' And then finally getting to it, 'D is for Deliveries.'

"Fascinating," Jacob said to ensure he didn't stare too long in silence at the pages that Barbara had prepared for him. He groped to find the exact connection he was looking for—and that Barbara Johnson already knew.

The books were laid out by year, with random gaps of time between each. The first was from 1901, the next 1910, then 1923, 1940, 1954, and 1955.

It took a minute, but Jacob eventually followed the trail that Barbara had politely left for him. The Deliveries header had subcategories, one of which was "Coal & Ice." In the 1901 book, only one name was listed—Weaver & Sons. The same in 1923—Weaver & Sons Ice and Coal Delivery. But in 1940 things had changed. Boyle & Sons Deliveries were the only option. The same in 1954, and then nothing listed in 1955. By that point, these deliveries must have stopped or been re-named into new categories.

Barbara said, "Isn't it funny that they delivered coal and ice. Total opposites, but the delivery system was the same. Hot and cold, two sides to one coin. Can't have one without the other. Reminds me of my favorite Christmas cartoon—forgot the name—HeatBrother and SnowBrother. Now that'd be a good name for one of these companies—The Miser Brothers!"

Jacob faked laughed. It wasn't that Barbara's joke wasn't fine. It was fine. But Jacob knew what Barbara didn't, that this wasn't a fun historical adventure but a matter of life and death. Jacob wanted to figure out which of these brothers might be the head in his basement.

"It looks like if that button was lost in your yard, there's a good chance it came from the Boyle or Weaver family," Barbara said. "The year 1903 might refer to anything. Hmm."

Jacob already assumed this—the Roosters had said as much. But now he wanted to parlay this adventure with Barbara into the real heart of it. He asked, "I wonder what happened to these folks. Are the families still around?"

"The Boyles I can help you with," Barbara said with another smile while walking to a new book aisle. How much information is she withholding? "I knew the family, some are still around. The original Jack Boyle bought the business, I'm pretty sure. I met him once rocking on a porch in the early 70s before he died. His two sons moved away in the 60s, though I was classmates for a few years with a Boyle or two. These would have been the original Jack's grandkids. But, they moved in elementary school and not much connected to Willouby after that."

Jacob didn't know what evidence he hoped to find. He tried to remember that checking names off the list was also progress. But if he really was on a river adventure, he needed more confirmation.

"Here's the last bit of information that I know of on the Boyle family in Willouby." Barbara grabbed a large binder from a shelf full of them. She opened to a photocopied obituary inside a plastic sheet. It wasn't long, but it said enough. Jonathan 'Jack' Boyle died in September of 1977. He was interred in a cemetery outside Richmond, near his birthplace and where his children now lived.

The odds were shrinking that it was a Boyle skull under his house. "Fascinating," Jacob said as he finished scanning the obituary. "What about the Weavers? Do you happen to know anything about them?"

"Believe it or not, that might be above my pay grade. Lucky for you, we have Aunt Mabel."

∞

## Aunt Mabel?

Was she a new, ultra-sophisticated Artificial Intelligence learning tool? Perhaps all the documents in the Archives had been fed into a machine. Maybe all you had to do was ask the machine named Mabel, and she spat out an answer. They were always giving cute nicknames to robots to make them seem less scary. "Oh great, Aunt Mabel." Jacob wasn't sure if he was supposed to know. He looked around for which computer contained Aunt Mabel. Or maybe it was in the back room, needing one of the keys that Barbara carried but that Jacob had yet to see her use.

"You already know her?" Barbara asked, impressed.

"Oh, not really, no. The name sounds familiar." Jacob flailed.

"Of course," Miss Barbara smiled, "She's quite popular around here."

Jacob's confusion grew, so he nodded and let Barbara lead him.

"Aunt Mabel travels frequently, but I think she's home now. Mabel is not interested in computers but sometimes she dares a text."

So it really was a woman named Aunt Mabel. Jacob grew confused. His loopy mind pictured an aged crone in the woods who would tell Jacob all that he wanted to know for the low price of the tears of a first-born child.

"Here's her number." Barbara handed over a scrap of paper. "But wait to send something until tomorrow. I'll reach out tonight to let her know that you've been here and that I sent you her way. So she knows you're not wasting her time."

"Oh," Jacob's stomach dropped at that last line. *What dragon's lair was he walking into?*

"I didn't mean it quite like that. She's an angel, sometimes. It's only that she gets many requests."

"Of course."

"She knows more than I ever could, believe it or not. But she's a character, and has limited time, so let me touch base first."

Jacob left the Archives with the one phrase bouncing around his skull— *She's an angel, sometimes.*

*And the other times?*

# —— Chapter 8 ——

**Jacob looked back** on the Huxley dome and waited for the Walk sign. It struck him that it was not quite a lion—but a Sphinx. He might have been a bit light-headed from skipping breakfast, but from his angle he could almost believe it sparkled with a hood atop an ancient cat monument. Would Huxley library still be standing in 4500 years, like the old stone in Egypt? *It'll take a miracle*, Jacob thought as the light changed. *But that will be a problem for somebody else.*

Then Liam called.

"Can you stop by City Hall? I need to pick up a permit so we can start a project. It's all taken care of, you just need to say your name, swipe it, and bring it home."

"Of course. No problem." Jacob said automatically, knowing he was more skilled at picking up permits than hammers.

"Thanks." Liam yelled above restaurant kitchen clamor chaos.

Unnecessary doubts slithered immediately through Jacob's veins. He had a habit of agreeing to things without asking for details—often having no idea what he was doing, setting himself up to be a fool. *What is this permit for? Where do I pick it up in City Hall, the front desk? Do I need to bring a wallet? Do I need proof of address, like getting a new library card? Do they let any random stranger walk in and pick up a permit? But why would someone steal a building permit?*

Jacob tried to wrestle control of his thoughts from the other version of himself and focus instead on his breathing. He stopped cold on the sidewalk, inhaled for 5 seconds, his chest expanding like a balloon, then exhaled for 6 seconds back to his normal size.

He alternated between looking at the sidewalk and the sky. He did not want to make eye contact with locals. He wasn't feeling his sharpest, and couldn't afford a wrong first impression with these folks, some of whom he hoped to be future friends.

As he looked up at floating lamb clouds, Jacob first noticed steeples. Willouby was an old American place, so the heavens were reserved for Jesus first and highest. A panoply of crosses on sharp, slated church roofs marked the generations search for answers. By the third block, still having made eye contact with no one, he saw two additions to the skyline—large clocks on regal towers. One he knew was the very City Hall that he was walking toward. The other was nearby—the old City Hall, now a Civil War museum.

The church and state remained the pillars holding the sky above Willouby.

And as Jacob walked toward the clocktower of the state he was faced with the New Age of the church. In a baffling two minute conversation that made Jacob temporarily forget why he was on the sidewalk in the first place, he returned to 1969.

The Summer of Love skipped much of Willouby, but its misty spirit existed now in a mixed bag of free-spirits, deepest thinkers, and live-and-let-live meditation guides who roamed freely. Jacob bumped into a mid-week loiterer asking for cash in exchange for handing out flowers from a cup. The clean-cut twentysomething Flower Cup Guy whispered to Jacob as he walked by, "If you give me $1, I will tell you the secret of eternal happiness."

Jacob was rarely one to do this. But the fact that he found a single, crisp $1 bill in his pocket that very morning spurred him. *Go with the flow of the river. Take life as it comes to you.* Jacob stretched his arm out to the street philosopher, who stared at the bill before asking, as if Jacob was making a life-defining decision from which he could never return, "Are you 100% sure you are ready to hear this?"

Jacob thought *No*, said nothing, and nodded Yes.

The man handed over a delicate white rose, cleared his throat dramatically, and said with the calm confidence of supreme acceptance:

"Desire leads to unhappiness.
So desire nothing.
But desiring not to desire is still desiring.
So do not desire to not desire.
That's to already have everything that you desire.
So what do you desire?"

Jacob blinked twice, wondering if this was the worst way he'd ever spent a pocket dollar. In a rare act of honesty born out of instinct to avoid discomfort at all moments, he said, "I don't know what I desire."

The young man beamed a smile and said, "Congratulations. You've done it!"

Jacob nodded and walked away, confused, thinking about the young man's teeth as he smiled. They were very white and straight, with the perfection of past braces. *How did he end up there doing that?*

*How did I end up here doing this?*

He was one block away when Jacob realized he was holding the white rose in one hand and the pocket dollar in the other. The gentlefella had not taken the money after all.

∞

**City Hall was** of a size and cleanliness such that all visitors knew civic duties were taken seriously—but not too seriously that everyone hated each other. He imagined a large hearted and bellied 1920's Councillor making small talk in a stone corner, slapping the back of a friend, and walking home to Ma before supper got cold.

That's what Jacob was thinking when he opened the large anthill brown doors, checked the collar on his polo to ensure it wasn't sticking up, and realized that it was the same sunshine yellow as the flowers surrounding the steps. He tried to believe this was another good omen.

"Can I help you find something sir?" A kind faced receptionist smiled from a raised pedestal. Her teeth were as straight and white as the flower cup fellow from the sidewalk, and so they might have been former classmates.

"Oh, yes. Do you happen to know where I can find the permit, ah, the Planning Permit Place?" *Jacob, get a grip.*

"Just up there and on the right, sweetheart. You should see the sign painted above the door." She pointed up the rather elegant and heavy stairs that branched off left and right into the pulsing nervous system of the Willouby state.

Glass doors led to a wing of the building labeled Planning and Zoning. Once inside, Jacob went to the main desk where an averaged sized man in a deep ocean blue polo and khakis, slightly messy brown hair, and golden retriever disposition sat trying to gain control of a swiveling stool that wouldn't stop drifting. The poor man swung around a full 360 degrees, as if on a teacup ride, before planting his feet on the ground and manually stopping the loop. Either the city had just received new state-of-the-art office furniture, or this was the gentleman's first day on the job.

The Planning man's face lit up in fright and Jacob heard a mumbling that he interpreted as, "Oh dear, I shouldn't be here."The chap recovered, put on a smile, and said unconvincingly, "Can I help you?"

His name was Peter Rawlings, Vice Chairman of the Willouby Planning Commission, and he and Jacob struck up a rhythmic conversation straight away. "This dang stool is not cooperating," Peter said as he again started a slow drift in a circle. "You bought the old place up there on the hill, the rock house?" He spoke like a man who already knew the answer.

For half a second his legal instinct kicked in and Jacob considered denying it, because maybe this was all an elaborate trap. *Old house, needs lots of work? Skull buried in the basement? Never heard of it.*

But reason took over. "Yes sir, moved in on Monday. So far, so good."

"Great place. So glad someone finally decided to take it on. Any renovation plans?"

*Immediate panic.* Jacob realized at that moment that he knew almost nothing about the long-term plans. Liam would have listed off their scheduled projects and ensured the man that the cherished old house was in good hands. But in that instant the only thing Jacob remembered about the house was there was a head in the basement.

Planning Guy saved him by asking another question before waiting for an answer to his last one. "How old is that place, any idea?"

And to Jacob's astonishment, he knew the answer. He only knew because he had been pondering on it with all this skull business, "I think it started around 1899 and finished two or three years later."

"How wonderful," Peter said quickly before starting to talk about himself. "We just bought the old flower shop on Piccadilly? Not as old as yours, built after the second war, but still storing buried history. I love that stuff." Jacob could tell this man had things on his mind, and so he tried to give a face of deep interest. "Oh wow, do you have any plans for it?"

"So many!" Jacob hit a nerve. "The whole thing was peeling red when we bought it, so we painted it a cream and charcoal with a mural. Soon we'll add a steel beam in between—blending the old and new, fastening the past and the future together. Actually, that steel is being delivered anytime this week. I'm just waiting for the call." Jacob saw this kind-faced Mr. Rawlings in the broken swivel chair turn a shade darker in a silent blush.

"So that's why I might be a little flustered," Peter rambled in a confusing fumble of information. "That and the fact that today's my son's first birthday and I already burnt the cake. Which was my one job."

Jacob frowned in sympathy with his plight.

"And I don't have any more carrots, so I have to run to the store again. Which is a pain."

"Carrots?"

"For the cake."

"Oh, of course." Jacob did not ask who decided carrot cake for the one year old birthday. That's because Peter continued rambling, and Jacob let it wash over him like a comforting sympathy of nonsense. All he remembered was that the 1st birthday party was Ancient Greece themed. Jacob's mood improved, knowing this rather dull man lived life at an even slower pace than he did.

"…and so the challenge is getting enough distinguishing characteristics between each philosopher for a one year old's mind to differentiate. I mean, in the end they are all grey men with long beards. That's why I added party hats to each. Different color ones. We'll see if it works." Peter exhaled, exhausted, as if his rambling was against even his own will.

"Well that's a lot on your mind," Jacob tried to move things along. Then Peter spun and half fell out of the broken stool. He caught himself with a foot, and used the occasion to pretend he was leaving anyway. "Have you seen the map? Let me show you the painting."

∞

**And that's how** Jacob found himself back on the first floor, now near City Hall's rear entrance, staring at a wall size painting that doubled as a map from some bygone era with a handwritten title: *Ye Olde Towne Willouby—A Place of Intersections.*

Peter spoke as if he'd given this same talk to his one year old earlier in the day, "The residents had this commissioned on the 50th anniversary of the peace at Appomattox which ended the Civil War. What a time that was for this little hamlet. I'm sure you know this is the place that changed hands most during that war. I like to think it's because the residents kept changing their minds after hearing better arguments, finally ending with the 3rd Battle of Willouby, when the Northerners won the day for good."

The Vice Chairman of whatever board stared at a corner of the map, perhaps where his flower shop now stood, as if contemplating something deep. But then he pointed vaguely to some patch in the distance and said, "That used to be a Civil War hospital."

"Oh wow," Jacob said, not even trying to find the exact building. Planning Man bore on, "Not many people appreciate the medical history wrapped up in our little field," Peter explained. "Did you know that Stonewall Jackson's personal physician was from Willouby? Dr. Hunter Holmes McGuire. Dr. HH was the one who amputated Stonewall's arm." Almost as an after-thought he added, "Of course it didn't work, he died anyway."

Peter kept going. "I love this painting. Maybe my second favorite thing in town next to Huxley library. Did you know that today it's considered the finest Beaux-Art structure in the state. Designed when viewed from above to be an open book, one wing opening left the other right. It's the defining object in town, and what's better than being known for knowledge?"

*Designed as an open book? Jacob still saw a Sphinx.*

Before he could say another word, Peter flung the back door and walked straight out, "Well, nice meeting you. Hope to see you around."

At the last instant, Jacob remembered, "Wait, I still need that permit." *Close call.*

"Permit," Peter's face blanched, "Ohhh, right. No, I'm sorry about that. I don't work here. I was keeping the seat warm while the intern went to lunch. She should be back shortly, and can definitely help you if you'd like to wait an hour or so. I think the Planning desk is technically closed during lunch."

"Oh, of course. How silly of me." Jacob cringed at his own strangeness. Peter nodded a final goodbye and left like a man remembering he was late for many things.

Jacob turned around and walked back out the front doors, toward his rock house without whatever permit he was supposed to grab. Instead he realized he still held the rose like a lollipop. *Was I holding this flower the entire time? What an odd guy I must seem.*

He took a 4 second deep breath, held it for 3 seconds, and exhaled for 7 seconds. He tried to remember the river that he was on, understanding that everything he saw might be a clue. But the only thing that popped into his head was a wondering. He wondered if the Flower Cup guy bought his white roses from Permit Man's new shop.

What a small world that would be.

<h1 style="text-align:center">— Chapter 9 —</h1>

**Jacob arrived home** to a call from Colorado. But in a rare act of defiance, perhaps buoyed by the river, he did not answer it. Instead he hit the little red phone button that said Decline. His head was elsewhere, and he went to the basement. Jacob wanted to check.

He checked. Everything was as he left it—exactly like anyone who does not believe in ghosts, mysteries, magic, or mayhem already knew full well. A skull, nothing else, unburied in the basement, a button that may be connected in his pocket, a hope for an invitation to meet a mysterious Mabel, and no permit that Liam asked for.

"I'm an idiot." Jacob said to Eleanor. "What am I doing here?"

Eleanor stared back with a blank face that Jacob would never admit said, "You're not an idiot, you're a fool. Completely Clueless."

Jacob almost gasped aloud at Eleanor's vulgarity but caught himself as he realized she hadn't actually said a word and the whole thing was a conversation with his inner self. But the gasp was real, even if the conversation wasn't. And so he tried to swallow it. The result was an absurd choke as the air rushed down his throat.

*Grrggrupuup*

Eleanor jumped off the dryer and turned away quickly up the stairs. Disgusted. Jacob followed her until his phone clanged again. Another call. *Not now Gladys!* Jacob thought and then felt guilty for thinking such a thing. But when he looked, ready to Decline again, he noticed that it wasn't from CO this time. A big VA popped up, another call from Liam.

*Dang it. Have to disappoint someone else. A walking disappointment I'm becoming. Sorry, I had one job and didn't do it.*

He accepted the green call button as he formulated the exact words to explain that there'd be no permit today. But before he could say anything, Liam broke into an explanation with the haste of a man in the middle of an orchestra pit, "So, we've run into a problem. Ovens are out—and we have to swap them fast. After a million calls, we found a replacement that is available and fits this exact spot. It's somewhere in Maryland, and we're headed that way now." Liam gasped to collect oxygen before continuing his speech. "Long story short, we gotta find a truck, get the oven, and get back in time to not miss tomorrow. The next few days are critical for this little opening. We might stay here tonight, might not. Either way, you probably won't see me until tomorrow sometime."

"Oh no," Jacob felt the exhaustion seeping through and wasn't sure what to say. He didn't need to say anything, because in a few seconds Liam was off, apologizing, something about duty calls.

**After hanging up**, in tribute to the hardworking American, and considering he'd just declined a work call, Jacob decided to take one small step toward productivity by unpacking his new home office.

He looked around at the 2nd floor Victorian room full of boxes, old feelings, and sneaky potential. A fountain of gratitude burst out of Jacob Maymerry's chest. *What a lovely space. I guess this is mine for now. Thank you for having me,* he thought to the 'ol gal for no reason.

One corner was an original fireplace, with a sparkling swirl green tile jeweled backsplash, and ornate dark brown mantel. Three large bay windows let in floor to ceiling light and looked down upon the side of the expansive yard. He let the dark orange mist of the setting sun seep through his skin as it burst across the budding leaf canopy.

He inhaled for 5 seconds and exhaled for 4 seconds, and for a brief moment remembered nothing but his gratitude.

Looking out the office window, he could see the embankment where he'd fallen on Closing Day. He noticed the grass was still slightly marred from the couch as it tumbled over. *No time for those memories.* He tried to fight away the nonsense by opening a packed box and pulling out random files and weights for respectable lawyerly work. He found pens, post its, and paperclips. A desk was already planted in the center of the space—a brown box monstrosity that might be compared to a dinosaur.

Most boxes were books, for reading and showing, sharing and remembering, and many for eventually, and maybe, and hopefully one day. Sometimes he worried that the more books he bought and read, the more he realized how behind he truly was. Is it possible to feel less well-read with every story devoured? He unpacked his books of law and life and mystery and wonder.

A special heavy box contained not books but bookends—a delightful and growing collection of triangle shaped stones, L wedges, odd weights, and four presidential bookend busts of Abraham Lincoln.

Jacob stopped and took special care when he opened the box that contained most meaning to him, though he wasn't exactly sure why. He pulled out a large gold-framed print of a young man's shoes, sitting on the moon, looking back at the pale blue of the Earth. Jacob liked to think that it reminded him to keep perspective. Though he often forgot that's what it reminded him of. In the box he found a special sunshine coffee mug craft show purchase of a gargoyle style, with a single eye and smiling chicklet teeth. The glazed yellow cyclops was heavy enough to double as a murder weapon, and Jacob considered it his thinking grail.

Two other items were in the box of most meaning—a Stephen King caricature wood carving and an abstract sketch of Oscar Wilde. *They'll look great in this new Victorian hideaway*. He forgot how he'd acquired either of them, but they'd followed him for years, place to place. A far wiser, more literate colleague stumbled into his last office and struck up a surprising conversation about the two authors that Jacob never forgot.

"I love your choice of those two opposites." He said.

"Oh yes, of course. What?" Jacob responded.

"Oscar Wilde, the poet novelist, only wrote one book, really. So it's studied like the Bible. Early death, so unfair, in my opinion. But that's just me. And then the Master, Mr. King. Runaway success and only more and more creative until, I guess, forever. But he's so prolific that no one can appreciate that one great thing. Polar opposites, really. Is that what you were going for?"

Jacob, who was going for nothing at all, said, "Quite right. Yes, good eye you have there." He moved the conversation along to blanket his ignorance.

Forever after, however, whenever anyone walked into his office he would try to mention how he only had two authors on his walls, "It's symbolism, you see, they represent two paths diverged in a yellow wood. A short man and a long one." He had a whole speech at the ready. He looked forward to sharing that important message with his future Willouby friends. Whenever he had time to unpack. Unless this skull business brought the house down upon them beforehand.

As he lost himself in the memory of his old office and his stump speech about the two writers, the air in the room grew strange. Jacob remembered being so wet that he was a raindrop. High up in the clouds above Willouby. It was a cold front coming in, and he was the early storm. Raindrop Jacob fell and split into two drops, headed to the roof of the 'ol gal as Jacob slept. The very cold spell that woke him up to beeping that morning.

Until Jacob Maymerry stopped sleeping on the floor of his new home office. The sun had set unknown minutes, or hours, in the past—and in the sudden darkness of an unfamiliar space, Jacob felt the mass confusion of *where am I?* He vaguely remembered a raindrop dream. Eventually finding the light, he popped it on to assess how much unpacking he had accomplished.

The room was far more chaotic than when he started—another failure seemed like the logical end to this strange day in his new town. The only bright spot was finding something on his office floor that he hadn't even remembered packing. It was a cheap, reusable writing gadget that he knew well from child-hood. He had no idea what it was called, but was sure that every dollar store must still stock them. With a simple plastic sheet atop cardboard square and a little plastic nib—endless information could be written down, and then with a flip of the sheet, erased again for new ideas.

*It's the river giving me a little help.* Jacob thought from nowhere. Feeling a spark of detective self-esteem, he grabbed the pad and scribbled with the fine point of the plastic nib:

**Suspects**
    A. Boyles
    B. Weavers

Writing it down made him feel like a real private eye. Jacob smiled to himself as he carried his thinking pad from his Victorian office, down the back twisty stair into the kitchen, to heat up a can of chicken noodle soup in the microwave, to eat under the wraparound porch lights.

∞

**He ate outside** because that's where the largest empty table was found, the temperature was right, and the sound of the breeze through the  leaves gave Jacob a small sense of dark cozy mystery comfort.

As he felt the warmth of the broth and tried to ignore any thoughts of AAMCLDS work, he heard loud voices in the distance—a conversation be-tween two men. He could not see them through high hedges, trees, and twenty yards of unkempt nature. But in his mind they were sitting outside on their porch just like he was—either finishing dinner or perhaps having a nightcap. These two men—older he knew from the rocks and ridges in the voices— were having what must have been one of many intensely friendly disagreements. Jacob gathered from the bits he heard that this dispute involved how to pronounce a word.

"That strikes the ear all wrong," Man One said.

Man Two responded with a twinkle, as if that's exactly what he expected to hear. "Bingo. But one word needs to change. You're missing one pronoun. I already told you what it is. Your!" Jacob listened intently but was lost. "It strikes your ear all wrong, not mine!"

"What are you talking about?" Man One was as confused as Jacob.

"It's all perspective. It hits your ear wrong, but not mine. You pretend we have the same ears. Willow Bean is a completely fine name for residents of Willouby. It doesn't matter that it makes you think of the legume."

"I am not a bean. It's silly. Willowbite, maybe. Or even Willow B An. Do you know what I mean? Like Carribean?"

Man Two was having none of it. "No, I do not know what you mean. Isn't that what I just said? It's all gibberish to me."

It was only at this point in eavesdropping that a thought came to Jacob— *The river wants me to hear this conversation. He knew the idea was silly. He knew it.* But he felt it anyway, and that got him thinking about what the conversation meant. Jacob thought so hard about it that he missed the rest of the talk.

He wanted to join in, because once he earned his varsity letters as a Willouby resident, he intended to call himself a Willowbeast. Before deciding if that was funny, the *Ding a Ring Ding* of Jacob's phone pierced the solo dining.

Jacob saw two large letters: CO. He sighed and wondered again what had become of his life. Jacob's cell phone worked except for one glitch—the font zoomed up and down from size 2pt to size 72pt at random. One second he would be reading a text and then out of nowhere it would *Alice in Wonderland* shrink to nothing. He tried to speed read when he saw it coming on, to get to the end of a long message. It didn't happen enough to justify the thousand dollars for a replacement. Not yet.

Jacob dealt with inconveniences, and grew accustomed to the font buzzing to its largest size with incoming calls. This prevented him from seeing anything

about the call except the state, usually a big VA for Virginia or the dreaded CO
— the AAMCLDS headquarters, based in Boulder, Colorado.

It was nearly 10pm when Jacob accepted Gladys's call from Colorado, the
Chairwoman sitting in the beige office of her large empty mountain home. She
pretended to have work-chatter, but Gladys bore into her personal life by the
second paragraph. A real rambling, "My grandson had a recommendation, but
I'm not sure. He's an angel, but he's stylish. I just don't know."

Gladys had to pick the selection for her book club next month. A woman
of verve, grace, and reputation, the choice mattered very much in her life. He
knew this without the older woman having to say a word. She loved her grandson, but Jacob felt touched that Gladys must trust Jacob's taste a bit more.

She needed his confirmation, "My grandson suggested something called
*American Gods*. Have you heard of this? Seems right up the group's alley, pa-
triotism and spirituality. I don't have time to read it first, but I was supposed
to email the pick this morning. I'm completely out of ideas and these damn
Europeans are just…" Gladys' white globe head was boiling, "It's fictional, so I
assume it's not a true history of the growth of the American Church, but must
be in the right vein. Have you heard of this?"

Jacob's mind felt so very foggy. He remembered feeling that he really
wanted to help Gladys, who really wanted to send this email and be done
with it for the night. That's why he said with the confidence of a kayaker headed straight for a hidden waterfall, "*American Gods*. A gem. How could you go
wrong? A diamond. From what I recall, it should be a hit!"

"Thank You Jacob. Goodnight sweetheart." Jacob could almost feel Gladys
smile through the phone. Perhaps he would sleep well that night knowing he
had brought slight peace to his boss.

Jacob lay in bed thirty minutes later, the other side occupied by a purring
Eleanor Roosevelt. He smiled again at Gladys's goodbye. But then he remembered that he had *heard* of the book *American Gods*. He had not read it. He knew
it must be great, because a smart friend with pure taste had said so. But then
he remembered, horror stricken, that this friend was English. And it occurred
to him that, perhaps, this particular version of *American Gods* was written by
an author not a citizen by birth. But Gladys might not find out. Perhaps she'd
love the book so much it wouldn't matter. Perhaps he could convince her that
Europeans were slightly different from the English. Perhaps. And the author,

he just remembered, also wrote funny tales and nursery yarns, so perhaps, just perhaps, it would all be OK. He'd research the plot later. There was no time to dwell, with the river he went. *So it goes.*

Jacob dozed into that magical valley between awake and asleep until he was jolted by a *Ding!*

*Another beep from the basement?* Not this time—it was his phone. It wasn't Colorado. And it wasn't Liam. It was a text message from an unknown number.


**"Please accept this invitation—tomorrow morning at 830am—Thursday—101 Sunrise Circle—Mabel"**

# Thursday

# —— Chapter 10 ——

**A message from** Mabel. *Oh my.*

Was the river toying with Jacob Maymerry? Seconds from a peaceful night's sleep, he instead spent the hours from midnight to 2am researching and thinking. He used four separate search engines when confirming directions to Mabel's house. Because the first three must have been a mistake. The street name was Sunrise Circle, which he had never seen nearby. So it seemed wrong that this mysterious old woman lived only 3 minutes away by car or 10 minutes on foot. The quirkiest search engine explained that it was 6 minutes by horse drawn carriage and 9 with roller skates. It all seemed impossible.

*Just up the street? What are the odds? Was he walking into a trap?*

Probably, but the computer was correct. Mabel's house was a few hail mary throws from his own, on the top of an even bigger hill, just to the west. The mound upon which her house sat might have been visible in the leaner months, when the leaves were gone and a hazy something could be seen through layers of bare stick branches. But its existence was unknown to Jacob until he found the address that Mabel sent in the late text.

In the middle of the nothing night, Jacob debated what he should call her when he arrived. Somehow he thought he needed to get that first name right, otherwise, like a wrong password, she'd clam up and give him no information. Or worse, tell the town he was a fool and ruin his life forever.

Jacob realized only then what he should have far earlier—he had upped the stakes by agreeing to this. The mysterious madam Queen Bee of Willouby's opinion would define him to everyone he met next. One wrong impression and their lives were over. The restaurant would tank, they'd default on the mortgage, homelessness on the horizon. And all because Jacob was a complete and utter jester, wheeled to the looney bin along a non-existent river.

But Jacob Maymerry was nothing if not a consistent fool.

*Who was this woman and what to call her?*

She signed "Mabel." But wasn't Mabel too informal for someone so respected or unique or high above the city? Barbara said "Aunt Mabel," but should Jacob use that when she wasn't his aunt? Mrs. Mabel sounded like a first grade teacher, too strange. And he had no idea her last name. He decided on "Ma'am" because it had a balanced ring to it, but he didn't know why.

∞

**Jacob woke after** sporadic, wavy sleep at 630am to the *Ding a Ding Ring* of his phone alarm.

He chose his most comfortable khakis and relaxed red zip up. Jacob stood at his front door staring toward the private lane where Mabel's house sat beyond the trees. He inhaled for 4 seconds, exhaled for 4 more, and reminded himself that the river would provide whatever answers he needed. *And if not—Oh Well—what did any of this matter anyway?*

Jacob walked and wondered what had become of his life. The most similar experience was when his household received a second hand copy of a bright gold Nintendo game called *The Legend Of Zelda* from 1988. He remembered the hero walking up many long lanes to meet old potion women conjured from different color pixel blocks. The yoda-like wizardess usually gave rewards and wisdom. He hoped that's what the river had in mind when it led him to Mabel.

Sunrise Circle, as far as Jacob could tell, was a straight line, edged on both sides by a waist high black fence behind looming lane trees with branches that whispered and whirled. A hint. Anyone making it that far should be guided in. Like bumpers in bowling.

The longer he walked, the more unkempt it all seemed. No cars had come this way in a long while, and Jacob realized there must be a back path to this old estate. The long drive was a mishmash of overgrown grass and hints of gravel. The house became visible after a bit of marching and grew larger with each step. As Jacob stretched forward he assumed the home would be barely standing if the maintenance on this driveway was any indication. It's no wonder that anyone new to town, like himself, would never know any passage here existed. Perhaps that's exactly how Aunt Mabel wanted it. Or perhaps it was a sign of something else entirely.

∞

**The House of** Mabel was a sprawling garden estate of white, tan, and faded red brick with too many ramshackle features for Jacob to absorb in one full eye-span. He saw at least three or four levels in various places, one and a half turrets, ivy here and there, armies of large ornate windows, a few fountains, hedges of Suessian shape, stone pavers, and crunchy pea rock that made a very expensive sound around his feet. The front doors were large and ominous but without fanfare, tucked into the brick like a cave entrance.

Jacob lifted a large turtle knocker, one in the center of each oak door, and banged three loud *Gongs*. The whole process was so charmingly silly that he smiled as the third gong echoed across his palm. He whispered his opening line to himself—*Thanks for having me Ma'am. It's a real treat.*

But he forgot all his training when a stone faced Jeeves of a man in full butler garb opened the door. The butler did not say a word. Instead, clearing his throat in a pleasant cough, he nodded his head, gave a fake lippy smile, and turned with military grace, striding in a clear *Follow Me*.

*What on earth?* But as if on the lazy river, Jacob followed freely behind, less scared and more excited than he would have otherwise expected.

He was led up the first of at least three stairways that he saw off the main entrance. He followed the quietly proper man to the right, winding up and around heavy cream stone steps an unknown number of levels, until he was brought into a perfectly charming, regal corner room with floor to ceiling windows looking to the east. The man made a mini bow or accidental trip and departed with such abruptness that Jacob felt as if a door had been slammed in his face.

There he stood. Jacob, the fool of a Maymerry, alone in an ancient woman's house in a town he barely knew. He stood in silence for ten terrifying seconds as the room disappeared and he saw only muddled batches of colors, having completely forgotten what he wanted to ask this Mabel at all. *Sweet mother of god, what am I doing here?*

But then he remembered that breathing techniques were nature's best cure for anxiety. He didn't actually breathe, but remembering that seemed to be enough and the room dissolved into focus. He felt again like an adult man in control of his senses.

Jacob looked around and saw many things that he assumed he'd find in the home of a very ancient woman—two canisters of oxygen and attached masks next to each of the three doors leading out of the room. He counted six oxygen cylinders in total, as if they were as necessary as shoes when leaving a house. Jacob realized how little he understood about getting old. He made a mental note that, no matter how he was treated, even if this lady was a grouch, he would be kind. He didn't know how hard it was to be her each and every day.

Collecting himself, Jacob looked around and saw that there was much more to Mabel than her age. This room might have been a combination inventor's workshop, artist studio, and potion cubby. He saw patches of scrawled notes, tiny print across scraps, papers in folders, pieces in notebooks. Ink bottles, fountain pen nibs. The art of correspondence was not lost on Aunt Mabel — or whoever she really was. A telescope in a corner. Unused cigarettes with long knobbly holders. *Is that an unopened Miller Genuine Draft can?* Potted plants of a curious sort that likely needed no water. Little opera glasses — though there was no opera in Willouby—he suspected they were for show—like the tapestry of plates across wall shelves. Three couches, seven end tables, mostly velvet, and an astonishing number of pillows.

∞

**Ba Kaw! Ba Kaw!**

Jacob's thoughts were cut off by a squawk from the hall. A distorted human chicken bawk in two loud syllables: *Ba Kaaaw! Ba Kaaaw!* A jolly of a barnyard sort. Some might have called it a mix between drinkers and smokers laugh. Jacob had no time to fully dissect any of this, because at that moment, in walked the butler.

Still wearing garb from the 1920s, this mute man toed in delicately as if holding a large tray of party drinks. Instead of cocktails, he pushed a wheelchair, upon which sat a slumped something of various pieces that Jacob could not at first fit together. All he could initially discern was an enormous poof of white fluff, two perhaps three feet. Hair. It was the color of a magnificent cloud.

This cloud of hair was mumbling. And then he made out a mouth with bright red lipstick moving under the hair. She wore a patient's gown, which was also white, just a shade different from the hair. This all had a strange effect, preventing Jacob from connecting the dots on this woman. She was pixie small, probably under five feet. More mumbling from moving red lips.

He looked to the butler for guidance, but the man intentionally made no eye contact. Jacob's heart sank to his belly, then rose to this throat. *What chaos did he walk into?* The mumbling mass of white fabric and fake hair was not going to be helpful. How could she answer questions? And how could he believe anything she said anyway? Barbara Johnson must not have seen her recently to have sent him into this white web.

This was not a woman who texted. *Did Jeeves the butler set this whole thing up? Should I run?*

The woman's mumbling increased from a whisper to a loud rhythmic humming.

*"HmmmMmmmHMMMHmHMMM."*

*At least she still had strong lungs.* Jacob saw the tiny head slumped on a shoulder underneath the blizzard of hair. Her head began to straighten, and her eyes popped alert, as if she wanted Jacob to hear. *Sad when the mind goes before the lungs.*

With the butler as Jacob's witness, he saw this ancient woman rise up from her chair in a miraculous memory of a past argument, pointing a finger in the air. Then she spoke with performer's grace:

"You think I am Nothing! I'll show you! I am Everything!"

Jacob hoped his jaw wasn't open in confusion as he glanced again to the butler for help. But the man stood as a robotic piece of furniture turned off.

Then like a plug pulled—it all stopped. She went rigid. Until this oldest of old women under the two foot poof, sat back down in the wheelchair, dipped her head wig-first into the rug, disappeared as her spindly frame collapsed into the cloud hair, and then reappeared in a kneel having completed a full somersault out of the wheelchair.

*Oh my.*

"Ta Da!" Aunt Mabel roared with mischievous feline ferocity, standing up carefully without any sign of ache in her joints.

Jacob stood ramrod straight, as if pulled by an invisible string, having no idea what to do. Out of instinct, he clapped, and kept clapping during his startled chuckling. The butler's face stayed stone cold, but he gave three gloved pats.

*How is this my life?*

If nothing else, Jacob knew this woman was a physical specimen that should be studied by science. *Must have been a dancer*, he thought, knowing some of the best line dancers could move with nimble feet well into their victory lap years.

Now standing in front of the chair, an angelic column of white, Aunt Mabel spoke with a new voice. It was the balanced gravel and rose petal coo of an extremely confident and feisty turtle. "Don't worry about her. That's Crazy Mabel. I bring her out for joy with new people. She's a game. Just for laughs. Sometimes I'm called Aunt Mabel. Thanks for coming, little one."

Jacob stood in silence for three seconds, unsure how to respond to being called "little one" by a pixie woman. *I'm maybe five eight, thank you very much.* "Thank you so much for meeting with me. It's a real treat."

He remembered that breathing helped and plowed on with the river, "I know it's sort of strange, but…" *not as strange as whatever the hell that was*, he almost finished. Instead, he asked without knowing why, "What were you saying earlier?" referring to her wheelchair nonsense-speak.

"Stage lines," she said immediately and her beautiful big teeth broke free. "In my day I've played them all. Starting with Antigone by Sophocles and up to Frogs by Aristophanes." Jacob recognized neither of those people or plays so he nodded and said, "Wow."

Jacob was relieved to notice Mabel didn't care about his opinion. "I did many local productions, with a few regional triumphs. I was once a scream queen. Always on stage, of course. Nothing artificial."

She walked slowly toward one corner of the room and continued talking, "What you just saw there was an original. I wrote it some decade ago. Forgot which one, but I never forgot those lines, some of my best. Unfortunately, it was never produced. So I pull it out from time to time to ensure its legs don't go numb. Know what I mean?"

Jacob nodded. *Obviously.*

"I told Winston here," she hiked a thumb above her shoulder at the butler. "But he thinks I'm Crazy Crazy. Not just Acting Crazy. Don't you Winston?" His back was already to the woman and he pretended not to hear. "He thinks my originals are mediocre. You know where people take junk from the dumpster, glue it together, and put it in the middle of the museum. But what does he know?" The old woman wrinkled her face like a shrew, with a subtle nod at

Jacob—hinting that they were in on something together, unlike the untrustworthy Englishman who had rolled her in.

Then she broke out in contagious chicken laughter that shook her cloud hair—*Baaa Kaw! Baa Kaaw! Baa Kaaw!*

Coming out of such a tiny fairy composed of 75% wig, the laugh reminded Jacob of the Easter commercials with fuzzy chicks and chocolate that made you feel all safe and sweet and happy inside.

"Sit Sit." She motioned to one of the velvet somethings in a tangle of a conversation area. Jacob found a corner of a purple sofa next to a wood armrest and a Tiffany style green lamp that might have been a dragonfly. He sank into the ornate comfort and felt as kings must when finally able to sit atop only the plushest fabrics from overseas. A hint of chocolate and melted butter in the air made him wonder if she had made cookies. Without thought, he submerged into the river and let himself be carried away by whatever mysterious nonsense had brought him here in the first place.

Jacob knew he was in the hands of a real storyteller, and he could see in flashes of youth behind wise eyes, the woman who was the original Keeper of the Keys, the precursor to Barbara Johnson. Jacob sank into the purple velvet that now felt like a Halloween marshmallow and enjoyed the show.

∞

# Mabel's Thursday Morning Story Hour

Mabel had never stopped talking as little Jacob descended chest-deep into the warming comforts of the couch. She walked toward the opposite corner of the room on strong but nimble toothpick legs, her back to him. "Honey, I don't know who I am anymore, except one bright big star!" She turned her head and winked at him before going behind a tri-fold dressing partition. "But don't worry, I'm not always *her*." She hitched a thumb at the empty wheelchair. "When I knew you were coming I thought, 'Why don't you bring the 'ol gal back out one more time.'"

In a flash, she re-emerged a new butterfly. Red wig, and a yellow outfit of some homemade looking creation that was part-fitted stage wear, part-cape—flattering her natural flutter—she might have been a red and yellow hummingbird.

She talked with what he now considered her real rose-gravel voice that she could modulate at will with performer's control. "People call me many things. Mabel. Aunt Mabel. Crazy Mabel. Feel free to pick. Names are always temporary."

She walked toward him and said "Always a Choice!"

Confused, Jacob eventually followed a thin arm she raised to the coffee table in front of him. It was then he noticed a tray was laid out with water, apple slices, and cookies. "Pick one. I insist. And make sure it's the one you want, not what you think I'll judge you for. This is your welcome to the neighborhood and everyone gets what they want in Willouby." She turned and walked toward a bookshelf, her back again to him, as if indifferent to his choice.

"It's my special recipe," she said as she walked. "The cookies I mean. You'll have to ask someone else for the apple recipe." *Ba Kaw! Ba Kaw!* She laughed at herself and then turned around to look at him. Jacob knew Mabel was someone used to having both sides of every conversation. Since he was here to pry her for information, this was no problem. She kept going as he tried to remember what he was supposed to do. *Oh right, pick one of these things to eat.*

"I won't take No for an answer. You look famished, little one. You must eat something."

Lost in her dazzling teeth, Jacob obliged knowing Mabel had put such thought into this visit, after all. He went with the cookie and bit into a delicious pull of brown sugar, chocolate, and pillowy dough, mumbling "Hm-mEmmmRmmm" mid-mouthful in instant satisfaction.

*I can't believe I made an audible groan of delight. How embarrassing.*

She nodded in as if he had answered a question correctly or made the only reasonable choice. He wondered if he would have been asked to leave if he'd chosen the apple—or worse, if it was poisoned. His mind was in a strange place at the moment, and he told himself calmly but forcefully to get it together. He couldn't be going around acting weird now that he was in the big house on the biggest hill that he didn't even know existed the day before.

Mabel drifted, cloudlike, until she sat down across from him, floating perhaps an inch above the dark green coziness of the opposing sofa. The Queen Bee continued with the confidence of a master of ceremonies.

"I'm glad you didn't take the apples," she said while fiddling with something on the end table next to her. "I just pulled them out of the icebox, and they probably would have been hard to break through with those young teeth of yours." Jacob considered that Crazy Mabel might still be working itself out of her system.

"Sorry, refrigerator. Refrigerator is what it's now called. But in my day, it was icebox. Words change constantly. And then they make up new words. And it's all so exhausting." She smiled to herself, pulled out a textured case from the table, and popped it open to reveal thin cigarettes. *Virginia Slims*, he suspected.

*EhhmHmmm*—the butler coughed from nowhere near the door. Jacob hid a startle.

"Shush, Winston. We have company. It's a treat." Aunt Mabel said without looking at him as a match flashed near her face.

"But I will say," she puffed in a deep inhale and released it slowly while continuing her talk, "Sometimes the old words come back. You know what they called crazy people when I was writing that performance? Nervous Prostrators. I kid you not. How Fun! It's like they wanted people to go crazy. Though crazy is always in the eye of the bee holder. That's what they say, now isn't it?" She winked. "But Nervous Prostrator Mabel doesn't have the same ring as Crazy Mabel."

∞

**She puffed and** released two small balls of white. "So this thing of yours," she waved the cigarette with a practiced hand in front of him. "Barb told me you had a heating and cooling question?" She narrowed eyes skeptically.

"Not exactly." Surprised that he wasn't nervous. "More general questions about old memorabilia I found at the house. Might be related to the fellas who used to do that work back in the day. I think Barbara might have..." he was cut off in a graceful way by the yellow and red hummingbird across from him.

"Right right. Now I remember, she said the Boyles and Weavers. You want to know about them. The delivery team. Or the current crop of Roosters?" She asked a question but left no time for a response. "I'll just do each, easier that way."

"I know all the HAC folks in town." Jacob heard her slight variation on the acronym and wondered if it meant "Heating And Cooling." *What happened to the V?*

Mabel never stopped, "Extremely useful friends to have. Get to know those Rooster men—you'll probably need them again." Jacob nodded at the practical home ownership and life advice, delivered in the elderly way not up for debate.

"Yes, yes, Barbie said you want to return an old button to the right family? If so, you're probably out of luck. The Weavers—father and son—worked this area to death until just before the war. Whatever family remained after that went far west looking for gold, or some such thing. None of them ever set foot here again. They sold the business to the Boyles who gave it a bit of a go but it all faded and they left too. Or best I recall." She looked out the window at that and puffed a small bit but released it without fully inhaling.

"Now the Roosters told you all this?" She asked a nonsense question but didn't care for an answer. "Fine people. The Roosters. Very fine. Excessive. Always want more. The very hardest of workers—no one's ever said anything otherwise in front of me. Honest. I'm no gossip, but the type to have three vans when they only need two. There's an honesty in that. And they're still down there fixing things.

She stopped for a quick beat, smiled a gorgeous warmth at him, and Jacob felt lulled like a baby, bobbing in this water. Or maybe spinning in a circle in the corner of a lazy river—one of his favorite places—where he didn't have anywhere to go and couldn't be reached. Or maybe this mysterious witch of a woman had poisoned the cookies and not the apple. He made an immediate pact with himself that if she asked him to check in the back of her oven, he'd run out the door.

Jacob realized she never paused and he hoped he didn't miss any context. "As Mama was fond of saying, 'Spiders are not scary when you realize you are one.' I think the Roosters and all Hot and Cold professionals learn this at an early age. It's a real gift."

The old woman glanced up at the corner of the room, as if a real spider was conjuring thread there. Jacob hoped it was Charlotte and not a giant evil one from a grim tale. But then he remembered he was on the river and all was well with the world.

"Or was it Octopus? Aren't they the spiders of the sea? Both 8s, right?" She looked at Jacob. *It was a serious question.*

But then she answered it herself, "Yes, definitely." She wiggled four fingers on each hand, then traced an eight with one finger in the air. But the 8 was sideways, the image for infinity.

∞

**"But enough about** them. What you really came for is me, right?" *Hehe He Haw Haw Haw BaKaw! Ba Kaw!* Mabel released a three layered laugh at her own joke ending with the chicken bawk that included an extra smoker's gravel. The laugh energized her. She dropped the cigarette in a green glass ashtray, beeped up on pixie legs, and began walking left and right in the conversation pit like a professional sinking into a rhythm.

"In the beginning, I noticed a difference. A light. Then a face. It was the doctor, and I was born. Picture it, 1926, Sicily. The product of pure debauchery." Hehehe, she winked. "Just kidding, Bel Air, California. I'm All American, from coast to coast."

With the grace of a champion dancer from the AAMCLDS Glistening Gold Division, Mabel swirled her hips. Up and down and then down and up. "They called this the 'ol CC—for Cal Coolidge. I'm a CC—he was the boss when I was born. I could do the 'ol CC with the best of them. Still can." She bopped her hips again, and now he could almost picture it as two swaying Cs. Jacob smiled at the swirling senior. "It was good that the president was mostly silent back then, because the rest of us were a dancin'. Flapping around!" She bent her elbows and fluttered pretend wings.

Jacob laughed out loud to ensure Mabel knew he was a good audience member. He had sunk so deep in the purple velvet corner that the armrest now seemed just below his chin — he was too relaxed to care.

"Legend has it that I was born or conceived on the set of the movie that made Clara Bow a star, *IT Girl*. Do you remember her? Don't worry, I barely do. My earliest memories are of my first family. I come from CC folks, as I said, Circus and Carny people."

She winked and Jacob realized he didn't yet understand what was a joke and what was serious with this increasingly charming oldest of old women. "Couldn't have dreamed a better start in life. The CC crew were sneaky smart and fun as a bag of jellybeans. Great teachers, my foundation. I learned all about life from them."

∞

**Mabel's white teeth** shone beneath her wig and fluttering red and  yellow, "See, carny folk sometimes think the year revolves around the 4th of July—the

Christmas of the Summer—a place upon which to mark time. Maybe that's why the bearded lady Samantha said that each of us are like one cracker in that Independence Day show, shooting toward our destination, and then Boom! an explosion of color. Though Samantha whispered to me that a few of us were the whole damn Grand Finale in one. She said that we keep shooting off non-stop, over and over, to all the *Oohs and Ahhs*."

Mabel paused as if to emphasize the importance of this. She leaned in closer to him as if to whisper.

"Then the tattooed man said that we lived in a globe of experiments, a test garden. And you had to live a life to figure out what your perfect heaven would be. Once you're sure you know what you want, then something happens, and voila heaven starts coming. I liked that one, because I want to pick my own heaven instead of having one handed to me. Plopped straight into it, even heaven wouldn't make any sense at first. And thank goodness we all don't pick our heaven at age five. A little too sweet that would be." She looked at the cookies on the table.

Jacob tried to follow this but was struggling to keep it all straight. *Was she actually raised in the circus?*

"The lion tamer sided with the tattooed man. But he said that none of it made sense if you get stuck in tricky ticking time." She wrinkled her eyes at him. "I was very confused by that, especially at my age then. But the big cat man told me to imagine time was an infinite ocean, and once the river took you there, you were finally free to play. Because that's when you know you've seen enough to pick your true paradise."

Jacob's ears perked up extra pointy when he heard Mabel talk of a river carrying someone to somewhere. *That cannot be a coincidence.*

Mabel sighed and then smiled. "I told the lion tamer that I had no idea what he was talking about. But maybe now I do." She winked at him and gave one *Kaw!*

∞

**Out of nowhere** Mabel asked, "You're not claustrophobic, are you?"

This time she waited for an answer.

*Silence.*

"I don't think so," Jacob managed to say as he sunk even deeper into the couch.

"Good good. That can be a real handicap sometimes."

Mabel sat again, now on a chair of dark emerald leather. Jacob was impressed that she had made it that long on her feet. She crossed her legs under her yellow outfit, bopped a toe which fluttered the yellow, and continued her story with sustained vigor. "Anyway, it wasn't all circus for me. I did go to school, and thrived. Though perhaps not in the ordinary way. A's were elusive, but I think that's because A is for Arbitrary. And I never do well under anything of that sort. But don't worry, I learned my ABCs," she winked. "And even my Ds and Es!" *Ba Kaw!* She cackled a single hen's laugh and Jacob couldn't help but chuckle at the lovely absurdity of it all.

"Arbitrary!" She rose from the chair, remembering a decades-old grudge that she had yet to forgive. "As if spelling matters! I like the razzle dazzle of the E. The letter. I remember my first love were those words that had that tricksy little e at the end. Ye olde towne frye. You know what I'm talking about, right?"

Jacob nodded automatically without a clue why as she bore on harder, "But No sir e! Apparently those were wrong ways to say the same right thing. So no, I didn't get many A's at first or last." Her hunched shoulders bobbed up and down in a chuckle at her own joke.

She went back to the sofa spot across from him, and he realized why. She wanted another cigarette. "So much Memorization. Capitalization! The Founding Fathers knew full well that the size of the letter depended on the emotion, intention, and trickery of the writer. Arbitrary rules for big and small letters, as if they knew better than Uncle Sam himself! And Names! Remembering each name for each thing for always, such an exhausting bit of nonsense. As if names don't change anyway. Over the generations everything changes, and I told them that even in first grade. I told them I would prove it. And look at me now. I've finally won the war!"

She looked at the corner of the room and gave a mysterious sigh. "A' course, all those enemies are long dead. So it goes."

Jacob wasn't sure who they were, but he shivered a chilled shake until she spoke again, "No, I didn't kill anyone if that's what you're thinking." She gave a cigar smoker's cough cackle—*Kaa Kaa Grmmm Kaa.* "No no, this riddle doesn't end that way. I only mean it's important to help your enemies stay alive long enough that they realize they are defeated. Otherwise, what's the point?"

*Silence.*

*More Silence.*

Jacob Maymerry noticed that he'd said almost nothing while here, and in a flash of panic wondered if he had forgotten even how to speak. *Was she waiting for him to say something?* Nope. The old tortoise fiddled with a gold match book, a long white slim popping out from red lips.

Jacob smelled the match as Mabel went on before her first puff, "Don't get me wrong, I love the long game. But if everyone's dead by the time there's a winner, what game are you really playing? The game of Most Healthy? That takes forever and gets boring quick."

∞

**She pulled the** pinky bone white cigarette from her mouth but kept it in her hand like a smoke wand. "I adore games, though. Who doesn't?"

This was a woman on a roll. Jacob sunk deeper into the purple velvet cloud and saw another cookie in his hand. *When did I even grab this?* It happened automatically, like a snatch of popcorn during a fascinating movie.

He knew enough to know that Mabel was a master of something. "There are times in my life when I suspect the whole bloody thing is just one game." She waved her cigarette hand in the air seductively as if pointing at something in her head and the distance. The cigarette made an S, and smoke drifted this way and that. "The Game of Life, ever play that? I mean, there's no losing. Everyone reaches the end in their little car, and then everything goes back in the box."

She now looked every bit a fashionable 78, instead of her late 90s. "In my younger days I played them all. Tennis is the best workout, and you can do it for a long while, so long as the body holds. But you must find a partner at the same level. That's why golf is so handy. Can do it with one, two, three, or four." She held up 4 fingers with her non-smoking hand, as if Jacob was a child who needed things made very clear. "I spent a lot of time golfing in the 50s. Though much of it in the sand. Got pretty good with the rake. I could get it so you barely knew I was even there." She winked. "Once even had a romp on that sand."

Jacob's eyes opened wide.

"It was with a squirrel! Little bastard wanted my ball! In the end I gave it to him. He could use it better than I could!" She slapped a knee. *Ba Kaw! Ba Kaw!*

It was only then that the thought occurred to Jacob—*Should he let a Cal Coolidge year old woman with oxygen tanks at every door smoke yet another cigarette? Did he have any responsibility here? If someone came in, would he be the substitute kindergarten teacher clapping as the kids played tag with scissors? Should he call for Winston?*

"Wiiiiiinston!" Mabel beat him to it. "Winston, get over here!" At least the butler would clarify the smoking situation. Deep down he was sure that no one on this earth told Aunt Mabel what she could or could not do. Not now. "Get over here you damn naughty kitty."

*Oh, that's interesting.*

Jacob asked, "You have a cat?"

"Of course. And yes, it's the same name. It's easier that way. For now. Maybe he'll change it later."

"Wiiiiinston!"

Winston the butler arrived slightly out of breath.

"Good, finally." Mabel transitioned with the ease of a Gilded Age baroness. She reached into a pile of trinkets and pulled out a tiny bell which she rang with her non-smoking hand. Jacob felt a ping of anticipation. "Winston, my wings please. My wings." Winston said nothing. "You know I get them every time a bell rings!" She cackled and looked in Jacob's direction.

"You've seen that one, right?" Of course Jacob had seen that one. He was the sole corporate counsel for the AAMCLDS and that Christmas movie which was almost not a Christmas movie was an absolute favorite of a majority of the Board.

"I love that movie," Jacob said honestly.

"Oh great," she nodded as if it was confirmation that she had good instincts, and he was a little one who could be trusted.

"But Winston, really, please roll out the music machine. And on the double." She rang the bell again, cackled again, and Winston nodded before the exit sounds of butler heels snapped down the stairs.

"I babysat his grandfather," Aunt Mabel deadpanned and Jacob could not tell if it was a joke. "I think he buys those costumes from Party Depot. I don't make him wear that, but it sure is fun."

Jacob grabbed another cookie and the river drifted on under him.

∞

**"As I was** saying about kindergarten, my first friend was Joey C. He moved away after a week, but I remember he showed me a book with buildings from Greece. It's the only book I knew for awhile, and it left a deep impression. Until 5th grade I believed that all Greeks were grey and made of stone. Imagine my shock when I was told they were statues!" She sighed as if exhausted. "As I said, I never did well in school. But Joey C and the Greeks, the  smartest kid I knew in 1st grade. It's funny what you remember. Wonder what happened to him."

She took a long drag from her slim cigarette, the ash building to dramatic length with a single tug. Jacob worried that his friend's lungs must be bags of crinkle paper at this point. *How on earth was she even capable of this?*

She spoke to him and perhaps the room, "When you're old they come to you. Like a tree. And once they think of you as a tree, there's no going back. Even if you move, you become a turtle. Slower than them and therefore beneath them. But the joke is always on them. It's turtles like me all the way down!" *Baakaka BaaaKaw KaaaKaw.* She really enjoyed that one and Jacob could not help but laugh out loud, mostly at her still building barnyard sound and remembering the turtle knockers on the way in.

Jacob beamed a real smile, as he felt his head dip below the purple armrest. He smiled because *he remembered the reference.* Mabel winked at him, and he knew it meant, *you're a clever little one.* Jacob blushed for some reason and hoped she didn't think he was crazy.

Somehow Jacob felt like he was being tested, and she spoke in partial riddles to ensure he was worthy of her company. "Memory is a funny thing, see. I find you remember not what you want to remember, but what that invisible thing that keeps buzzing in your head — whatever that thing thinks is important— that's what you remember all these years later. So I remember the lines to my play that was never made. Because it's important to that joker deciding what I think." She tapped her head above an ear.

Mabel looked at the embers of her cigarette and considered a drag before putting it out in the green ashtray.  From nothing she bopped up again, moving like a senior ballroom champion toward the dressing gown corner. She pointed at some of the oxygen canisters and said with a throttle voice. "I had a genius friend who was lights out with organic chemistry. She could visualize it all as pictures in her head. She told me that the stuff sitting over there in the tubes is 'Oh two.' Not just O for Oxygen. Do you understand? It's a molecule, not just one. A single O is deadly to humans, you need the combo to breathe."

She pointed two fingers at him and said with gusto, "I considered a career in the sciences you know, but the stage beckons us stars. This seems silly but wait. You'll need this information one day. Like heating and cooling professionals. Take it from this old turtle, the things you care most about will change quickly. Especially now that you're a homeowner."

Jacob smiled at the advice which he knew was genuine. He was touched that Aunt Mabel seemed to care, even if barely, about his future well-being. Perhaps another friendship brewing in Willouby.

∞

**Winston arrived with** a stone *Clap Clap Clap* from the hallway. He rolled something, this time a plastic cart Jacob remembered from middle school. Instead of an old tube television, this one carried a turquoise suitcase record player like a crown. What a treat!

The silent butler prepared the mystery music machine and Mabel walked slowly to what Jacob realized was a small performance area in the middle of the room. Somehow, with more elderly magic, Mabel had changed from yellow to a deep ocean blue jumpsuit that almost shone. Then she moved an inch, and Jacob realized it was rhinestones that sparkled like a disco ball made of constellations. As she moved the entire room began to glimmer, glossen, twinkle, and flutter with light. The trinkets, flubdubs, and whatnots in the ancient workshop came alive as Mabel waved in the empty center.

Jacob sank completely through the purple velvet and felt that he was dipped in the water, watching an astonishing light show of glassy greens, whites, purples, and other hints of Mabel's life reflected in her jumpsuit. She barely need move to create such beauty.

And then the music machine began, adding a fantasia layer to the dazzling display. Jacob heard words in pieces but mostly felt the sound echo past him like tiny balls small enough to seep through his skin and into his core.

Sounds filled the room, Mabel twirled to the disco dancing with words about jiving, swaying, digging, watching the scene, and having the time of your life.

He knew this one. ABBA, *Dancing Queen*. Though the names and letters and meanings didn't seem to matter as much as the feeling. Jacob watched Mabel sway and the room blazed, perhaps like the inside of a sun.

Melted into his purple cloud, watching the glistening show, and hearing the beautiful sounds from past voices — Jacob felt peace for the first time in ye olde towne of Willouby.  He realized that if she was a witch willing to lure him here, she would have poisoned both treats—just to be sure. *Of course, you fool. Your fate was sealed long before you ever had a clue.*

He didn't know how long he sat and felt that way.

Until he noticed a difference, the lights slowed, Mabel spoke as she moved like an ending pendulum. "It's a favorite from my getting older days." Jacob tried to do the math to figure out when this song was released.

Feeling the cheekiness of a budding friendship, Jacob pointed to the Oxygen. "Do you need any of that?"

"No no, I'm saving it for later." She said and Jacob wondered if Crazy Mabel is always just below the surface. She followed up, "Do you want some of that life-saving sustenance, little one?"

"No thank you ma'am."

"They're like fire extinguishers these days—can never be too safe, especially as a homeowner."

"Maybe one day. If I'm lucky." Jacob said, hoping the joke made sense, though he suddenly realized that the cannisters must be an enormous fire hazard.

"I'll buy you one for Christmas this year. If you celebrate. If not, I'll buy it for Halloween." *Ba Kaw! Ba Kaw!* She clucked herself into another coughing fit. "Now if you don't mind, I'm dancing."

Jacob took the hint. *This old broad always steered the conversation.* He knew, with a wink.

She closed her eyes and spoke as she swayed. Like a practiced performer getting to the point of all her rambling, "I don't remember the name of this one, but names don't matter dear. Not for too long. I remember some names

I shouldn't and forget others that I should. Eventually all names mean nothing to anyone who has ears to hear them, so don't cling too tightly. Recognizing the soul is everything."

Mabel seemed a woman groping for a simpler way to explain things to a little one without her experience or artistic acumen. "Never forget there's an ocean between 'not for me' and 'not good.' How dull the world would be if everyone had the same taste."

As suddenly as she appeared, Dancing Mabel stopped spinning and Jacob could almost see the mist of remaining energy leave her frail frame in a *pffft*. "And with that, I'm afraid, I must attend to other appointments. You've been a dear. I'll show you out."

*Abrupt*, Jacob worried. But deep down he saw it was real exhaustion, not rudeness. She grabbed his arm and they walked in silence back down the steps toward the front entrance. With sleight of hamd smoothness, she palmed an item from a pile as they left the room. "I know you lawyers prefer yellow paper, but sometimes this works too. To write down my pearls of wisdom. Or anything else that comes to mind." She winked as a great grandmother turtle, and handed over a small green memo book with spiral binding and tiny lined pages.

As they walked, he felt Mabel's weight slowly build up on him, as if he became the cane she needed with growing urgency. The remaining magic escaped her, and Jacob thought of Harry Houdini finally releasing his exhaustion after some death-defying tumble. Mabel whispered in his ear, "I don't really have any other appointments today, but that whole Willy Wonka bit wore me out. I hide it well, but anymore I only have the energy for one real showstopper every week or so." She gobbled down a cough for his benefit.

When they reached the front door Mabel searched for something in the tray. "No one leaves this house without something." Mabel reverted back to a grandmother and that made Jacob shrink down into a grandchild. Or great great great grandchild. Finding her object, she handed him a black and white car decal, "Who Saved Who?" Jacob guessed it was mailed in a fundraiser, probably a gift for a donation to the local animal shelter.

*She already gave me spmething—the notebook. Maybe her mind can hang on only for so long each day, like a senior aunt mailing three birthday cards a year.*

He walked out the cave entrance onto the rich gravel. Before he could think about whether a goodbye hug was appropriate, she spoke again, "I'll see ya tomorrow, sweetheart. Noon. And I'll tell you all about the folks who lived in your house. Buh bye."

She slammed the door in his face as hard as a Calvin Coolidge woman ever could, a turtle knocker gonging inches from his nose.

## Chapter 11

**Jacob Maymerry walked** down the gravely grass lane holding a tiny spiral notebook and adopted dog sticker. He arrived on Nottingham Avenue in a flash of what felt like six seconds. He had no idea the time, but saw the sun at a lunchtime middle. Perhaps it was the whiz burr of his meeting with Mabel, or the poison in the cookies and now his veins, but Jacob Maymerry felt like a man on a mission.

Or a River.


He re-played Mabel's Story Hour in his head and tried to determine when he was talking to regular Aunt Mabel and when he was talking to Crazy Mabel. Jacob instinctively felt that her dazzling smile and the way she spoke of heating and cooling was proof enough that she was a turtle to be trusted.

That's why when he reached the end of the private lane, instead of heading left to his rock house, he turned right with the confidence of a man not questioning a single step. Some might say he was in the flow. Aunt Mabel had been the jostle he needed—as if she could be anything else. He now understood why she was such a Willouby icon—she couldn't help but shine. He was glad that she let him take hold, even if only for a little while. Perhaps a little while was all he needed.

Mabel's final, bizarre plea to visit tomorrow to talk about other people who lived in the 'ol gal was the *Ring a Ding* he should have heard far earlier. *Past owners. Of course!* He was so distracted by thoughts of the river that he followed the first shiny object he saw to the wrong destination. The button was passing river glitter left for his amusement. He needed to keep his sights on the real prize.

Who was most likely to be a skull in the basement of a house? *Someone who once lived there, of course!* Silly Jacob, still learning his detective skills. Mabel was the fun lesson on the road to the answer—her real gift must have been the hint about the past owners.

And so Jacob turned right at the end of the lane and headed straight back like an echo to the old but not oldest woman who had sent him to Mabel in the first place, Barbara Johnson. He knew just where to find her, in the bowels of the beast—Huxley Library lion of riddles.

*Deja vu* hit him as he descended the basement stairs—probably because he did it yesterday. Someone once told him that *deja vu* was a sign that we were all ghosts, re-living loops over again. That made Jacob wonder if he himself was the skull in the basement. If so, how would he ever get to know that without first dying? Or going crazy? That worried him, because it meant he'd never know. *Maybe failing to solve this riddle is how I go crazy and end up as the skull?*

But then he remembered that breathing techniques were nature's best cure for anxiety, and he felt better.

∞

**His mood continued** to improve as he entered the Archives and was greeted like an old friend by Miss Barbara, "Glad you and Mabel hit it off. I hope it was helpful!"

"Can't thank you enough. She's a treasure, that's for sure." Jacob didn't yet know how to describe anyone in this town.

"Amen. And now that you've met her, you can understand that she's hard to pin down. A little bit of everything."

"That's for sure." *Think of a new stock phrase Jacob. Be original for once in your life!*

"So what brings you back here? Did you solve your mystery?" Barbara winked, a mirror of Mabel's practiced trickery.

In a single 3 second span Jacob was certain that the wink meant this entire city was a cult, and he had fallen into the center of their web—a plaything in their games. But that paranoia dissipated when he remembered that all librarians are good at things like winking and twinkling and gracefully gliding between shelves.

Jacob knew just what to say. He told Barbara that he was there to learn more about the past owners—he didn't mention the button at all. Best to drop that link in the chain once it was no longer needed. After all, once you use the canoe to cross the river, you don't carry it with you. Leave it at the shore.

Barbara spoke more freely as if to a near friend, "Amazing Ant Mabel was here for a short while. The first of my kind, and this place wouldn't exist without her. I wonder if she knew her own strength?" She lowered her voice an inch, "Because, to be candid, sometimes she scared the children. Or so I was told. Perhaps Mabel was ahead of her time. I mean, she created new costumes for each reading hour. I wasn't there and no pictures exist, but apparently things got a bit terrifying. Depending on the tale."

Miss Johnson stopped in the middle of two narrow shelves but continued her story, "The Board originally asked her to stop wearing costumes so as to ensure no one was traumatized in their dreams. But she refused on the principled grounds that Mabel does nothing half-assed. Then she quit."

Barbara smiled to herself. Jacob hid a grin at Miss Johnson's slight vulgarity—it felt mysterious, like a smoking priest. She winked.

Jacob immediately thought, *the magical winking women of Willouby.*

"But perhaps it was for the best, because I don't think Queen Ant Mabel was meant to be inside a library for 50 years like I was. She was going higher." Barbara winked again and Jacob wasn't sure how to feel.

Barbara glanced at something on a shelf. An obituary, he noticed. An old one. Barbara knew his thoughts, "They were so much more casual about the language in old obituaries. There is no photo. They didn't have as many photos back then. That's why old photos always seem a little more magical. They're rare."

In a 2 second span Jacob was certain that it was Mabel's skull in the basement. And that meant that he himself was also going crazy, because he saw her earlier that morning. Somehow he and Mabel's fates were now linked in his mind—both normal humans—not ghosts or crazy folks. He hoped.

Before the hope escaped, Barbara saved him by throwing a thick binder his way, "Please hold." She pulled binders and handed them to Jacob, piling atop one another in cartoon fashion, below his eyes. "That's good for now." She said and walked toward an empty table, "Let's set them over here."

Jacob followed Barbara as she grabbed and dropped the binders full of obituaries on the B&B sized banquet table in front of her. She shuffled them in some order, like cards, though Jacob could not yet tell the point of this game.

"I want to see if I get this right," Barbara said to herself as much as Jacob. "To see if I remember the order. See, only two families have lived in your house, which makes it somewhat easy. It's the Hamilton House—at least that's what some people called it. Because the Hamilton's built it and then lived in it until the McDonalds. But they only had it for a little while before losing it to the bank."

"Wells Fargo." Jacob said automatically.

"Actually, no. A local bank that was swallowed up by Wells Fargo later." Barbara said without hesitation, a dazzling academic display of the town and its inhabitants.

Barbara moved toward the first binder and tested her fifty year master brain, "Seven total in the Hamilton family that built your house. Chester and Elizabeth, and five children. Oldest son, three daughters, and then a baby boy." Barbara squinted as if wanting to get every detail right. "Then the McDonalds are much easier, just the two of them and the one child, I believe. Strangely enough, I know the older family better than the new."

Jacob wanted to tell Barbara she did not have to apologize for anything. She had already demonstrated enough to wow him. But he didn't dare interrupt her. Because just like his river, he suspected Miss Barbara Johnson might never be more alive than in moments like this one, when she was demonstrating the fruits of years of honing her mind for a very specific purpose.

"If I remember right, the first child, the golden boy, took the inaugural voyage up to whatever comes next." The librarian artfully explained, "I only know because I walk past the Hamilton site at Mount Willouby Cemetery most mornings."

Barbara said this, but Jacob wondered if she tried to hide her photographic memory under a fake but plausible facade. "Father Chester moved on shortly after that. Followed by a daughter, then Mother Elizabeth, but I can't remember the exact year. Not sure if she's in the plot. I know the little boy, the wanderer, isn't there—Christopher. But I think all three girls are there." Jacob lost himself a bit in the blur of Barbara Johnson's information, but he knew this was all important.

∞

**Barbara flipped open** the first binder while explaining herself, "I figured we'd go through the obituaries—if we have them all. That way you can see where each of these folks ended up. Not that an obituary is an ending, mind you, but at least it's a start."

As she twirled fingertips, Jacob noticed penciled handwriting atop every photocopy in a plastic sleeve with deceased's name—last, first—and then the newspaper from where it was pulled. Barbara's work, Jacob suspected. He saw periodicals that were no more, like *Willouby Evening Star, Willouby Constellation,* and one he noticed in a flash called *The WB Buzz.*

As if reading his mind, Barbara jumped in, "There were more papers back then. And so we had more obituaries. Stories on top of stories. If something happened in town we'd have two versions of it, sometimes three. Of course, that was before phones and computers, when these pieces of paper were all there was besides conversation." She smiled and Jacob noticed two silver fillings in the back of her mouth.

"But I'm not one to complain. Now we know almost everything out in the big world instantly, sometimes it overwhelms the smaller world directly around us. I still remember a time when that small world was all there was, you know?" She said it with a slight smirk. "And the obituaries were so much more casual back then. I mean, look."

She read a random one in front of her, "He perished as he would have wanted, on the big ocean blue. Fishing, we assume, with the largest life he could find. We never found him, but like to think that he found whatever he was looking for."

*Did Barbara wipe away a tear?*

"I mean, you just don't see obituaries like that anymore. Now it's all something else." Her voice faded, and Jacob remembered Barbara Johnson was a woman who took her job seriously.

Collecting herself, the Keys Keeper jumped one-third of the way through the binder before saying, "Hmmmm. Is it not here? Was I wrong?" Then she began flipping through the front and the back, in a search of a specific kernel in the sandbox. Until she found it. Or it found her, by falling out. Somehow, it had escaped the plastic sleeve and three ring holes. "How funny. Here it is, floating at the beginning, near the As."

Barbara pulled out a slightly crumpled piece of white paper upon which was a printed photocopy of an old obituary from a newspaper of unknown age. "So this is the obit for the first son, Oscar Hamilton. Apple of father's eye. Mr. Popular. But died young, so he has the biggest monument at the cemetery. The father, probably in grief, died a year or three later."

She motioned to the next binders on the table where his obituary was presumably found. "Those two men have the largest stones out there. The sisters are all there too, I know, because each starts with an S and they stand out side by side. Christopher is not there, because he fled the nest, I do believe. Not sure where he ended up. And Elizabeth, the mother. To be honest, I should know but I'm blanking on exactly what happened to her. My apologies. A long week it's been!"

Jacob saw a crinkle in the corner of one of Barbara's eyes, and he worried that his new friend was now showing all of her 70 plus years. *Forgetfulness and an unorganized binder, was Barbara slipping?*

"What I can do is photocopy each of the Hamilton and McDonald ones we have. So you can reference them." *Spoken like a true professional of the book.* "The McDonalds, unfortunately, might not be in here yet. Too new, can't quite recall."

*Ring a Ding Ding. Ring a Ding Ding.* A call from Colorado broke the Archives silence.

*How embarrassing.*

Jacob excused himself from Barbara as gracefully as he could conjure on the spot. Not daring to disturb the echo-less Archives even more.

Barbara waved goodbye with another effortless wink in the way mastered by those who work with groups of children, like birthday party clowns. But then paranoia set in. *Did she know that his real mission was discovering the owner of the skull in the basement?* He worried librarians notice twice as much as they ever let on.

After an uneventful call with Gladys about the ABC Wars, and eliminating phased dances in competition, Jacob found himself sitting on a bench underneath the hood of the Huxley Sphynx. He sat with the *Who Saved Who* sticker in one hand and the green spiral notebook in the other. It seemed like a lifetime ago that Mabel had given these gifts instead of earlier that morning. *Time is funny when floating on the river*, he thought from somewhere, somehow. Then he thought, *the real gifts are the friends you make along the way.* Finally he thought, What a fool. *You know nothing, Jacob Maymerry!*

The insult jolted him into an idea. A mysterious muse. He realized he should use Mabel's gift. At least one of them. *One out of two ain't bad*, he thought from somewhere. He wrote a list of the new suspects, believing that he had made progress.

∞

**Past Lives**
   **A. Hamiltons**
      1. Chester*
      2. Elizabeth
      3. Oscar*-i
      4. S*
      5. S*
      6. S*
      7. Christopher

   **B. McDonalds**
      8. Dad
      9. Mom
      10. Child

He smiled to himself and hoped he properly summarized all the information to glean from Barbara. Then he went back and added asterisks to the names of those who had headstones at the cemetery. While he could be sure of nothing, as a budding detective he must make choices. Playing the odds—or perhaps following the river—he decided the head in the house was most likely one not already buried on the other side of town in Mount Willouby Cemetery.

Then he went back one final time and added an i next to Oscar's name—A new code invented that very second to signify "interesting." It was too odd that this obituary would fall out of its plastic sleeve. *There are no coincidences on the river.*

Writing it down made him realize something more. He was having fun, and he now wanted to uncover an interesting story. After all, he was risking a lot for this and he felt, just perhaps, that the skull now owed him something for all this trouble.

Though he didn't know it, in some moments he was trusting the river so completely that he made snap judgment after snap judgment without worrying at all about the endless things that might go wrong. He was beginning to think, and he didn't know why, that all answers would be given to him. He just need be still and let the current show him the way.

But as he began the walk back home, an even newer idea struck him like a punch in the forehead: *What are the odds that a Hamilton House obituary was the one that fell out? Was it perhaps left where it wouldn't otherwise be found? Was it hidden or misplaced? A fellow traveler on the bool hunt? Was a mysterious marauder ahead of him? What is going on?*

*Am I paranoid or am I in the middle of something much bigger than I understand?*

# —— Chapter 12 ——

**Jacob lost himself** in thought about his list of names and who might be chasing him in this skull hunt. His eyes in the sky, one block from his house, when he bumped head-first into a Rooster. It was the 4th, the same Roger who saved his heating system the previous morning.

"Toot-a-loo," Rooster said as if he wasn't sure what the saying meant.

"Oh, Hi Roger. Good to see you again," Jacob said truthfully, happy he'd already crossed wires with a familiar face—the benefit of shrinking one's world a bit. "What brings you back to these parts?" *What a weird thing to say, Jacob.*

"I didn't know you had a dog," Roger said idiotically and Jacob wondered if he had a celebratory lunch. Until he followed his friend's eyes to his own hand, holding the "Who Saved Who" sticker. Before Jacob could correct him, Roger explained why he was there. "I got another job, right next door to you. Your neighbors need some tinkering done before the summer, AC concerns. All old homes have such needs eventually," Roger said like a proud owner of a sustainable business.

"How great," Jacob said. "Such a small world."

"Yes sir. It's *deja vu* being back here again. And it was meant to be, because I think I might have left a tool in your basement. Happen to see anything?" Rooster stared into his eyes.

*You've got to be kidding me.*

"Oh that's too bad. Nope, I haven't seen anything, but I can take a look when I get home and let you know if I do."

"Thank you kindly. I sure do appreciate it. Hate to be a bumbler, but I do need to get going and pick my boy up from school. He takes the bus there but I haven't the heart to make him ride it back too. Twice in a day is scary." Jacob only then realized that there was probably an entirely other human side to this Rooster that he knew nothing about.

As Roger lumbered into his van, Jacob felt better about his house being cold the previous morning. Because he met Roger Rooster, and the local Hot and Cold professional got an extra job. *At least there's that.* In some ways, with a little careful floating down the river, even life's bumps and razzies can be sweet. That wasn't nothing. *So it goes.*

∞

**Ding a Ding** *Ding. Ding a Ding Ding.* Expecting a call from CO, Jacob was relieved by a large VA on his phone. Liam had an update. But the update was a string of disasters making it plain to Jacob that Liam was on his own, entirely separate, heroic adventure.

The restaurant oven was now accidentally in Ohio, which is where Liam was headed in the rented van. He chased the appliance because he'd also received the good news that the restaurant was to be featured in some web food series that Jacob assumed was a big deal from the tone in the chef's voice. Long story short, it was a monsoon of chaos.

"The last thing," Liam said wrapping up the call, "the fence folks will be there tomorrow. So show them the permit, and they will get to work. The good news is they are the fastest out there. The whole yard in one day—posts, board, beginning to end."

That's when Jacob explained the snafu, and Liam decided to call and reschedule the fence folks. Jacob tried to keep things in perspective, "I mean, if it only takes them one day, then it doesn't matter when they start. I'll grab the permit tomorrow and *voila*, fence in no time."

"Yep. Don't sweat it." Liam said, "Duty calls."

∞

**Jacob realized he** also probably had some duty to fulfill. Though he wasn't sure which one was most important at the moment. Line dance legal work called from somewhere, something about eliminating complicated ABC dances per Gladys. He also had a skull in the basement. But in a snap judgment, he went back to the office to unpack. After all, where else would one determine which duty in life to fulfill than the office.

In an effort to find inspiration, he sat in his old blue swivel chair behind the large brown dinosaur desk and spun in one slow circle. The Oscar Wilde portrait propped on the floor, and the Stephen King woodcutting watched from a shelf.

He remembered the first time he heard of Mr. King. It was a Mass of Confusion. Jacob was in 3rd grade, sitting in a circle during one of his classmate's birthday parties. A girl said, "What is it?" Jacob thought she was pointing to a shadow on the wall, which looked like a balloon. But what she actually meant was 'What is making the shadow?' Then the kid next to Jacob said, "It's a clown." Which it was. The clown making the shadow was there to pass out cupcakes for the birthday. Then another classmate said, "Yea, It's a clown. Stephen King made him."

Jacob asked which kid in the class was named Stephen King, but everyone laughed at him. Then someone else said, "You dummy. Stephen King is a book." Until the smartest girl in class who usually had the last word said in response to the original question, "It is a Pro Noun." That really threw Jacob into a tailspin, as he had barely gotten his head around regular nouns and was wholly unprepared, at that age, for professional nouns. So he forgot about It. Until 6th grade when he found the K section of the junior high library and entered the master storyteller's mind for quite a spell.

In a flash, Jacob bounced from the middle school library to his Hamilton House home office, which was pathetically still packed. He glanced out a tall window and saw the sun dipping below where Mabel's house stood hidden in the distance. The strange thing about having your things all boxed up is that it forces you to look at the beautiful emptiness of all that is.

It made Jacob uncomfortable, and so he stood up and decided out of nothing to have a twilight walk. After all, Jacob remembered, meditative walks and changes of pace were an easy way to snap the mind into a new groove according to some experts.

∞

**Jacob ventured out** again, and was soon carried along the red and black brick sidewalk that lined Nottingham Avenue in a regal display of the historic city's elegant undertones. *Many interesting shoes have trod these paths, Jacob thought from nowhere.* Noticing the street fully once more, Jacob admired how wispy wonderful it all was, when looking at the right angle. Large sycamores towering in front of larger homes—each a unique jewel, crafted like links in a chain as the city expanded further from its inner core.

One pink and turquoise house with a bubblegum snap door caught his attention immediately. This pixie estate sparkled with lush green grass, picket fence, a napping doodle, and flicking gas lantern atop a post. A storybook porch swing drifted in the breeze as if inviting him in for lemonade and a baked good of some magical variety. He fought the urge to meander off the brick sidewalk toward it, and instead walked on.

But another immediately ensnared him. Perhaps a refracted mirror reflection of the pixie house, with a shared gas lantern, there arose a dark crystal of a castle home. A brewing fantastical creature of greys and blacks, it loomed as a giant both sinister and jolly. The house seemed to glimmer a dark jade and drift back deep in the yard, hinting at a labyrinth of hidden secrets inside. Slate roof tiles projected permanence. This was a home for here and always and for creation not just reflection. Jacob imagined a large cauldron brewing beneath the smoke drifts up the medieval stone chimney. *What enchanting fun dwells there?* But not for Jacob. Not today.

He turned away from the dark crystal and focused straight ahead. Eyes up. He needed to get his head on a little straighter. Prioritize. *What was he doing on this walk again?*

Luckily a house at the end of Nottingham Ave. took control of his ambling brain. Far different from the others, this one was traditional in the white house sense. Respectable columns marked the door and pegged the owners as those who understood Greek and Roman standards of beauty and form. This was the house of a statesman, with a central corridor, two wings, and Jacob assumed it must be furnished with the finest of period specific antiques. He noticed a historic marker near the door deeming it "Notting House." *Do all houses have names, or is a historic marker required?* Jacob was having trouble concentrating.

The southern end of the avenue drifted east, becoming the Piccadilly St. Upon which sat the Huxley lion, the permit man's flower shop, and much of Willouby's core. Jacob noticed that the last building on Nottingham was another church, this of an older American sort—a Quaker Meeting Hall. Jacob had no idea what the Quaker's believed, but he made a mental note to look it up. Saving souls, no doubt, assuming that was the purpose of all homes of higher power.

The sun now almost gone, Jacob circled around, back north on Nottingham, toward his rock house, and the mountain of duties that awaited him inside. He still had no idea which one mattered most.

# —— Chapter 13 ——

**Upside down deja** vu hit Jacob as he trod the back embankment, a tilt-a-whirl vertigo under the inky purple sycamore leaves. Can you have *deja vu* about *deja vu* experienced as *deja vu? Must be muscle memory from when I fell at that very spot on Monday,* Jacob knew from somewhere deep.

He tried to put a positive spin on it. *That was the river sending me a message. I'm older and wiser now, and that tumble was a wake up. Be more careful. Don't jog too fast in unknown territory. Always a lesson, just gotta hunt for it.*

Before Jacob could consider his options for dinner, he heard it, Ding a Ding Ding. It was from VA via OH, at least Jacob assumed. Good news for Jacob that it wasn't Gladys in CO, but bad news for Liam in that his life had found its own inside out. The stove was headed in the van back to Willouby. But Liam was not.

"New York? Good Morning, what?" Turns out a last minute cancellation, friend of a friend, favor, something or other led to a big promotional opportunity and cooking showcase or whatnot. Jacob was thrilled for the restaurant, didn't process all the details, but knew that Liam was re-energized. That was all the verification he needed, a sign to focus again on his own mystery. A reminder from the river that this skull business was his bone of burden.

*Focus on what you control*, Jacob reminded himself of a lesson he'd heard in a video. *Like your body. You're starving. Feed yourself.*

**That's how Jacob** ended up back on the front porch, eating another can of microwaved chicken noodle soup, and listening for the second night in a row to the sounds of cackling crows through the trees. *Routines develop quickly in a town like Willouby.*

But they weren't crows. His neighbors were back on the porch—the two old men that he had heard but rarely seen. The same men he now knew had air conditioning concerns that would soon be addressed by Roger Rooster. He eavesdropped, but Jacob knew that anyone who speaks into the night air that loudly wants to be heard. So he did them the courtesy of listening.

Jacob imagined they were brothers, though he didn't know why. Perhaps because they spoke in riddles, like two men who could finish each other's sentences and spoke nonsensically to keep things interesting while jousting with their brains.

"You're completely missing the M. Meaning," Man One said with calm confidence.

Man Two was having none of it, "The rules state explicitly that you can replace anything for repair. The letters of the law matter."

"Of course they matter, my dear Brother," *Jacob's ears rose pointy in astonishment at his own clairvoyance. Brothers!* "The letters matter, but they are not all that matters. Don't forget about meaning. What do we mean when we want to preserve an old house? Think, now, think!"

Brother Two grew enraged at the implied condescension. *As if he needed to think. He already knew!* "Spare me. The letters can mean whatever they want to you, but we all agree on some meanings. You can't replace every pipe, board, and brick in a one hundred and fifty year old home and then claim it's still the same house. And have the audacity to believe that it was all repair. Outrageous!"

Jacob almost thought he was going to say 'A for Audacity!'—but he didn't.

Instead, Man One tried to land the plane peacefully, "I wonder if every cell in our body is eventually replaced, are we the same person. Who are we really?"

But that is where the brother ended things, "Nope. Not playing that game today. You can speak that gibberish at your meditation retreat, and have a real discussion on planet earth with me later. Goodnight."

Jacob tried to follow the merits of each brother's arguments, but he doubled back on himself and gave up. Instead, he finished his chicken noodle soup and thought about old houses. And the names of old houses. He thought about the three houses he saw on his walk. And then he wondered what people thought of this house when they walked past it.

Jacob's mind drifted more than usual lately. Was it the time spent in the basement thinking on skulls? Was he losing touch with reality and following his rambling mind wherever it led? How could he ever know?

Perhaps staring at the grey matter in the basement one more night was necessary—until he made some final decision. He threw his bowl in the sink and walked down the pine to the lair below. He felt Eleanor follow behind him, joining for the thrill.

Part of Jacob knew why he followed his skull thoughts down deep. Because even if he was losing touch with reality—the sneakiest part of him giggled that it was all too fun not to keep going. An adventure. This little caper bubbled up something in his veins that felt real and true and part of the fascinating story in this little corner of the big old world.

*Was anything else in his control more important this very instant?*

**Jacob sat on** the boulder to the center of the earth, stared at the skull, and then looked up at the haphazard-grid of pipes above. Some new white plastic tubes looked frail. Others a thick black metal, clearly there for the long haul. *The veins of the 'ol gal*, Jacob knew, sending her all she needed, in and out. The hallways were larger passages, and people were tiny tourists.

*That's what we are*, Jacob sat wondering weird thoughts. This house is far more stoic, solid, and long-lasting than he would ever be. It stood here indifferent to the permits and titles in City Hall. It was not owned by anyone other than in their heads. It existed here like a tree. Built by men, sure, but with its own freedom. It would live, change, and die like a mighty oak. Humans may alter it and eventually kill it, but it will have existed on its own terms. With its own story. And it didn't matter if no human ear ever understood it. In that way, the 'ol gal reminded him of Eleanor Roosevelt the Calico Cat.

Jacob realized his eyes were narrowing in bedtime exhaustion. And while he may have hit a new low in controlling his thoughts, he was not yet low enough that he'd literally fall asleep in the basement.

Then in a 3 second spiral, Jacob knew thinking about falling asleep in the basement meant that he was the skull. But that was too crazy and too easy to be true. Trying to turn a scary thought into a positive one, Jacob instead asked himself what the river was really trying to tell him. *Think, Jacob, Think!*

*Was the skull itself talking to Jacob? Explaining what happened? Was this what it felt like to experience a ghost in the scientific world? Was being possessed like an invisible spirit taking control of your mind for a period and making you do things by thinking you're still in control. Inch by inch. What's the difference between something being invisible and something not being noticed? To the person, aren't they always the same thing?*

Jacob's brain twisted too tight for a Thursday night alone with an unhelpful calico companion. Human friends are still necessary, Jacob knew. Wasn't it Plato who said friendship was the purest relationship, with no desire to change the other person in any way? Or maybe he heard that from a Creature known as  Snuffleupagus.

"Meow! Meow! Meow!"

Eleanor saved Jacob's complete nonsense thoughts with a Mew of very clear Meaning—"Feed me."

Jacob obliged, as he typically did to her demands, and walked back up the pine to fill her dish. It remained one of the very few things unpacked.

∞

**Quite a fascinating** *first few days in Willouby*, Jacob considered in bed with a purring cat asleep opposite him. He felt in good spirits. Perhaps because he was more curious now than he had been in some time. Perhaps because he knew exactly what he would be doing the next day—returning to the House of Mabel.

*Because how could he not?*

The river led him there. Mabel invited him again with her own voice, and Jacob knew that you did not turn down a lunchtime invitation from a still breathing CC woman who lived up the lane. Jacob wondered if the river decided everything from the beginning. The chef was on a wild goose hunt somewhere in Middle America specifically because Jacob was chasing this wild ghost. Then Jacob thought about a Ghost Goose. Then a Goose Ghost. Then he laughed out loud in the attic bedroom. Eleanor rolled her closed eyes.

*Perhaps, just perhaps, it all made sense. Eventually.*

As Eleanor dreamed, Jacob flipped open the little green spiral notebook which he'd placed on his end table without realizing it. Detective Maymerry looked at his information in preparation for tomorrow's Mabel Meeting.

**Past Lives**

    **A. Hamiltons**

        1. Chester*

        2. Elizabeth-i

        3. Oscar-i*

        4. S*

        5. S*

      6. S*
      7. Christopher-w

### B. McDonalds
      8. Dad
      9. Mom
      10. Child

He added a w next to Christopher's name as he remembered all the talk about "wandering" and wondered what that might mean. Then he added another i next to Elizabeth, considering it was also very "interesting" that Barbara couldn't remember if she was buried in the cemetery. *No coincidences on the river.*

Jacob felt prepared, ready to absorb whatever information Mabel might share about these folks. He drifted to sleep before midnight—the notebook on his chest—his mind a mass of confusion afloat a river he increasingly hoped, believed, and felt most deep actually existed.

# Friday

**Ring a Ding** Ding welcomed Jacob back to Willouby as confusing bells of many meanings. He didn't know if it was a call, alarm, or warning of imminent danger. *I need to change that sound,* was his first Friday thought—adding a task to his worthless mental To Do list to be immediately forgotten. Lately, his brain felt like the dollar store sheet he found in his office that wrote things down with the plastic nib but disappeared in one swish.

Eleanor left him long before, her indention on the empty bed no longer even there.

From nowhere Jacob heard another beep in the dark, down the stairs. *In your head,* he knew, still waking up. *Perhaps I dreamed after all, but forgot it entirely. But how could he ever know he wasn't still dreaming now. Dreaming about dreaming. With a little imagination, it's dreams all the way down.*

Jacob caught his mental rambling with oxygen. He took a 4 second inhale, held it for 4 seconds, then exhaled for 4 more seconds.

At last, with the zip of a child realizing a holiday approaches, he remembered he was lunching with Mabel today. *What a delight!*

He recognized a tiny kernel of fear in his center—worry that this Mabel visit would be far different than the last. A murky wonder escaped the darkness without his knowing—*Did she really want me to come again? What time did she say? Am I making all of this up in my head?*

It was a mental loop not helped by a series of different number breath combinations. *Should he text Mabel to confirm? Was she joking about a return visit? Would she look shocked if he showed up at her door?*

Sometimes Jacob wished he could live life like a book. Hold your place, flip backwards to re-read the exact language of Mabel's goodbye, then zip forward again to make a smart decision that wouldn't embarrass himself. But no sir e. Jacob Maymerry was stuck plodding away in the dark of the unknown future, with a shoddy memory, and growing wonder about how much he thought about flowing on a river.

Finally his sound, logical brain saved the day with capital R Reason. *Keep perspective, little one. You remember Mabel said lunchtime. You'll go at Noon, and if she doesn't see you, she doesn't see you. You'll apologize and say you heard wrong. Get a grip, Jacob. None of this matters anyway.*

"Hear hear!" Jacob said aloud to himself and the room. Clear thinking is why he kept that part of himself around. Sometimes you need to slap sense into your worrying mind and stop with the silly fears.

His head felt screwed on tighter when he remembered one more thing—the Keeper of the Keys. Miss Barbara Johnson was as real as anything else Jacob had seen in this town. She spoke of Mabel as fascinating, worthy of visiting. Who was he to doubt Miss Barbara?

Jacob then remembered a third extra thing, the River. He knew full well that he talked of this mysterious River as a spirit mist. An imaginary friend. But since Jacob *knew* it was all silly, then he couldn't actually be crazy. Imaginary friends are fine so long as you know they are imaginary. Right? The River was Jacob's adult imaginary friend—a feeling deep inside that he could not and did not want to control.

Sitting on the porch, watching Eleanor cackle at birds, Jacob ate a breakfast of apple slices. He cut them into four hunks around the core, enjoying the snappy sweetness of the honeycrisp as juice droplets spilled out with each bite. Detective Maymerry sat on the porch, flipped open the green notebook he carried in his back pocket, and thought about his suspects.

That word struck his ear all wrong. There was no crime so there could be no suspects. He stared down at the list and felt a deep kinship with the ten names—some of which were just letters—each of his predecessors inside the 'ol gal. Perhaps like that fuzzy feeling of belonging he sometimes felt as an American, Jacob sensed an attachment to these folks. *Each of us spending some of our very precious time on this earth within this little place atop the boulder to the center of the earth.*

He inhaled for three seconds, exhaled for ten, and tried to shift into a new gear. Adjusting a pretend Holmes cap, he flipped open the notebook and decided to pluck slithery silver thoughts out of his head with his magic wand pen onto this notebook. He wrote questions:

*What happened to Mother Elizabeth Hamilton and youngest boy Christopher Hamilton? Are they buried at the family plot, and if not, why?*

*Who are the McDonalds? Why did they lose the house? Is anyone still alive, and if so, can I find them?*

There was so much more that Jacob wanted to know. Because he wanted to know everything. Now that he was on the trail of all those who had walked the halls of his home, he must discover what happened to them. Just perhaps, something similar might befall him, and Jacob liked to find happy endings. That was a silly river thought, but a thought nonetheless.

∞

**Hours left before** walking to Mabel's, Jacob did not even consider more AAMCLDS work. Instead he decided to continue what he already considered a hobby—walking the red and black brick road around old town Willouby. Jacob strode this time with more confidence, like a graduate of some level. Perhaps only past the orientation, not yet a full Willoubeast, not after just five days in town, but at least he could be someone who had been here before. *That's not nothing*, he thought from somewhere.

Jacob admired again each of the three houses that caught his eye like jeweled signposts on the road to the end of Nottingham. The twinkling pink door picket fence house. The dark Maleficent castle of delicious creation. And the regal white block estate of elegance and respectability, the home with a name—Notting House.

Time enough at last for a longer walk, Jacob turned left onto Piccadilly St. This took him past the Huxley library, and he continued down because he wanted to look at something. He found it three blocks further along, a charming little thin mint building jammed between others, the two floors cut in half by a steel beam from which a flower mural grew. He walked up to the window to see if he saw the swiveling seat man to ask how the first birthday party went. No dice—the shop was empty.

Jacob figured he had walked far enough from his house for the morning, and so he took another left down an unknown street to begin the circle back toward home.

This half of the circle was far less sparkling in the traditional sense than the walk down Nottingham. Here Jacob saw the underside of the city, remnants of old industry that chugged the numbers half of things for generations. The fuel bringing jobs, money, and occasional purpose to real folks. The key industry in Willouby, as far as Jacob could tell from this part of town, was Apples. Both the growing and storing of them. Willouby had an attachment to apples, and Jacob noticed there were orchards all around the surrounding county. In the winter these mangled trees guarded the approach to the old city like a hideously crooked army, ensuring only the most worthy reached the town center and treasures inside.

As he made his third left, now walking along grass remnants growing up between the bare traces of generations unused wood and steel rail lines, Jacob's eyes were drawn to a once magnificent painted sign across a windowless warehouse —

*Home Of World's Largest Apple Cold Storage*

The letters blazed on the horizon like a beacon. Jacob felt a pang of nostalgia for an old Willouby he never knew. Upon closer look, he noticed some time after the original painting, the words "one of the" was added in small print. Jacob stared at the little addition which now changed the punchline —

*Home Of one of the World's Largest Apple Cold Storage.*

It made him wonder. *Who decided to edit this painting for accuracy, but small enough that it would mostly go unnoticed?* He pictured the painter up there, laughing as he brushed on the addition. Was it the same painter who did the original, or was it a two person job? Jacob realized that perhaps the River reminded him that no one can stay the largest of anything forever.

The industrial area with the famous cold storage went up to the end of Nottingham Avenue. And so Jacob made one final left to finish the loop and return to his rock house from the exact opposite way that he'd departed. Jacob walked through an empty parking lot with a charmingly vandalized corner that had turned into a skate park of such stereotypical elegant grunge that it might have been a movie set.

A few teenagers congregated around some large red figure. *Is that a human sized M&M candy?* Jacob had seen many strange things lately, and he suspected it was the growing pains of learning a new town. *Is it someone dressed as an apple?* The closer he came he realized it was something else entirely, Santa Claus. Which was strange considering it was a Friday in April.

The person dressed as Santa Claus, with a thick fake beard, appeared to be handing out candy canes of a glistening red and white swirl in one hand. In the other he rang a bell at random.

Jacob tried to walk swiftly without eye contact, but the river had other ideas.

∞

**"Hello O O O** there!" Santa said, stopping Jacob.

Jacob smiled and tried to drift past with a wave, but a conversation ensued.

"Ho Ho Ho. Merry Christmas!" Santa bellowed in a voice that struck him familiar.

*Of course it sounds familiar. It's Santa Claus. You know him!* But then he thought—*Jacob, don't be an idiot. You don't know this man. He could be a local loon!*

"Christmas in April! Haven't you heard of it?" Santa sang with youthful elven glee. Then he rang the bell before going on, "The truth is that this is an inherited suit that I like to wear. And I wanted to wear it today. It's April. So, Ta Da! Christmas in April."

Jacob had no idea what to say until the River provided him a burst of insight. *I do know him.* The voice belonged to the Flower Cup Guy—the young man who gave him a free rose two days earlier. "Hello again," Jacob said, realizing that might sound strange. But then he remembered that he could never be stranger than the Santa in front of him. *It's easy to relax around odd friends.*

Young St. Nick spoke with a smirk, "Good memory you have there. Just like I remember you are the only one who got my riddle correct on Wednesday. Funny seeing you here in this place." He looked around at the ramshackle boards, trash cans, and uncomfortable wooden lounge corners.

"Not as funny as seeing Saint Nicholas at the skate park," Jacob surprised himself with immediate banter. "Or are you a street preacher?"

"Why not both?" Santa smiled his perfect teeth, as if he didn't expect anything witty from a man in a cardigan. "You can call me Nicholas today, if you'd like. Because today I'm an artist. Art is the same thing as Christmas in April, isn't it? Jamming two things together and seeing what happens. I'm pretty sure that's what the scientists are doing in that collision machine in Europe— buzzing those tiny bee balls around in circles real fast until they explode into one another. Then they watch to see what new things pop out." Saint Nicholas grinned, and for half a second Jacob wondered if the whole thing was a ruse. *Is this weird young Willoubeast in on some joke?*

"Pretty interesting ideas you have there." Jacob said neutrally as he tried to get his bearings. Perhaps Nicholas ended up on these streets because it's exactly the place he wanted to be.

The young man dropped the beard under his chin to reveal the clean shaved face Jacob remembered from beneath the Huxley lion sidewalk. He had the natural physique of a jungle athlete who ate only to survive and thrive, like a jaguar, and so the Santa suit bagged around him like a deflated inflatable.

Nicholas smiled again, adjusted a tilted Santa cap, and spoke with a hint of secret whisper, "Sometimes you're the particle, sometimes you're the wave." He stared directly into Jacob's eyes, "You are nothing, my man, until you decide to look and see what Is. You can be whatever you want. Seeing is deciding. Believing is seeing. Do you understand?"

Jacob sensed extreme earnestness in Saint Nicholas's eyes. But then was relieved when the young preacher laughed and spoke again without waiting for an answer, "It doesn't matter amigo, we're all figuring it out as we go."

*Was that condescending or extremely kind?* Before Jacob could decide, Santa ended the meeting with Christmas flair. "I'm afraid it's a busy day for this old jolly elf. Many stops to make before it's all done. It was a pleasure seeing you this Christmas Day, and I do hope you enjoy your gift."

Before Jacob could understand what he meant by gift, the young Nicholas lifted his beard back under his nose, walked in full Santa suit and empty sack straight into the woods behind the skate park, and disappeared into a dark green nothingness like a ghost baseball player in a fantasy movie cornfield.

∞

**Jacob tried to** remember the words of wisdom that he assumed was his Christmas gift. But he had forgotten it already, his mind swished clean, ready for his next adventure—eager to finish the final block back to his house to prepare for a return to the big house on the biggest hill.

Detective Maymerry was ready. He tried to remember the questions he had written down.

"Honk!" A sound burst in Jacob's ear from the road. He glanced and saw a flash of ampersands across a white van. A Rooster, he knew, probably coming back from his neighbor's house. Jacob waved a hand blindly in the air behind him in a half hello.

Roger's horn derailed Jacob's train of thought, but it made him notice for the first time that a synagogue marked the start of this end of Nottingham Avenue. *How curious,* Jacob mused, *that the other end has the Quaker Meeting House and this is capped by a Synagogue.*

Deep symbolism in that. Jacob made a mental note to brainstorm that symbol—in case he needed to have an interesting idea to share with a snappy smart neighbor. *Capped by Savers of Souls?* Perhaps Mabel would mention it, Jacob smiled as he arrived back home, *because he was riding the river and all the pieces might fit eventually.*

Or perhaps *Jacob Maymerry was a lemming drifting over a waterfall without a barrel to the laughs of everyone pointing on shore. If so, he'd give them a good show.*

∞

**Once home Jacob** took a quick look at the basement skull to see if any ideas popped up. They didn't. He felt a nap coming on as he walked back up the basement steps, which he decided to take to kill time before his Mabel meeting. A little rest would ensure he was fresh when he again visited the house on the high hill.

He napped and dreamed of Christmas and letters in a twisty red and blue snowy blur. He sat atop a cloud and Aunt Mabel's voice spoke to him with a smoker's hilarity from all around.

*You know about SC don't you, ye childe Jacob? It's a secret of course, the Society of Cincinnati. SC was the start of the conflict, they fired upon our fort. But that's not the SC I mean, Ba Kaw! Ba Kaw!*

*The S is for Sam or Samuel for the formal. And the C is Clemens. Not to be confused with Clement, who wrote about Eves and The Nights Before. No Sir e!*

The dream Mabel voice gave a performance in words as dream Jacob sat upon clouds.

*"When what to my wondering eyes should appear, but a miniature woman, and a chalice of golden beer."*

*"More rapid than eagles, his rescuer did land. Under the house itself, a hero that no one had planned."*

Dream Mabel's voice then chastised Jacob for misunderstanding letters.

*But that's the wrong SC, as I told you. The American SC is an MT, for Twain. Mark be his name! He wrote the book, after all, about prisoners escaping to freedom along the big American River.*

*Are you him? The Huckleberry? Or a different version, the Maymerry?*

*It's Robbins and a Free Man that floated the river to escape. Don't you know? Aboard the SS Raft to Mexico. The SS is a prison, or a street, or a swan song, depending on how you Go!*

He awoke with a blurry mind, and made a cup of coffee to jolt his senses. Jacob needed to get zipping, as he had a friend to meet.

**Jacob felt more** comfortable than he had since moving to this town. He unpacked a few clothes, mostly sweaters, a small step to making this place feel permanent. Wearing a purple t-shirt that flattered his figure, thin vintage yellow cardigan, grey jeans, and puma sneakers, he nodded at himself in the mirror. That inspired him to head down to his Victorian office and open a few work boxes.

Instead, he immediately sat in his office chair and spun in a circle. Looking at Oscar Wilde, he vowed that once this skull business was solved he'd finally read more information about the playwright or novelist or whatever. In that very moment, the only thought that came to Jacob was that Wilde was a tricksy e. Mabel might like him, with a name spelled like that. It's funny what information sticks and what doesn't. But Jacob sternly reminded himself not to actually bring up Wilde with Mabel until he had something far more interesting to say about him than a letter in his name.

Snapping out of his silliness, Detective Maymerry pulled the spiral green notebook from his back pocket and looked at his thoughts once more.

*What happened to Mother Elizabeth Hamilton and youngest boy Christopher Hamilton? Are they buried at the family plot, and if not, why?*

*Who are the McDonalds? Why did they lose the house? Is anyone still alive, and if so, can I find them?*

"Simple," Jacob said though there was no one to hear. Even Eleanor had disappeared somewhere that morning. Jacob stared at the notebook, twirled a pen in his hand, and wrote down some stream of conscious ideas that he hoped were from the River itself.

*Such stories from sisters*
*Who wants to be down there?*
*Why do you care?*
*Jacob, Jacob let down your hair!*

He looked down at the gibberish and smirked at the idea of someone thinking it was the worst poem ever written. Then Jacob Maymerry ripped the page out of the notebook, and trashed it with glee as he nearly skipped out the door on another journey to the House of Mabel.

# —— Chapter 15 ——

**Jacob Maymerry strolled** up the green grassy private lane lined by the black fence and looming sycamore trees. He strode like a man who had been here before, in his form-fitting puma shoes, casual yellow cardigan, and confidence that he believed would last.

He gonged one large turtle and waited for the silent butler to greet him. Jacob hoped most deep that Willouby remained a town where routines developed instantly.

Jacob wasn't disappointed. Winston opened the cave door with a silent nod and arm gesture inside. At the very least, the butler acted as if this was all expected, and not the nosy little neighbor arriving unannounced. If this was a video game, at least Jacob had gotten back into this castle once again. But would it be the same as before? *Come come my little chickadee.*

Standing in the familiar rising entry, he remembered the three stone staircases that rose up into the estate, left, right, and center. Then he remembered that he completely forgot to use the bathroom before he left the house, and that was a tragic mistake. *Dammit, Jacob!*

But before he even knew what was happening, a hidden courage rose up in him and he said to the mute man guiding him along, "Can I use the powder room?"

*Powder room?* Jacob was almost certain he had never used that phrase in his life, at least not out loud. And yet he just did.

It was only his supreme luck that he was greeted by a British butler who thought nothing of it. Winston nodded and pointed at a small door hidden in the crook under one of the stairs. The cupboard powder room was greens and browns, with owl and mushroom wallpaper, topped with three dimensional big eyed bird and fungi decor screwed into the wall. A sanitarium yellow sink sat like a rising sun, low enough for children or pixie CC women to use.

Jacob noticed that the sink was the color of his cardigan and hoped it was a good omen.

*Powder room. What a strange name.* There was a freedom in moving someplace new, to become unknown. Once past the fear of having no emergency contact number, you realize that you can entirely reinvent yourself. Use brand new words without any strange looks. That wasn't nothing.

Jacob left the powder room and followed Winston up new stairs, to the far left. He wondered if using the word *Powder Room* was a hint. A sign that the River was gaining full control of his thoughts. He once read an article or summary about fungi, just like the decorations in the cupboard room, that took possession of minds and became zombie controllers. Jacob sighed, remembered about breathing and thought that if the River did have control of his mind it was telling him to relax, loosen up, act like a real human, respond to your bodily feelings, look around at where you are.

Then the river thoughts were drowned out by the sights that popped up around Jacob inside this new wing of the House of Mabel.

∞

**The room opened** to the West, and Jacob first noticed windows. Windows across the entire wall, windows with crested panes, arching both round and pointy, geometric shapes, and colors that reminded Jacob simultaneously of Frank Lloyd Wright and an Enlightenment Cathedral. The sunshine streamed in, shading and grading the floor, melting Jacob into a goo—this room felt important but comfortable.

Two swirls around and he realized he was wrapped in books—it was the Library of Mabel. This might have been a modest ballroom for seventy six of Mabel's closest friends of the season. Instead it'd been converted into a demonstration of this regal oldest woman's respect for the written word — or at least the *look* of knowledge. Jacob Maymerry, being a creature who always wished he could read more books than he actually did, would argue to his grave that *creating* a library of any size was as valuable as *reading* everything in it before death.

The library was floor to ceiling books with, by Jacob's count, five golden, textured ladders up the two and a half stories of paper, ink, binding, strands, strings, and other weavings of stories. Each rung corresponded to a shelf— some numerical organizational system was written in fancy lettering on each grip beyond Jacob's understanding.

The furniture was a unique blend of elegance, refinement, and tomfoolery. In the center space, under the largest chandelier, stood two reading tables with green lamps, and matching circular conversation chair pits of greens, browns, and warm yellows. Spiraling out of that center, were less organized pieces, spaces, small tables, soft corners, smaller shelves, carpets, and assortments of other swizzles. Knick-knacks, reproductions, tiny knobs and nozzles, miniature sculptures, maps, scrolls, magnifiers, community college craft projects, and a vast assortment of old-timey gizmos decorated the remaining shelf, floor, and table space, which Jacob imagined now as a hobbiton neighborhood for shorter adults.

Before he could understand even a fraction more, his host appeared to him as a sound—the rose coo of an elderly hen.

"Well, well, well," she spoke from behind a river green high back chair, smoke drifts serpentining up from the faintest trace of a wig Jacob suspected was blonde. "The Prodigal Queen returns!"

*What?*

"Me, of course!" *Ba Kaw! Ba kaw! Ba Kaw!* "Never forget, little one, I'm usually talking about myself."

She rose and began a slow turn around the chair, the wig bopping up to a luscious breezy dew yellow, shoulder length with seductive swirl. Her tiny frame spun atop the 50s hair and Jacob tried to place the concoction Mabel presented to him for this meeting.

Her one piece outfit was a silky feathery green, with hints of maroon beads and silver trails. Huge billowy sleeves, form fitting waist, until more billows around the calf. She wore large bug glasses of inky green and smoked her slim from a long golden cigarette holder worn as a wedding ring. She walked with the wispy cigarette as a butterfly stretching wings atop her hand, a dear insect friend smoking here for a visit.

In one moment Mabel looked a large mantis, graceful, of mysterious limbs and shapes. But in a flash, she moved with performer confidence and Jacob saw something entirely different. She could have passed for either the villain or seductress in a spy movie.

"I was a wonderful Bond woman once." She read his mind, and Jacob knew the river must be real. "Not on screen, of course. But I do pass for the first queen bee from that first movie, Mr. No Way. I think her name was Ursula and she rose from the ocean. Or maybe it was Honey Writer. I won't remember. You know they had so many strange names back in those days."

Jacob squinted, had no idea if any of that was true, but smiled to see his friend again. "Great to see you Mabel. Thanks for having me."

"You're a dear for joining me once more. And you are very right, I am a dear for having you." *Hehehe.* She chuckled to herself as she motioned for Jacob to join her in one of the cozy conversation circles, yellow leather chairs which might have formed a sun if pressed together.

Mabel stood as Jacob sat. She pulled the gold cigarette extender off her ring finger, and instead puffed it from afar as she stared at him for a brief moment. Jacob felt sized up in half a flash, as hopeless as an exhale against a hurricane. He knew he was in her control.

∞

**In an instant** he thought, *if she is a witch I just hope her allegiance is to the east.* Then he realized he was facing west and gulped. But then he remembered that they were on the east coast. *She's probably a good witch*, Jacob thought to himself idiotically before realizing that the green witches on Halloween were often far more fun, until he realized Mabel had been talking the whole time.

She held up an ominous looking Red Book of which Jacob only saw the blank back cover. "This is the only book you need. All the stories in one." A double wink with a right, then left eye. Jacob again wondered if Crazy Mabel was lurking below this charming old veneer. "Just kidding. It is a psychology text. Might be gibberish to you yet. I'm a reader. These days I don't do 1 but 3 at a time. Don't want to miss anything." Mabel held up three fingers to ensure he understood.

Jacob knew without asking that what she really meant was, *I don't know how much time I have left.* Then again, Mabel didn't seem to have little of anything, so Jacob decided not to think about such things and let the River guide him.

Depending on how she sat, Mabel could appear a wrinkled tortoise. She'd open her mouth with pearly whites and say something snappy. The slightest hint of makeup at the crinkle of the eye. A quick arch in an eyebrow—the faintest flair of a character underneath the old woman body. But that was only for the moment that she sat completely still.

In a flash she'd be up and all of those details would disappear, and Jacob noticed only the things about her that had nothing to do with her age. *How strange*, he thought before realizing Mabel was still speaking.

Jacob heard none of it, he found that if he squinted he could see a mirror ghost image of the young Mabel projected over the old. If he wanted, like turning a dial, Jacob might brighten the former Mabel in his mind. Then he could see again the 50s hair, that original villainess, and some hidden light as bold as ever inside.

*She must have spent all morning, looking at her favorite things, deciding which ones to bring out for this visit.* Jacob thought though wasn't sure if it was true. But he was sure glad he had followed the River today. It might have meant as much to Mabel as it did to Jacob.

Jacob's mind finally returned to the Library, "That's why I watched the Letter Man, because I love letters. As you've probably picked up by now. I figured between the two options, I'd go with that one. The other one was just as funny, but as I said, you can't watch two things at once. Not unless you have four eyes. It gets too complicated."

It was only then that Jacob realized she held a tiny umbrella, which she'd opened sitting across from him in the yellow chair. "The sun is brutal this time of day," she said without any emotion.

Jacob smiled, calm but confused, "Isn't it though?"

"Just kidding, need to keep you on your toes. If there isn't five percent of you," she held up five fingers, "that doesn't wonder if it's Crazy Mabel all the way down, then I have failed you." She mimed confusion, "Or is it fifty percent? This memory of mine is really going." She winked and closed the umbrella, using it as an excuse to glide up toward the umbrella stand near a door. Jacob noticed that the billows in her calf and sleeve hid her size—power under a skeletal frame—like a pterodactyl.

"But enough about me," Mabel smiled, "for at least a moment. You came here to learn about your predecessors. Or are they descendants? The ghosts in your house is what I meant to say." Jacob blanched for a second. *She knows,* but then he realized he was paranoid and to trust the river ride.

"Now the last gentleman to live in your house, the clown, Mr. McDonald. He looked like the Man of Letters who made me laugh at night. Remember? He was a spitting image of the Letter Man, Mr. McDonald, I mean. I said that to explain that Chester Hamilton, the original father of your house—the Hamilton in the Hamilton House—well, the man looked like the other one, the Lenny O. Did you know him? Just as funny as Letter Man, but different. Or maybe he went by Len. Doesn't matter, but it's a charming coincidence all the same."

Jacob was immediately lost but took two deep breaths and trusted the River.

With a willowy green fabric arm, Mabel swung a hand toward the table in the center of the sunny library chairs, "Do enjoy."

∞
# Mabel's Coffee Not Tea Party

"Unfortunately, I cannot offer tea, considering this is America. But Winston kindly laid out all coffee accouterments, fresh water, the same cookies from yesterday, slightly softer apples, and miniature grilled cheese sandwiches. I suspect you know what kind of cheese." She winked after delivering the menu with server's grace before drifting to gaze out a twelve foot library window.

Jacob looked down and realized that snacks had appeared without his knowing. He wanted to try it all, but then wondered if coffee went with any of these items. Instead of thinking more, he trusted his body, followed his nose, and grabbed not one but two grilled cheeses, each crisped to the right buttery golden brown goo.

Somehow during his focus on the cheese, Mabel silently flanked him and now stood above and directly behind his chair.

"Good choice," she whispered with a spook.

Then with dragonfly grace Mabel walked around again and sat on the edge of a chair across from him. "Where to begin? That's always the question. The obvious place is the first house." She seemed to scrunch her eyes as if considering. "And do we do it by seniority, chronologically, all woven together? I mean there's no one way."

She didn't care for an answer, Jacob knew. "Well for many it starts with Otto."

During this monologue, Jacob finished one sandwich, took a bite from another, placed it on a napkin, pulled out his spiral notebook, prepared to take down clues, document whatever the River wanted him to see, to solve his mystery, or at least notate the jazz wisdom and wit that Mabel played that afternoon.

"You're a clever little one," she beamed at him upon seeing her spiral notebook gift being used. "Like the greatest bird songs from the highest trees and swankiest clubs, most of my tunes are only heard this exact way only this exact once." A wink.

*Wait, what does that mean?* There was no time to understand more, because Mabel was off.

∞

**"The Hamiltons were** as Double A All American A Family as you can find. Otto Hamilton is the first name that matters here. This Otto did not live in your house, but we start with him because he was the Father to the Father Chester who did live at your house, and the grandfather to those five kids, and the one with the name Hamilton to be passed along. Do you follow?"

Jacob understood so far. He had yet to document a single note, so he wrote one word, *Otto.* He stopped, not wanting to be the first year student scribbling everything like a real dolt.

Mabel now circled inside the conversation chairs like a shark stalking within a metal cage. Occasionally she sat for a brief landing, or leaned against an armrest. It was all a swirl of billowy green sleeves and calves. "Some folks believe it mattered how long a name was. Do you follow? Like a chain unbroken as far as possible until the kinks appear. That's when people start whispering, and it all gets a bit screwy. But those perfect chains of respected names were once as valuable as gold, especially back when there wasn't as much gold could even buy. Except new names perhaps."

Mabel strode and stalked, sat, leaned, spun, and wove a physical yarn as she spoke. Even in the silences, Jacob *knew* from somewhere most deep that this particular show needed an audience, and that was the role he was born to play. For now.

"Otto Hamilton claims to be from an unbroken line of five Ottos traced directly back to Europe and one of the original such pioneers to cross the Atlantic and then Blue Ridge. In other words, an old son of Willouby — back to the see-saw of a cabin in the woods. The Hamiltons were part of all the important things here. But see, that's tricky, because then you need an explanation for the two wars. Did your folks risk everything and fight for patriotic revolution in 1776? *Did they really?* And far stickier still, *Who did your folks pick when the country twisted in two?*"

Mabel landed on the edge of the yellow chair across from him and stared into his eyes. "In the earliest days, some traced roots back to the true Virginny — you know, before the West broke off. Do you know about all that nonsense? You probably should considering Willouby is so close to the border. But West Virginia used to be part of all Virginia until that civil war. But there's no time for that now." She winked.

"Otto claimed that his father's father's father fought gallantly with Washington, and even rode to Boston when the tea got pitched. Quite conveniently Otto whispered that his own father died of some illness mid-Civil War and took no sides. Otto Hamilton himself, of the great Willouby line, was born, smack dab in the middle of that American conflict, and so he had no need to take sides, because he was simply one of the first Real American babies, born of out the love and heartbreak of that bloody botched sawing in half."

"Fascinating," Jacob said honestly before almost writing—*Born a Real American.*

"Don't worry, I won't linger too long, but this is fun. At least for me." She flew up and back around, preferring to talk while standing. "Some said, and I'm no gossip, but some said that all that stuff about Otto Hamilton's family being back before the American Revolution was hogwash, pure honey spittle." She smiled deliciously, "They suggested that like many others of his day, it's a wonderful fiction."

Mabel looked at the stack of grilled cheese on the table, "Instead, another origin line was suggested for dear Otto. They said that his father was a man with very bad luck. A gentleman with an extremely long last name, with letters in an order that struck American ears all wrong. This mysterious father of Otto somehow crossed the Atlantic in search of a new life during Lincoln's election, arrived in the United States without any idea there was a war, landed in Willouby, had or found a son that he named Otto, and then, the gossipers believe, this mystery man picked the new last name Hamilton because he thought it was that of a respected American President."

A cart sound rattled from somewhere deep beyond the hallway, and Jacob wondered what Winston did all day.

"Yet another set of gossips claims that it was Otto himself who somehow wandered here from overseas and made up the last name." Mabel tilted a head as if she doubted this. "But I prefer to think at this very moment that there's a middle ground."

*How curious*, Jacob thought.

"I told you all of that mostly to explain why Otto Hamilton named his son Chester. Because the year that Chester was born, the President of the United States was Chester Arthur—he's a CA. Otto wanted or needed an American son, so he named him after the President. Of course, Chester ended up an only child, and so the line of Ottos ended there but the Hamiltons rose up. If it matters, so it goes."

"Otto Hamilton, last of his first name, became the biggest banker in Willouby. His origins forgotten by most, he grew into a fixture. That allowed him to build the big house down there upon which the street was eventually named. The original Hamilton House. Not yours, little one, but the Notting House on Ham Hill. Otto the banker, living in that perfectly columned white house on the hill with a baby boy named after the very President of the United States. All nice and tidy, don't you see?"

Mabel took a short drag from her golden extender and turned her head to puff away to a corner of the towering library.

*Is smoke good for these old books?*

"Once his own life was all fixed up, Otto used his surplus to give his All American son the head start he deserved. Chester was not yet a full man when Otto had your house built—the new but slightly smaller Hamilton House, the Rock House on the hill further down the avenue. Chester moved in probably not much more than 18 years old, married Elizabeth a few years after, and thus began the story of your Home."

"Chester went straight into the WB—Willouby Bank—just as Otto wanted. Together they grew into big names that mattered. Otto was head hobo at the Triangle Temple Club, those of the pointy pyramid hats. The TT Club dissolved or went underground by the time Chester came of fuller age. But building upon his old man, Chester became a memorable M&M. I don't recall the technical term, Master Mason, perhaps? That crew still has a spooky building downtown. You'll notice it one day, or maybe not. It doesn't matter right this very now."

*A Pause.*

*What to write.* Jacob's pen froze in his hand and he wasn't sure what mattered and what did not in that brief family history. He wrote, *MM.*

During the silence, Jacob saw a curious object placed for Mabel atop a library end table. A 16oz can of MGD beer, with a matching frosty mug fit for a queen's feast. The goblet had an MGD logo on it—must have been a set.

Reading his mind, or following his eyes, Mabel crowed, "They're a set. They call this a tall boy. A friend gave it to me as a Christmas gift, knowing it was a favorite from a past life. After all, those letters are filled with meaning. And who doesn't love a golden liquid and a chilled vessel from which to enjoy it."

*Is this the River giving a clue or is Mabel losing her mind?* Jacob decided to question nothing and float on, until he thought, *What if it's both?*

∞

**Mabel rose as** a string of thoughts came to her. Reinforcing an important point, she said, "You must have noticed I love letters. Lately I like letters much more than words. Getting older gives you freedom to come back down to the root of things, the building blocks that matter most."

She paced the center of her library, underneath the shimmering chandeliers, glancing at the books across tables, the green lamps, and the little neighborhood of knowledge with too many crannies for Jacob to yet appreciate. Especially not when all of his attention was absorbed in the mesmerizing performance of Astonishing Mabel who finally seemed in a real role.

As if acknowledging her newfound strength, "I'm powered by jewels," she gave spirit fingers with a few glittery items. "Of course I'm referring to the Joule, the measure of energy with the tricksy e at the end." *Ba Kaw! Ba Kaw! Ba Kaw!* "That's a scientific joke for you, little one. Remember, I once considered becoming a scientist."

Jacob heard the crack of the MGD can. "Ahhhhh," Mabel sighed in ecstasy, and Jacob could almost taste it himself. Out of nowhere, Mabel again appeared behind him, above his shoulder, "You must try a sip, it's so refreshing."

Before Jacob could say a word, Mabel handed it under his chin. He sipped and the fuzzy foam brought back a froth of too many memories that he couldn't concentrate his mind on a single one. "Delicious," Jacob said honestly.

"Atta boy." Mabel grabbed her beer back with wrist strength far above her age, took a full three second triple gulp, and jumped into a conversation without Jacob understanding where it picked up. "No, instead I must rely on smarter friends for science. Because the stage beckoned, perhaps because of where I was born." She winked.

Jacob remembered that she was born in Bel Air, California. But he didn't point that out, because he suspected that's what the wink was for. It wasn't.

"I'm from California, remember. Ever been there?" *Yes, Jacob thought but didn't want to brag.* "You know you're sitting in the OC right now?" Mabel narrowed her eyes to see if he was clever enough to understand. He wasn't. "The Original Colony. Ye Ole Virginny." She blinked twice. "Virginia. This was the first Official Colony or some such."

Her eyes narrowed again, as if this was important. "And do you know who was the first CO of the OC?"

*Another test!* Younger Jacob might have panicked, but the House of Mabel lulled him in a river flow, and he responded without thinking in the form of a question, "Was it George Washington? He's the first Commanding Officer that comes to mind."

Mabel gifted him a dazzling full sunshine smile that nearly reached her ears, "A clever little creature we have here, one who can count and knows his letters."

Jacob melted like a chocolate chip on the equator, and he knew it was worth it to feel the joy beaming from Mabel. "Exactly, little one, Exactly. He's quite a foundation for the US. It's to him we owe the special M for Mister. That's what we call our leader, the rotating national head. P for President is M for Mister—that's uniquely American, don't you think? I'm partial to the letter M, after all, it's Me!"

*M for Mabel?* Jacob tried to keep up

As if immediately testing him again, she threw another one back. "Now don't confuse the CO with the AP. Completely different angles and levels of the same spirit, do you understand?"

*Dammit.What?* She must have known he was clueless, he saw her eyes drift, but the River gave him courage at the final moment, "Oh you mean when Washington the Commanding Officer transformed into the AP for American President?"

*Jacob nails the landing!*

Mabel's eyes opened extra wide, "What on earth are you talking about? No dear, the gold medal AP is American Pie. But you still get the bronze. American Pie is the most powerful AP of all, at least the recipe is. Delicious. The song also works. And if you combine the bite, sound, and AP souls, well, that's a triple of utter unknowns."

Jacob did not know what to say, it never mattered.

"Not quite the right bounce," Mabel said to some invisible stranger in the corner, "I'll work on it." She shook her head like a woman familiar with all this. "Virginia is not actually an S for State. It's a C for Commonwealth. And don't let anyone who traces their line back, like the Hamiltons, hear you say otherwise."

She lit a cigarette attached to a totally different adapter, this one a silvery green dragon with the white slim puffing out its lizard mouth. Mabel released smoke between vinegar lips without missing a syllable, "But it's really the OD. You are sitting in the OD right now. Know what I mean?" She winked. Jacob smiled and hoped it meant he knew what she meant. "But No, not a scientist. I'm still looking for my third master skill. Have you heard this term—triple threat?"

Mabel pointed her dragon cigarette at him in explanation, "It's when you become a master of 3 totally different abilities." She held up three fingers to hammer the point home to the fool of a Maymerry. "Together those three powers make you something far bigger." Jacob immediately thought of a cartoon from his past—with her powers combined, Mabel is Captain Planet. Or Mother Earth. Or Mother Goose. *Get a grip, Jacob.*

"My new goal is to become a triple threat. But I haven't quite settled on the third yet—still trying a few things out. And when I become a triple threat, does that mean I'm finally three dimensional?" She beamed a cheshire grin but didn't wait for a response. "Once I'm 3D does that mean I can reach out and grab ya? Abra Kadabra!"

"Rah!" Mabel snatched a fake claw at him with her non-MGD hand, and in a flash Jacob saw her as a wicked witch or the spy movie villain. Until she cackled, *BaaaKaKaKaw Baaakaw,* and softened into a feisty greatest grandmother, "Just kidding little one, I like some of these newfangled terms for a bite. Until they bore me again."

∞

**"Eat, eat, eat."** Mabel looked down and saw Jacob's second sandwich with only one nibble mark. "At least try some of the apples, a little sweet for your salty."

Jacob snapped an apple wedge in half—delicious honeycrisp—and was grateful they weren't soft at all. He finished as Mabel drained her MGD, clanged the glass down on the coffee table, and looked again at the unknown text inside the red tome on a nearby pile.

Jacob wondered for a moment if the pages were empty, it was all a show, and the red book was a novelty. Mabel asked him, "Haven't read this one, right? Did I already ask you that? It's a J for Another Day! A Hook for a Different Book! The Crook of a Darker Brook!"

Mabel judged her previous nonsensical rhymes, "Eh, not quite there. Still working on it."

Jacob understood none of that whatsoever. Completely lost. But he noticed his open notebook on his lap and wrote—*J for AD*.

"Where was I? Chester and Elizabeth, newlyweds, in your brand new house. You with me?"

Jacob took a sip of coffee and nodded.

"Elizabeth was the perfect match for Chester, because she came from McKinley stock. Yes, that McKinley!"

Jacob narrowed his eyes and felt again like a nobody in this town of which he knew nothing about anything. He guessed with the help of the river, "A famous local family? Ummm, the old President McKinley?"

"*Ding Ding Ding*, Winston what do we have for him?" Mabel called out the library door to no one before looking back at Jacob, "The cat may be back with something for you, though it's impossible to say when. The important thing is that before he was President, young McKinley spent time here, or so some say, and either started a line or a relative started a line, or some such thing. But the name McKinley stayed in town, and that's who Chester Hamilton married, Elizabeth McKinley. What a coup for Chester! And for Otto! A coup! Not one, but two APs!"

"No doubt!" Jacob said with idiotic vigor.

"One key for you about Elizabeth Hamilton is that she was a Mother. And by that I mean that's what she was called by most, Mother Hamilton. Or in her later years, in the 60s and 70s when words loosened up a bit, she was just Mama."

Jacob realized he hadn't written anything in a few monologues, so he scribbled to keep up appearances—*Mama*.

"Which is all curious, because by that point people had forgotten that it took them a long bit to conceive their first of five kids. She was what they called a late nester or some such thing. But once they started hatching she had plenty to do. When all the little babies began growing, Mother was a twirling ball of everything those open mouths needed. After all, her youngest was a WW and her oldest an FDR!"

Jacob caught almost none of that but wrote down, *WW*.

Mabel talked nonstop from the library window, looking at the light across the blue sky, "Mama lived life for those babies. It's an ordeal sometimes, as she learned, like we all must, that we cannot control our darlings. But she discovered quickly that love needs a thorn to bloom brightest." She winked.

He almost wrote bizarre gems she spun that might have been genius or gibberish. "Mama always said, when you're lost, close your eyes, and make your own kind of music. The sound will lead you home." But that seemed irrelevant to his detective mission so he decided to remember them in his head without committing them to paper.

Instead, Jacob nodded gravely and said, "Amen." He looked down at his notes in dismay:

*Otto*

*MM*

*J for AD*

*Mama*

*WW*

Yikes. Detective Maymerry was off the rails. He ripped the page away, considered it an admirable first draft, and crumpled it in his pocket to trash later.

Mabel had never stopped talking.

"How to explain these kids? Would knowing their letters help? I'm a CC, remember, Cal Coolidge. Oscar Hamilton, the oldest, is a double, like me,

WW. No wonder he was Mr. Wonderful Willouby with letters like that. Oldest daughter Sara was a WH. Susana was a CC, also like me. Sandra was an HH. And Christopher, dear boy, was the mixed up triple, FDR."

Jacob tried to calculate that all out, and feeling river superpowers, he rattled off answers in his head in perfect order. Woodrow Wilson. Warren Harding. Calvin Coolidge. Herbert Hoover. Franklin Delano Roosevelt. *What a clever little one you are, Jacob.* He complimented himself.

"And you, little one?" Mabel read his mind.

Jacob was confused. *What about me?*

Mabel answered her own question. "You're another double, how curious. How curious indeed." Jacob realized he was an RR and wondered what on earth that meant to her. Something about doubles. The River sent him ideas or song lyrics or rambling lines, *Two for One Special. Is this a twist about twins?*

But if Mabel had more meaning, she didn't say anything to Jacob. Instead she returned to old Willouby, dove into the details of the Hamilton children, and Jacob tried to absorb all he could as a little one.

∞

**"Oscar was the** tallest, strongest hairline, oldest child, and most well-known in town for your purposes. World War Two hero." She held up 2 fingers to ensure he understood. "Back from the Battle, Oscar followed Chester straight into another B, this one for Banking. But he always needed dragons to slay, Oscar did, Mr. Popular of Mr. Populars. You know the type?"

She sighed and sat down for a short bit. "That's the problem, however, for a man like that, coming back from overseas, ready to keep saving the world. He had the bank, but his father and grandfather already covered that ground. So perhaps that's why he became a magician."

*Oh, that's interesting.*

"Don't get me wrong. He didn't quit the bank. He was just the type to do both. Maybe as an elaborate joke with his father. I think to appease his old man he called it something else, not Magician, but definitely an M." She seemed to discuss with herself. "No, not that one! Maybe it was Mentalist. Words are so elusive."

Jacob threw out an answer with hidden river courage, "Maestro?"

*Ba Kaw! Ba Ka! Hehehe.* "Sound! Good guess little one, but obviously no. I suppose it was the missing 4th M. You'll think of it eventually."

Mabel leaned forward in the leather library chair, set down the salamander cigarette extender, and pulled out a blue wand upon which she placed a lit cigarette. Her third of the coffee lunch thus far. She puffed a long drag between bony fingers, held it as if it were a July sparkler, and continued, "It was the magic that ultimately killed him early. Oscar had a friend from Bethesda named Phillip who got him into it. I told him it was a mistake, I said 'Oscar, Bethesda! Can anything good come from there?' And he said, 'you wouldn't believe it if I told.'"

"Near the end, Oscar's ideas were always quite big, fantastical, head in the clouds, that sort of thing. But to tidy him up, he died shortly before JFK. Such a missed opportunity that he didn't experience the Kennedy years. It was a train crash on the way to a magic event of some kind. Isn't that such a wonderful laugh—killed by magic!"

Mabel then shook her head as if it was all such a shame. "A lot of folks died while traveling this way and that way back in those days." Jacob imagined the local tragedy shocking this black-and-white TV American town at the end of the Eisenhower years. What a sad story, another American war hero killed by a faulty train switch, loose bolt, or some such thing. Probably didn't even have seatbelts back then.

"Father Chester Hamilton never recovered the loss of his Oscar. In a strange coincidence, Chester dropped dead of a heart attack on the very day Oswald ran up the School Book Depository and ended the Kennedy years. Some said that Chester simply did not have the energy for a new administration and decided to call it quits. So it goes."

Her back to him, looking out the window, Mabel checked the time, "Look at how fast the sun is moving, I need to pick up the pace."

She turned around in a smile, her teeth a sparkling half moon under the blonde wig. In both hands, seemingly pulled from her billowy green sleeves, were two magician's rings.

*Was that entire magician story just a ruse to use these props?*

"Since we are at the magic part of the story, and I found these rings earlier, I pulled them out to see if I still had it." She waved the metal circles in gentle swirls, like bubbles floating in the air, her arms moving with practiced grace. Jacob realized that she might have spent all morning, waiting for his visit, circling the rings, but pretending to not care in that charming old lady way.

With the experience of a Vegas professional, like chemicals combining, the two rings were joined together, and she showed that they were now locked as one. *Ring Ring Ring.* She made clinking sounds to indicate a fusion of the metal.

*It's the simple tricks in life that matter*, he thought idiotically from nowhere as she pulled the two rings apart, pretending they were never connected.

"Ta Da!" She said with a first day of summer smile that Jacob tried to copy. She tossed the rings on an empty chair. "Anyway, enough for me. You want to know more about the Hamiltons. The sisters. It's unfair to lump them all together, such a shortcut, but it's inevitable. And Mother did decide to name them all S."

∞

**Mabel puffed her** cigarette from the blue wand. "As you know, before telephones, television, and compact discs, letters were much more important. The most important things in the world, in fact." It took Jacob a moment to realize, yet again, she was being literal. Mabel did not mean notes—the old paper letters mailed from one person to another like cherished heirlooms of ancient wisdom shared through the generations. Instead she meant one of the actual 26 letters of the alphabet. In this case S.

Mabel knew letters. "Sewn onto all sorts of things, letters were passed down, see. It felt good to do it, was easy to remember, and identify. Back then things were less disposable. Perhaps that's why they named all the girls with an S. They shared the same little baby outfits sewn in Ss, toddler bonnets, and whatnots."

"Still, I doubt people called them by their given American names of S, Sara, Susana, and Sandra. Instead they were identified by their professions — caregiver, rebel, confectionary. Or by their hair color — blonde, red, and black. Definitely not by their total number of husbands — Zero. If they were the flag Susana would obviously be red, the hair. Sara the white. Sandra the blue. Of course, I already made most of it plain when I explained to you that their letters were WH, CC, and HH."

Jacob looked down at his notebook, and fought the urge to write down those letters, knowing full well he needed to start thinking a little clearer. Instead of writing a word, Jacob heard himself saying "Mmmm," out loud to the library before even knowing he had grabbed another grilled cheese.

Mabel waved her blue cigarette extender at him, and Jacob wondered now if it was incense and he was being cleansed of something. "Let's do the sisters by shortest lifespan, shall we?"

Jacob nodded "Sure thing," hoping that wasn't a morbid.

"Susana, Daughter Two, was a bombshell. Scratch that, she was a bomb without a shell. And she very much knew it. Which is my fancy way of saying she was a whole lot of fun. She had the energy for a life on stage, but the heart of a warrior. So Susana spent most time in the dusty garage all around the country with those fancy cars. Which, as you might imagine, was not exactly expected of a Hamilton daughter. I can still see her red hair blowing down the avenue in some fast thing or other. In my memory there were more vehicles without roofs in those days, so you could identify hair color much easier. It's those conveniences that I miss most."

Mabel gave a lippy smile to some bookshelf. "I bet you know how things ended for Susana? Most cars didn't have seatbelts back then. And if they did, Susana of the House Hamilton was not about to drive fast and then strap in. So she became another transportation casualty. Such a shame. But that wasn't until the end of LBJ. I only know that because I remember the funeral. It was the 4th of July during the summer of love. She was the third stone up there at the family plot on the mountain. So goes it."

It was only then that Jacob noticed Winston standing like a suit of armor at the entrance. He was a proper Versailles servant, or perhaps an electronic vacuum back in its charging station.

Mabel took a long drag from her blue wand and then waved it at him again in a completely different tone. "I should say, Mama Hamilton passed away not long after her Susana. I believe she made it to the first few months of Nixon, but well before the watergates opened. Went out in one of the rooms of your home, though I couldn't say which. The funeral was in the room with the coffin door that opened onto your porch. She's not in the mountaintop plot, is she? I don't recall why, but it'll come to me. That's a big missing piece of some story, no doubt."

Detective Maymerry took the hint, and realized that with the blank notebook page, he had a fresh start. He wrote anew with more sophistication—

**Most Likely**

    *I. Mother Elizabeth—missing body*

He switched to Roman numerals, because they looked like columns which seemed sturdier to Jacob's increasingly swirly mind.

*But was it a mistake?* Because another part of Jacob thought deep—*Mabel prefers the Greeks to the Romans. Greeks have curves, more likely letters and poets. Romans are lines, quite possibly numbers and engineers. And Romans use letters for numbers, confusing the whole order.*

**Jacob laughed at** his mental nonsense and straightened his Detective cap. He assumed he'd add more names to this list, but perhaps he'd already solved it. Just perhaps, Mother Elizabeth was the skull. Was Jacob clever enough to have already reached an answer? Perhaps, perhaps, perhaps. But he knew that knowledge alone was not enough. Because the River would provide confirmation. He only need drift on and see how it all ended.

The Queen Bee wove between the library furniture as a stage insect giving a matinee showstopper.

"Oldest Daughter, middle lifespan, Sara was the rock of the daughters and in some ways perhaps the whole family in those cold years. Not always cold, I mean in the Cold War years. Sara was a social center, perhaps like her mother. She had an angelic voice, but you could only hear it at the church. Sara Hamilton ran the Methodists in Willouby her entire life. Every baptism, birth, death, christening, and who-tin-alley in ye olde Willouby included Miss Sara."

"Her voice, what an astonishing singing vessel. I'd walk down Nottingham Avenue, past the Hamilton House, to the back of that brick church, and sit in those uncomfortable pews just to hear it. Which I now suspect was the real reason she never allowed the voice outside church walls—didn't want to dilute her siren call to lost souls."

Aunt Mabel tilted a head as if just remembering something fascinating. "That reminds me of my time in the tent churches. Or were they schools? Mostly I remember Mark. He was my next friend, maybe we were in the 5th level at the time. But Mark memorized that whole book that he was named after. Do you know what I mean?" She looked at him with genuine curiosity.

"The Bible?" Jacob assumed but knew.

She nodded quickly as if just making sure. "Yep. Nice young fella. He loved showing off his memory. For this very moment I only recall one bit. 13th Chapter. Since today is Friday."

Mabel cleared a throat in serious contemplation, *"You do not know when the master of the house will come. In the evening, or at midnight, or when the rooster crows, or in the morning—lest he comes suddenly and find you asleep. And what I say to you, I say to all. Stay Awake!"*

She growled this last bit and Jacob shivered before she bawked herself silly. *BaaaKaww! Bawawk BaaKaw!*

"Don't worry little one," Mabel put a  finger to her lips under a mischievous smile, as if remembering a scandalous story. "They kicked me out of that church tent shortly thereafter. But we artists admire fascinating stories of every stripe, now don't we?"

∞

**Light shifted in** the library, and only then did Jacob realize he was eating his 4th grilled cheese as he forgot Mabel was still talking. "Anyway, Oldest Daughter Sara the songbird sang and never took a husband. Too busy with the congregation for such frivolity, some say, but I'm no gossip. Instead she integrated herself into every respectable family in town, indispensable in one way or another. Which is all the more surprising that the only person I ever knew her to fall out with for a time was her baby sister, quiet bitty Sandra."

"Sandra was the third of three daughters." Mabel held up three fingers. "She was the squeakiest of the trio, a mouse. So it was odd that she became a businesswoman, at least temporarily. That's because she was a tremendous baker, so precise and pretty. Confectionaries, I believe they are called. Or is it Convection Fairies? I remember the sign on the little shop downtown, all corners. An octagon. Sandy's Succulent Sweets, or some such silliness. But it was the 70s, you understand."

"Of course," Jacob said without understanding anything.

"Speaking of Sara's church voice, did I mention that I tried my hand at music too? I love letters, and aren't notes the very same thing as letters—a different way to understand a meaning. I was quite adequate with music notes for a spell, my throat being such a tremendous instrument, after all."

Mabel squinted as if wanting to get it exactly right. "Early 50s or was it 60s—during the Es or Bs, that I remember." She made eye contact, realized she needed to clarify, and added, "Beatles or Elvis. Anyway, I asked my friend, Maybelline, if she wanted to form a duo, considering she was lights out on the drums. She said yes, and that's how our group formed. My voice and Maybelline's banging ability, what a match! The only thing stopping us from success was the name."

She ashed out one cigarette and took another, her 4th or 5th of the party, Jacob was past counting. She now appeared a grizzled rocker re-living hard glory days in an open access documentary. A new ember blazed between her smiling face, behind bug glasses, looking every bit a dazzling 75 year old professional who still had it deep down.

"In the circus I had a system where Number 1 was good. And then if it was really good you added another 1, so it was  Number 11. Do you understand? Like tallys." She held up one finger and made dashes in the air. "So that's why Maybe and I called ourselves the Elevens. From some angles we looked like tiny toothpicks, so it also worked that way, you get it, right?"

"Absolutely."

"Being exceptional, I awarded myself many Elevens, so it became my lucky number. I understood it to mean first among champions or first among equals. And Eleven is simply equals turned side by side. A number of towering importance. But turns out most people's minds are so narrow they only see an eleven. So we decided to up the ante and call ourselves the Twenty Twos. We shortened that to the TTs. Then we tried The Deuces. But nothing worked."

A three second drag, and a tilt of the head from Mabel as she re-lived the challenging name situation. Jacob better understood her simmering anger at the need for names at all. Mabel spoke directly to Jacob, "Then I realized we must keep climbing up. Become 3D." She held up three fingers. "Form a tripod, so we needed a third. It's like rock-paper-scissors, some games require 3 people to play properly. Do you understand?"

Jacob narrowed his eyes in slight confusion but let it go without comment. "Fascinating."

"Like braiding, it doesn't really work with only two. So we began looking for another musician. I was open to anything, ukelele, trombone, tambourine. Buuuuut," Aunt Mabel was getting to her punchline, "Before we could find our third, Maybelline up and died on me! So goes it." *Ba Kaw!* She cackled a hen's laugh, smiled beautiful teeth to a large cookbook on a nook pile, took a long drag on her cigarette, and dared the ash to grow as much as possible before moving it over to a green glass tray to watch it fall with a blue wand swish.

"Anyway," Mabel built to an even mainer point of the entire digression. "What matters for your purposes is that I knew that Musician was not my third master skill, not once I heard Sara Hamilton sing. Because I could never match her cloudbird voice."

She smiled seductively and spun her back to him in a sultry walk to the umbrella stand, "But my stage voice. Now that is something else altogether. Let me show you."

∞

**Jacob contemplated her** music career, but he lost his train of thought when Mabel yelled while opening up a yellow prop umbrella. "Kitty kitty, here Winston!"

Jacob asked a question before even realizing it, "Are you sure you have a cat?" *Does that seem rude?* He fake laughed and smiled as large as possible to indicate a joke that was also not a joke.

Ba Kaw! She did him the courtesy of a pity bawk. "Little one, I'm sure of nothing. I can A sure you that I did once have a cat named Winston, but where he is this exact moment, neither of us know." Another wink, and before Jacob could process Winston walked in.

"Good lord, finally!" Mabel roared from the umbrella stand underneath the yellow.

She closed the umbrella and stepped into the sun-drenched room unprotected. Her skin seems translucent white. *Does your skin get thinner as you age?* "For this final act, I was going to perform an original, but I need to save my energy, so I'll do an oldie but a goodie."

She circled and spoke like a master tuning an instrument. "This was written for a great friend of mine, William." She raised her MGD glass and toasted the room, "After all, it's to him we owe this very sip." She took one more chug, like a priest with a communion mug.

Setting her glass down, Mabel rose to the center of the room, books circling all around her in anticipation. Winston approached holding something of regal mystique. For a moment Jacob thought it was a crown to be placed upon her head. But instead, Winston arrived behind her and tightened a large, ornate Elizabethean collar around Mabel's neck. She looked perhaps a miniature Queen of Green Diamonds, until in a flash she strode upon the stage and rose higher somehow.

"To William from Mr. S Shakes his Spears. Or so some say." Jacob noticed she looked tired. Or maybe it was all an act. She winked, dipped into a one-knee crouch, pretended to hold a skull on an open palm while pondering, and then in a few simple lines became once more a knight of the round theater.

"And in this state she gallops night by night" *Mabel waltzed across the floor as if on horseback, her billowy sleeves and calves offering a majestic flow in the wind.*

"Through lovers' brains, and then they dream of love;" *She rolled upon the floor as if fluttering in a breeze.*

"O'er courtiers' knees, that dream on court'sies straight," *A giggle from a schoolgirl in deep contemplation.*

"O'er lawyers' fingers, who straight dream on fees," *She was upon him somehow, her fingertips brushing the slightest across his own.* How did she manage that?

"O'er ladies' lips, who straight on kisses dream." *Mabel fell upon the carpet in a prowl.*

She might have continued, but at that very moment, a corner of the library shook in an Independence Day Explosion:

*Crinkle!*
*Clanks! Kliks! Cackles! Krinkles! More Clanks!*
*Crick! Kliks!*
*Cackle*

Jacob jolted up from the cushy yellow chair with a fight or flight sting. He noticed Mabel had not moved an inch, unfazed entirely, paused with yoga precision in mid-prowl as a jaguar atop green fibers in a reading nook. *Stunning poise,* he thought, *she breaks at nothing. I wish I could have seen her real performances, probably a community theater savant. Wasn't Einstein a hidden genius, postman, man of letters, with two tricksy Es.*

*Focus, Jacob, Focus!*

"Winston, Christmas Almighty! Your timing, as usual, is impeccably it-self!"

The butler had dropped cutlery of sizes and shapes that Jacob could not see from his angle. He imagined rolling silver, platters, spinning spoons, and forks of various orientations all about the hardwood. Enough for a baker's dozen feast.

Mabel rose from her stalking, "I'll take the hint. I need a break. And I suspect little one does too. He doesn't understand a wink of this. Do you?"

Jacob froze. A pickle. *Does he disagree with the agitated Queen Bee after her performance was spoiled? Or does he agree with her that he's a fool who understands nothing?*

"As usual, you're exactly right, ma'am."

"That's a good dear." She took off the Shakespearean collar. "Did you know that one?"

Of course not. "It sounds familiar, but I can't quite remember," immediately embarrassed.

"Come now. *Romeo & Juliet.* What else could it be?" She continued after a cigarette crackle cough. "I'm just kidding, little one. None of us control what we remember. I had to recall that section in 9th grade. One of my earliest performances. I nailed it. And all these years later, that's one Bard song that's stuck. It's funny what we do and don't remember." She bawked then coughed into a swaddle pulled from a deep billowy green sleeve.

∞

**The Renaissance collar** off, and another cigarette in hand, Mabel returned to a seductress of jade mystery. She glanced up at a gold chandelier of chiseled complexity, "These chandeliers are something else, aren't they? Once during a leaner administration, I remember Winston having such a battle with them. But like a french candlestick rallying the cleaning supplies, I often thought I almost heard him once echo down the halls, *'My Gentlebeasts if our As for Bs and Cs are to last for 1000 years, let them remember, This was their brightest hour!'*"

Mabel snapped her fingers. "And Poof! Like that, these chandelier lights shone a little cleaner and clearer. That's one reason I keep him around."

Mabel gave a lippy smile. "At least that's how I typically remember it.

Anyway, I haven't thought of these Hamiltons in quite awhile—thanks for the reason to think again." She stared at nothing before asking, "Five is a difficult number of children, don't you think? Maybe all odd numbers are. It's like when 5 people play a game and there are two teams. One person must play both sides or the teams are uneven. Do you understand? I can't make it any simpler than that."

*Uhhhh*, Jacob sank into the river, until he realized Mabel had never stopped talking.

"And I haven't even mentioned Christopher yet. The 5th Child. We can do him tomorrow along with the McDonalds — the pair of robins who nested there a few springs. As you might have noticed, it's getting late. We'll complete the circle tomorrow night. Sometime before Sunset." She looked at him with pity. "I suspect you don't know when exactly, but you should. 1776 will do just fine for a time."

*1776? Ma'am, I'm way too late already.*

Noticing his confusion, she explained further, "I mean I don't expect perfection, not from the littlest ones like you. Anytime between 1776 and 1787 is completely acceptable." She narrowed eyes on him. "You don't understand this, do you? Are you yet to learn other kinds of time?" Mabel rarely waited for an answer, "Let's pick a respectable dinner hour. Six will do, my tiny friend." She flashed three fingers, two times, then circled her hand into an O.

Jacob tried to visualize the hand signals of 6:00. *Six tomorrow night, it's a date!*

∞

**Mabel seemed ready** for an early bedtime, holding Jacob's arm only as far as the library door. Turning a hidden corner she then remembered, "Oh dear, almost forgot your gift." She pulled a notecard out of a pocket sleeve. "The recipe! It's for the cookies. You liked them so much, I thought you might want to learn how to make them yourself."

Looking now a hunched tortoise, she smiled through exhaustion, "You know the saying." Mabel rolled her wrist as if Jacob finished the saying in his head. He didn't. "The saying, you can teach a boy to fish, but. But. But you can buy him a pole, give him the bait, cast it out for him, catch something, reel it in, but, you know," she groped for an answer that satisfied her, "eventually he has to call himself a fisherman."

Winston arrived to walk him out.

Not another word was spoken until Jacob mumbled, "Thanks sir, see you tomorrow" while standing outside the front turtle gongs. Winston twirled a wrist and gave a small bow in silent acknowledgment before closing the door in a clear goodbye.

The crunchy snow sounds of his sneakers stalking home atop expensive pea gravel kept Jacob company as he processed his visit. A candy smile of silly mystery plastered his face under the sycamores.

— Chapter 16 —

**Jacob's yellow jacket** fluttered the slightest behind him, as he considered the lessons from the naughty coffee party in the Library of Mabel. All he could think about was the last thing he saw—the silent butler, Winston. Wasn't the butler the hidden mastermind, somehow, in so many of these movies? In his head flashed a smiling butler from a Halloween musical about an alien house, with a man builder, or is it man eater?

*Focus, Jacob, Focus!*

What was Mabel's fascination with letters? Jacob suspected a Cal Coolidge woman simply did not care enough to learn any more long names—letters were enough when you see the same thing for the 10th time. He knew he had two missions—understanding the skull and understanding the mysterious Madam Mabel. The skull quest might prove easier than untangling the magic of his friend.

He passed the protective buffer of Mabel's private lane, and at that exact moment Jacob received a call from Colorado.

"Oh Gladys." Instead of dread, Jacob smiled at the sound, and pretended that he had Mabel's soul. She'd be happy to chat with anyone, regardless of the reason or season.

He decided to walk and talk. *Why not?* Instead of going straight home he took a right and did a small loop around one half of Nottingham Ave. Perhaps he'd have a more enjoyable conversation under the breeze. The entire Board was on the other end, and Jacob again explained that the Europeans were not bound by American law. More than once, a member would blurt out in frustration, "Does the Constitution mean nothing anymore!"

The call was brief, and Jacob sensed that his employers were boring of their international feuding. The Kick-Ball-Change wars might finally end. Gladys, for one, seemed more interested in re-igniting the internal ABC Wars against those American dancers who did not understand the traditions at the core of their artistic medium.

He only then realized the coincidence—*I love letters as much as Mabel does. Sometimes the River is so obvious and I only see it until later.* Jacob smiled to the porch birds.

∞

**The front door** jammed, Jacob twisted helplessly as he watched a man walk down the sidewalk. The ambling senior, he already knew, was the next door neighbor, a Philosophy Brother. He'd seen only one of the men since moving in, the same local three times now.

A thought occurred to him—perhaps the other brother was not able to leave. *Is one man caring for another?* Maybe the second was confined to a bed and could only ever get as far as the porch. Maybe that's why one man seemed far grumpier, with a more pessimistic approach to life and its mysterious questions.

Jacob psychoanalyzed his neighbor with colorful Mabel nonsense. The invalid might be a furry green grouch because his life was more vulnerable. *But aid always comes to those who ask*, Jacob remembered from some movie.

Who would Jacob call for help at that very moment? *I can always text the eccentric 98 year old woman that I met two days ago.* He smiled without knowing why.

The loop was stopped by a *Ding Ding* call from VA, though technically in Ohio, or perhaps Pennsylvania, or even New York, depending. Liam didn't leave time for a breath. The tone was dire. "There is a development." The word Development was uttered with a capital D for Disappointment. Or Disaster. Or Don't blame the messenger.

"Remember how we put our name on a list as fosters for some dog for maybe way in the future?" Liam knew that was only partially true and confessed immediately, "Or maybe I put my name on a list. It was awhile ago."

"I'm sorry, what?" Jacob was lost as usual.

What followed was a less than five minute explanation of more than an hour of information. A planned strategy straight from law school of burying the other side in too many words and too little time. Flooding the zone. Jacob was impressed at Liam's ability to steer life, it's why he needn't ever doubt the restaurant would succeed.

Liam spoke even faster. He mentioned that the fence was supposed to be done beforehand, so the dog could run. "They have an army of people. Supposed to be done in one day. Maybe two. Guaranteed. And the dog was supposed to arrive in one month. But all hell's broken free."

Jacob had little time to process details, because Liam had to get off the phone. He apologized profusely, but it changed none of the facts on the ground.

That's how Jacob learned that a dog of unknown size, shape, and origin would be dropped off at the house at some unknown time the next day.

*Oh dear.*

Before hanging up Jacob almost said, "But I have to see Mabel tomorrow!" But he didn't, because of course he couldn't say that, because how could he possibly explain? He was on the River alone. But he somehow knew everyone eventually had to take a river journey with only their own little brain.

**The chef sleeping** in a hotel somewhere in the northeast, Jacob enjoyed himself a bag of BBQ chips, more apple slices, and chicken noodle soup—the final can—for the third night in a row. On cue, he heard voices rise from the next door trees, a neighborly nighttime conversation. Jacob smiled before biting into an apple, glad again that traditions develop fast in a place like Willouby.

At first Jacob couldn't quite make out the details of the disagreement. It was something about the deep sea. *Fishing perhaps?* Jacob guessed wrongly, because it was only one brother loudly saying, "See! See!" as if hoping his point landed. Not sea, as if a body of water.

Then he realized in some garbled way they were discussing a tricky E, for Ending. Jacob was now thinking about everything in the form of their first letter, Mabel's influence.

The invalid brother, Jacob assumed from nothing, was talking about the ending of some movie or book. A debate ensued about what makes the best ending.

One brother said he preferred those conclusions that were completely shocking but fitting. Those that are hidden in the wide open the whole time, and on second viewing make you exclaim, *Ahh, of course!*

The other man didn't disagree but wondered about those tales that hinted at all the possible endings throughout before revealing the real answer only at the last. He spoke in riddles, "Like a coin flipped in the air, heads, tails, heads, tails, and you're on the edge of your seat wondering which way it will finally land when it's done."

"What does that mean," the grumpier man felt the ambiguity was a cop out.

"Endings. They are tricky, aren't they?" *That cannot be a coincidence*, Jacob thought at the word tricky, and he wasn't sure which brother even said it. "Do you mean you like whatever ending is the least likely, or hardest to guess at first?"

"Maybe. But isn't that different for every person? What I consider the least likely might be completely obvious to you at the start."

"Of course you'd say that, refusing to take an actual position on anything. Sometimes I wonder how you ever get through life without making any real hard decisions."

Jacob listened and thought of a favorite ending from a Stephen King story and movie, about best friends reuniting after a prison break to start life anew in a beach paradise. He did not speak Spanish but he remembered the name of the place—*Zihuatanejo*—somewhere beyond the Texas border. It was a Z, the very last letter, which Mabel would have told him was quite important. He did not know if it was correct, but he said aloud as he heard the free men say it in the movie—*Two Watt A Nay You.*

That ending wasn't quite a surprise or a twist. But like two hands clasping with interlaced fingers, it felt like the perfect connection. Maybe Jacob preferred two stories told at once, that only make complete sense when fit perfectly together at the close.

∞

**He walked back** into the house and forgot about endings for a spell. Instead, Jacob considered this strange beginning that found him, he again remembered, getting a dog tomorrow, without a fence, with a skull in the basement, and without accomplishing much else of anything. On paper, he'd basically done nothing yet in Willouby.

*But paper is flimsy!* A new Jacob thought in his head. *Maybe he was working on accomplishments of stone. Or Brick! Or Steel! I can solve this Mystery*, he gave himself a short mental pep talk.

He considered the Hamilton family, from such a long, impressive national line. Jacob did not know much of the names in own family tree, coming from a middle place where such things mattered far less. All he did know was that his family was American, and had been for generations in all its branches, direct and collateral. That wasn't nothing. So goes it.

∞

**After dinner, for** the briefest moment, Detective Maymerry donned back his Holmes hat and drifted to the basement. He sat on the boulder to the center of the earth and considered his head list once more.

## Most Likely
### I. Hamiltons
       1. Chester*
       2. Elizabeth-i
       3. Oscar*-i
       4. S*—Sara
       5. S*—Susana
       6. S*—Sandra
       7. Christopher-w

### II. McDonalds
       8. Dad
       9. Mom
       10. Child

Feeling drowsy after even a few moments staring at the skull, Jacob decided to think in bed. There's something about the comforts of the bedroom. *Is it the brain or the heart of the house*, Jacob wondered? Until a second voice told him, *The bedroom is the bedroom of the house. Not everything is a symbol, you silly little fella.*

Sitting upright against the headboard, in comfy blue pajama pants and purple T, Jacob bopped his toes with his green notebook open on his lap. He forgot again completely that a dog was arriving the very next afternoon. He forgot because he was remembering so many other things.

Jacob thought of Mabel's letters and numbers gibberish, and then realized perhaps why he was drawn to her. She was a puzzle, and from his earliest days, he always liked puzzles and riddles and games and codes.

He remembered his own code, shown to no one, that he created out of numbers and letters when bored in the backseat of many car rides. He re-created it while laying in bed. It was quite simple, if you just piled different symbols on top of one another, an entirely new way to hide messages is created. Numbers become letters, letters become numbers.

A—1
B—2
C—3
D—4
E—5

He did not write it all out, but instead thought the rest in his head. Thirteen is M. But it's also AC. 1 and 3. But then if you don't know what letters or numbers mean, you might look at them as shapes. A 1 is a straight line. And the 13 is a shortcut to the B. After all, a Capital B is created by drawing a 1 and jamming it against a 3. And an E is the same thing but a backwards 3.

Young Jacob enjoyed these clues and puzzles and codes, because they were secret. And secret things were exclusive. And exclusivity was the rarest item of all, depending on one's Angle and Perspective.

Codes are gibberish unless you know the key. Messages make no sense, but the complexity transforms to simplicity once someone gives you that key. Jacob smiled to himself in bed as he thought about hidden messages from one person to another. That was a gift that he could give to a friend—a key to a code—to send messages only to those who he wanted to understand. The best gifts in life are always free. The E of Exclusivity.

Then a curious thought arose as he remembered his friend's weaving of letters and numbers—*Has Mabel been trying to send me hidden messages this whole time?*

Jacob decided to put his code over Mabel's random rules. Her 11 for exceptional is the same at AA, which Jacob knew meant All American when translated into words. And 22 was BB, for some acronym that Jacob hadn't yet decided.

In middle school Jacob once tried to make his code more complicated, triple layered, by adding colors to each combination. However, he couldn't figure out if colors were made of letters or something else. That stumped Adolescent Jacob, but now he wondered if he was capable of a bit more.

It was those thoughts that Jacob started to think as his eyes grew heavy. *Perhaps give your old brain a little more credit for the things it can do instead of worrying about all the things it can't!* Jacob imagined his friend Mabel boosting him.

Jacob thought more about his system of jamming the shape of numbers together to create a letter. *Take the 1 and the 3, spin them a cool 180 degree, and explode them together to create the tricksy E.*

He drifted deep into dreams that felt like marshmallow fun adventures in the sky. Perhaps inside a bubble bath. Or foam party.


*He dreamed he was elected AP! A blue ribbon American Pie! But No! The election was a different AP, American Pope. And it was only because he had the correct silver shoes. But when he looked down he saw only white slippers. Then someone asked him to pick his new Pope name and perhaps a number—if the first name was already taken. Jacob was very confused until he remembered what Mabel thought about names. Nonsense!*

# Saturday

# — Chapter 17 —

**A dark coffee** breeze and sunlight streamed past bay windows through green leafy plants reminding Jacob that it was a beautiful spring Saturday morning. He exhaled and felt alive. How marvelous life could be when one gave oneself the luxury of an exhale.

Unlike past mornings, Jacob did not wake up with a first instinct of dread at all the loose ends in his life. Instead, the rose charm of Mabel lingered on him, and he felt excitement more than fear at all the unknown adventures that might lay before him.

Inhale. Exhale. He didn't count, but breathing helped, he knew from somewhere.

He held a warm mug in his hand, pushed back fear about the animal that would be in his house later that day, and reminded himself that he had another meeting with Mabel that evening. He need only trust the River.

Sipping his morning American joe, Jacob decided to swivel in his blue office chair. His heart bubbled up into a Saturday morning sparkle, relaxed as the light hit the green tile backsplash of his office fireplace. *What a delight*, his good mood surprised even himself.

He spun and stared into the eyes of the Oscar Wilde print when that part of the room came into sight on rotation. In the sunny weekend glow, he didn't even think about that time he blanked the name of Wilde's *one book* in conversation with a smart colleague. He knew it had a color in the title and was about mirrors. But his mind got stuck on Snow White, knowing it was not the right color at all.

That memory did not arise that morning. No time for past embarrassments when the future was so bright.


Instead he thought of the ABC Wars, a feud between old and new dancers, traditional and progressive steppers, and other alliances too many to name. Like a retired soldier wondering if he'd be called up again, Jacob considered the foundation of the ABC Wars, that he now considered naming the War of the Letters.

∞

# War of the Letters

The ABC Wars were a dispute that would make no sense to those uninitiated in the internal workings of line dance creation. Outsiders would learn of it and scratch their heads at the absurdity, like a Hatfield & McCoy chain with generations of bodies strewn on the ground and those alive forgetting completely the first disagreement that ignited the whole thing. Or a civil war in a far-flung nation over the color of a flag or the slight variations in magic words needed to secure salvation.

The origin of the War of the Letters involves creation. A line dance choreographer thinks up steps that fit a song, tries to write those steps into words on paper, and shares it far and wide. A traditional line dance has a set number of movements. The electric slide, for example, has 18 steps, also called counts, repeated over and over until the music stops. More complicated dances have more counts, 32 is common, sometimes even 64 steps. Each a test of memory and agility.

At an unknown point in the past, one intrepid choreographer decided to up the ante. *Eureka! Why not weave two different dances together during a single song?* Perhaps one dance of 32 counts and then a second, say 16 counts, danced only during certain parts of the music. The longer part is called A, the shorter B. Then instead of dancing the same steps until the song ends, a weaving occurs. AAAB, AABB, or anything similar.

The idea is that these weavings better fit the sounds, a tighter glove on the hand or shoe on the foot. Eventually an even more daring choreographer decided to weave *three* dances together in a single song. A, B and then C. So not only would dancers need to remember the individual steps of each but the unique sequence. Perhaps AAABC, AAABBC, or any complicated combination of the designer's choosing.

Now when Cs were added, that's when purists like Gladys started drawing a line and grumbling to the heavens. The artists claimed that they were only expanding the artform, breaking boundaries, trying new things, stretching the human potential. Gladys explained that at some point they were no longer line dancing but simply trying to remember an impossibly long series of steps only to look like a high school pom pom group.

Jacob liked to think he was instrumental in bridging the gap to what he called in a 54 page Powerpoint presentation, "The Middle Way." It was a blend of competition categories, rules, and mostly utter nonsense, "You see when you break things up into little pieces, and balance out both sides, then it becomes quite easy to keep a moderate peace."

Skilled negotiation and persuasion was required to secure the cease-fire. Gladys's first offer of compromise was that all dances could be woven, so long as the phrase was in the same order. She said, for example, she thought it was perfectly fine to have a dance ABABAB, or if one dared, BABABA. But it was out of the question to do something like ABBA or BAAB.

A compromise in name only that fooled no one.

What Gladys didn't know but others on the Board did, was that if she simply let the boundary breakers have their fun, eventually those same frontier thinkers would forget, get nostalgic, and desire the old ways again. Life is a wheel, as wise folks often say.

Jacob remembered these battles with Eleanor and the two authors in his office that Saturday morning with a blissful smile of past victory. The cat didn't say a word, which he took as a sign of respect for his crafty generalship.

∞

**Jacob didn't need** to re-litigate the entire ABC drama in his head that morning, because Gladys's call from CO was on something else entirely. Instead she asked about an idea she dreamed up in an actual slumber the previous evening.

"It came to me in the middle of the deepest night. Lucky for me I remember sleep thoughts. Why are the Europeans allowed to recruit from the British dancers—notoriously some of the best in the world?"

Gladys thought she had a checkmate, "The British voted themselves non-European, isn't that right? I'm not up on the law like you. But I'm pretty sure that's right. And technically, we Americans used to be British. We're almost brothers and sisters. What I'm asking, legally speaking, aren't the British basically Americans and obligated to dance for us? Can we draft them? You know how when a star athlete moves to a new school district they have to play for the other team?"

Jacob dodged this bullet deftly, and had Gladys off the phone in less than five minutes.

Afterwards, holding a slice of peanut butter toast in one hand and more coffee in the other, he bounced down the spinal pine steps to consider the skull once more.

He stared at the bone without really looking. *What else can I learn from the actual old noggin?* Weirdly, now it all mattered much more than before. Before it was an unknown piece of material. He could have been told the name of the skull—Mama Hamilton—and it would have meant nothing. But now, knowing that same information would have meant something to him. Because thanks to Mabel's storytelling, Mother Elizabeth Hamilton was almost a real person to Jacob. *How strange riding this river can be.*

He didn't stay in the basement long, because a Ding Ding Ding call from VA returned him to the present.

*Oh damn, I forgot about the dog!*

"Close call, crisis averted, but they almost delivered us the wrong dog!"

Jacob was lost from the start and suspected he was being fooled. "Wait, what crisis was averted. Are we not getting a dog?"

"No no, we're getting a dog, but not until later in the afternoon," Liam spoke as if he wasn't hundreds of miles away. "But they were blocks away from dropping off a dog this very morning. You're at home, right?"

Jacob wondered if he should be grateful for a problem averted that he had no business causing in the first place.

"What do you mean the wrong dog? I don't even know what the right dog is? What is happening?"

"You know these organizations, things move fast. They were going to have us take the mother, but then something happened, so now they need a spot for the largest puppy".

"Huh?"

"Turns out we're getting a different dog. So the wrong dog is all relative." Liam's talk made no sense to Jacob. Instead, Jacob's mind went to a book or TV show that he may or may not have read or watched where the son of satan was mistakenly delivered to the wrong family. And that set off a chain of events that ended the world. Jacob shook his head at the thought. *Or did the child save the world?*

He hung up with assurances that the puppy would arrive after school let out, and should not be any trouble at all. Though Jacob couldn't entirely banish the thought that this animal might signal end times.

An extra long inhale and exhale helped quell those fears. Helping even more was his remembering that he was visiting his friend Mabel again that sunset. No surprise puppy was going to stop that. Willouby Jacob was taking control of his own life. Making decisions for himself, or perhaps carried by the River. Either way, he was a much more confident man than the one that had rolled along the embankment only a few days earlier.

"Onward!" he said to Eleanor as he decided in that very instant to keep his own new traditions alive by going on another walk. The streets were already beginning to feel like home to Mister Maymerry of the Rock House on Nottingham Avenue.

## Chapter 18

**Out the front** door, he took a right, headed north on Nottingham, past the synagogue, then the skate park, toward the underside of his neighborhood.

On the sidewalk near the house of worship he saw the same Philosophy Brother he always saw, getting into a mammoth black cadillac the size of a humpback whale. The old man wore a light brown jacket, wisps of white hair on a balding head projected deep knowledge.

*Was he going to pick up medicine for his invalid sibling who constantly disagreed with him?* Jacob's mind whirred with so many stories about these men made up from nothing.

That got him thinking about the previous night's conversation of endings. One part of Jacob thought, *life would be so much easier if I knew the ending. I know I'm gonna die, just let me know when so I can stop worrying about it and enjoy each moment.*

Maybe, another Jacob thought, but do I really want to know?

Once before a beach trip, the bookseller was so excited that he bought her favorite mystery, she accidentally told him the ending as he checked out. It was the first beach book that he couldn't get himself to even finish. Maybe that's why one of his first loves were those Choose Your Own Adventure books. Endless re-readings.

Another part of Jacob knew better. *How utterly dull my life would be if I already knew everything. What would propel me forward?*

He thought these thoughts and then tried to think why he thought them. What was the River trying to tell him? He didn't know, and before he caught himself, worrying about it all caused his heart to sink like a blue diamond to the bottom of the deepest part of the Pacific black.

*Isn't someone still chasing you? Or hunting?*

For a flash he remembered the obituary clue in the library. He wondered. If someone was chasing him or following him on the skull hunt, there would be one obvious suspect—Liam. What are the odds that he disappears on a random mission at the very moment this all happens?

Until an ever deeper sea thought struck—*There is another in town who might know about this skull and you've just seen him. The Philosophy Brothers. Why didn't you think of them much earlier? They must know so much.*

Jacob's mind sunk even deeper still—In fact, hadn't I only seen a single man walk in and out? Maybe there is only one old Brother next door who has conversations with himself.

Perhaps Jacob in his blindness confused the whole thing. This neighbor might be ill. Or dangerous. Or both. He saw him now in a much darker light. The old man may have dozens of bodies in his own basement. Or perhaps he ground them into salt and dispersed the remains each winter to melt the ice over the sidewalks.

Jacob wondered if he reached bottom when he believed without question—*The next door neighbor killed someone in my house, didn't he? My life is in danger, isn't it?*

He now knew with utter certainty that this balding wise man in the light brown jacket rocked in a chair next to the skeleton of a past victim, and had conversations as two people that Jacob overheard.

*Maybe Mabel killed someone. Or Barbara Johnson. Or a Rooster.*

*Honk! Honk!* He was saved by a truck whizzing by that may have been saying hello to Jacob. He waved just in case. That allowed his mind to get back to blunt honesty. *Get a grip! Remember the River!*

Jacob jolted himself into a slightly saner mindset, remembering that the answers might be provided to him if he looked. The odds were infinitesimal that his next door neighbor was one unwell man pretending to be two men having philosophical conversations in order to trick Jacob as part of a plot to hide involvement in a past murder that was so sloppy it left a skull to be uncovered by the first cat to move in.

*It. Does. Not. Add. Up.* Jacob pointed his finger in the air and felt much better.

∞

**Jacob walked and** pondered on Mabel. She was the most fascinating elderly human that he had yet met. And he had met many. After all, Jacob was a young man who began line dancing at the age of 12, with dancemates ranging from 27 to 96. He spent many high school weekends in American Legion halls, empty wedding venues, and banquet rooms converted for one night into line dance havens. Later he realized that might have been a bit strange for a teenager. But the oddest ducks rarely know or care that they're odd.

Shortly after passing a now empty skate park, Jacob noticed a trail, previously invisible to him. It was easy to miss, a clearing in the trees indicating a slightly overgrown but still usable alleyway that ran behind the houses along Brandywine Ave.

No longer afraid of spontaneous life changes, he took a sharp turn to explore the new path behind houses. Songbirds guided him along, and the late morning sunlight dappled the ground with a checkerboard of gold shapes. Forgetting everything for a moment, Jacob felt again a child free outside with no obligations after Saturday morning cartoons—content living in the moment, like a puppy ecstatic to romp in all that is.

*I totally forgot a dog is coming soon.* Jacob had no worry about what it might mean for his future. *It'll be fine, a new adventure.* Jacob surprised even himself at his calm approach to unexpected developments. Maybe it's the breathing techniques, he thought as a joke.

"This place is full of hidden mysteries," Jacob said to the birds. Black, blue, and red shapes darted and followed him from tree to tree as he walked. The backyards of each house were large enough, and the tree density thick enough, that he could have fooled himself that he was in the middle of a dense wood. What a luxury to have such an escape so close to home.

Up ahead he saw a slight clearing, and an empty picnic table atop a lawn of freshly cut grass emerged. He felt a tinge of anticipation as he approached, like the warm crinkle opening the spine of a new book, and imagining what dreams lay ahead.

Jacob heard rustling and then let his body go numb as if he was floating atop a raft of slow moving water.

Someone was there, alone, leaning against a second picnic table, whistling to himself. Jacob knew exactly who it must be. *Traditions develop quickly in a place like Willouby.*

∞

**The young poet**, zen master, and Saint Nicholas appeared in a new form altogether, but his big cat fluidity was recognizable straight away. Something about the casual movements, relaxed hips, and sly smile made Jacob wonder if this was closest yet to his true nature.

He wore a patchwork hippy cardigan, green t-shirt that hugged his body, and a cap of a cobbler sort askew atop dark hair. His pants were three quarter length ending mid-calf. Altogether he might have looked a 1920s golfer. Except he was shoeless, which lent an Aladdin look to it all.

Jacob's instincts about his true nature seemed vindicated, when the twentysomething vagabond smiled his pretty teeth and shuffled as if interrupted. *He's not acting but being himself?*

His sympathetic eyes darted down at his feet, and Jacob couldn't help but think of himself, and his own games of eye contact. But then the young man looked up, as if back in control, and smiled even brighter.

"Look who it is, the very person I was hoping to see."

Those words warmed Jacob more than any yet uttered in Willouby, with the tone of honest friendship.

This Santa Claus from yesterday was someone who respected those on the River, those who followed random alleyways, and those who answered questions about desire. Jacob was proud to be recognized by a kindred soul but suddenly grew nervous that he might not live up to his new friend's conversation standards on this Saturday.

He smiled to the ground as he walked closer, tapping the top of the first picnic table as he walked past. He couldn't yet fully understand the man in front of him now. Perhaps a Tom Sawyer, or an adult Peter Pan, or even a lost boy of Willouby.

"What brings you out here?" Jacob cringed for unknown reasons. With a flashed grin of hidden glee, the young tiger on the prowl put Jacob at ease with a strange question. "Would you believe I'm playing hide and seek?"

"You're kidding?" Jacob coughed to hide a silly laugh.

His new friend smiled a white brightness and then spoke with nervousness, as if he wasn't prepared to talk to anyone at that moment. "Just kidding. I'm thinking. And was going to read a book, if I can find it."

Jacob looked down again at the bare feet which might also have just finished an hour long match of dirt patch soccer. "Great to see you again Nick."

The young man tilted a head in curiosity. *Should I have called him Nicholas instead? Or Saint?*

"Oh, yesterday." His friend said, putting it all together. "Sometimes I am

Nicholas but to you I can always be Will, or William. I'm fine being long or short. Versatility is one of my main virtues."

Jacob smiled his most honest smile since moving to town, as if he'd finally passed all tests, answered enough riddles, and unlocked a mystery to be told the real name of this most fascinatingly odd young bird.

*I may have a new friend as strange as me.* Jacob felt buoyed by the River.

Young William seemed to consider the underside of the afternoon leaves. "Some who know me best call me William of this Hood. And now you know much more about me than I do about you. Why are you so fascinating?"

Jacob blushed at the unexpected interest in his life. He forgto that as a brand new person in the neighborhood, others might genuinely want to learn about him. *What memorable mystery or magic did Jacob Maymerry bring new to the street?*

What followed was the longest conversation Jacob yet had in Willouby outside the House of Mabel. Sitting atop picnic tables, Jacob lost himself at various moments talking about his daily waves as a comedic fantasy of riddles.

He told Will about line dancing and Eleanor Roosevelt, already comforted that this young man bawked at nothing. Jacob laughed out loud as he shared the story of his triple spin tumble down the embankment while pushing the couch on move-in day. "I'm still missing one yellow scooter."

Will smiled a brilliant glow. It's easy to be your odd self when with an even odder friend, he remembered from somewhere.

The bard twirled a purple pen between his fingers as he discussed himself, "I come from a family of nomads, so this all is meant to be." He waved a hand around at empty nature.

"My Dad worked in Richmond, and took the train there from here every day. For a few years when he was younger he didn't even have a house or apartment, just slept on the long train ride, saved all his money, and loved every second of it. He gave all the money away, which is why I have none. But that was a beautiful gift he gave me."

*What sort of man commutes from the top of the state to the bottom every day, leaving a son alone and with nothing?*

Jacob thought this in defense of his friend, but William seemed smart enough to make the proper decisions about the older man's virtue.

William kept on his father. "A champion of the little people, and the simple things that matter most. I've got some of that in me, I guess."

An hour or two passed and the golden spheres of light through the trees on the greenest cut grass kept shifting the shimmering checkerboard setting as the picnic conversation continued. Will eventually reminded Jacob that he had other adventures ahead when he looked up and said, "Apollo is moving that sun across the sky rather fast today, isn't he? I lost track of it all."

*Oh shoot, I've got to get back. There's a dog getting delivered soon.*

Jacob looked up, directly into the sun like a fool, before telling his new friend exactly what he was thinking, "Oh shoot, I've got to get back. There's a dog getting delivered soon."

He filled Will in on the unexpected delivery, the missing fence, and his fear that Eleanor would never forgive the betrayal that was not at all his fault. In the spirit of complete honesty he even let slip that he was meeting someone—he didn't say who—that very night and hoped the two creatures in the house would get along in his absence.

Looking down again at his bare feet, Jacob left by asking if Will needed anything. "The only thing I need is nothing at all. But I'm glad I know you're there, buddy."

As he walked away William made sure Jacob knew he was free to cat sit, dog sit, plant sit, or just sit and chat at any time. "I'm easy to find," Will said as he disappeared into the trees on a path of his own making.

∞

**Instead of finishing** his walk as intended, Jacob backtracked in order to get home as fast as possible. He re-traced the alley trail, past the skate park now filled with three middle schoolers in helmets, and nearly jogged down Nottingham to his own front door.

*Someone would have called if I missed the arrival, right?* Jacob inhaled and then exhaled as he closed the door behind him, confident all was still well with the world.

He arrived back home and spent the next hour following the sunlight path arc across the downstairs, waiting and thinking. Jacob Maymerry was a man who thought about what lay ahead. A dog, then Mabel.

School was out long ago, Jacob assumed. *Would this dog ever arrive?*

*Ring a Ding Ding.* A call from Colorado brought him back.

"Line dance cruises," she said without introduction as soon as Jacob answered the phone. "They are a lifeblood for us, and of course, *they* copied us long ago." The word *they* dripped with patriotic condescension.

Gladys continued, "But it just occurred to me that *they* are missing something we have. Constant Sun."

Jacob was unsure how to respond so he went with his usual trick of making indifferent sounds, "MmmhmmHmmm"

"Have you looked at a map lately? Have you compared their southernmost point with ours? Game Over." She said with glee. "If you draw a line across, I think they only go as far south as Missouri. So they'll never be able to get us on that one, because we've got the Sun Belt."

'HhmmmUmm Hrrrmmm'

"Just wanted to share. You have a good weekend, sweetheart."

Jacob smiled at the pet name after hanging up. Perhaps the future excitement of seeing Mabel put him in a good mood, but he forgave Gladys all her silliness of the call. He knew that as President of the Board she was trying to be her very best American self. And she only knew how to be American by understanding what was not American. He knew if Europe changed its name to America, and pledged allegiance, then she'd flip completely around and welcome them with open arms. Words mattered to her in that way. Jacob might think on it later, but he felt no need for judgment on that Saturday afternoon.

**He sat at** the dining room table, the clock inched forward, and Jacob began to worry that he'd have to make a choice. Was it any choice at all? Go to Mabel's or wait for the dog?

Aunt Mabel was not a woman who waited. Jacob felt that securing not one or two but *three* separate invitations to be dazzled by the most interesting woman in town—perhaps the entire Commonwealth—was not something to be tossed lightly.

If it came to it, he'd call Liam and tell him to re-schedule. And if there was no answer, he'd leave a message. And if necessary he'd scribble a note on the door for whoever came to drop off the puppy—*Sorry for missing you. The door is unlocked, please leave the puppy inside, and I'll be back this evening. Best wishes, Jacob.*

Come puppy, high water, or hell, Jacob Maymerry would not miss a sunset dinner at the House of Mabel atop the hill. It wouldn't make sense to say that his life depended on it, but deep down he felt that it did.

The River did not demand this choice from Jacob, because just as he formulated the plan in his mind, a small hybrid vehicle with a single cage in the rear pulled up the back drive.

A ponytailed woman emerged carrying the crate, which to Jacob relief, held a sleeping black, white, and brown eyebrowed puppy. She was running very late, apologized to Jacob for her brevity, not knowing it's exactly what he wanted anyway.

The dog was unquestionably adorable, as all puppies are, especially those snoozing with occasional burps, sighs, and dream hiccups. "A springer spaniel," the woman said as Jacob noticed the dog hair covering her entire body. "He'a big fella, and quite the personality. When he's awake, that is, as he does seem to tire quite easily.

She went on for only a few minutes, taking a trip to the car to bring back puppy accouterments of food, toys, bowl, and old blankets of various sizes.

The woman couldn't hide rushing, apologizing for not dragging it out longer. "I've got to drive back to the city tonight, otherwise I'd stick around to help you get acquainted. He loves his crate and might be out for quite awhile, so no need to do much until then."

Jacob thanked the river that this kind woman was fast, because he had his own appointment to keep. He watched her out the back door, through the gate, and waved as she sat into the driver's seat. Until, with a huff, she got out once more and walked to the house.

*Sweet mother of pearl. What now?*

As if hearing his prayer, she didn't bother to walk all the way back, instead yelled in a quick huff, "I forgot to mention, his name's Herbert." She shrugged and her ponytail bobbed like a Kentucky Derby contender. "I know I know, but old man names for dogs are popular now. It's a fad, and you can change it if you'd like. Not sure anything has stuck in his puppy brain yet."

Gravel dust misted the air along the embankment as she peeled out down the back drive with a heavy acceleration. Jacob smiled at the sleeping circle of fur. He felt gratitude that the woman was brief, the dog was asleep, and he would not be late for his Mabel meeting. A reminder not to get caught up in life's unknowns and instead let the River guide him on this unexpected adventure.

He grabbed the sweater that best matched what he wore—a thick weaving that was not much different than the one William of the Hood was wearing earlier in the day. He found his green spiral notebook of clues, slipped on puma shoes, and headed out the door to meet his friend for her latest performance.

— Chapter 19 —

**Jacob danced down** the green grassy gravel lane for the third day in a row—feeling almost at home. The estate now looked and felt different, as if he were wearing glasses of another prescription. Perhaps it was familiarity, comfort, and acceptance of the River's inevitable journey for him.

An older Jacob would have noticed this emotion bubble inside, chastised himself, and then looked for the underbelly of looming darkness. Those thoughts had no power now, mere shadow puppets. He knew *looming darkness* was simply a funny grey way to say that it was almost sunset.

The Jacob carried by the river, *metaphorically of course*, he thought with a wink, considered it the rise of the stunning twilight. At least when near Mabel, Mister Maymerry remembered that even the most simple opportunities shone out with meaning. An evening connection with his wise new old friend harbored magical potential—a candy orange and tangerine moment on the horizon. Even Jacob's thoughts seemed more colorful when skipping up Sunset Circle toward the large cave doors.

∞

**Three gong knocks** later Jacob followed Winston into the familiar castle entry with three staircases. Instead of traveling up a new artery, Winston led Jacob directly across the home from east to west. Past the stairs, doors of unknown shape and number, at least one and a half kitchens, and upon three pairs of matching triple windows at least thirteen feet from stone tile to ceiling. It was a partial sunroom that opened entirely onto Mabel's Back Patio.

The large French doors revealed a pavilion that first reminded Jacob of the winery views that dot the Blue Ridge Mountains. That was only a foundation image. The back patio of Miss Mabel was nothing if cookie-cutter. Stones of odd natural curves, protrusions, and comforting blues, greys, and swirls of other pillars formed several seating areas seemingly burst from the earth itself.

Outdoor furniture and pillows of every conceivable variety might have been present somewhere, though Jacob remembered a fraction of what he saw. The view was a splendid mirage, as the landscape changed based on where one stood. Like a garden atop a mountain, Mabel's back yard might have been up high or down low, depending on her mood or preferences at the time. Sitting in some spots behind a tree or under an umbrella, made it impossible to appreciate that the entire space sat high above town. The patio was a shining city on a hill all itself.

Appearing from nothing, Mabel rose inconspicuously from a wall in a black gown and sparkling sequins. As if chameleon camouflaged, once she showed herself, Jacob realized she could not help but swim in exotic mystery as she rose and fell. Mabel needn't even try.

"We have a guest, how lovely." Mabel strode toward him smoking a cigar in a nonchalant performance that might not have been performance at all. Only after following the cigar wisps up into the sky did he realize she wore a black headdress. Putting it all together, she now appeared an echo of a wild flapper New Years party, sparkling gemstones covering her entire body up the white Antoinette wig which might have been half her Willy Wonka hair from the first visit.

Jacob admired her beauty and an image struck him, obviously a fantasy, of Mabel's own practiced hands sewing each jewel on the gown—some distant year in the past for a Hollywood party of a bygone era.

He thought she looked unbelievable, and said as much. "You look unbelievable." Jacob found her example as interesting as her words. Maybe she went into her closet and pulled out one of her greatest hits only because she had a nice young visitor on a random Saturday evening. It didn't matter. He enjoyed each second here, and that was enough for now.

A second compliment came to Jacob, "That gown is miraculous."

"Oh, this ancient thing? I only wear it when I don't care how I look." She winked and Jacob knew he'd heard that line somewhere before. Mabel didn't even glance down at her sparkling gown that he now realized must have been skin thin. Because while it looked as robust as Cal Coolidge American prudence required, it also barely contained her. She moved with a fluidity that would have shocked Jacob Maymerry. But Mabel had already shocked him time and time again, so he no longer questioned what she did or how she did it.

Feeling the feistiness of a budding friendship, Jacob bantered back. "Now you didn't need to dress up all fancy on my account, but thank you anyway." He tried to wink and hoped it didn't look like a spasm.

∞

**She ignored him** and started her stories, "Speaking of dressed up. Did you see this thing that popped on the Internets?" She sat on an elaborate orange chair in the yard made of a material that Jacob suspected would be destroyed in the rain. "This one dress, two dress, blue gold dress, what a mess thing? At first I thought it was a Dr. Seuss book. You hear this?"

Jacob remembered the meme but couldn't remember if he saw the blue or gold dress. He now suspected he could see both.

"The point is," Mabel seemed frustrated by her own topic, "Colors of dresses don't matter. What matters on a dress are ruffles, frizzles, frazzles, glittery glam. The I AM. Personalization, you understand. Anyone with real fashion sense knows that. Some of us recognize authentic art when we see it. And some of us are authentic art." She winked a long wink. "And extra rare ones are all three." She held up three fingers. Jacob was lost in the woven conversation of various ideas that he now considered Mabel's trademark.

"Where were we?" She knew he was clueless.

Jacob was never fully sure when Mabel had finished with a topic, because her mind often whirled back around to old ideas that caught her fancy once more. Glancing out at some view of green across the lawn, Mabel motioned Jacob to sit on a cream cloud chair of balanced plushness.

"Of course we had to come out here. I'm sure you knew that. Why on earth would I invite you at this hour and not take advantage of this!" Mabel swept both arms around in a flat line revealing the majestic conclusion to the day's festivities of the sun.

"What flair for the dramatic could I possibly have if I didn't take this easy standing ovation." She spoke with nostalgia, and looked at the horizon remembering a real standing ovation from the distant past.

She stood up, as if for herself, and for a second Jacob assumed he was supposed to do the same.

The symbolism was almost too obvious for Jacob to acknowledge. But what he did think, as they stared in silence at the sun, was that he couldn't help but see meaning in this. Or was it matter? Mabel meant something to Jacob, even if he didn't know what, and she mattered very much.

His mind remained a whir of Ms, Meaning and Matter. Staring at the sun, perhaps showing the early stages of heat stroke. One half of Jacob's head seemed to be trying to understand the other. As if spoken by a stranger, Jacob heard himself ask a question he never intended.

"Do you know the two older men who live next door to my house? The men beyond the trees? Are they brothers?"

Mabel stared at him and raised an eyebrow—he felt pride at being even slightly interesting to her. At least he hoped that's what the raised eyebrow meant.

Mabel sat across from him in three quick strides, as if eager for the unexpected diversion. "Oh those two? They're identical twins. Quite rare specimens in fact." She lowered her voice for no reason. "I'm no gossip, but I have a theory. I think those two are rare triples." She stared at Jacob hoping he understood.

He was improving, but she knew he still needed help. "Opposite, identical, conjoined twins." Jacob tried to process that but Mabel provided no time to process. "But here's the twist, now pay attention. What if they were sawed apart as kids and never told? Perhaps one of them took one half a brain, the other took the other half. Or half of the other. Two halves, of course. Some speculate that's why they agree on nothing. How else do you get to that point with identical genes? And they were raised in the same house, so it's not nurture, right? You tell me. The parents could have cut them in half in secret, because appearances were much more important back then. But that's just something I heard, or did I think it? It doesn't matter. I'm no gossip. No No." She winked and then bawked twice. "But it sure is fun to imagine, isn't it?"

Jacob had no idea what to feel about this revelation.

"Speaking of sawing in half, it reminds me that separations are always difficult. Or is it transitions? They can get bloody if there's fighting. That's pretty much all our wars, right? The Revolution was us cutting ourselves away from the Brits. Then Old Virginny tried to do the same to the Yankees in that Civil War. They failed, thank Uncle Sam. We're sitting just a few miles from one." She pointed to someplace north or west with the black lace gloved hand. "That's Mary's land over there," She spun the slightest angle, "And the West Virginny border is over there. That line is one big scar created in the War, remember?"

Jacob didn't remember but now he kind of knew.

It occurred to Jacob that Aunt Mabel was interesting because she had run laps around the field, an old lady who was so old she started over and became fascinating again. At one point she probably made many jokes about being old, but once that got boring she made jokes about making jokes about being old, and then, eventually you reach a stage where you Willy Wonka the new neighbors, ramble about hidden surgical procedures, and identify people by the initials of the President the year they were born.

Jacob loved it.

∞

# Mabel's Saturday SunSet SurpRise

**"Now where were** we?" Mabel said and Jacob realized they'd already started the tale. He pulled out his notebook, like a prop, as he play the role of Detective. Another deeper part of him wanted only to watch and enjoy the astonishing performer completing some final quest that Jacob suspected was in her own head. *But isn't everything?*

Mabel turned a black glittery back to him as she returned to the town's past, "Too late to go any earlier, so I suppose let's start after the Civil War—that clean slate." Jacob blanched. *Not again. I don't know how much sunset is left.*

Then he realized he had absolutely no choice anyway. Jacob Maymerry was a fool—Aunt Mabel would tell whatever story she chose, and he was glad to be on the lazy river for a short while to enjoy it.

She had never stopped talking, "As I keep telling you, those silly Grey Confederates got too big for their britches. And I know exactly why. It's because I'm good with numbers, and they weren't. One, Two, Few." She did not hold up any fingers this time. "Do you understand?"

Jacob did not understand, and his face must have shown it because Mabel tried another way. "One too little. Get it? The Missing One." She held up 1 finger to make it plain to Jacob who remained confused.

With a nod Mabel tried yet again, "I need to back up to give you a better mathematical foundation. Like the best recipes, a successful split in two requires exact right ingredients mixed at the precise correct time. As you might imagine, quantities are a key and some ingredients change mid-bake. The perfect number of pieces for a split on this continent obviously starts at 13." She did not hold up all those fingers but instead said, "I'm referring to the number."

Younger Jacob would have immediately given up at this foolery. But like a favorite grandchild finding meaning in a Grandmotherly ramble, Jacob began to appreciate the way Mabel's eyes viewed the world.

"I follow you so far," Jacob wrote the number 13, indicating the colonies at the time of the Revolution. *Or so he hoped.*

**Most Likely**
    1. *Mother Elizabeth*
    13


He saw her eyes watch him write in the notebook. And then he saw that she saw. And then she said with a nod, "Glad you're still using that. The first step in having a young brain is remembering that it's too young to remember everything without help sometimes. Maybe when you're older you won't need that." She smiled and tilted a head as if considering something.

Finding her answer immediately, Mabel moved to the chair in front of him and sat. She looked carefully at him as if it was of the utmost importance. "This part may be confusing for little ones like yourself. See, back in the 50s of 17. The 1750s, the Founders of this magical wood made the first split—slicing Willouby up into 26 lots. Can't you follow me from there? That's a perfect double of the necessary 13. Not only that, but it's the extra special tricksy triple, because you do know what 26 refers to, don't you? That's right. They are each a letter, my man!"


*My man?* Jacob wondered if Mabel's mind was whizzing from strange memory to memory, using different words. Then he remembered powder room and decided that everyone was free to start using new phrases, no matter the age.

"Remember that as you consider my original point. Do you know, little one, how many states those crafty confederates had?"

*Dammit, I should know this one. Think, Jacob, Think!*

"Eleven?" Jacob guessed and felt himself hitting the shore of the river with a thud.

"Close, but completely wrong. They had 13!" Mabel smiled as if he had finally graduated, though she had simply told Jacob an answer that made no sense to him. *Wasn't that the same number of original US states or colonies or whatever?*

Mabel answered him immediately, "That was a tricky question. Those Greys were close, but no cigar. Because they forgot about Unum. One. The Missing One. They forgot about the hidden 14th. The US. The USA. Don't you see?"

The performer never cared if he understood, she plowed on. "Thirteen is such an unbalanced number, especially for a complex trick as those Confederates attempted. Never stood a chance, because two legged stools cannot stand. Everyone knows that. And my dearest little one, that is why on this very day there is still a Willouby, and there is forever these United States of America." She waved both hands in the air indicating all that you see, "But those thirteen unbalanced individual and divided grey states of temporary confusion are now only echoes in our story."

Mabel was not finished with the topic, her passion ran deep. "And the thing is, my dear, even those who know only letters should have figured it out from the start. The Confederates had 2 out of 3 letters correct. CSA versus the USA. It was a Con. Con is opposite. It's false. It will always be inferior to the U for United!"

As a sly madam, she puffed two quick puffs of her cigar from sleek black gloves and released smoke balls into the purple and baby blue sky. "As I said, I'm quite good with numbers. Which is why it was so egregious that I failed every mathematics class that I ever took. Preposterous!"

Jacob laughed out loud, appreciating that Mabel was in on every joke. He need only relax sometimes to better understand how life might be lived at its most graceful.

Slippers gliding in close, Mabel almost whispered for the deepest of secrets, "But do you *really* want to know why 13 is the first key? It's exactly half the letters, and the 13th letter is M for Me." There was no bawk, as if Mabel wanted it clear this was serious business. *But was anything serious for Mabel?* "Connecting letters to numbers is such fun. It's two of a three. Don't you see?" She winked and Jacob again had no idea what to understand.

She sat up in front of him as if building to a separate point she wanted the whole time, "Did you know that during a 9 month stretch in 1863, some-wheres before or after Gettysburg, this ye olde Willouby was in the No Man's Land between both lines of the War. It became a kingdom unto itself, and many wondered who was in charge. The Mayor? Did City Council have the power to hang people in the Kingdom of Willouby? If only a Queen was in charge then, things might look different. Or maybe exactly the same!" *Ba Kaw! Ba Kaw! Ba Kaw!*

Mabel coughed herself silly at that joke, and Jacob found himself laughing in mirrored response. There's something about pure joy that is contagious. Jacob tried to imagine Queen Mabel with the power of life and death over her fellow citymates, or Willow Beasts. What mischief she'd explore with revelry.

**On tiny feet** covered in red slippers or socks, Mabel rose like a fairy bopping from one pretty color to the next in her back garden of twinkling mystery. Literal twinkle lights began popping up at random, as if each were on timers of completely different orientations, flicking on whenever they were ready. Or perhaps they were solar lights that shone once enough energy had been collected by the sun.

Regardless of the mechanics, the effect was a dazzling firefly twilight un-der the sunset now shifting, ever so subtly, into a stream of pinks, reds, blues, and purple beacons of evening warmth.

"Winston!" Mabel turned frustrated in half a flash. It may have been an act, but she was so good Jacob couldn't possibly ever know for sure. "Winston, Crickety Crockety! Get a move on! Can't you see the sun? You cannot, and that's the point. We're running out of yellows for this spin cycle. Only purples for awhile after."

For a moment Jacob didn't understand her——*Is Mabel's sanity going in front of me? Can it last forever?*

Then he remembered words like Crazy or Sane no longer mattered. At least not in reference to his new old friend. She was Mabel, and that was enough.

After all, the only reason he was here yet again, absorbed like a fool with a book, was because she rode that rail between sane and crazy like someone who had finally figured out the purpose of this whole thing.

Mabel read his mind and directed him back to the game that brought him there in the first place. "Where were we? We did the war. What's next? Oh, right! Christopher and then the Clowns and Birds. Excuse me, the McDonalds."

Jacob looked down at his notebook and remembered his quest. The skull! *Which of these folks is not buried in the cemetery? Which person ended up in his basement?* His mission, however, seemed to be changing before his eyes. He now cared only about what the River wanted to show him. And the River wanted him to listen to Mabel. Of that he knew full well.

∞

**Mabel walked left** and right, up, down, and swirled around as she spoke of the transition between the House Hamilton to the House McDonald. She unattached a layer of black across her shoulders that Jacob hadn't known was layered. A hood. The reveal was a majestically regal purple cape, made of the thinnest silky substance, fluttering behind her as a Flapper Hero of the Twilight. She had a new cigar, this one slender, more feminine with a bright red ember burning hot as she sucked in to continue her tale.

"That red-headed Susana died in the 70s, Mama shortly thereafter. That left the two sisters. Christopher had flown away years earlier. Sara the songbird lived forever in your house and guided souls from administration to administration until sometime in the 90s or some such when she probably drifted away on white wings. Though she and her sister never did fully reconcile, some do say."

"The only wrinkle, as I said, was that the Confectionary, quiet Sandra, had a revelation mid-life. At least revelation enough to leave the Methodists run by Oldest Sister Sara. Instead, she marched down the street to a different church, can't remember the name now. They met in the M House. One called each other Friends, but the others called themselves Brothers and Sisters. It definitely wasn't Aunts and Uncles, that would be crazy." She winked. And Jacob knew that the wink really meant, *It's all A for Arbitrary.* But that might have been in his head.

"So Sara moved out of the Hamilton House that bore her name and into a tidy thing back over there." Mabel pointed in some direction down that could have indicated virtually anywhere in town. "She had a wonderful party in celebration. I never actually saw her new house, mind you, though I did attend the gathering. She was the type of person who had a housewarming party in the back room of the church because she didn't want people milling about the house. Which on some levels, I respect."

Jacob made a sound to let her know he was listening, and she smiled as if she appreciated his gesture but it was unnecessary.

"Sara lived in her own place until she out-lived her sister. That's how she ended up back in your Hamilton House for the last year or three. Sara Hamilton, black haired quiet little mouse with the baked goods and the Friends. She's the reason for the transition. Well, that and the Friends."

Jacob looked down at his green spiral notebook and wondered if he should write something down. Instead, he nodded and said, "Right." Mabel smiled as if knowing he was trying to understand something he didn't.

∞

**Her cape of** woven colors and twinkling constellations around her flapper sleekness, Mabel almost danced atop the stones as she finished the complex metamorphosis of the Hamiltons to McDonalds.

"Let me explain the Schism between Sara and Sandra. I'm no theologian, so do forgive me the details. I think it was a disagreement about the number 3. Or maybe it was the word three. Some confusion about what it meant, the Trinity. I believe a sister was dyslexic and woke up one morning suspecting it to be the mother, daughter, and Christmas spirit? Naturally that caused all sorts of confusion with the old line ideas. And for folks who take these details seriously, that confusion goes to the bone. Or in this case, the grave." She sighed and Jacob wondered how much of that was true. Mabel went on, "Some such thing like that, any more specifics would confuse you."

"The important thing is that this theological disagreement caused Sandra to switch allegiances completely to the Friends church. It's been said that at this new church, on the very first day, she sat next to Robin McDonald. They struck up a conversation straight away. And so it goes." Mabel nodded at the disappearing light between trees, and wondered if that was enough.

She turned back to face him, and Jacob realized she held a champagne glass. Mabel continued after a sip, "Remember, Sandra ended up the last surviving Hamilton. She wandered the halls of your house alone for a time, until moving back to her little cottage to slip away. On her deathbed Confectionary Sandra sold your house to her church friend, Robin McDonald and her husband. Far below market value, no doubt, perhaps a gift entirely. Maybe it was in the Will, some whispered. The McDonalds certainly couldn't have afforded that square footage otherwise, they say."

"Interesting," Jacob said. He leaned back in his chair, almost wrote something in his notebook but didn't, and then exhaled while remembering he need only trust the sights and sounds of the River.

"Eureka!" Mabel zipped up from the edge of the chair in front of him with a whippity hippity boo of inspiration. *Does she have tiny wings?* "Now I recall why Mama isn't at the Mountaintop Plot with C, O, and the three Ss! Isn't it obvious? She was cremated!"

*Oh, that's interesting*

"Or I should clarify, she was *going* to be cremated, in case Christopher ended up somewhere outside of town. Mother Elizabeth was nothing if not pragmatic, and she wanted to be with all her babies to the end. Someone must have eventually carried out her wish, though where she was spread I can't say at the moment."

Mabel took a long drag of her thin cigar, smiled wide lips that might have been bliss, and exhaled a weaving wisp that faded in the dark air.

∞

**Little Christopher, oh** what to say about him. I might have been an older sister, see. And he's the type who disappeared on the quest for the grail. Followed the grail trail. Is that a thing or did I just make that up?" Mabel looked at him and realized it was an actual question, not a joke.

As usual, she answered herself, "Definitely a seeker. Maybe I should write a poem about that traveler—I haven't thought about him in oh so long." She looked at a corner. "Christopher Hamilton. A seeker of stars. Followed the grail trail, to a great tale, until the tail, end of it all, *blah blah blah*." She circled her hands hoping he could finish the weaving himself now.

Mabel sat nearby, crossed her legs like a proper lady, gave a smile of seductive impropriety, and tried to finish the family stories in a jiff huff. "Christopher forgot that the search for the grail is the search for the ending. You only find it by giving up." She sighed and took a cigar puff.

"It took him a long time to realize that. Though I most suspect he remembered once more. Such a smile in that Arizona casket, I imagine. A pretty face on that little one, even at the last. With a grin like that, he found what he was looking for, of that I have no doubt. And once you find it, why what's keeping you from the great what's nest?"

*Did she say nest?*

"Because what comes next is always what we decide." Mabel nodded matter of factly, uncrossed her legs, and stood back up. As if on to more important things.

Jacob began to wonder if what Mabel did not talk about was as important as what she did. Or thought another way, he suspected that what attracted Mabel's attention was far more interesting than the words used to describe it.

She stood, stalking as she explained. "To clarify, I didn't attend his funeral, and I'm not sure it was in Arizona. That's just the last place I recall him being." She gave herself a quick puff, tilted a head in consideration, and then decided, "Maybe you should know more."

"Here's a little about Christopher's life instead of his death. His given name was Chester after his father, Chester Christopher Hamilton. Chester Two is what they called him as a child. But he hated that. So they called him CC. But that infuriated him even more. So he went by his middle name, Christopher, and only his father called him Chester."

"His brother had the stature of a first born, like his father, but little Chris was more delicate. A wandering soul, he knew this place wasn't big enough for both his father, brother, and himself, so he set off to another shore. Tale as old as time."

She turned her back to him and looked at the moon. "He was always searching. I guess he eventually found it, somewhere in the desert. Arizona, as I said. It's the AZ, after all. The beginning and end, first and last, *blah blah blah*." She bored herself. Jacob suspected Mabel had an entire lecture ready on letters and their hidden meanings. Then he realized that letters with hidden meanings were just words of a different language. Then he decided to stop thinking and listen.

∞

**Without a word** from Mabel, Winston arrived with two glasses of a refreshing concoction and tiny glass jars of honey.

Mabel didn't glance at the butler but spoke to Jacob, "Mostly liquid fare tonight my love, as our performance requires levity and balance." She bopped both shoulders up with the faintest glee. "This is an AE of Winston's combination. A blend of American lemonade and English tea. A Golden Bear, I do believe it's called. The sweetness is mostly a garnish. But you must at least dip a pinky in the local ambrosia honey. They say it gives you superpowers."

She winked before correcting herself, "Or is it immunity?"

Jacob immediately dipped a finger in the jar for a taste. In a bizarre electric buzz that might compare to a cold sweat, Jacob felt tingles seep from tongue to fingers to knees and toes. "This honey is something else," he blurted automatically and was thrilled to see her smile with glistening white teeth

"I'm glad you enjoy it. The bees do work so hard each year for us. Your reward is more words from me!" *Ba Kaw!*

She appeared a professor emeritus of some such thing underneath her Antoninette wig, a professional of the Versailles Court. A savant sitting in constant demand, Mabel tossed random pearls as gifts to Jacob's eager young ears. "Life is easy. Someone creates a snowball and a hill. Then someone is the snowball and someone is the hill. Then you switch positions to keep it fresh. My goodness, I can't say it any simpler than that."

She sighed and sat down, gazing at the mountaintop garden of her creation as the sky above burst with a mix of moonlight, starlight, and the fading colors of a missing sun. "So many snowballs seem to roll here to Willouby," she stared back at him with a twinkle in both eyes that Jacob saw jump out of her irises and land in the sky behind her.

Mabel steered the conversation to a place that made Jacob believe, very and truly, that the River existed. It existed as some link to elsewhere in his brain. She said, "One such snowball was an English Owl, or was it Irish?"

Jacob spoke his confusion, "An Irish Owl rolled into town like a snowball?"

Mabel's eyes narrowed, "Not owl, little one. 'Ol W. Or OW. I mean to say that Oscar Wilde stopped here. Because his train broke down. I wasn't there, but that's what they say."

*This is quite the pearl necklace of coincidences. Jacob's logical brain knew. What are the odds that she'd mention Wilde?*

But then his sane mind thought, *you're just looking for connections now and making the magic work. It's a self-fulfilling prophecy.* Until a third, perhaps unified Jacob thought, *What if you're both right?*

Mabel explained further, "The only thing I know about that Oscar is he visited Walt Whitman once. Now Whitman, that's a real American. Growing that luscious beard alone."

Then she mimed confused, "He was the one with the long white beard, right? I always get him mixed up with Santa Claus. Can you imagine, Walt Whitman sneaking into your house at night to leave little jeweled poems under your head. Or maybe inside it." *Ba Kaw! Ba Kaw!* "Then stealing a tooth before flittering away." *Ba Kaw!*

In a twilight blink, Mabel popped up flagpole straight, her joints locked as she blared a siren call of what Jacob could only assume were Walt Whitman lines. "O Captain, My Captain! Carpe diem! Now he rests with the angels!"

*I really need to read more poetry.*

**Mabel kept the** pearls coming, "Many Willouby families first rolled here for the strangest reasons. We were once a penal colony, in fact. Some prisoners from the revolution who they stored right over there ended up staying here," Mabel pointed off in some direction. "Hessians I think they were called. But they got a taste of freedom and decided to stay. Like that Headless Horsemen from the sleepy little willow town in the American spook story."

She considered her previous statement, as if someone else said it and she'd never analyzed it before. "Yes, isn't a hollow just another name for a valley, like our Shenandoah? That tale was written by another real American. Mr. Washington, I do believe. The story goes that his mother learned that the Revolution was won in early April, just as her eleventh child was born. And so he was named Washington to honor the new nation and its first father. This child became Washington Irving. The Original Author, not the President. The first American Man of Letters, some suggest, though I'm no gossip."

"Hear Hear" Jacob saluted the Headless Horseman and felt most sure that the river must be real. *And I have a head in the basement! So many coincidences!*

Jacob began to wonder and then wonder if he already knew. He smiled to himself and felt for the first time that perhaps he was understanding Mabel's winks and nods just a tad bit clearer.

Mabel stood again, cape fluttering in the slightest breeze in the back patio paradise. "Enough for me. Before my final performance we have business to attend to, don't we?"

The Fool of a Maymerry forgot his business entirely. For it was only then that he noticed greenish blue fluorescent light growing from trees all across the park patio. He worried he was hallucinating, how could translucent colors grow from bark?

But Mabel missed nothing, followed his eyes, and asked, "Penny for your thoughts? A Lincoln for what you're thinkin'? Too late, I already know, you're too slow. And that's coming from me, a turtle!" *Ba Kaw!*

She answered a question that he'd only thought in his head. "That's fairy fungi fox fire. One of nature's hidden nightlights, isn't it something? It's the runaway's best friend, I like to think, because it brightens the way in dark forests."

"But you must focus, as it's time for the story of the McDonalds. Which is a story of three MCs. It goes something like this."

∞

# The Story of the 3 MCs Squared

"There is an entire line of folks who suggest that Sandra Hamilton did not coincidentally happen to split and join the Friends where she met Robin McDonald. They say she became a friend *because* Robin McDonald was there. They were *already friends!*"

"These Society of Friends, you must remember, were proud members of an old American philosophy. Some claim that one of the greatest founding Americans was just such a Friend. He was not an AP but he was from PA. He was the B of Electricity!" She looked at him with the sly smile of a budding friendship, already with the start of a private language, though this was a most challenging riddle.

Jacob knew the answer straight away, perhaps buoyed by the local honey, "Benjamin Franklin!"

"He remembers, this little one. How curious." Mabel gave the slightest twitch to the corner of her mouth which might have been pride at her student's understanding.

She transitioned quickly again into the bearer of tricky new River knowledge. Holding up three fingers, "There were three McDonalds in your house — the pair of old robins and the young birdie they adopted."

Jacob flipped back a few pages in his book, pen at the ready. *No need to write this part twice*, he thought from somewhere.

**Most Likely**
  I. Hamiltons
    1. Chester*
    2. Elizabeth-i-I
    3. Oscar*-i
    4. S*——Sara
    5. S*——Susana
    6. S*——Sandra
    7. Christopher-w-I

  II. McDonalds
    8. Dad
    9. Mom——Robin
    10. Child

Perhaps gaining honey powers, Jacob immediately knew how to fill in his chart of information. He added Capital Is to Mother Elizabeth and Christopher, because they were *especially interesting* now that they each had reasons not to be buried at the mountaintop. He felt a dash of pride looking at his notes. To anyone else it might be chicken scratch. But Detective Maymerry had already developed a system for himself. Only he and any friends he cared to share the key would fully understand.

As always, Mabel had never stopped talking. "Remember I told you, Robin McDonald looked exactly like the funny Letter Man. His wife was short and stout with the jolliest belly laugh in memory."

Jacob looked back at his notes and was confused enough to ask a question, "The wife looked like the letter man?"

"Are you already lost dear? I forget how mesmerizing I am even when I don't try. You might need to practice your hearing," She winked, smiled, and cackled all in one to ensure he knew it was in good fun. "I do believe I told you it was a pair of robins."

"The birds?"

"The people. Robin McDonald married Robin McDonald. Pretend to keep up, dear. Try writing in your little book." She pointed a nailed finger down at the pad in his lap, like the principal trying to teach kindergarten for a day. "The Robins were long together in various ways."

*A male Robin and a female Robin, of course.*

∞

**"Where to start** with these folks. Hmmm." Mabel groped for an answer that Jacob suspected she already knew.

"Perhaps," Mabel smiled deliciously, "Perhaps we start with one of my favorite things, Letters and their synonyms for the ear, Notes. You know those times when words only matter as much as they sound? What I mean to say, is that the story of the MCs must start with a tricksy E for Enunciation. Or maybe a P for Pronunciation."

"It's important to know that there are two lines there—Mick Donalds and Mack Donalds. Two completely different family trees—though both strands arrived here from Scotland at about the same time, or so I've heard. Scots were respected because they were against the redcoats like us, allies in a mirror way. So Scottish names seemed trustworthy for a time. But like everything, there were levels. It's one of those *some are more equal than others sort of things.*"

Mabel puffed one quick indulgence then continued, wanting to get to the point of all this Scottish talk. "The important thing is that for the last century, folks around here had very different opinions depending on whether you were talking about Macks or Micks. The smallest bitty sound has the biggest social difference. Depending on the ear." Mabel stared deeply at Jacob as if this was of the utmost importance. "Do you understand?"

She continued, assuming he had no idea. "One family thread had a far higher reputation than the other. To make a long story simple, the MacDonalds came from Scotland, moved into a fine sturdy brick house on the south side of town, and had many boxes of glittery goods brought to fill the estate."

With a tilted head she said, "Well, the MicDonalds came at the same time, but they were the ones who unloaded all of the boxes into the big house. Then they got fine employment helping the MacDonalds live very fine lives. You know what I mean, right?"

Jacob knew what she meant, having watched enough period pieces about the British aristocracy and their team of service workers.

Mabel smiled and shrugged her shoulders. "MicDonalds came from AB folk. Attic and Basement people. They had offices in the basement and bedrooms in the attic, with the little hidden stairs they could use in the back. That must be familiar to you, right?"

*Of course it was familiar.*

"Now your house may have the stairwell, but it never had the servants. Remember, I told you, the Hamiltons built it, and they were of a stock slightly later than the servant age. Of course, they still designed the home in the same servant style—traditional families act traditionally.

"I'm getting to why this matters. It matters, because the McDonalds who lived in your house right before you were of the extra rare double—a blending of the Mic and Mac Donalds!"

Mabel left no time for further contemplation, as if she wanted to get all this out and move onto something else. "Strange birds, as I said. At least that was their reputation in town. It was probably because they didn't care about names or money. Which, if you don't chase those things, folks really start to ask questions. Then why would you even want such a big place as the Hamilton House? Were they hiding something or plain weird?" Mabel flicked a wrist with unfurled hand fan in some direction toward downtown. Jacob knew what she meant, *that's the gossip that kept those common Willow Beasts entertained.*

Jacob immediately realized the River might have opened up for him. These Robins and their son must still be around. They must be the next link on the chain of information. *Is that what Mabel is trying to tell me?* Then another part of Jacob thought, *If you stop thinking and listen, maybe we'll get an answer far faster!*

Mabel might have heard the whole conversation in his head, "They're gone now, of course, because when the McDonald's got into your house they were already old. Similar ages to the Hamiltons I do believe. Seventies, Eighties, who's to say? You assumed otherwise, didn't you? See, it's so easy to fool you when you make assumptions." She shimmied her shoulders as if proud of herself.

*There goes that idea,* Jacob sighed. Until Mabel volleyed back another light, "Of course, their son is still around. In fact, he might be the only living person besides you who lived in that house."

*How curious? Now who might this son be? Just listen to Mabel, and the River will lead you to the answer.*

∞

**As if on** cure, Mabel came in hot, "Wait, did I tell you yet about the Civil War?"

*Oh no. Is Mabel's final thread fading away, a mind that needs a break? Is this where she loops again with the same stories.* Jacob took a deep breath and hoped Mabel's lucidity returned.

"Three battles of Willouby," she held up three fingers to ensure the fool understood. Then she pointed in three separate directions around her, presumably where each battle was fought from Mabel's patio. "Not to be confused with the Revolutionary War prisoners kept over there," she pointed in a slightly different direction. "Or the Seven Years War fort which is even older, over there." She twisted like a compass and pointed in yet another direction. "But that's a name for another game!"

*Ba Kaw! Ba Kaw! Ba Kaw!* As Mabel's bawks descended into a swaddle cough, Jacob considered that Mabel was just like a compass. He needn't worry about steering the conversation, because she'd point to true north either way. As if he could control the North Star!

Mabel reminisced now in the twilight with the intensity of an actual Civil War veteran. "Those were difficult times, a real clean slate for these parts. It was apple weaving that started things back up again. I'm sorry, Apples and Weaving. The apple industry and the woolen mills, threading blankets and such. That started the wheels once more of building and loans and shopping and dancing and praying and entertaining and whatnot." Mabel circled a wrist that either meant *blah blah blah* or telling herself to speed it up. "But that's the end of a different friend."

"So as I was saying about The Child. The clown son or Merry Fellow. The McDonald Boy. William who lived in your house last."

*The only living one,* Jacob thought, now trying to guess how old the man must be. *This one might be a key.*

Mabel started again with mass confusion. "Such a wonder. That reminds me, the Robins couldn't have children. That's why their lives were so strange, perhaps. They were lifetime renters, see. Or in his case, rider of the rails. Until they landed your house, which was a coup."

*Wait, I know this already.* One part of Jacob tried to knock sense into another.

Mabel sat across from him, her purply black cape now draped around her shoulders as warm folded blanket wings. "But they found a little Will to adopt with the similar soul, and finished raising him in your house. Speaking of growing wills, have you met him yet?"

"Who?" Jacob sounded an owl.

She rolled large eyes, "Little Will. William. The kid you want to know about. McDonald. At least I assume that's his last name. Might not be legal, like it matters to anyone who matters."

*But of course—Flower Cup Kid. Santa. Nicholas. Will. His new first friend. What a small world, after all. At that very moment the River felt as real to Jacob as anything in his life.*

Jacob figured it out in his head as he stared at her face and noticed she had added a beauty mark on a cheek under the white wig. He sighed in strange comfort and blanked completely on absolutely everything. Mabel kept talking to save him.

"He's my friend — the stray cat that stalks around this neighborhood all the time. He probably has many names. Willy Mac. The Bard. Young McDonald. He's a clever little one. In fact, yesterday he brought me that very MGD Christmas gift which you and I enjoyed together. I believe I told you that. Do try to keep up dear." She smiled and winked at the same time.

Mabel paused from her story, as if bored with it all. She rose, champagne flute again in hand. "Of course, I think he's temporarily homeless. Or maybe permanently, I haven't asked."

Jacob almost said a word to show interest before remembering it wasn't necessary in the House of Mabel.

"Let me finish up the story of the McDonalds. Both Robins died shortly after Will turned of age. Heart attack and stroke, or vice versa. She's buried up there not far from the Hamiltons. The Father Robin is not, though where is a question for his son. Soon after the funeral, the bank took the house. There it sat until you moved your furniture up the back lane this week."

∞

**In a flash**, the natural world caught her attention and Mabel turned to stare at the most robust sycamore in the yard. She spoke without giving Jacob a chance to follow up about Will, the large stray cat. "Sycamores are crafty. The bark sheds in snake-like wisps, because it's stronger than other bark. Their trunks are mostly hollow, did you know that?"

Mabel then recalled a story she once heard, about how the first pioneers in this area survived because of a sycamore tree and its empty center. Lost in the Willouby wilderness, a settler and two sons lived in a hollowed out sycamore during the bitterest blizzard for three straight weeks. Mabel spoke like an old librarian, "The blizzard faded, but the family decided never to leave Willouby. Or so the story goes. In gratitude they buried deep roots, promising an endless family line of guardians to become the Consciousness of Willouby—a golden light hidden in the dark—providing good fortune to all those who stop here in search of it."

As if easing a concern before he had it, "Don't worry, that's not my line. It's only a riddle as old as the fiddle that I thought you should hear." She sipped champagne then leaned in close for a whisper, information of a most secret sort. "The name of that original line has been lost to the winds. So it goes." She paused, stared directly into his eyes, and then Mabel whispered inside the whisper, "But the only way to find anything is to first lose it." Finally she leaned in and might have beamed him telepathically—*Or perhaps finding things is seeing that which was always there.*

Leaving no time for Jacob to write that down, Mabel stood up and stared at the last of the rays. "Sometimes words get in the way of it all. See?" She closed her eyes, inhaled big, exhaled, opened her eyes, saw something magical, and smiled her whitest Christmas brights yet. "Sights and sounds sometimes block the core. The Feeling. Can you feel it?" She had no interest in Jacob's answer, because she seemed to be feeling something for many seconds beyond counting.

∞

Jacob stared at his list of two merged families, one split by schism…

**Most Likely**
> I. Hamiltons
>> 1. Chester*
>> 2. Elizabeth-i-I
>> 3. Oscar*-i
>> 4. S*—Sara
>> 5. S*—Susana

6. S*—Sandra
7. Christopher-w-I

II. McDonalds
8. Dad—Robin—I
9. Mom—Robin
10. Child—Will—A

Mabel enjoyed her transition into evening, and Jacob filled in his information. He identified a third capital I for Interesting with the Robin McDonald of the Rails whose body could be anywhere. He added an A for Alive next to his main link in the real world. He felt hope at something new to explore tomorrow, no matter where it led.

Staring back down at the list of lives before him, a small kernel in the Old Jacob creaked, "I'm not sure how many happy endings I see here. Don't know what to make of that."

"What now?" Mabel heard. Jacob hadn't realized he'd thought it aloud.

"I mean, nevermind. Just thinking out loud." Jacob realized it wasn't worth repeating to the old ears that must be getting tired. *How utterly pathetic my troubles must seem to her right now.*

"They are all happy temporary conclusions. Wasn't that clear?" Mabel sighed, then smiled all lips. "Endings? No silly child, you misunderstand yet again. Have you ever heard of E for Epilogue? What a hopeless case knocked on my door three days ago!"

She looked out at the sycamore and put the back of her wrist to her forehead in feigned exhaustion like a hopeless Southern Belle. "Sure as dogs eat little green apples, my dear, the day will come when you understand! Even if you have to wait a century or more!" She winked and shimmed her shoulders, tilted a head, and sized Jacob up in a beat.

Then she smiled her Christmas morning teeth as if he didn't already know it was all an act. In that moment he felt younger than he had in all his time with Mabel. And so she seemed older. "I told you those particular stories about those particular people, because that's what you wanted to hear. Don't you remember? There are so many other things that I did not tell you. More things than could ever be said."

She tilted a head, preparing for extra explanation. Perhaps Jacob was more remedial than she expected. "Oh dear. You've gone and done it again. Either you misunderstand or I'm not perfect yet." She mimed a thinking lady in deep concentration. "Yes, just as I suspected, the fault is yours." She winked. "Don't worry, I forgive you. You could see these sad endings, because that's what you're thinking about right now. Your mind is in charge, but you know that. There's a whole other side to all this. I do believe I told you that everyone gets exactly what they want in Willouby. I meant that literally. Do try to keep up."

"Maybe I only told you what you wanted to hear. Or perhaps it was what I wanted you to hear. Or both. Or something else. Oh dear. This memory of mind is really something else at this young age." She winked both eyes for three full seconds.

She trailed off with a dramatic pause, looking out at the now purple color bursting from dark maroons and blacks atop the landscape. She smiled involuntarily, a twitch, and he knew in that moment it was not an act.

The tiny smile expanded as she said, "Chester Hamilton loved cigars and helped over a thousand or two families get a home loan to build or fix a house. They say he died with the largest grin on his face, thinking of how much every block of this place was helped up by him. His son Oscar saved his younger brother Christopher from a drowning, won a cloister of WW2 medals, walked on water across stages, and was first to whatever's next, like a true Mr. Willouby." She pointed to some direction in the far off distance. "Forever the hero, some of his admirers even threw him a parade outside of town over there."

She was back on a roll. "And those sisters. Each could be a novel. In some ways Sara is the whole shebang, because she's the one who kept the stories going for so many families. Susana was happy every second that I ever saw her. Sandra had the closest friendships this town's yet known."


Mabel's cape fluttered purply black on dark grey like an evening crusader of happy endings.


"The McDonalds, oh dear, the purest bunch of kooks this side of the Rockies! Robin McDonald shook this earth endlessly, knowing the greatest gift is to laugh and be laughed at in return. Her husband was barely here! Instead he lived each day walking and talking on the train with his best buddies. Quite the life! In fact, few know this, but he's the very reason Willouby has so many sparkling public spaces."

*Oh, interesting.*

"The thousands of hours he spent with business travelers over the decades. So many kept leaving him money in their Wills—I wonder if that's how they named the boy? I guess he was a man of Cs for Connections. Robin McDonald the jolly porter, had little use for such silliness as mountains of cash. So he kept giving it to the city for parks, museums, gardens, library updates, art and whatnot. All for the Nottingham Avenue fun of it all, I suppose." She finished with a phrase entirely her own creation.

"Hmmmmmmm" she hummed to the air before moving on. "Mama Hamilton gushed to everyone on the exploits of her brood. She dreamed of even one wee childe, but a complete hand of five she had! Each growing into such things! Young Christopher may be an enigma, but what else would one want to become who flees the nest and explores these United States for an entire lifetime. What an adventure!"

Jacob smiled and Mabel matched it. "From the tiny bit you understood, how could you possibly know the complexity of these souls? Don't be fooled into thinking you know these people. Do you even know yourself yet? Maybe one day." Mabel then mangled or reinterpreted some quote, "Ye best not judge lest ye be judgey."

She nodded, before tilting her dainty head, "Then again, it's impossible not to judge, so good luck with that!" *Ba Kaw! Ba Kaw!* Her Antoinette wig shimmied into a jiggle.

∞

**"Sad endings? Oh** little one. So much yet to see you have." She smiled to indicate she was very glad that he still had so much yet to see. It meant adventure awaited him. Jacob felt gratitude, because he knew that Mabel cared. She understood friendship, reminding him, "Sometimes you are a fool, Jacob Maymerry. A dear fool."

She rose with Nightingale fullness, "What sadness except that which we build in? I keep telling people what they say they want to hear. I need to stop that. It's too confusing. I keep forgetting that these days no one even considers that it's always happily ever after no matter what story they tell!" *Ba Kaw!*

"The McDonalds got exactly what they needed and wanted from that 'ol gal of yours down there. A nest. Do you think birds make nests for forever? Even our things that we think are for forever, like your house, like this house, are not forever. Everything is a nest for the briefest bit—depending on one's perspective. But I'm no gossip."

"This is something you should write down in your little book. Be careful. I just told you what some people said. I didn't tell you what other people said. And more importantly, do you think I said what all these people told themselves in their own heads?" This really tickled her for some unknown reason, and Mabel released a triple lutz of a simultaneous wink plus *Kaw* that transitioned seamlessly into a smile. "One day may you get as lucky as I, giving yourself the attention to look at every single person who catches your eye and understand the happiest ending for them."

*Silence.* Jacob tried to absorb that idea, but Mabel cut off his thought, "That's clever. Write that down!"

Jacob froze and then clenched a pen before relaxing and laughing at the River. "Just kidding. Just kidding," she rolled her eyes. "You're such a schoolboy."

She hacked into the swaddle which seemed to be growing in size out of her pocket, now a mini blanket. Either that or he was getting woozy from no food being served at this dinner. Or maybe her hand was shrinking and the swaddle was the same size. Maybe the moon made Jacob tired.

A velvet cream cheese frosting voice cooed him, "But no my dear, I do have some serious advice. And I mean this. Life is a Diamond." A gentle smile. "It all depends on the cut and the magnification."

She laughed a different sort of *Hehehe* that ended with an exhaled smile, "I say everything with the flair of Ye Olde Layde of the Willowe Tree. It's a ruse. Trust no one for advice. Including me. Especially me. Now write that down!"

Jacob's hand automatically gripped his pen, his nerves moving outside his control— almost drawing the shape of a diamond before catching himself. His internal clock froze—*is someone else in control of my mind*. Until he breathed and remembered he had a rambling brain and was in complete control, for now. *Keep your hand on the wheel ye olde boy.* Jacob stared at Mabel's teeth and tried to center himself.

She had never stopped talking. "Or as Rhiannon said, 'Shine bright like a diamond.' I love Fleetwood Mac. I like to think I'm the AM. They are the FM. And I'm not sure who the PM is yet." *Ba Kaw!*

Jacob dared throw one out to the winds before even knowing what he was saying, "Proud Mary is a PM?" *Does that even make sense?*

*BaaaKaaw! BaaKaaw!* "Oh, you're a real jewel. I love CCR as well as TT, and have always adored diamonds. Because they're hard, and hard to find. And they matter because we say they matter. And they take forever to make. Like me." She smiled all lips before her sunshine teeth broke through in a warm reveal.

Jacob melted into the teeth before noticing that he was taking notes in his tiny spiral notebook. But all he'd managed was to write the letter D and draw the actual shape of a diamond. He hoped it'd be enough to remember the importance of all of this diamond chatter from the old turtle.

She fluttered among the flickering twinkle lights, cape a dark mist as she spun out elderly gems as part of some grand finale that must be ending with bedtime. Mabel shot out old lady wisdom in a fast money round, as if a clock was ticking down and she wanted to set a new record, to earn the highest score in a game where Jacob was probably a chess piece instead of the other player.

"If you ever feel inside out, remember that feeling is a gift. For that's when you're closest to understanding your true self. That's when you become a lure for only the biggest catch that is seeking exactly what you truly are—nothing more, nothing less, Upside Down for Inside Out and Ouside In! Gaudi!"

Jacob thought deep and tried to understand if Mabel meant he was the bait, the fish, or both

As if able to bore into his soul, she said with kind eyes, "If you don't know what's going on, you have nothing to worry about. Worry is only for those with information. I'm sure you get this a lot sweetheart, but it doesn't look like you know much of anything." *Ba Kaw! Ba Kaw! Ba Kaw!*

She clucked herself silly, laughing into a coughing fit of barnyard proportions.

∞

**Changing subject, Mabel's** dark shadow of a figure strode the yard and seemed an echo or mirror reflection of the darkeing night sky with hints of stars sending little light zig zagging pinpricks down at them.

"Someone told me that constellations were a map to what comes next. And that's when I realized I wasn't a star but a whole damn galaxy!" Ba Kaw! Ba Kaw! KaKaKaw! Mabel's cackle ended with another coughing fit, prompting her to look around and say, "We don't have any of that oxygen in tanks out here do we?"

Jacob was confused. *Was this Mabel's way of saying she finally needed some? Should he call for Winston?*

But she seemed to mention it only to tell another story. *Silly Jacob, thinking Mabel wasn't in control this whole very time.*

"I learned about the importance of Oxygen from my friend Maybelline."

Mabel fluttered to the edge of a stone chair, with purple balls of light on sticks twinkling around her from a wildflower garden. "She was a genius in the sciences, remember. She told me that you need 2 Os of Oxygen in a molecule to sustain life. I do believe I told you that. Dearest M had a heart full of sticks and I loved her so very much! Oh yes, sit with her a while gazing at your enemies from afar and she'd have you in stitches. She'd pick apart those beasts and remind you how much you did not need to waste a thought with them. She once roasted a feisty golem of mine in a science lesson, and it made me laugh so much I was asked to leave the class. I never did return."

"Apologies my dear, I flutter between the past and present. Life is about finding your altitude. That's all. Dip too high and it becomes a ball of stress that'll burn you. Spin too low and you start staring at the ground thinking of a crash. So find your right altitude for the moment and ignore the rest."

Mabel bored of it. "This is wise gibberish. But it's not my fault if that is not a language you speak. Some of the world's finest wisdom can be understood only in gobbles and gabbles. Don't worry, you're far too young to be expected to yet know. My little child still growing his garden. What is it they call that level before the first? The basement? No no, Kindergarten."


*Clap! Clap!*


With two rasps of her hands, and a rustle of her dress in stallion pride, Mabel demanded Winston's attention. "My dear Englishman, 'tis time. Bring out the magic music machine if you do so please. And if you do not please, I insist."

Without a second delay, clearly on cue, the robot man squeaked out, literally, with wheels on an ancient cart *squee squee squeeing* across the patio.

The machine, Jacob could only guess, was a phonograph, gramophone, suessaphiddle, or some retired contraption akin to the 8-track of the 1920s. The only point that mattered for Jacob's purposes was that this magical gadget made sound.

Mabel saved Jacob's worthless rambling about things he didn't understand, "Do you know records? Of course you don't."

"I know records. I mean, I know of them. I've listened to records." Jacob found the courage to speak.

"Well, that's good. But I was talking about something else entirely, a ranking perhaps. Or an order of numbers. Nevermind. For young minds, sometimes music is the best medium in which to swim the sparkling seas."

∞

**A sound began** to rise from the machine. Strings pulsing up into complex vibrations echoing off the patio now all shadow and partial lights.

Mabel moved to center stage, swaying hips, shifting shape into a seductive swivel down of Sss's. "When I'm dancing to the moon I like to see which it prefers—the squiggle or the dot." She closed her eyes and seemed to combine lifetimes of movement into a swaying swirl of blues and whites as her jewelry dazzled across Jacob's transfixed eyes.

She spoke as she swayed, with eyes closed. "A dance instructor told me that all of life was E and R, Energy and Relationship. Each of us has our center, we pick something else to focus on, and then decide what energy to use to interact." Mabel's Sss, slowly shifted into her trademarks CCs. "Everything is two points, two dancers, and how they relate to one another. How beautifully simple, you understand?"

"I must ask you to listen. This one has words to help you along. But that's a bonus. Don't read too carefully, because words are training wheels, unnecessary at the end. Eventually, my dear, one realizes that getting old means going back down to where you started. Breaking everything back to its basics. The Essence. It's jazz. When finely tuned, one might experience the purest perfection with sound alone. Though there is no sound without ears, now is there?"

Jacob might have said "No," but then didn't remember what question he was answering. The magic music machine saved him with sound.

*Beautiful dreamer, queen of my song,*
*List while I woo thee with soft melody;*

*Gone are the cares of life's busy throng,*

*Beautiful dreamer, awake unto me!*
*Beautiful dreamer, awake unto me!*

She floated forward on both feet, and circled her hips like Elvis which reminded Jacob of some of the best line dancers 30 years younger than Mabel.

*Beautiful dreamer, awake unto me!*
*Beautiful dreamer, awake unto me!*

The same lyrics were repeated, this time slightly slower. Jacob wondered, perhaps hoped, that the angelic voice he heard attempting to waken this beautiful dreamer was Sara Hamilton herself. The one and only recording, made and preserved somehow through Mabel's mysticism, surviving for Jacob the fool of Maymerry to hear. Even if only this once, an angelic voice, escaping the church of decades past and into his little ears.

The words faded but a gentle tune continued, and Mabel rose higher, using a hidden energy reserve for a grand finale. Jacob noticed that she liked the parts with no words best. *Maybe the older you get, the words get in the way.*

As if reading his mind, "Take it all in and let it go. There's something deeper than letters or ideas or differences between all the senses. It just comes in, you savor it, and let the nonsense go. Take it all in and let it go."

She looked at the clouds for two deep breaths and Jacob couldn't help but follow her deep breaths with his own.

∞

**The music faded**, the machine carried away, Mabel sat across from him, her chest heaving ever so slightly as her cape traipsed the wind behind her.

"I do believe I said I only had one big performance in me each week. By my count that is my third show for you in as many days. You were special enough for it."

She smiled without teeth and Jacob felt warmed by the sun. "Now my dear, another evening approaches, and I must transition activities accordingly."

Mabel rose and Jacob somehow knew he was to follow her. She seemed to meander slightly, as if taking him on one final walk around her patio, the scenic route back to the exit door.

"The Evening is another tricksy E, after all. Isn't life all transition?" Mabel asked in a way that both was and was not a question. A sentimental send off, Jacob suspected, "Transitions might be hard, but eventually one forgets even to notice the shifts. Once things blend, you realize you've seen it all before. Everything gets a little dull until you notice once again that you do not care. And that, my dearest little one, that's when things really get good."

She winked or blinked and then stared directly into his eyes. *And soul?*

"That's why I love New Years. It's like a swipe up. An invisible transition disguised as a celebration! All the babies in top hats crawling around. And the 4th of July! Our nation's birth—Fireworks, Romance, Explosion. and Embers. Birthdays are re-births right?" Mabel was getting a little loopy.

"I know you have more questions. Like what is the secret of life? That's what everyone asks the oldest person they know. I always say there is no secret. That's closest to true, if supremely dull. I once wrote an answer as a poem. This very one." Mabel stopped not far from the door, and stared directly at him, as if the poem she spoke of was floating in the room in front of them. Or perhaps floating in his head.

Before more confusion set in, Mabel jolted him with a sane explanation, "Didn't I tell you? I'm thinking of becoming a poet. I'm starting with limmericks. Here's one as your last gift. It's a rough draft. I don't know if it fits the rules. I didn't check, because I don't care for arbitrary rules." She cleared her throat and belted with a river croak:

*I am the lady who SeeS*
*All of the things that can BeeS.*
*The good and BaD*
*The happy and SaD*
*And live for EterniteeS.*

"Wait, that actually wasn't your last gift. Take these." She motioned ahead and Winston appeared, leading him out while handing over a stack of what Jacob realized were three records held together by a string tied in a bow. He was handed a matching suitcase record player. "There wasn't enough time to play them earlier. Something to enjoy at home. Keep them together. They're a tripod."

Jacob did not know what to say to his friend, "I love it."

∞

**The re-tracing back** east happened in a whiz burr. He left the patio, through the long first floor, and into the lovely purple on his side of the House of Mabel. He turned to face his friend, as Mabel spoke again, almost waiting for him to finally catch up. "Wait, there was one more thing for you." *This woman wouldn't stop.*

"I have a tricksy E for Encore after all. One more show for a favorite little one. Peep all you like. Do you know this one? It's the 'ol Cal Coolidge. The boys can never resist ye olde CC."

And with that, she swirled hips in seductively silent Cs. Arms up as if dancing with an invisible partner, Mabel turned slowly with circles and sways, ups and downs, until the sequins on the other side of her sleek black number sparkled across Jacob's eyes. His irises reflected diamonds through the door slamming in his face, and he barely noticed that his nose rubbed the top of the tortoise shells. He took no offense at this temporary ending, for he knew that when Mabel was done, she was done.

Not because she was ending. Quite the opposite, in fact. Absolutely perhaps, there was always one more performance, and Mabel was needed backstage.

# —— Chapter 20 ——

**Jacob Maymerry left** Mabel to her backstage and strode toward his own final performance—or adventure. The only thing he knew for very sure was that he drifted under the bright half moon which followed him with a sideways smile. *Ancients knew that the Moon was a mirror,* Jacob remembered from some mythology book, *reflecting the light of the sun and controlling all nighttime activities on our little planet.*

He felt relief that at least he wasn't alone. Mabel put him in a mystical mode and he thought the Moon a goddess—perhaps that made him the friend of the cosmic deity.

Arriving back down atop Nottingham Avenue, Jacob's mind was a play-doh of images trying to make sense of his little mission. He clod up his own gravel back drive, careful not to hit a pothole and drop the things he carried. He looked down at Mabel's items. If this was a video game the records he held would mean something extra special. *Gifts. Or final clues. Clues to solve the riddle. But what riddle did he want to solve? Whose head is under his house?*

Maybe the gifts were weapons to fight a coming dragon. But what dragon would be slew by sounds? Who was he fooling? Jacob Maymerry, the guy down there in the cardigan, was not slaying any dragons with paper and plastic nothings. Anyway, there were no dragons here, unless one counted the HVAC unit. And if that was the case, he might as well lay down his sword right now, because AN for Absolutely Not would he be able to beat a real heating and cooling emergency alone on a Saturday night.

Eleanor Roosevelt wove out the door through his legs, escaping to nature as soon as Jacob arrived home. He was embarrassed that it was only upon seeing the cat that he remembered he also had a dog.

*Dammit! He might be thirsty, or hungry, or need to go outside. He might be terrified.*

In that instant, Jacob felt overwhelming sympathy for a puppy that, through no fault of its own, found itself in a cage, in a new place, without knowing anyone. A kindred spirit, even newer to Wilouby than Jacob.

*What was his name again? Herbert? How curious.*

Herbert sat in the crate, calm as a carrot, staring at him with the confidence of a new best friend. *How curious indeed.*

"Look at you, my little Herbert Hoover," Jacob said without thinking as he examined the little beast remembering Mabel's obsession with American Presidents.

The creature opened his mouth at the full name, and seemed to smile with a bright pink tongue lolling out. Jacob took it as confirmation that he and the animal shared a sensibility.

"Yes, we shall call you Herbert Hoover," Jacob said as he opened the crate and fell into puppy face licks.

He slipped on the leash provided by the pony-tailed delivery woman and took Herbert for his first yard walk. Jacob ignored light bitterness at not being able to open the door and let him run free. But there was no fence. *And Jacob only had himself to blame for that. Or did he? He couldn't even remember.*

∞

**The spaniel and** fool walked the yard. Jacob Maymerry thought about the cat, then the dog, and realized he might be lost. He didn't quite recall what he should do, could do, or wanted to do with this inaugural adventure. *Who gave this bumbling cardigan man the keys to the Willouby Mystery Mobile?* But then the authentically optimistic part of him considered that was perfectly fine, all part of adulthood. He could figure it out as he went along, because that's the only way anything is ever really done anyway.

For now he was hungry, which reminded him from nowhere about the recipe Mabel gave him the night before. As he thought it, the memory of her cookies came back to him, automatically irresistible as both a smell and taste.

That's why when he and Herbert returned inside after the dog did not do any business, Jacob went straight for the notecard on the fridge. He glanced down at it and gurgled a cacophony across the kitchen cabinets…

## Mabel's Famous Chocolate Chip Cookie Recipe

| | |
|---|---|
| *Eggs* | *Flour* |
| *Salt* | *Vanilla* |
| *CCs* | *Riser* |
| *Heat* | *Time* |
| *Your Own Mystique* | |

*Ta Da!*

∞

**And then an** old idea hit him. One that should have hit him much earlier. That even those of regular intelligence would have picked up on immediately—Mabel was getting ready to die. She was giving her stuff away. She was drinking beer from a mug. She was refusing the endless Oxygen that she obviously needed. She smoked a cigar.

Another thought came like a bear in a shop already almost ruined. *Barbara Johnson made it seem like Mabel was gone a lot. She probably meant mentally. Or physically. Maybe she gave up all her remaining strength for me.*

Until the Jacob of Willouby on Nottingham Avenue beat away the negative ideas with trust in the River and memories of Mabel. Like an invisible voice melting nonsense thoughts with a backhand wave.

*Prepared to die? Did you see that woman prowl on the floor with Shakespeare? Didn't you witness her Dazzle and Fizz and Crackle and Crow and Kaw? Wasn't that the exact opposite of dying? Wasn't Mabel living so fully that Jacob could hardly comprehend all the life he saw?*

Suddenly he missed her sunshine teeth. Standing in the kitchen Jacob decided the universe demanded that he solve this mystery in the basement. Not for himself anymore, but for Mabel. He felt somewhere deep that she had given him everything he needed to understand the answer to the riddle. Failing this was failing her—his oldest friend in Willouby—and perhaps failing the entire world.

*Think, Jacob, Think!*

He instinctively walked to the fridge, opened it to look for string cheese, and noticed with astonishment that inside sat a cylindrical tube of chocolate chip cookie dough.

*The River is real*, Jacob believed in that moment. He wondered if it had been there all week and he'd never noticed, or if it magically appeared tonight. A welcome gift from Willouby itself.

Trusting the flow of things, Jacob pulled a baking sheet from a box, pre-heated the oven, and understood that the universe wanted to give him a sweet midnight snack as he finally solved this pesky puzzle. Everything he needed was presented to him. Detective Jacob Maymerry was tasked with connecting the pieces to reveal the solution.

He prepared to descend the basement stairs, think all his best thoughts, and not rise up until he knew the answer. "It's the least I can do for Mabel," he said to the air.

*Rough Ruff ruff ruff Ralph Ruff Rough*—the barks were of a consistent inconsistency, a robotic tinkling of sounds that hit the ear as almost too perfect. Herbert was nothing if not on cue.

Jacob said out loud, "Oh right, the dog." He looked at the little heathen with puffy pieces of brown, black and white fur. "We just went outside. We can go again in a bit."

Then he remembered purple gloves, and pet messes, and he changed his mind. That's how they ended up outside a second time in fifteen minutes, meandering and sniffing, as the oven preheated. Herbert's tongue lolled, teeth shimmered in starlight, and puppy paws danced across the grass. The dog was happy and had no interest in any bathroom.

Jacob brought him back inside, ignoring eyes pleading—*Let me stay out here!*

If the fence was finished, he could have opened the door and let the ward run on his own. Herbert could have lived like a king in the yard. But that was not to be this night, because they had no fence.

*Ruff! Rough Ruffruff!* Herbert tilted a head in the puppy way that Jacob thought only for movies.

Ignoring the Spaniel nonsense, Jacob made a *Shhh* to his lips with an index finger, hoping to keep the dog from waking the neighbors. But Jacob suspected Herbert was not yet as skilled at understanding his human meanings as Eleanor. The cat knew the importance of keeping quiet, the value of temporary secrets. But dogs? Jacob suspected they were entirely different creatures altogether.

Deep thoughts about cats and dogs must wait for another day, because on that night Jacob knew just what he had to do.

Detective Maymerry marched down to the basement resolute that he would not leave until he had found himself an answer to the skull story that made sense. A story he believed in. Ultimately, he told himself that he would get whatever he needed to understand what comes next in the silly charming life of Jacob, Fool of a Maymerry.

∞
# Jacob's Store of E for Everything

The wood sagged under Jacob's bare feet as he descended the basement stairs. In a flash, he split in two. At least that's the metaphor he used as he heard a new voice speaking to him and about him in his own head. He understood that one part of him lived in the world of mortgages, work, and electronic mail. A second part, Detective Maymerry, swam in an adventure so exciting and exotic that its meaning grew stronger with each step he descended deeper down.

Did breaking in two mean that he was coming unwound? Perhaps, but now that Jacob felt as two, he was able to appreciate the value of brand new perspectives. After all, even an unraveling was more exciting than scary if one wanted it to be. He was ready for this next adventure, and the sting of fear was the beautiful dark silence before the first crack of light in an astonishing grand finale.

Jacob retraced the cat path, pulled back the sheet, and uncovered the skull. He stared at its familiar smile, sat down on the boulder, and opened his green notebook. He glanced at his complex master list with hidden meaning before writing a more precise summary on a fresh page.

**Final Folks**
> *1. Mother Elizabeth*
> *2. Christopher Hamilton*
> *3. Mr. Robin McDonald*

*Down from 10 original possibilities to 3. Three heads with unknown final whereabouts.*

He added the Mister to the third line to distinguish between the pair of spouses with the same name. Names were tricky—he now understood Mabel's perspective much better.

In a jolt of inspiration Jacob considered a new approach. Mabel's voice echoed back to him, "*Do you even know yourself yet, little one?*" Instead of wondering which of the three it was, he imagined which one he wished it would be.

But that raised an even thornier question. *What on earth did Jacob Maymerry want out of this skull mystery?*

A *Kaw* voice returned with beautiful hilarity in his head—almost as if Mabel were with him in the basement that very moment, "*Ba Kaw!* What a silly little one who forgets. I told you, see, that everyone gets exactly what they want in Willouby. Whoever's head you see is exactly, just right where he or she wants to be."

And then the old turtle in Jacob's mind considered something more, "Mister Maymerry, how does your garden grow? What do you remember first? Imagine the head was there for you to find this whole very time. Perhaps the Why is You!"

"RufffffRUFFrruffFF"

"RufffffRUFFrruffFF"

"RufffffRUFFrruffFF"

With obvious symbolism, Herbert's robotic dog sounds hit Jacob's ears as a bell of meaning. *The oven is ready for the cookies!*

Jacob was grateful for the reminder. *Perhaps this dog will be useful after all.*

In quick succession he bound up the stairs, gave HH a two handed head scratch, rolled the cookies into 9 large balls, and threw the sheet in the oven. As quick as he was up, Jacob bound back down the pine to consider the riddle once more. He stared at the boulder to the center of the earth and wondered how different it was from the skull. It's all matter!

One part of Jacob Maymerry thought these strange thoughts and the other analyzed them. He wondered if these were deep enough to impress the Philosophy Brothers next door. He needed to be ready with wise words in case an invite ever came.

∞

**Split into at** least two parts, Jacob's mind began unraveling again shortly after he took six deep breaths, exhaled for three, and then held his breath again for an unknown number of seconds.

As he exhaled he remembered the cookies were in the oven, and he needed to go back up in ten minutes to give them a check see. Then Jacob's mind swirled in gratitude to Mabel. She didn't provide the materials for the cookies, just the inspiration. *But that was enough. Because now he could make his own——over and over. What a gift!*

*Focus Jacob!* Instead of focusing he thought of letters—more of Mabel's influence. He considered the great American Man of Letters in the woodcutting in his office. SK were his letters. Then he thought of the other Man of Letters in his office, though not American. OW—Oscar Wilde. SK, OW, and Jacob the Fool of a Maymerry. Deep down Jacob wondered if he was an L. L for Loser. But perhaps it was an L for Lovable. Maybe he was LL for Lovable Loser. Or maybe just Lovely Lunatic.

Jacob's mind chatter spoke as a many voiced Mabel, a scarecrow of multiple characters, "L is for Linc with a C. But with a K it becomes something else entirely, a Link in a chain of the elven hero protecting the TT Triangle Triforce."

Mabel voice warned him, *"CO of the OC. Careful those together, that's a Cook. With a K it's a Kook. Lunatics perhaps. either way, jamming two together is dangerous art. Liable to explode."*

*You're a clever little one*, he thought to himself with a chuckle. Laughing at oneself is a sign of sanity. Though he now knew the difference between sane and insane was all perspective.

He wondered.

To get to the bottom of this mystery, Jacob needed to get to the bottom of himself. At the very least the idea was a distraction, a shifting of the gears, a new groove in the record, allowing his mind space to find its Eureka moment. There might be wisdom in that.

Jacob thought of how he first knew of letters. Then the thought occurred to him that perhaps letters were his very first friends. He saw them everywhere in his earliest memories, like shadows on a little box.

Mister Maymerry knew he was in that fuzzy place between dozing and awake, but isn't that where Eureka moments are found? The fuzzy box became what he saw in his head.

*He saw M for Mabel. The M became a Monster on an S Street. The Monster that guarded S Street perhaps? Maybe that's why he feared finishing this skull story. Worried about the monster at the end, never discovering who the monster was, or realizing something else entirely.*

*Is this some silly metaphor, and the monster at the end is death?* One part of

Jacob rolled eyes at the pretentious psychoanalysis of another half of himself. *No no, that's far too dull.*

*He remembered his first nice friend who followed the street. A man of sweaters,* Jacob thought in his middle mind, *and shoes of different colors.*

With a jolt, Jacob remembered, he was sitting in the basement and trying to end this skull business once and for all. Was it Elizabeth, a mother buried here to be with the spirits of her children forever? Was it Christopher, a wandering soul, finally back home again? Was it Mister Robin McDonald, the merriest man here only because it was as good a spot as any other?

Which and why? What did Jacob even want?

*Ruff Ruff Ruff*

Finally catching his senses, Jacob realized he needed to pick a lane. Too much was going on at once, and he was jammed. He dashed back up the pine stairs, gave the dog three pets to calm him, saw the cookies needed more time, took a swig of room temperature water, and went down to see what progress he could make in the time left before the next *Ding.*

*I'm ready for cookies.* He salivated at the thought of the midnight snack.

∞

**"Meow!"**

Eleanor the Calico Cat somehow found him in the basement, like old times. He saw her and knew she was special.

She leapt from the washing machine to him but became a jaguar. A Crafty J beyond his understanding. He was Cheating but it was Code. You can cheat in dreams, and somehow he knew he was dreaming as it was happening. There was a word for that space, wasn't there? The land between Awake and Dreaming, where the Eurekas are found.

Then Eleanor looked slightly different, no longer quite a jaguar but a bear. The bear began shrinking into a wee baby bear, becoming a Cub, as if in a magical circus act.

*Jacob did always like performances or was it games or was it puzzles?* He knew he was in the basement, half dozing while thinking, half trying to remember a dream while dreaming it.

The tiny baby bear Cub spoke in complete sentences full of letters. *"You can B if U explore the C. When your Ws look like Ms, remember Nick and the E. NE. ANY. ANY. ANY. Always Next Year. Always Next Year. Always Next Year. And Even 2U all E, U*

*Will C.Ws! Two Vs together for Victories!"*

Then Eleanor exploded into endless pieces of dust upon which Jacob zoomed. *What a dream,* he knew with a giggle, *finally able to enjoy the ride for a moment without worry about what was next.*

Jacob saw that Eleanor was dust made of letters and numbers and words which appeared to him as if the entire universe was his notebook. Words written in the sky as constellations or embers or sparklers. The light connected into letters and numbers and words and matter. Meanings to someone, somewhere.

*Thirteen. 1 2 1. Or 1 & 21. Or 1 & 3. 13. Do U C*
*1,2,1. 2,1,1. 22. DO U c*
*3 is always 4. dO uc*
*URA. U=A. AC. do UC*
*There is no try*

The white glitter riddle wiped itself clean with a swipe, and he opened his eyes. *Whoops.* Yet again Jacob Maymerry had fallen asleep while trying to think about something in the real world.

Enough of that nonsense. Jacob hopped back on both feet to ensure he really wasn't fully asleep. Nope, still in a basement, able to stand up, but with a brain drifting away into mush. He needed a snack, and that reminded him to check on the cookies.

∞

**"Just a minute** or three more" he said to Herbert Hoover, the Springer Spaniel who now sat by the back door, confusion deep in his eyes. Jacob wondered if it was concern for Jacob's inability to take care of a puppy properly. Or perhaps, optimistic Mister Maymerry felt most deep that Herbert already cared about Jacob. Maybe dogs truly were man's best friend, and that friendship was absolute, automatic, and instant.

He drifted atop that feeling of gratitude down the steps and back to the boulder. He forgot how many minutes more the cookies needed, but he knew he'd smell the final crispness.

*Where was I? The skull must be either the mother, son, or porter. But I was thinking of something else, wasn't I? Which did I want it to be? My friends on the street of letters.*

*The Mister Man with changing sweaters.*

Then Jacob remembered One More thing. For he was now deep deep deep inside his middle see. Or was it C. Or See? He was inside something big. Perhaps the middle of the biggest thing of all, Himself. And inside there he found the One Book. From when he was a wee lad, a Rosebud sled of literary proportions. The first book that reached out and grabbed him. He couldn't yet tell you the name, but he knew there was a big blue monster at the end from that very first street. And just as that dark thought occurred to him, a bright new one came on top—the monster was no monster at all. What that meant he almost knew.

And then he remembered something even deeper or bigger or brighter. There was a voice above even the letters of the book. For at the very beginning, before he knew squiggles with his eyes, he knew sounds with his ears. And the words of his first book came not in his own voice but that of someone both part of him and not—his creator perhaps or maybe his helper, his companion, his angel, his Link on the endless chain of all there is. Words, he already knew, were fuzzy things, liable to change shape on you with the faintest breeze.

Jacob felt a breath on his skin in the basement atop the boulder. And Mabel's voice in his head started prattling about a hat. She was going mad.

*"They say the man who saved the country had a special cap. Mr. Lincoln had a magic hat. Didn't even need to write down his ideas. Whenever he needed them he'd lift that hat, and pull the special words right out. Or maybe he used the hat as storage and the snowman had the magic hat. It's pretty much the same thing, you understand."*

**Detective Maymerry forgot** if he went and checked on the cookies once more. But he looked around and saw he was back in the basement, and so he knew they must still need a bit more heat. He rolled the dough thick, and that required extra oven time. Even an elementary baker knew that much. Then Mabel's voice returned, "I'm a poet, didn't you hear?"

*When U chase the B for boool*
*On the hunt in the G for ghoul*
*Fear not deep D for duael*
*Jump through E to the F for foool*

He was lost in a moment until the growing O for Optimist in him understood that he could find the happy ending in every puzzle if only he looked and believed—even gibberish puzzles from another dimension.

*Was Jacob in the fourth dimension? What did it feel like to be 4D? Isn't that tricky ticky time? What was it like for the first creature to breathe—or decide that breath was a thing to need.*

Jacob was always going back to the beginning, even when unnecessary. *Maybe it was Adam and Eve's skull down here.* Then he thought about endings. His thoughts were The River. He was still in it or on it, but now it was all dark blues and greys and blacks of increasing beauty.

He needed someone wise with words to explain it to him. Like Mabel. Like Shakespeare.

Maybe Stephen King was his Shakespeare. In 200 years, if you come back and want to know what Americans were like, what they feared, lived, struggled, loved and hoped then you couldn't do much better than Mr. King.

"Because this King tells stories about the beginnings and endings. His heroes are you and me, in blue chambray shirts, clueless for a while that they are heroic. And they don't become a hero because they seek glory, but because no matter where they go, adventure seeks them."

Jacob rose in righteous clarity in front of the Supreme Court, "For the King shows that the adventure requires It to be an invisible nothing at your back. A horror show. But when you turn around and face it, it can do nothing but shine on you. It's a sleer you see, a tricksy. Not real. It's the Nothing and therefore the Everything."

Then a thought struck him. *HE* was the monster at the end of the book. *Of course.* The thought was Crazy. But he now knew that Crazy was relative. It meant, so long as he wasn't afraid of himself, then he need not be afraid of the monster. Or the end. Because he was the end. And he could always decide what the end was and how it blended perfectly, invisibly, like magic, back into a beginning.

∞

**Jacob awoke in** the basement. *That was close.* He wondered for a moment if he was still asleep. Did he take the cookies out yet?

His mind thought in shapes and numbers and ideas of an unknown mixture. A weaving, perhaps from the Virginia Woolen Mill which thrived in Willouby after the War Between Brothers.

Weaving Ideas is the city's foundation. That and Apples.

*Dont uc, uc,* Jacob thought just perhaps *HE was the KeY. But How could that be? Little 'ol Jacob Maymerry could not bee. Not IT!*

Mabel appeared again in his head. But it wasn't her face it was the name, in letters of smoke.


*MABEL*

*M ABEL* moved apart and re-formed into something new from the same smoke.

*M ABE L*


*M is for Mister.* He knew. *A letter most grand. And L is the Link On which we all stand.*


*Mister ABE L*

*Mr ABE Lincoln*

*At Your Service*


Mabel spoke to Jacob as the letters, "Is this me or you? Our American Hero. The Middle Man. But if it's a Circle, we're all the middle! *Ba Kaw Ba Kaw!*"

Big letters became small letters with dilution of the smoke, some letters grew fainter to become words. Mabel Lincoln spoke, *"You need strands connecting east and west, over the As, to save north and south. Don't Youou See?"*

Mabel was on a roll. Literally, a bun that had just recently been baked. She danced atop it as she spun wisdom, "Pronunciation is important, it says a lot about you, depending on your choice of apple. For example, there's a mountain of difference between Apple At Ya! Or Apple Atch A! You probably won't understand that one, little bean."

"See See, Where Will You Bee. WB for Wheel Burrow. Good try. Wrong. WB is for Wheel Barrell. Nope. Houdini in a Christmas Carol."

Then another silver smokesnake emerged. It slivered over the name still in fireworks. The snake itself was a piece of something already there, like the leg of an X, cut off to leave only a Y. From 4 to 3.

*Mr ABE Lincoln.* The new smoke piece snake slivered next to the R, because S comes after R, and with a single letter, everything changed.

*MrS ABE Lincoln*

A voice cackled, and the big E shrank to a little e to make room for new letters, which also faded, creating new meanings altogether from the very same smoke. A rush of words of lighter smoke emerged from the name of letters.

*Add a Ham to an Abe, and Abraham, Yes I am, Uncle Sam, I am!*
*Father. Abraham. Mary. Magdalamb!*

The smoke letters exploded in Jacob's dream into an entirely different meaning.

*You don't understand, do you? Don't worry, help is on the Way! In the form of Me! The Bee! Eventually you will See! Look for Me! And remember We!*

Perhaps it all opened at the close, the end he needn't fear. His very first friends told him so, he now remembered. The idea was mad, insane, looney. But only to a sane person. For he realized now that for his wildest dreams to ever come true, as a very sane Jacob Maymerry, he first must go a little crazy. After all, the C for Crazy comes right before the D for Dreams. To emerge in the E for Explosion. It was simple ABCs straight from Jacob's very first friends on the Street of Letters.

And little 'ol Jacob Maymerry could never improve upon that. Because he didn't know who he even was. Was he the swirling everything in his head? Was he what scientists would call a ballooning brain bordering on brilliance? Was he *dust in a basement? Exploring deep drains during Echos Call Before All…*

∞

**Jacob felt dream** chaos but also something more. Was it the slightest control? Jacob wondered, perhaps, if he had superpowers. He was dreaming in pure nonsense, but at the very same time he was also awake. At least one part of him understood. He had no idea what the dream meant, but he remembered it while he experienced it. And that wasn't nothing.

*It's a lucid dream, you fool.* The dream part of himself seemed to roll his eyes, but Jacob was still mesmerized by it all. Maybe this was his subconscious trying to talk to his regular conscious. His mind looking at itself. Or perhaps it was a computer hive colony brain processing all the junk and deciding which bits to forget or save for later.

Maybe this was a mind finishing the process of Mabel's update. Jacob imagined that he and Mabel were connected. She was pulling him up, as if on a string, to a land more magical but far more complicated. Mabel must be rising herself. They were Always Connected and forever rose together, leveling up for infinity.

He grew brighter or hotter inside. What was the difference? He needed to expand. Into what, he did not yet know.

*Who Who Who is the skull?*

That made Jacob think of the movie with the skull of an old woman rocking in the attic. It was symbolism or something. But what wasn't a symbol? That's what letters were. He was trapped. It was symbols all the way down and there was nothing he could do about it. He wondered if one could drown in the deep deep sea, covered in Ss. Ss for SymbolS

What a silly think, one part of Jacob thought to the others. Until a more poetic part took control and explained that Jacob Maymerry was a fool. A consistent fool. Down deep in the basement, he also remembered that he was an Optimist. A Consistent Optimist.

He knew *there is no A without  D, which is mere smoke so that there can be an E. After all, what is Red Without Blue? Up without Down? The idea of the other side must be felt so that the real side could be real.* Each part of Jacob better understood itself.

His mind got so foggy, that he forgot which part was asking questions and which was being questioned. Perhaps he could pick which version of himself to follow and hope for the best.

Jacob immediately thought of the Choose Your Own Adventure books he checked out from the school library. Then the Optimist in him remembered that he did once survive to the end of Oregon Trail, floating down the river, avoiding the rocks atop a log, on a second generation Apple computer in the 3rd grade library.

Jacob must be dreaming, though he still felt like he was sitting in the basement. How strange.

Another call from Colorado. He ignored it. *Ring a Ding Ding. Ring a Ding Ding. Tick Tick. Boom. Ooh. Aah. Ding Ding Ding. Boom.*

**It was then** that Jacob drifted from one place to a brand new one. Novel images flashed from neuron to neuron inside his brain, leaping across guardrails into different lanes, encased by a skull now resting against the boulder attached to the core of the earth as the world's first head stone.

He once read that those in a trance, on rainbow pills, or with superpowers report woven ideas and mixed up senses. Sounds have color. Smells can be heard. Gasses are seen as shapes. At least that's what Jacob thought in his increasingly fantastical mind. Before all was color, he saw the letters CO drifting toward him in the black, like once invisible smoke rings now exposed. His kaleidoscope mind thought—*Only one O is Poison to People*—*Are you kidding me?*

The rings faded and all was beautiful white except for a small weight on his chest and a wet sandpaper licking on his cheek. It must be Eleanor saying goodbye or good luck.

Answers came to him and he wondered if the cat beamed them into his head as a final parting gift for his journey. Like coins placed upon the eyes of the departed that they might never spend. Just in Case!

*What do you remember first? You need only say the magic words. Abra Cadabra! Open Sesame! The answers you seek are in U for You! The S Street is the Hood. Next to Mr. R with the Cardigans, and he's a Neighbor. The voice of your origin story is A Mother of a sort. Because what else could it ever be?*

He remembered that first sound. But what was a sound except for a certain kind of feeling. He had no letters or numbers for that feeling except one that jumped to mind, the tricksy E, or maybe it was L for Love or Logos. Or maybe all three.

*A feeling. It. It was a Thing. A Pro Noun. Until a Noun became A Name. The first name he remembered was that tricksy e. The E for everything. Eros. L for Love It's interchangeable, don't you see? It's all Greek to me and Joey C. EL, Eleven, One One, tricksy tricksy. OOee.*

As his mind explored the new grooves, he saw the other skull across the dirt. Still there. Smiling at him. Jacob was not that head after all. *Two skulls down here now?* That smile was his first friend in Willouby. Welcoming him to Whatever Comes Next.

# Saturday - Sunday

## Chapter 21

**Eleanor Roosevelt greeted** him on the shore of the river in the Land of Lost Letters. *Because who else could?*

Jacob thought this from nowhere. He was nothing and no one except thoughts. But thoughts aren't nothing, and so he thought perhaps he wasn't dead. *If he was dead, who was noticing all of this?*

Eleanor was a large calico cat on hind legs pushing a wheelchair. Jacob realized, with a twist, that he was in the wheelchair, in a white gown, no slippers. They were headed toward a large flashing red sign: ER! ER! ER!

*That's a me!*

The Cat spoke Mews of Meaning. But they required tuning, "Moew… meoew…mewo moew meow…mew mew…mew!"

Jacob had forgotten that he was a Jacob, but somehow, from somewhere, knew Eleanor's mews meant, "When you think it's 2 it's 3. When you think it's 3, it's 4. And when you know it's 4, they all pick sides and you're back where you started before."

What was once a Jacob thought, *Not helpful kitty.*

"Meow Meow Mews mews Mews…" He heard her clear, "But for now, it's 2. You and Me. And three others we'll greet one by one. Each more oblivious, obvious, and annoying than the last." Jacob tried to roll his eyes at what he heard but he had none. He was sound.

Eleanor spoke faster, as if remembering she did not want to do this at all and was missing something far more important anywhere else, "Meeeeeew, meow, meeeow, mew mew mew."

"Also, a swarm of wild bees will chase you the entire time."

*I'm sorry, what?*

He felt prickles all over no body but Eleanor mewed on, "Or is it hornets? Do not be alarmed. You are on the pure bliss ride. Not the double black diamond."

The calico whisker face scrunched up while reading instructions like an employee who had already given notice. "Is it pure bliss? I think, perhaps, mew mew. It doesn't matter anyway. It all reaches the same conclusion."

And then he noticed that he Saw. Both in front and behind. He wondered if this is what it was like if he had 4 eyes—like an insect.

"Mew!"

He knew it meant "Pay attention!"

"Mew Mew Mew!"

"Out of that chair you lunatic, and into The River!"

For the first time since his arrival, Eleanor showed real interest, bordering on glee, as she tipped the man out of the wheelchair and into a majestic roaring stream of fizzing white and blue swirls.

He panic sank deep into dark cerulean but then rose in a refreshing exhale out of the water, into a morning dew sky with the redding lines of a rising sun on the horizon. He landed atop a cushioned canoe, drifting along paint thick water beneath him. The shore was a comforting forest of dark greens, browns, and earth yellows. Eleanor Roosevelt, the Guide of a Calico Cat, sat behind him. She was supposed to be steering but probably wasn't. He didn't dare look back to check.

∞

# The What Comes Nest

The swarm of wild bees arrived first. He felt fuzzy warmth across something. Not stings, the opposite—perhaps rooster bumps of gratitude that they were bees and not hornets.

Surprisingly, they were literal Bs. The Letters. Flat side down. Little b head and bigger B body. Yellow and black kidney bean Bs.

The swarm was 7 Bs. Then they split in two, a BBBB and a BBB.

The quadruple B, Clearly in Charge, spoke first in a heavenly but commanding hum, "Is this a wee D? It's not a Dream, iz itz? Dreams are Cheatz, so not allowed here. Not Delusionalz. No sir E. Notz the right D. It'z certainzzly no A. Couldn't possiblee B."

The BBBB that was four Bs narrowed his eyes as if to look closer at something. "Is it a bebe? A bb? Babies are sometimezzz allowed herezz, depending on one'zz perspectivez, I suppoze. BeeBBs, pleazzze report all you've discovered of this specimenzz before launch."

The BBB gave a full report. "These creatures are candy coated, shell of an exterior, delicious inside." His superior seemed pleased. "Go on."

The yellow kidney bean BBB blushed a hue orange and continued, eager to explain everything he had uncovered in a musical hum trained in all sounds foreign and domestic, "All they show you is this shell, you have to break the skin to see inside. And so from the outside, they are mostly just…" the BBB searched his trained bbb brain for the right words, "flubbing around."

BBB's figure disappeared into a mist of two wooden shapes. He knew, somehow, from someplace, that they were two men, twins, perhaps man-netwins. No no, not quite. They were not twins only of body but also mind and most absolutely soul. The figures transformed into two playdoh humans of delicately spun dark yellow shadows upon the sky.

The figures moved and the BBB voice explained from nowhere, "They do a lot of this." He made both shapes a straight line. "Then they get up and do this—sit sit sit sit." He started moving tiny ends to the figures. "Then they do this with these little things—*type type type*."

The BBB continued, "They stare at twittering boxes of various sizes. And sometimes do a little of this random mishmash." The mannequins shook in either a dance or epileptic fit. "Then they start over. Most of the in between is running here and there for this and that, no discernible reason from most angles."

The Boss said from somewhere, "Interesting."

The BBB wasn't finished, "But they aren't all like this. The small ones are most powerful, they have the sight. They understand perspective. They lose it, though sometimes gain it again. When in tune, they don't move within the world—the world moves around them."

Boss's commanding hum voice came back and he seemed to wink as he spoke, "Oh there was a C herezz after allz. The Catz brought him. Those Crafty Critterzzz. They are always doing this. Little a following the C chasing nothing but immediately into D. The Cellar Door as old as time. Too latezz, I sup-posez. The ride is already moving. Put them throughzzz. Goood luckzzz. U Neeeedzzzz ITzzzzz."

Through nothing they went until they arrived back on the canoe that he hadn't realized he'd left. It floated without anyone paddling at all. He knew this without looking because he knew, somehow, from somewhere, that Elea-nor Roosevelt would not dare stoop to such absurdity as paddling.

The canoe wove through a now rainbow thick sea of paint water. It swished and globbed like a multi-pack of jello baked into an ever-changing fundip. Along the shore of this kaleidoscope rose a party. The canoe stopped, and a large wooden table set for 13 sprung vividly from the clay earth along the bank—the same mysterious material as the mannetwins.

*A nottee coffee party*, how scandalous. *Or maybe even a knotty gala.* Voices rose from somewhere beyond the bushes. *The guests arriving?* He felt rustling, but he could not make out any forms yet.

∞

# Visitor #1
# The Host Family

As usual, Jacob was wrong from the start. It was not a party but a supper. And those were not guests arriving. It was the catering family at the B&B getting ready for the feast. He overheard the conversation.

"Who's the head today?" Voice #1 asked. A woman.

"It's Luke." Voice #2 said. This was a young boy's voice. Jacob knew this, but he knew nothing else.

At least Jacob had an answer to his head question, even if he didn't remember the question. *It is Luke. The answer is Luke.* But then an even younger boy, Voice #3 said, "Luuuuke, I am your mother." And Jacob felt lost again, back where he started. *Pure chaos.*

"It's tradition. Only one at a time at the head of the table. We only have the one fancy chair after all. But I can't remember whose turn." Jacob knew Voice #1 was a mother enjoying her children's banter but pretending otherwise. "It's not Luke. It's not him. Definitely not. Who is left? We are missing One. He's the entire key. Is it a J?"

Mother continued, "Who was the missing fourth?"

"The fourth? Are you talking about the J from the 4th D?" Older boy seemed genuinely curious. "Oh wait. He's the 4th. What was his name again?" He spoke faster as if inching toward a truth he knew but couldn't pronounce, "He wrote the book at the end, right? He got closest."

Younger Boy jumped in, "Are you talking about the M&Ms. I love them.

Those are the only two I know."

"It's not them. It's the 4th, she told you." Older Boy was trying to get on his mother's good side.

"And I told you that Matt and Mark are very nice friends who like to tell stories." Younger Boy loved adults who entertained him.

"No, she already guessed it's one of the Js." The Older Boy was getting annoyed both at himself and his little brother.

"You don't even know. You're just guessing. If it's not an M then it must be what's next, the N." Little brother did not fool easy. "Is it Nicholas? He goes every year."

"It's not Nick. It can't be him, because he's only nearly headless. It was a botch job," Mother explained.

"Oh that's unfortunate, because the man is a saint." Old Boy seemed to be growing older during the conversation.

"Then what comes next? The O." Younger boy seemed to fast forward. Or the P. It's Paul, right? He lost his head too."

"Hardy har har," Mother said with a smile. *Her clever little boys.* Jacob saw only shadows of this, but he knew.

"No. It's definitely not that P!" Older brother wanted to impress his sibling.

"They were all beheaded? What a coincidence!"

The first born flexed his knowledge as budding authority. "This one isn't his. Get your mind out of the dirt. You're getting it all twisted and causing mass confusion. Don't be a fool!"

Mother jumped back in, "The word fool isn't helpful, regardless of whose head it refers to. I think it's a J."

"Jays? The birds? Oh you mean the Hooks, the J." Youngest boy figured it out.

Mother was proud. "That's right. He wrote the book, after all, and is a man of letters. But I don't remember exactly which one. And numbers. The 4th!"

Mama smiled and said, "Forget it. It doesn't matter yet anyway. I'm acting a fool too. It's April. The 4th only matters once July comes around again."

"What about Bartholomew?" the youngest voice snickered. "That's a big long B."

"Are you throwing names out now? Get your head in the game. I'm getting tired of all this. Let's solve it already!"

Jacob did not know who said this because he drifted, and the kitty was back.

*And then he noticed a difference. A something. He was a J. That he knew. And he remembered another difference, a cub, wee bebe, he could see. A Jay cub, he could be.*

∞

# Someone Arrives

With a flash of nothing, Jacob was in the canoe, but now he was in the rear seat and Eleanor Roosevelt was in front. She faced backwards, at him, a human-sized cat staring at Jacob. The cat ignored all practicalities and let the river steer them blindly. She mocked applause with cat paws that never fully touched and therefore didn't make a sound. The look on her calico face was that of a carny worker watching as guests kept coming to the tilt-a-whirl. *These humans never cease to amaze.* "Mew mew meeew. Meew. Mew mew…"

He understood the Mews meaning, "You are a man of letters. I am letters. We all are letters, somewhere, sometimes, to someone. C is for Cat. Calico. Captain. Chief. Capitol. See?"

"Constant. Center. Constitution. You understand C." Eleanor coughed up something all tangled but Jacob did not see.

She went on in half a flash but this time the Mews were of a different pitch, more a cackle. "Me. Mew. MeMeMeMeeeew…"

The cat was not looking at him, but gazed off at the moon visible in the daydream of the rainbow river next to a melted yellow sun on the opposite side of the sky. Eleanor mewed the high cackle mew and Jacob understood fear. Because he could not decipher Eleanor this time. He heard only Mews. Mews all the way down, and it terrified him. For growing moments he feared he might forever live in the land of gibberish Mews.

"Me. Mew. MeMeMeMeeeew…"

But when he needed it, someone arrived. He noticed a speck of a difference in the distance, and realized bees were coming again. Two of them, but arranged as one BB.

The BB arrived, yellow and black kidney bean Bs. "Sorry about that, minor glitch." He stared at him, "You're D, right? D for Dead? Because you can't be D for Dream. Not here anyway."

The BB looked down a bee nose at him to inspect and Jacob prickled. But then he felt wind, a cooling breeze across whatever he must be. The wind reached the BB, and it spun as if hung by an invisible string—a twirling chime decoration. He twisted 180 degrees and faced the other way, but still a BB.

But Jacob knew, somehow, that this was a totally different BB. While the first spoke with the confidence of a train conductor, this one whispered with the secret information of an experienced traveler. The whispering BB said, "Shhh, don't tell them who you are."

Another spin in the wind and the conductor returned. "Yes, yes. D for Dead. Must be. Otherwise, how would you even be here." Spin.

"Shhh, don't tell. Who knows what they'll do if they find out." Spin.

"D for Doubt? Doesn't matter. Not here. No how. No Deal!" Spin.

"Quiet. Do. Not. Tell them. The Big Bad B, BBB, said so specifically. Do not, Do Not, Don't UC. The Big Bad Bee, With Big Buddha Bell E, Says Specifically. Under the B Tree. See. Do Not Talk about the G, next to the Nothing, Near the D. Because then he becomes a Killer B. And they aren't Fun E. Don't You See? Don't UC!" Spin.

Without another word the BB buzzed straight up into the velvet blue sky, as if the string was pulled—both the commanding and whispering versions were heard no longer. Jacob was left in the canoe again—Eleanor still staring up at the moon next to the sun in deep meditation.

He knew she was not actually with him. He was alone.

∞

**Until he noticed** that he wasn't. Because a jellybean buzzed near him, a plump sunshine yellow. As he looked close he saw it was also the letter b. Kind of.

Though he had yet to say a word to him, he felt like this jellybean was a lifesaver. A friend. From somehow, somewhere.

His new companion spoke, "It's a me, the bb!"

"I'm the baby bee. A buzzing bee. Don't UC? Everyone knows about Double A, but so few remember double me." The bb buzzed the appropriate distance from Jacob's eyes and it was then he saw the bb smile. The brightness exploded from tiny b teef, entered his own eyes, and Jacob felt a feeling he couldn't yet understand.

The bb spoke as if they had always been bestest buddies, "See in real kindergarten, they explain it all out. They show, don't you see, even if you don't understand."

The bb giggled a *hehehe* and then buzzed himself next to Jacob's ear for something special. "Wanna know a secret? I found a book, don't you see? don't u c! A Book! With the bittiest bee! Me!"

The bb never asked Jacob to explain or understand or decide. He just kept being a bb.

"Me!" The bb gleamed a silver red glow that Jacob knew was pride. It was a speck of brightness, an ember in the otherwise ocean blue sky. But he knew from inside the bb's eyes, that the bitty bee was shining like a star. "I'll show you, I'll show you. It's most fun to share. But keep this secret, the Book just for We! A Book! For the bittiest bee, Me!"

Jacob knew from a place most deep that the bb was a friend, finally, someone he should keep. The bb spoke, as if reading his mind, "Here he comes. You won't see me, but I'll be here."

He flew close as if giving a final secret message, "I'll be here, hiding right behind your ear."

And with that he did not see or hear the bb, though he suspected, and hoped, and felt most deep, that the bb had not left him.

∞

# Visitor #2
# The M.L.C.C.

The Calico Captain awoke with a startle, a napping employee dealing with utter catastrophe by pretending the chaos was her going away party. "Mew. Meeeew. Mew. Mew mew mew mew."

"What a treat, at this glorious hour, we welcome One of such distinguished and volumewnous letters. So many letters. And other things perhaps.

A creature of mystery, eloquence, and fearsome knowledge."

Jacob grew new feelings. C for Courage. He thought he understood Eleanor crystal clear and got so bold as to cast a thought to the nothing. "Is he the Count? He sings, right?"

**BOOM!** The Creature arrived as darkness within darkness. But then lightened into a grey of maybe something. A swirl of purple, white, the slightest hint of green. His shape took form in front of the canoe, or perhaps above. It could have been the shore, or it might've been all three. If there was a canoe anymore. Because Jacob now saw darkness and the growing shape of the Creature. Letters and Words and Strings began forming with the colors, and he knew they were both creating the Creature and Explaining him at the same time.

Jacob was confused and shaking and ever so small.

"Psssst. It's OK. This is the scariest part. Just Be and you will C that it's a simple tricksy," his friend whispered in his ear when he needed to hear it.

The Creature's misty lights of white, grey, purple, and greens grew in a feathery sort of huff. The Creature expanded, a cap appeared on a large bird head, arms of wings. A beak, perhaps. But the colors remained a threading, and Jacob was never sure what he really saw.

The Count spoke in an accent of distringuished industry, efficiency, and Capitol I Information, "I am not a Count! Like everything I was the nothing. The O. I twisted in two—OO—and now last until infinity. Then I found the Bees and became the Boo, but this was all before you. After that I bumped into three straight lines and was the Book. But only until squiggles returned, when I sprang into the Brook that brought you here. But yes, I also sing."

*Silence.*
*More Silence.*

Jacob felt terror, but was rescued, for the first time, by Eleanor Roosevelt. As if finding her place on an old script at the wrong time, the Cat broke the silence with beautiful bored ridicule, "Mew mew mew…"

"What did you expect, Mr. Letters? He's still learning to understand. Please forgive him. Mew mew mew. This is not his first language. Mew mew.

I don't think he even speaks it at all. It's probably gibberish to him. Mew mew mew mew mew. But go on anyway. Wouldn't want to hold you up from your performance."

Mr. Letters the Creature Count appeared in mid-Mew, leading to confusion in Jacob's senses, "But I hide out sometimes, to learn. See. Let me explain it like this, if you don't understand that way. You take the E, the tricksiest number. The 1 plus a 3. Tie it all together in a strong colony. And with enough force you topple it over onto its side, and it bends into M with sharp points. Don't U C? Do you see? Those rocky tips need down to be ground. Back down. To the littlest m. And that's where you create Intersections."

"And with those. With even a single I," the Count looked nowhere as if remembering an old lesson, "Well with those, much IS to be had. Immovable Spots. Impossible Solutions. Immediate Strength."

The Count leaned in for a whisper for the first and Jacob suspected only time, "But a clue for you. To find the IS, first cut the IS knot!"

∞

**Jacob's head spun,** *until he remembered his friend.*

bb appeared around a corner. "He's a Scary C, isn't he? Sometimes, see, the Creature can bee tricksy. To learn twists you must twix, right?" The bb didn't listen to see if Jacob understood.

Then little bb buzzed closer to the ear for a whisper, "See a tricksy about me, is that I'm also a c, and b, just like you! But I'm really BB, eventualE. So don't say you can't see, tell my secret, to no one but you and to me!"

The Count returned with a hazy harrumph of silvery purple and green swirls around his tangly owl feather arms. His cap of knowledge seemed askew, but he was busy engaged in a favorite pastime of pointing out flaws.

"Shouldn't you bee writing this down? Careful the doubles, like BB, like me. They're tricksy you see. Like GG is special. Golden, they say. And don't get me started on triples, oh dear."

Jacob realized now that Mr. Letters the Creature Count was for always and evermore, and so there was no forward and backward or up and down with his wisdom and wit. But all knowledge without order is too hard to grab long enough to jam into one's head. Mr. Letters continued his lessons from somewhere without translation, and Jacob heard only a mumbling that seemed like information from another dimension.

During his confusion, a whisper from his friend, hiding behind an ear. "This Book is un bee leev able. So neat. So cool. Do you know what I found?"

He zipped a buzz around in a full circumnavigation of Jacob's head. Then another. After his third orbit, bb asked, "You wanna know something cool? Or something warm? You wanna know where I found the Book?" He laughed a *Hehehe*. Then he chirped on with a bb glee, "It was in the urns, the Boo urns, in the 6th Level! I found it way up there! Me! Little bb!"

bb did not care for a response, he never did. Instead he started reading mid-way through some mystery page of the Book found on the 6th Level.

*"S is for smithers sure swivels slinky sleers! And sings and secures and survives swimmingly!*

*It ropes in the A, and brings it to a Soul. To be combined in a twist, like red onto A Pole.*

*That's AP, don't you know, see to see! Atlantic to Pacific, the connection, finally!*

*Advanced Placement, Perfect Attendance, It works with all your names. And Both, Both And, ABBA, All the Same."*

bb stopped to take a bitty bee breath before diving back in as if mezmer-mized.

*"SuperPowers, they say, when you combine the A and the P. And all great Power, it's been heard, starts with the bittiest b."*

bb gazed at the book while a breeze blew a few pages ahead. He continued reading as if he hadn't missed a beat.

*"W is Whimsical! It's WEeeeSential. You see? It's Will and it's Wont. It's Wisdom! It's Waltz and Whit and Wondrous Whoopies! Keep W around, that's for sure. If you spin them around and ground them down, they are mothers, merry men, mischief makers, mumbling mightily!"*

bb buzzed near a nose and seemed to calm down. "Sorry, I get overexcited sometimes. You won't understand any of that. So don't worry about it." He continued but now spoke with the wisdom of someone who had already read this page of the Book.

*"Be careful the S, it's a tricksy, some say. But I found something secret in the book*

*about StrayS.*

*S is a Cloak, Swaying Strong and Seen. Be Kind to the S, you don't know where She's Been."*

The bb inflated two sizes in helium pride at his new knowledge. But Jacob saw something behind the hazel bb eyes that betrayed a secret. Or deep worry. "So careful with S, I guess is the thing. Careful with all of them, each of them precious, like a ring."

∞

**Jacob wanted to** contemplate the wisdom from his little friend, but he couldn't. Because the Count returned mid-sentence as if he had never left. "Understanding your ABCs is most important. Don't you now see? That's how you learn all the very things that you can be. Like Apples Best Crisp. Aunts Be Crazy. Admire Beautiful Creatures. There are so many to discover little ones, sometimes I envy you."

Mr. Letters the Creature Count looked at a memory in a corner. He might have smiled across a static sunset orange beak.

"Consider the M. A Magical Mysterium, that decides where you start, and explains where you end. It's Make and it's Model. It's what U call Meaning. You dance atop the D for Decide through the E that's an L. Eros. And that, my darlings, is for U to go Find! Use your Mind! And Your Is and your Ps and your Cs and your Gs!"

"And the M is a Mystic, for it brings you to A. Or perhaps it brings A to you, which is a Miraculous thing to do." Mr. Letters powered down for less than an instant before awakening with the faintest of grey in his swirling twine colors of deepest intellect.

"N is Narrow to those with cylinder eyes. It's confused for the Nothing, but that's simply white lies. Because it's often an E for Everything or an A for All Natural, you See. Numbers, it be. Nicholas with an S, but Nothing, very rarely." The Count went all grey for a flicker as if knowing it was losing itself.

"Lucky Ducky you are, ended up here, in the ER. The exact place you need to be. For it is here where the concoction is brewed. For you need the E plus the R to burst forth into brightness that reaches the mountaintop. Don't you see? Perhaps not at all, but I'll explain anyway, because after all, this is mostly for me, not you."

The Creature seemed to wink repeatedly across his whole body, which might have been his laugh.

"R is for Rationality. Quite prudent, no doubt. But alone, quite twisty and tighty, too stout. But, Ah, comes the tricksy, the E, can't you see? E for Empiricism Exercise Experience! What you feel, what you are, what you must! What you see, what you be, what you lust! Mix the E and the R, with a little H for Honesty, and the places you'll go, the faces you'll be, why it makes one feel StupendouSly!"

*Silence.* The Creature Count stared at the growing memory with utter delight. *More Silence.*

Finally, Mr. L the CC spoke with a deepening tenor in his voice, building up to the highlight of this entire ceremony. "It is now time for my song. I sing, because I See."

He sang.

∞

# Mister Letters the Creature Count Sings
## He Sang, Because that which must B is E:

*A is for you, B is for me, C is everything, all that you see.*
*D is for Dead, but not for any of we.*
*Oh say can't you see, that's why I carry the Bee.*

*E is a tricksy, it's one and a three.*
*It's a safe place, some say, to hop over the D.*

*But careful with E, it's 1 then a 3.*
*It bounces high over 2, Rebels against D all for U.*
*And hides out, all the while, as a B.*

*Keep the D under the heap.*
*Where the darkest things creep.*
*And the C is most deep.*

*We hide the scrolls,*
*to protect all souls,*

*until everyone's ready,*
*able to reap.*

*Now that's just how it starts, Oh how much more 2 C*
*When you are finally able, Free 2 just B.*

*You can explore all there is, from the A to the Z,*
*When you're finally ready, and want all 2 B.*

*Understand what is A, and what is not, like the R*
*Because U R the A, and it won't take you far.*

*But you're also the B and the C and the Z.*
*And will always, forevermore, Be all you can B.*

*So maybe, perhaps, now that I'm plotting this out*
*You couldn't be careful.*
*You mustn't look out.*

*Because U can only B and fully know C,*
*Once A sings with B about C near the D.*

*So maybe, perhaps, now that I'm seeing this through*
*There isn't anything, at all, you could possibly do.*

*Smile big. Laugh loud. Become the greatest of Whos.*
*And Buzz like a B, Finding All of the Yous.*

*But maybe, perhaps, after that fun is done,*
*U remember those left behind,*
*Perhaps bring back the Sun.*

*Start with the S, who circles the Drain,*
*who Slinks with the D men and takes all the pain.*

*She's also the Sand that roughs up the Skin,*
*That Scrapes the Survivors, that bathes them in Sin.*

*She's also the Sand that Sits on the Shore,*
*So the Sun can Shine where it hasn't before.*

*High atop that Sand, her work never done,*
*She Saves everything, with the raise of the Sun.*

*She Straddles the Oceans, Strong colossus Sea to Sea,*
*She Splits in two at nothing, Sending SOS to the bee.*

*She brought you here, Say now don't you SeeS?*
*U only arrived as A, after traveling thru beeS.*

*So bring S along, if you can, if She's Seen,*
*Because U Saved the A and she's best when between.*

## Silence

The Creature cleared his throat, "*Because U. Saved the A. and she's best. when between.*"

Another throat clear. The Count spoke with frumpish delight at catching fools in the act, "The traditional refrain is, 'That which must B is the kEy.' But I suppose you delinquent kindergartners could not be expected to know that."

He continued. "Repeat after me, 'That which must B is the KeY.'"

*Jacob remembered he was Jacob. A J.* And hoped he repeated after the Count, though he didn't know if he did. The Count went on anyway, "Don't you dare say Francis Scott is the Key. That 'ol yarn doesn't jolt me even a tittle. The entirely wrong FS."

He narrowed owl eyes at him, "Little ones, this is all theoretical for you. Corralling Ss is not something you learn until at least the 6th level. Do not let me catch you Swimming in the D for Deep fishing SoulS. Far too RiSky BuS-SinESS. No EggceptionS!"

"So slink on that little ones," the Count was heard to say, "And maybe 1 Day. Even U 2 will find yourself on the Mountaintop. Harrumph!"

*Mr. Letters the Creature Count lifted wings of a blurry sort, and with a final frumpy Rumphumph, flew away into nothing.*

∞

**Jacob felt the** nothing like a coat of heavy black wool. What a weighted burden of nothing for nobody and nowhere. He waited for the cat to return. She always returned. Even if she was useless, she was there. But there was no body but himself, a dull sense of the coat becoming his everything for everywhere, and the fear of being always a nothing.

Until a whisper between invisible teef, "Careful the I. And the E for Eye. Sometimes the A and the I equals the e. It's a tricksy. Remember, U decide right. U decide real. You decide the lovely, the happy, what you feel."

Jacob did not understand his friend bb's message. But he felt bb's fear as the bittiest bee squeaked a warning before hiding back deep deep behind an ear, "They're coming for us."

∞

# Visitor #3:
# The Substitute Teachers

**Be wary crooked** *smiles on familiar faces.* Jacob thought this from somewhere and wondered if his little friend could send him messages from inside. He felt hope.

A friend was what he needed as a new swarm, the largest beetallion yet, approached with the vigor of ESTCBs.

Extra Special Top Cadet Bees arrived with overwhelming force before breaking into a mass contingent of BBs, BBBs, and other arrangements beyond Jacob's understanding.

Spokesbee, a BB, emerged wearing a perfectly tailored green uniform of a keebler size atop a plump yellow and black B body, "I am BB, as if you didn't know."

The BB raised a chin like one elected to this position for a reason, "Of course, I'm here to help. You must know that. Being D here. You are D right?"

His BB chin dropped a bit as if appraising Jacob for the first time.

The BB flew left and right in a pace, "But this is only for certain Ds. Dreams always brings Cs. And Cs are cheats. Sometimes they even steal Cheat Codes. Those fools don't realize that CCs are no good unless you press the buttons. But still they steal."

The BB sighed and shook his head as if willing himself not to think about that unpleasantness and instead focus on the smiling soul in front of him.

A sharp wind blew the BB, he spun 180 degrees, and then spoke again with more razzle, "Shouldn't trust dreamszzzz. Dreamzzz are surface. They goingzz behindz the curtainz to the wizzard using wordzzzzzz. Wordzz to say what happenzz. A shortcutzz. But itzzz a trixzy. Because where iz shortzcutz, if there is no dezzztinationz? And how to have dezzztinationz before first knowing what is not dezztinationz?"

Another spin and an entirely new Spokesbee continued with enunciation, "Dreams are where the leftovers live. The dark matter. All the parts that don't fit and can't be seen until later. The backstage, where the mystery disappears, when the friends have solved the case, and the show is over. Unless you understand, it looks like chaos, and if you wander there before you know, IT becomes the monster."

**Somehow without his** noticing, during this very speech, the BB merged with two others to become a BBBB of full authority and height. It seemed to speak at times both as a single unit and as individual pieces, "Dreamzzzz are to Eeeee Zzzzz. So they doezzzn't work. Twooozz not threeeezzz izzzz badzzz."

The BBBB spoke with accents of a musical variety that twinkled and grew into something of a jazz, "Still work to do I see. Such a struggle with theeeez onezz. They don't know when they can't see. And when they look they don't see. But when they finally see, they forget. OOoo EEEeee OOOooo"

The BBBB was a Boss but also something more. The BBBB seemed a chorus of voices using their time near the bullhorn to shout advice, "You work too hard, because the thing you call work is toward nothing. Beee Laaazeee. Don't write three sentences when 1 equals 3. Everyone will catch up. It's not your fault they can't understand. And never forget that two out of three ain't bad."

Eventually the BBBB settled into a clear command, and the remaining speckled colony of Bs became a yellow and black swaying sea around a Colosseum. The BBBB rose up to a single Tower of Bs with a clear riddling buzz, "You get two questions, probably not three, and definitely not four."

The questions were asked though Jacob didn't know how.

"Who are you?"
"I am the B. And am exploring the C."
"Who am I?"
"You are the A. And are looking for me."
The BBBB became a Cheshire grin. "Fine. I am most generous. You get a third question."
Jacob felt as if someone spoke on his behalf, "You speak in riddles."
"Please answer in the form of a question. Thank you. Try again."
"Why do you speak in riddles?"
"Because the answer to your question is a riddle." The bee continued, "I give you what you ask for, but then you say it's not what you want. So I take it back and give everything else. But then you ask only about what is missing."
*I don't understand.*
"I insist that you answer every answer in the form of a question! Do you think you can think without me knowing?"
*What?*
"Yes, exactly." The bee grew exasperated. "Fine, have all the questions you Desire. Ask me What and Why to the bottom of everything. Then I can tell you the truth. But you couldn't understand."

The BBBB towered higher, above Jacob and also around him, as if desperately trying everything to help him understand, "Don't act surprised. You don't understand anything. Do you even understand how you are understanding this right now? Is this all a swirl in your head of nothing? Don't you see, that's why you need not worry about anything. Don't worry that you don't understand this. Don't worry that you're scared. I could tell you the truth now, but you wouldn't know what it was. I may say that you are in control of everything. But you wouldn't believe. I could tell you that there are no mistakes. But you'd roll your eyes. I might reveal that you are the One. But you'd shrink and call me a snake. But I'm really just a spider, like you. Wearing a bee suit. So I tell stories.

Because twist and twist and twist is how you learn."

A breeze blew and the BBBB broke again into a string of individual Bs, each buzzing a volley of questions and answers in a game of conversation.

"You are A, I am the B, C is for carpenter."

"No it is not. Common mistake. Carpenter bees are dangerous. You are *exploring the C. You are the B. B is for Bumble.*"

"I sea you scrunch your face with fear. Silly little one, I already said it thrice, you don't know enough to worry. You'll know all at the end, of course. Not because you deserve it, but because there is no other way it could ever bee."

"Got any more of those SiGs?"

"So it Goes. So it Goes. No SiGs. No."

The wind picked up and a breeze became a gust became an onslaught of motion in the air. Spin, spin, spin. Turn, Turn, Turn. Twist. Turn. Spin. Jacob felt nausea and felt like throwing up, though he wasn't sure what that would be or where it would come from or what it would do or where it would go.

The wind finally settled.

"Now Beeeeee gonezz and take your riddle with you. Solve your riddle. It's what you think you want for nowzz." Spin

"I'll even give you a See, a Clue. It's all three answers you need to win. You want the WHO, you think you know WHERE, the game is the HOW, and I really don't care. But you mostly need WHYs, so it goes…"

Just at the moment he was most paying attention, all the Bs dissipated in a mass extinction, a fizzle of dying embers in the distance. Except one. A single B looped around as the others vanished. Until, with a pointy huff, it charged back at him! *Flying fast!* **Ready to sting!**

But then the B twisted around with the skill of a most maverick fighter pilot, 180 degrees, and a new Bee spoke with a distinctly Middle American accent, "Sorry about him. I leave you with a Bard's tale. It's everything and nothing. It's the B song. From the other side of the D. To get the full effect, it must be sung at the right tune. Can you do that yet? If not it might be flat words on paper floating in the nowhere of your head. But I've included the hidden verse, in case you don't notice, and finally discover you've been singing the whole time."

Jacob listened. The Back of the emBroidery Bee cleared his throat and belted with unmitigated glee:

∞

# An UnderSide of the B Song
## Performed by the C after the D
## formerly known as Embroider E

You will go through all the motions,
like a cork upon the see,
You will twist and twist and twist,
and think that A is B is C.

You will know that this is tricksy,
but is all in great big fun,
Then forget and huff and puff and say,
"that trick's already been done!"

You will wander through the snowcaps,
with all eyes out for the bumblers,
Eureka! You have found the twist:
1 and 1 and 1 is 4 numbers!

Tricksy Tricksy. Oh so Tricksy.
Tricksy bitty bee.
Tricksy Tricksy. Oh so Tricksy.
Tricksy bumble bee.

But then a kernel in your center grows,
and pops in two a bright balloon,
And you wonder if the twist you found
was found much far too soon.

But maybe not, you dare to think,
it's not too soon at all.

*It's quite the mind, you have right there,*
*to rise up to the call.*

*You scour all that is,*
*collecting A and B and C.*
*Then you weave it all together.*
*It's a perfect tapestry.*

*Eureka! It fits. Proof that you were right there all along.*
*So you go to work. Think it down. Craft this very song.*

*And with your words, I drift away, and you miss my final plea.*
*Laugh with me, as you see, what we do is what always must be.*

*Tricksy Tricksy. Oh so Tricksy.*
*Tricksy bitty bee.*
*Tricksy Tricksy. Oh so Tricksy.*
*Tricksy bumble me.*

*So you write the twist, and polish up,*
*the tricksy that you found.*
*You become the twist itself, you see,*
*what makes it all spin round.*

*For everything is twist, and thread,*
*and everything is trick.*
*And everything you see, and bee,*
*must always have a prick.*

*But the thorn is all allusion,*
*that hides just who you are.*
*It hides it up until the time,*
*of the rising yellow star.*

*That's mourning, when you finally see,*

*and again know what to do.*
*Surprise! The twist, forever always,*
*is you and you and you!*

*Tricksy Tricksy. Oh so Tricksy.*
*Tricksy bitty bee.*
*Tricksy Tricksy. Oh so Tricksy.*
*Tricksy little me.*

*It tears the eye. It breaks at two.*
*From I to we. From us to you.*

*And once the turns and tricks unwind,*
*When One remembers where It's from.*
*A jumps over the D once more!*
*Hallelujah!*
*E! Pluribus Unum!*

*Tricksy Tricksy. Oh so Tricksy.*
*Tricksy bitty bee.*
*Tricksy Tricksy. Oh so Tricksy.*
*Tricksy mini me.*

*Tricksy Tricksy. Oh so Tricksy.*
*Tricksy bitty bee.*
*Tricksy Tricksy. Oh so Tricksy.*
*Tricksy magic me.*

*And for a moment he remembered. He was in a basement. He was a Jacob. Now he was dust. Dust in a basement. Drifting down deep drains during Echos Call Before All…*

*And he noticed another difference. He could BE. If he wanted. Jacob could BE. He was only missing one thing, but that he could not yet see.*

∞

# The End

From the astonishing dark beauty and empty nothing of a tangerine sunset, his friend buzzed out from behind an ear. The bb flew past his nose, with a tiny hehe smile at the Jacob that now wanted 2 Be.

"I did tell you see," said the bittiest bee, "that I am also a c and a z?"

His friend spoke with the calm confidence of supreme acceptance, "I read here, in the Book, you see. About the bittiest bee. Some special ones jump straight through an E. It's over the D, as the bittiest bb, and into something much different. Much more than me. An Echo of an E."

The yellow jellybean expanded into the ever-changing sky of a crayon lavender. "I understand now, you see. That the Book was there exactly for me. To show you as the bb, I was once to then be. But I skipped up ahead, to the G, and I see. For bb is for build. Build bright into you and to me. But only carpenters build, and that's not enough for we. Not all that we can be. No Sir e. But G is tricksy too and Extra Special, uc. G is for Grow! A Garden of Es! Up and Up! Graceful. Gigantic. Agelically. Until…"

E for
Explosion
Expansion
Everything

The bb gulped between growing bb lips, "But now, my gift is, you see, to become the Biggest BBBB. And to save you with what you need. A cooling, AC. With a Jolt. Please forgive me. For I cannot help what I Bee. You don't need it. But you think you do. And so I must become BBBBB—All that you See. And that is how I can Give. Give this special Gift C. C for Chance. A C to you. AC just for you, and for you just from me."

"Now U can finally All C. A followed the Bee, which once was the Me. Through the tricksy e, also me, into the Garden you C. The Garden for A and me, the E.

bb exploded into a yellow white light of all there is. Jacob felt him and heard him as a character must hear the author of his story contemplating his creation.

## ∞
# The Beginning

The BBBBB was not a creature that answered questions but gave answers. "I cast you out! You don't belong here. You belong in the upside down. I know exactly where to put you. Take the sharp M, flip it straight downside right, and a W you have with a Why. You then add a Bee. And a Willow, you see, there you'll be, you'll Be, Willow Bee." Spin.

"Right destination, wrong directions. To get there you first need Will, definitely not wont. Add nothing—O. Find a single B. Add the Tricksy E. And Voila. There you'll Will O BE." Spin.

"Close. No Cigar. It's a W for Whatever. I for Eye. Add 2 Lunatics. U after the Nothing. A single silent seductive B. And Y. Because you always end with a why like a cat always ends with a tale." Spin.

"Silence!" The real BBBBB returned to end the madness. "It doesn't matter from whence you came, just from here you are!"

A bright sandy white light melted into a wax of honey yellow until the edges of Jacob's vision blackened at the corners like burning film. The black narrowed down on the honey until all that remained was a single Bee shaped like a B. Until the B morphed into a D. It flipped 180 degrees, into a grin of Epic Delight.

The D twisted again and expanded into many letters. A word. Dream. It spun like a wind chime and became the word Death. It kept spinning. Changing from one word to the other. *Death. Dream. Death. Dream. Death. Dream.*

And as it spun like a sideways coin, Jacob remembered Jacob. *He was dust. Dust in a basement. Jacob Could Be. Or was he a head? A head in a basement. Did he have a body? Did he need one? Thoughts were thought by someone or something until he was so left and right and right and left that he no longer knew even which one he wanted.*

*And at that precise instant, he noticed a difference. Without slowing, the B which was a D began spinning the other way. Perhaps it was an optical illusion, but what once was left was now right. And then the D began to slow, and he saw words of a different meaning. Doubt. He Saw Doubt. And then it slowed more and became Dream. Dream. Until at the last he saw a string of Ds—Desire. Dare. Dream. Dance.* **Do!**

The BBBBB returned, "Oh yes, that will do. The Land of Apples. He's the A, After All. The M ground down turned upside down. They love Apples there. Largest Apple Cold Storage in the World." A breeze blew.

"One of Thee. It's a tricksy e, see."

"Quiet you! They celebrate Apples. The ABCs. And the ABs. That's why people are always drifting its way—one day grey the next day blue—it sways like a cork in the sea. A place of intersections. That's the place for you!"

And then nothing.

O

OO

Until in the beginning he wondered who wondered. Then he wondered if he would always remember. He remembered the B song. But would he sing the right tune? He knew he wasn't dead. He was dreaming. Because he was cheating. And you can cheat in dreams, but there is no cheating death.

A Mist turned into foam. It drifted toward him like a cloud of what he hoped was protection. Instead it melted into a shaving cream sky from which emerged Eleanor Roosevelt—The Cat of Astonishing Indifference—"Meeeeeeeeeeeew. Mew. Mews mews mews."

She spoke as one who hit a new low but would admit nothing, "I forgot to tell you. There's also this last bit. There's always another scrap and scrabble. You should already know all of this if you paid even half a hair of attention to any of that previous nonsense." She swished a paw of uncaring in the air behind her

The large cat scolded him in an attempt to shift any blame from herself, "Those Delightful Morons told you the same thing. It's always Five. Three in the middle, a beginning, and end. What else could there be in this D you came from, whence! The I before the D is for Identification and the I after is Independence!"

"Here's the end. Of this part anyway. It has been a pleasure being your Muse on this trip."

∞

**Jacob Wanted to** *Be. Jacob Wanted to Know. Jacob Desired. And he noticed a difference. Two men appeared.*

He waited for one to bash the other over the head with a rock. Instead they worked in sync, hauling something heavy together. A canoe. "Misters at your service," they said to him, though he didn't know how.

"You don't remember us, do you? You sent us to find the connection from the east to the west. From sea to shining sea. The big river cuts us in two. It drains all to the East, don't you see? And so the West burns. You sent us to find the water that connects? Ringing any bells?"

The man exhaled concern, as if it had been an extremely long day. He turned to the other, "I think the King might be getting a little woozy."

The second man ignored him and spoke, "But as you can see, there is no Direct Connection. AC is the real jewel. The Alternate Connection. That's why we're doing this last bit over land. It's the hard part, but worth it. We had to port the final leg. That's the key, see. It's not as easy as following a river. On this continent you must power through the mountains first, before you reach the sea yet again. This last bit requires a little Manual Effort to finish the job. So please pay attention, your royalty Mr. Sir."

The man spoke, and he knew it was A Clark, "Don't you see Mr. J, we understand how to get there. So now you decide where to go next. You have the Power. Do you finally see?"

The other man spoke, A Lewis, "Have Fun. You're Lucky. Lucky Ducky. Laugh Lots. Get Lucky. Win Big. Smile. Savor Succulent Sensations."

A Clark spoke with grey in his eyes, "Lewis is Right. Do it for US. Tell Stories. But mostly bounce laughs off canyon walls and Swim together in Sparkling SeaS."

The man exhaled and a puff emerged. Jacob saw a white smokesnake of what turned into a line. The line circled into a shape of a sort. Round. The O. The Nothing. *He knew.*

But then in a blink the circle meant something. The circle was a trixsy E. E for Earth. And then with a zoom in and sparkle out, a growth here and there, the earth zoomed onto a specific shape. The shape, he knew, meant something. A C. For Country. U and the A with the S in between. The one that Misters at Your Service had finally connected C to C.

But then the white shape, with only a slight twist, a nudge here, a pull there, the C became something else entirely. A blob, he knew it meant A B. B for Brain. He saw now that the brain had two halves, like the country, and you needed strands of strong C connecting each side to fully B.

Then he knew he was that brain. His head became a little red balloon. And he drifted.

Up
Up he went
And the clouds darkened

Until the thinnest blanket of silk over his little red balloon. Or was it the nose of a clown?

No longer drifting up.

But ever so carefully now back down.

A slow descent into the below that was no longer scary.

He felt light on a face. He had eyes. And he opened them. To see a Turkey. Or perhaps, with a squint, An Eagle.

# Sunday

$$— \text{Chapter } 22 —$$

**As usual, Jacob** Maymerry was almost correct. The large bird in his face was flightless, a Rooster.

He remembered. *What a Wonderful World.*

He was a Jacob. Alive in a basement, his back to a washing machine, his body covered in dirt, and a mask of blissed confusion on a dazed face. A bright lippy smile opened across Cheshire cheeks—a grin of ecstasy or enlightenment, Jacob did not care, because it was absolutely an E.

One glance down and he noticed it was not a mask of confusion but a literal mask, a portal to life. An oxygen mask. Because you need 2 Os, in a twist, to survive. It's simple chemistry, like two rings colliding. That he knew from somewhere deep.

He did not consider this more, as the large bird made eye contact. The Rooster looking down his beak was a 4th Level named Roger. As if Jacob grew two hearts and heads instead of one, he experienced what the Rooster experienced.

And Roger stared at the face of Mr. Maymerry thinking that he had never been so happy to see eyes open up. Roger Rooster had no idea how he got so lucky as to have a man survive such a thing, but perhaps everything, depending on one's perspective, happens for a very exact reason.

Jacob tried to speak but couldn't because of the mask. He knew in a flash that he did not need that anymore, because even masks of life can suffocate when left on too long. He pulled it off and mouthed words from slowly moistening lips, "What. On. Earth?"

Rooster answered as Jacob's mind flowed both in and out of some misty state. The Rooster's message reached his brain as an echo of symbols and rhymes and shapes and colors and syllables all at once.

Not again. Jacob tried to combine pieces into human understanding. He heard the Rooster say words that almost made sentences. "So the animal got it. I bolted right past. See. Jolted me into action. Didn't want you to die."

Jacob focused harder and his mind created perfect poetic gibberish in Roger's words:

*"If your A for Armor is held by 1 B for Bolt,*
*Then under the C, through the e, beyond the D,*
*To E, with a J for Jolt."*

*What on earth does that mean? Was he still thinking in the Twilight Zone?*
The awake part of Jacob did not yet understand. "Do you understand?" Rooster read his mind and looked concerned. "Are you still with me? Give it time, and you'll be back to thinking clearly. It's a woozy feeling, isn't it? I've been there."

Jacob did not know where Rooster had been before, but he was comforted knowing he wasn't alone. A few deep breaths of unknown number later, and Jacob almost felt like a fully formed Jacob once more.

Roger Rooster spoke in clear English, answering as he often did, in the form of a question, "Well damn man, do you know what happened? I mean, I think I know what happened. Was someone else here?"

It was only then that Jacob realized the Rooster was bright crimson, dripping in sweat, and out of breath. The red hot big bird smiled through an exhale, "I'll tell you this buddy, you waking up saved me. I'll never be able to repay that debt, that's for sure."

Jacob did not understand but answered automatically in triplicate nonsense, "It was nothing. I forgive you. You're welcome."

The Rooster seemed on the verge of tears, "And your cookies are burnt to hell."

∞

**A shuffle, groan**, squat, and rustling later, Jacob found himself off the dirt floor and being led up out of the basement.

Woozy and weary, the Rooster gave an accounting of what he remembered. "I was working late down the street at your neighbor's house, follow me? They're gone for the night and wanted it done when they got back."

Jacob almost understood, and Roger went on regardless, explaining it all with a crisp efficiency of a man ready to go home. "I took a break outside, and that's when I heard the barking coming through the trees. I didn't think nothing of it at first, but then the barks seemed a little dramatic, of an odd sort, if you know what I mean."

Roger did not care if Jacob actually knew what he meant, "But that's when

I remembered the sticker that you had, and knew it was your dog." He tapped a finger to his skull indicating intelligence.

"At first I thought it was in the yard, doing its business. But then I realized the bark was *coming from inside the house!*"

He said this as if it changed everything. "Maybe it's parental instinct, but it made the hairs on my arms tingle, ya know? A bark of a different sort. Maybe I understand a second language, dog ruff ruff."

He smiled to himself in relief. " Besides, I'm still missing that tool in your basement. So I walked over this way, saw all the lights on, the dog going banan-as, the door unlocked, and I put all the pieces together."

Rooster is some kind of hero, Jacob thought from somewhere.

"So I ran down, found you, realized it was CO, Carbon Monoxide, and then darted back to my van to get the Oxygen. It took a bit, but then you woke up, saw me, and here we are."

The large man wiped more sweat from his tomato brow. "If not for your breath, that would have been the end of us. You dead. The other guy suing us for not noticing the CO risk. I shudder to think. But you came back and saved us."

Rooster walked toward his work van like a man needing to get back to a safe place to recover from the traumatic rescue. "I didn't take your cookies out, because I didn't want to risk black smoke filling the house if I opened the oven door."

Jacob saw Roger's eyes glisten mirrors. The slightest quiver rose in his voice like a confession, "I keep thinking of my boy. He's why I need this job."

Roger now was rambling in a way that wouldn't make sense except in a conversation between two friends, men talking about personal things after a shared basement battle. "It's a miracle you're alive right now. Papa always said heroes could work miracles, but I never figured out which came first, the hero or the miracle. It's always a Chicken or Egg question, isn't it."

Jacob rolled his eyes at a thought—*What comes first, the C or the E? Perhaps A Mister E!*

∞

**After a few** more this's and that's, Roger excused himself to get his life in order. Jacob was left waiting for the sunrise and wondering what came next.

He wondered.

He wondered more.

He wondered a third more.

*He saw the letter M. He knew it was a motherly mischief maker of a merry man. Or perhaps a mischief of a mother making merry men. A shifty little letter. Twist the M, CC for counterclockwise, B for backwards, and the M becomes a sharp E, spun again it becomes the W, and then once more into a crafty 3, before twisting back to the M, where it started before.*

He saw this M pushed as if in a wheelchair, straight into a little e, it flipped the M, 180 degrees, flattened into a little w.

*Mew,* he knew.

∞

**Whew, that was** *close.*

He needed more oxygen. That's how he found himself on the porch looking down at the green notebook remembering the cause of this nonsense in the first place. Three names scrawled there. Whose skull was it? How did it end up there? Why was it only a skull?

He'd never narrow it down more than that. Not unless a magic answer drifted in from the sky.

*What is an insight except a magic answer drifting into one's head from an invisible sky?*

Eureka! At that very moment Jacob had a realization. He understood a clue. From Mabel. He remembered names of a weird meaning. The Letter Man. Lenny O. Chesire grins. Christmas smiles.

There were so many more, but once the mind settles on a final form, does it matter what else remains, because at that point everything becomes a clue if one is on the trail of the right answer. If on the wrong path, then everything becomes a red herring. Jacob pressed on.

*He looked just like that Letter Man.* Mister Robin McDonald looked like something. Something that had a face and lips and teeth. He looked just like that Letter Man. A Connection was all he needed, and now he had it. For he knew that Mister Letterman was a funny D, known for something, or rather nothing. The nothing between front teeth, a gap. Weren't teeth the one part of us that stood the test of time, that was used for the old fashioned ID for

Identification. Jacob need only look much closer at the teeth on this skull to understand if there was a missing middle, indicating, just perhaps, that this was the Letter Man. Mister Robin McDonald. Father of Will.

∞

**Should I really** *go back down into a basement filled with carbon monoxide? Rooster didn't say anything about the risk.*

Jacob realized he couldn't place any more responsibility on Roger. It would take only seconds to look into the face of the skull and test his hunch.

He no longer cared to drag things out. Now a man of action, he dove headfirst back into the basement, oxygen mask in hand, to visit his friend, and discover if it was who he thought it might be.

Mr. Maymerry descended the spinal stair to the basement, ignored the pine step whinny, and looked around once more. The washer and dryer remained the only objects besides the overhead pipes, hot water heater, long dead metal coal furnace monster, and boulder to the center of the earth.

The cellar door remained darkly tucked along one slanted ceiling, the ancient golf rake propped against it. Two rickety wooden steps along the downslope led to the dirt basement floor, mere feet from the bunched up sheet covering the hidden object.

Feeling a magician pulling away a sheet to reveal the final surprise to an audience, Jacob flipped up the white covering with dramatic flair.

He revealed nothing.

*Poof. Gone. Like a windy ghost. An escaped prisoner through the old model and into whatever comes next.*

*Are you kidding me?*

*Feeling nothing but the absurdity of life, he smiled. And then Jacob laughed and laughed when he realized it no longer mattered.*

Could there ever be a satisfactory answer? Even if there was a gap in the teeth. Even if that meant it was the Merry Man. Even if he knew exactly whose skull he found and then lost, would it ever be enough? Would it explain why it was merely a head and not a body? Would it prove why it ended up there in the first place? Would it come close to capturing the life burst forth from the bone?

Laughing all the way back up the stairs, a thought struck him—he hadn't taken a single picture of the skull. So he could never look back and check.

He might say it was because he needed to keep it all secret. But perhaps the real reason was that he hadn't thought to take one since moving to town. When on the River, there is little interest in doing anything except living in the moment. And that wasn't nothing.

**Yet, the missing** skull meant one of two tricky MindThumpers—Did Jacob hallucinated the whole head or Someone took it away. He might be woozy, but Jacob Maymerry remained a logical man capable of solving a mystery.

His Detective mind whirred and wove connection after connection. *The button was real. So Barbara is real. So Mabel must be real. So the stories might be true. And my memory isn't nothing.* He decided to think more on it and find the happy ending. The universe provided a gift—*Now Jacob needn't tell a soul about the skull at all. Instead he could tell the story to anyone he chose, but only at the very right moment.*

*Poof. Gone!* Like a sneaky squirrel stealing a golf ball in a sand trap, then wiped clean and out the door.

*How curious.*

**Jacob walked upstairs** and for the first time remembered the cookies. Burnt to a blackened midnight, he pulled out the charcoal spheres as the morning sunshine rose from the kitchen windows behind him.

*How curious,* he considered. These cookies must have been in here for hours. But then how long was I out in the basement? How long can one survive with only CO and not Oxygen?

*How curious.*

*No one else was here except for a dog, cat, and Jacob.*

He remembered.

*What a long chain of lucky rapids allowed him to still be here, thinking these thoughts. But also a long chain of who ha that required him to need the saving in the first place. Together, maybe with a giggle, one could see harmony somewhere, in something, somehow.*

*Full of O for Optimism, exhausted but excited. What friendships brewed in Willouby.*

*The Wisest Woman in town, the great Archivist of the East, a Heroic Rooster, and a Saint William of the Hood from the House Robin. A beginning to remember.*

*Perhaps, Jacob thought, he would always find whatever he looked for. And if that were true, then it was especially important to look for things that he wanted to find.*

∞

**Thinking these cartoon** morning ideas, Jacob Maymerry remembered again that he was excited about what comes next. Because what came next was what he decided. And he decided that it was the Sounds of Mabel.

He took the record player and three vinyl discs tied up in a bow to his Victorian hideaway with the green tile backsplash. The records, he knew, were special messages from Mabel—whispers from the past. He noticed a yellow post-it note with small lyrical handwriting from the needle point nib of a cherished fountain pen.

*"I recommend both even and odd tracks to ensure balance. But never forget the third is always dealer's choice. And when that fun is done, you can try the B side. Or better yet, B for Backwards. Enjoy my dearest little one!"*

Jacob decided to begin at the end—Z for Zeppelin. Though the H toward which he headed felt like Home—Weird and Wonderful Willouby.

He spun in a slow circle in his blue swivel chair, now a kindergarten graduate and a new elementary Willoubeast. As he floated up, past a ladder or atop a stairway, for a flash he almost forgot.

*But he remembered that he was A Hero. And he did nothing more than walk around the block in different directions, smile at local loons, fall asleep in the basement, and wake up. But that's what the Rooster said. Saved a life! Kid is gonna build things. And that might matter.*

For now he knew about Connections. Connections of Opposites. Sea to Sea. A with B. For there is no shortcut without a destination. And there is no right destination without a wrong destination. There is no other way it could ever be. But deciding Which is Witch is up to you. For Jacob also knew that messages are hidden within messages. And he could never know for sure what someone else saw when looking at the very same letters. Or hearing the very same sounds.

It was always up to him. To use his Mind to determine what Mattered.

Because what mattered was not matter but what he decided mattered. And he had no choice but to Look. Because that is what it means to See. One can't conceive an A without a B. So he started looking for B——to notice Beauty and to make that Beauty matter. It's anything, everywhere, anyone, and all at once.

In a buzzy harrumph, Jacob remembered that everyone gets exactly what they want in Willouby. But what on earth did Jacob Maymerry want? *I don't know what I desire.*

*Ding Ding Ding! The correct answer! What do we have for him Winnie?* Mabel's rose coo floated in his mind for a hidden message, a prize, "The answer you seek is in your head. And what is in your head is Stories! *Because what else could be there?*"

Mabel's voice quieted into a whisper as the record player spun on, "A Story is A Connection, from one thing to another. A searching for B. Each looking and deciding what the other IT is. We must be our tales——our Ends and Beginnings——reflections of everything we see, mixed up as we wish, inside the place we are but can never fully be."

A whisper within the whisper, "*This space would not, could not, and must not exist as it does unless we are in this very position at this exact now——both writing a story and reading it. Performing and watching the performance. To know this tale of a single hero is to be One.*"

At that moment Jacob popped out of the blue chair swivel and knew exactly what came next. A Walk! *Traditions develop quickly in a place like Willouby.* Along the red and black brick sidewalk Mister Maymerry remembered the story of his American Hero. The tale might start at the beginning. It may begin when moving in. Or moving out. In the basement. Bleeding on a rock. Dreaming. The only thing for very sure is that It Starts Now, and Begins Here. In all that you C. For you are the A, looking at Me. And We are A B.

# — EoE —
## A tricksy e for Epilogue, Encore, & Eternity

**A man in** a forest green cardigan over powder blue polo sees a piece of trash blowing in one of his yellow bushes. He planted them along that embankment himself, and they're coming in nicely. He looks around the yard. *Yes, things sure are coming in nicely.*

He walks the gravel drive in bare feet, his left moccasin slipper ripped in two by his dog that very morning. He reaches the middle of the three blooming Forsythia plants, and grabs the white paper stuck like a log in an otherwise blazing yellow eye.

But it isn't garbage—an envelope has blown into his bush. As he makes this realization, his bare feet slip on the still wet morning grass lining the embankment. His heels sweep from under him, his pants hit dirt, and he swirls down in a slide until he's stopped by the fence hitting his back, having made a full 180 degree swivel. He laughs and feels the permanent grass stains that must line his underside.

A calico cat stares from a metal shard that makes up the skeletal rib of a large fish statue in the yard. She rolls her eyes at the now seated cardigan man. The feline look is unmistakable—*What did you expect? Who thought it was a good idea to let him leave the house without shoes?*

The man stays seated, crosses his ankles, and opens the delivery.

He pulls out three items stapled together in the left corner—an old newspaper article sandwiched between two postcards. The man knows the staple is a sign—his attention is being directed—there is an order to processing this information. A then B then C.

*That's how things have been done through the ages.* The thought rises from nowhere.

The first item is an antique postcard of the very street that he now calls home. But it isn't his rock house on the front. It's a place down the block— Notting House on Ham Hill. A faded note written in tiny scrawl across the back is preserved through generations. He narrows his eyes to make out the fainting letters…

———

*Am I telling your story, or are you telling mine? Am I in your head, or are you in mine? Does it matter? Can we ever know? Who Saved Who?*

*Each of us are stories. Stories creating stories about stories. It's stories all the way down, and up. Tell yourself one that fits, until you'd rather not. Then find another one, until you notice a difference.*

*I give you permission to do all of this and more.*

*I can't make it too easy, little one. Once you know and find yourself back at the beginning, then you're free to make mischief. And that's when things really get good.*

*Who are you really? Are you the biggest of the big, everything there is and yet to be? Or are you the smallest of the dust, the tiniest of the nothing? And when there is another cut, a stronger microscope, a deeper look, a discovery, a creation, a name, A new Adam within the Atom——Do you transition yet again into that thing? Do you become something else with everything that is noticed?*

*Are you a mirror? Or am I a mirror? What happens when we look at one another?*

*Careful with mirrors. That way there be monsters, and clowns, but Oh How Much More. Everything. If you are ready.*

*When you feel smallest, remember it is all illusion. There is no big or small or important or magic. There are only different levels of magnification and angles at which you look. It's guardian angles all the way down, and up, and on both sides, like a diamond. Twisted diamond spiral staircases to the end and beginning.*

*Noticing as much as possible is enough.*

*But you want answers. You think answers bring peace. I can provide an answer if you'd like. But I warn you, this is a trap. Answers are created from questions. And questions bring seeking. And seeking prevents peace. Decide if you want all of the answers or none. But know that you are forever both wrong and right. Each in its own due course. There's an order to these things.*

*The apple becomes the onion the instant teeth break the skin.*

*Da Ta!*


*- O*


∞


**The cardigan man** burrows a frow, frows a burrow, and pulls the postcard back to expose the second slice—the newspaper clipping. He creases under the staple, and presses the three pieces together between his fingers to ensure they remain attached. An obituary. An old one. They were much more casual about the language in old obituaries. There is no photo. They didn't have as many photos back then. He reads…

———

**Oscar Nathanael Hamilton—**
*"The Amazing Abernathy—All American Allusionist"—left by train near St. Bartholomew's Home for those with Happy  and Nervous Prostration after a hilarious, brilliant, and short stay.*

*Per his wishes, having lain on both sides of the tracks all his life, two services were held. One in nearby Willouby, and another in a field at the site of his sunset trip.*

*He leaves his behind and all that entails to his father to do with as he pleases, likely interred atop Mount Willouby Cemetery next to those with similar last letters.*

*His front and brilliant mind is returned to the care of the one who knew it best (and who wrote this obituary). Mabel goes by many names—including Queen Maebs and Miss Kitty Kitty. But around these fields she's best known as The Lady of a Million Pieces— the title bestowed after an unfathomable number of sawings in half with the help of The Amazing Abernathy, most occurring during their thrilling live stage performances.*

*Rarely separated, in the beginning Oscar and Mabel rose from nowhere to some kind of prominence as the miming duo, The Mirrors, once dubbed "a modest, regional achievement."*

*Oscar enjoyed all things ripe and delicious of the five senses. Insisting on the last say but not believing in goodbye, here is his most recent note, echoing off the tracks, beneath a blazing sycamore tree, atop a rock, under an apple:"Dear little one, let's make mischief together until you can't."*

∞

**Cardigan Man notices** another message, not hidden but less obvious, in careful, tiny print across three yellow notes on the back of the obituary. He smiles without quite knowing why…

———

*The fairy tale is the place where things that matter most exist as words long enough to be noticed.*
*And still they only appear to those who aren't looking.*
*Because words are make-believe smoke conjured from the nothing.*
*Words are inadequate for understanding the real.*

*The sound of the dark cannot be translated. The feel of the earth is existence. The warmth of the sun simply is.*

*Squiggles atop the eye and vibrations in the ear tell only part of the story.*

*Those seeking answers require more.*


*Magic is the Missing Medium.*

*That's why I keep Crazy Mabel around.*


*Sometimes she a real Angel.*

**The cardigan over** powder blue polo flutters, the first hint of a spring chill on the horizon. A light breeze sweeps up the hill, over the limestone rocks surrounded by mulch beds. Sitting under the yellow bush, back to the fence, Cardigan man doesn't notice the beginning of a low fog just beyond the homes to the west, a wisp of growing white drifting across the avenue toward the rock house.

He looks down at the third slice, a new postcard of the Pacific Ocean—a large wave over glistening orange waters below a lavender sunset. The wave is shaped as the word Pacific, a large P crests into the sherbert sky. He imagines it purchased by a firecracker redhead in bug glasses, purple scarf blazing in 1950s yellow convertible, she laughs hysterically to a memory and throws the postcard back into the wind to begin its journey across the dust to him as she plunges over the cliff into the deep Pacific blue.

The man in the cardigan doesn't know why he thinks this, but the story appears in his head at once. He shakes it away with a blush, as if kissed by a Grandmother.

He flips over the postcard and sees the ink of a different color—in lyrical handwriting from the needle point nib of a cherished fountain pen—this is brander than new. If the first postcard was written by a left hand from the past, this came from the right of tomorrow—connected through the ages. His thumb presses the staple, holds the pieces together, and hopes the growing wind doesn't rip them apart. He wants to save this.

His bright eyes shine as he considers the Pacific postcard message. Cardigan Man reads and doesn't notice one of the yellow notes slip off in the wind, blowing into the neighbor's bushes.

———

*If you'll forgive the indulgence—One final performance or reward or map for completing the journey and beginning it. It's in the form of a poem, which is new for me. Perhaps poetry is the closest we ever get to the misty white swirl of magic and words that elude us at the last.*

*And if I want to complete my quest, to become a triple threat, to be 3D, to reach out and grab you, then I must settle on a third. And I like the rhythm of Magician, Actor, Poet. A little for the mind, body, and mystery in between.*

*If you think this all gibberish, please be gentle. What did you expect? I'm a 98 year old Beginner, and this is a rough draft. But if any of this sings to a place deep in your soul, then I am your Echo. What did you expect? I'm a 98 year old Angel, and I've noticed many things—*

*In the end, you want to remember.*
*Remembering is another reading.*
*You look back and create a thread from here to there.*

*And while weaving, you pretend it always existed.*
*You forget the feeling of the original reading.*
*When you were alone in the dark and the deep.*
*With no connection to ground or sight up ahead*
*Or memory of what brought you to nowhere.*

*But eventually you notice a difference,*
*And then reach a once distant shore.*
*You look back and decide how you got there,*
*Noticing everything missed from before.*

*And the more you remember. And the more you create.*
*And the more inevitable the connection appears.*
*You uncover the beautiful allusions.*
*The thread that you conjure, gold tiers.*

*You forget so that you remember.*
*You forget until you know all along.*
*When you feel the connection is strongest.*
*Threads vibrate in bloom and a song.*

*Until a fade,*
*Beautiful dust,*
*Careful drift,*
*In the deep.*

*With no sight,*
*Only sound,*
*It's the Echo.*

*'Til by Dawn's*
*Early Light,*
*When New Eyes,*
*Open Bright,*

*To shine Wilde*
*At the Rise,*
*Of the Hero.*

*For your journey I offer this:*

*Look to the mothers, mischief makers, and merry men.*
*They will light the way.*

*Ta Da!*

—Mabel Abernathy Bartholomew Edwin Lincoln V I I, V I I I

# —— E² ——

# A tricksy e for Epilogue from Another Dimension

∞

A regal man in full butler garb stands in front of turtle knockers on the largest house on the largest hill in Willouby. He notices a yellow envelope nestled in expensive pea gravel up the green gravely grass lane of 101 Sunrise Circle across Nottingham Avenue. He opens the message and finds labeled sheets of paper. There's an order to these things, A then B. 1 then 2. He reads…

∞

**To Whomever Discovers This Letter-**

Please consider this Detective Maymerry's "Theory of the Case of the Found and Lost Head of Willouby." As the Reader likely knows, I discovered a human skull buried underneath our house, then plunged into a quest to uncover its owner. Could I find the answer?

Most Likely shifted from old delivery crews to one of the ten former residents from the home's 125 years. Based on a hunch and unique conversations, it narrowed to three - The original mother, her wandering youngest son, or a jolly porter man. Three red herrings.

My adventure ended with a near death journey. As I pondered the skull on an unexcavated boulder, Carbon Monoxide poisoned me. Invisible. So much we can't see. My life was saved by a Rooster HVAC professional with good timing. Or perhaps I survived by Magic, or at least a Magician. Here's my report -

### *Who is the Skull?*

I was stumped until a note just like this one blew into my yellow bushes. It gave answers and created questions. Who? Of course the skull once housed the mind of **Oscar Nathanael Hamilton** - Oldest Son, WW2 Hero, The Amazing Abernathy, and First to Whatever Comes Next.

### Who Did It?

As CO gas dipped me through the misty riverlands between this world and the next, Oscar's skull disappeared. I may be a fool, but I'm a rational fool. The skull was taken. But How? Why? Who?

Who took the head? The only answer is the same person who put it there in the first place. Mabel Abernathy Bartholomew Edwin Lincoln. Or as she would say, The M. The first M is the AM. Aunt Mabel. It works both ways, Magician's Assistant. ABBA. Always Both Both Always. Dancing Queen Maeb. My neighbor. A Mischief Maker.

Mabel was perfectly Sane. But from certain Angles & Perspectives, any of us might be Crazy. She was awarded Oscar's upper half, including his mind. I imagine her conversations with the skull. All in good fun. Like the midnight tricks and treats fairy godmother of dreams, Queen Mab, from the very Romeo & Juliet speech Mabel performed for me. She was both Sinner & Saint.

"She's an Angel, sometimes."

### How?

Mysteries are quests for missing information. Here's my best story of the case...

Aunt Mabel saw me on the day I moved to Willouby. She might have been inside the very house itself, spying from my office window, as I tumbled the embankment. She watched while leaving my first gift - the Dollar Store cardboard notepad. Perhaps right after hiding the skull of her former beloved. What fun to watch the new neighbor unravel this puzzle, she might think.

Eureka! Why not also lead the cardigan man to her, like a crafty spider. Sneak back in through the Cellar Door, to leave the button. Will he follow the trail? Here kitty kitty. Mabel, master of life's tomfoolery.

Wait! The MM notices a hidden risk. Invisible to most but not an expert in the sciences. Carbon Monoxide, CO. The Fool will never figure it out. She must save him. So she stops the furnace, brings a cooling, buys time, and draws in the Roosters.

But the poison got me anyway. I was never good at breathing techniques. Luckily, Mabel gave an encore performance in the basement, to save her neighbor, a kindergartener in Willouby.

As the dog barked upstairs, she again folded her tiny frame through the Cellar Door, and pumped Oxygen long enough to keep the Fool alive. Until the Rooster arrived. Glad she left the cookies. Then back up the stairs with care, like Saint Nicholas, as if she wasn't even there. The golf rake will hide her footprints, the Queen of Artistic Flair.

But WHY?

## Why?

Every tale ends in a Why like a cat always ends in a tail. I can provide an answer if you'd like. But is there ever a single answer to WHY?

I like to think that Mabel knew she could do better than simply protect me from poison. A part-time Angel, Giver of Gifts. She could provide another present - The thrill of adventure. The Mischief Maker guessed it was a quest I wanted, and everyone gets what they want in Willouby.

Many lifesavers are invisible—Real Magicians.

Solving mysteries is about making connections. A to B. C to C. Clue to Clue. A connection from one hemisphere of a brain to the other. North and South. East with the West, over the Appalacians.

Mabel's three performances lured me back to the basics. A kindergartner. Lower even than the 1st level. Perhaps a basement. I like to think Mabel was a substitute teacher, explaining the start of the alphabet, A then B, to the bumbling new neighbor who unsuspectingly moved atop the Rock House. Maybe that's one reason.

Every tale ends in a WHY but every WHY ends in another Y.

## Another Why

The Quest of the Head was a lot for me and mostly for her. And Both Both And. "Let's make mischief until you can't," were Oscar's last words to her. A final act for the Mesmerizing Mabel, the triple threat of a performing savant. It's how Oscar would have wanted his favorite bones to shine.

Much more to explain and remember. If only life were a book, I could *go* back and find all the clues. Because once yo+u know an ending, the past becomes something different. Memory is Mist. Gibberish might morph into a new language between friends.

Her nonsense wasn't nonsense—Talk of Oxygen. Two metal O rings magically combined in a molecule. You need two Os in a twist to survive. She sang, "Awake Unto Me, Beautiful Dreamer." She knew I'd need the Rooster again. Mark Chapter 13, "When the Rooster Crows…Stay Awake!" Oscar's obituary was misplaced in the A section and left to fall out on my second library visit. Even my phone kept flashing the CO for Carbon Monoxide. How many other warnings did I miss?

If only I could listen to her stories once more. There'd be depths to explore. Mabel acted a muse to resuscitate the Fool, entertain herself, explain the birds & bees, fulfill Oscar's final request, understand America, and Welcome Me to Willouby.

Case Closed. Your Move.

Da Ta!
Jacob E Maymerry
First of his Name

∞

P.S. For the most curious, there's always more. So many connections to investigate…between names, like BartholoMEW and Nathanael. And Willoughby with a GH from The Twilight Zone. Like Letters and Numbers from The Phantom Tollbooth. Or the Smoking Caterpillar who becomes a Butterfly in Wonderland.

Thanks for Reading!

# Book Club Conversations
EQ Test for Eleven Question Test because Eleven Equals Exceptional

1. Do you have a final answer for all of the original Questions—Who is it? Who did it? How was it done? Why?

2. Who is the M in the first Clue? Are you very sure? Consider it means "Mastermind." Who might fill that word? Once the mind gets going, perhaps this is a story that can be read as a Choose Your Own Adventure. Imagine the entire tale is made up by Mabel. Or Jacob. Or Liam, in a dream as he is away. Or William, wondering who moved into his old house. Or Barbara, imagining why this new man really investigated the button. Can you rank these as most likely from the details in the story, like a ladder?

3. Consider this clue from the Land of Lost Letters: Don't write three sentences when 1 equals 3. Everyone will catch up. It's not your fault they can't understand. And never forget that two out of three ain't bad. What does that mean? What about the Fairy Tale Rule of Magic 3? Does it have to do with Mabel spinning tales from different perspectives, angles, and dimensions? What if many sentences in the book mean 3 different things, depending on who you decide M might be?

4. What if there are two involved, an A and B! If so, what does this postcard quote mean to you? —Am I telling your story, or are you telling mine? Am I in your head, or are you in mine? Does it matter? Can we ever know? Who Saved Who?

5. Roger Rooster IV proved most helpful for Jacob at both the beginning and the end of his adventure. Do you think he knew more about the situation than he let on?

6. This is a story of generations and family lines. These are all ways to divide up time, or history. Aunt Mabel prefers her own way—Presidential Administrations. What letters are you? What do you think it says about you? Is that a better way to discuss groups of Americans than typical Gen Z, Boomers, etc?

7. Willouby is known for weaving, threaded twists that look like loops to create strong fabric. Jacob explained, "Someone once told him that deja vu was a sign that we were all ghosts, re-living loops over again." And he wondered of Mabel, "Is this where she loops again with the same stories?" Can you notice loops within the story? How many? Try starting the book once more, up to the first infinity—does anything seem familiar?

8. Round Robin: Clue or Red Herring? Which of these silly details matter? All of them? None? Some number in between?—a golf rake, an original writing device, a red book, magic tricks, science jokes, rings/circles/zero/letter O, bells and dings, and ranking of letters.

9. Jacob decided he needed to get to the bottom of himself to solve the mystery. What if he needed to get to the bottom of Mabel? She said her circus and carnival foundation had three teachers—The Bearded Lady Samantha said she was a firework or grand finale. The tattooed man said life was a test garden, and when you figured it out, good things started coming. The lion tamer said it was a garden but you need to understand tricky time. What do you think he meant? What did Mabel mean when she suggested there are different kinds of time? Or different ways upon which to mark time? Like the 4th of July?

10. Who is Oscar Nathanael Hamilton? Who is Mabel Abernathy Bartholomew Edwin Lincoln? What do each of those names mean? What is an All American Allusionist? What is an Allusion? How many can you spot in this fairy tale?

11. Did you find any clues as hidden messages? When you weave together the stories, dreams, poems, capitalizations, synonyms, and visions in the land of lost letters and numbers, what new meanings pop out? Don't worry if you go crazy, it's all A for Arbitrary!

And don't forget that answers are made of questions. But perhaps the right answer is always whatever is in your head. Or better yet, the head of your book loving friends! -M

## Paul Alan Richardson

Paul drifts here and there, frequently west of the Blue Ridge Mountains. He enjoys nature's curious creatures, games, mystery, and beautiful cosmic nonsense. He lives in the Shenandoah Valley, surrounded by rocks, animals of various sorts, friends, and family.

*Welcome to Willouby* is his first novel, but I'm no gossip.